LOVE IN THE TIME OF CORONAVIRUS

20/20 in 2020

Richard Lanoix, MD

To Alexandra Jaramillo: My great love, life partner, muse, inspiration, and wife.

To my lovely, wickedly talented, gifted and creative daughter, Héloïse Simonneaux Lanoix, for her brilliant editing, cover art and design.

CONTENTS

PART 1: FIRST WAVE

MARCH 23, 2020

"Dr. McKenna. There's another one in room 17!" The charge nurse exclaimed as she entered the room. "What?"

"EMS just brought her in," she said. "69 years old. Doesn't look good. Her oxygen saturation is 82% and breathing at 44."

"Shit!" Dr. McKenna said. The charge nurse couldn't see the smirk on his face through the mask and face shield over it. That grimace only expressed the tip of the iceberg of how overwhelmed he was at that moment. It was the culmination of four consecutive 13-hour shifts of events just like this one. Then again, the charge nurse was also wearing a mask and face shield, and Dr. Bodhi McKenna had instinctively learned how to read the eyes peering over the mask that said: "Go build a bridge and get over yourself! We need you in room 17 now!"

Dr. McKenna was standing over a 55-year-old man, holding on to the endotracheal tube that he had just placed in his windpipe and squeezing an Ambu breathing bag to oxygenate and ventilate the patient. The tube would be attached to a breathing machine that would perhaps keep him out of Death's clutches. The man's last words to him, eked out with great struggle in between rapid, labored breathing and dry, parched lips were: "Please...tell...my...family..." a long pause, a deep breath "...I love...them...Please."

The man knew intuitively, just as everyone in the room knew from experience, that his survival was unlikely. Death was already in the room to register him for later pick up. The man also knew that he would die alone in the hospital without the comfort of anyone to hold his hand and share his last moments.

"Can George or Ileana take it?" Dr. McKenna asked, still holding onto the tube poking out of the man's mouth.

"They're both intubating other patients," the charge nurse said. "The patient's crashing! I need you now!"

"Then get someone to replace me. Quickly!"

"Where's respiratory?" the charge nurse asked.

"Looking for a vent," Dr. McKenna replied. "We might be out."

"Where's Michelle?"

"She ran out to help with the patient in 11."

"Give me a sec," the charge nurse said, checking the ED tracking board on her mobile. "EMS just brought in another patient. I'll get one of them to bag so you can get to 17." She ran out.

Dr. McKenna looked down at the patient. The man wasn't that much older than him. Dr. McKenna wondered if he would meet the same fate? That was the question that he, and everyone else in the emergency room asked themselves every day. Sure, they wore PPE- masks, face shields, caps, gowns and gloves- yet there were reports of emergency medicine staff contracting and dying from Covid-19. *Weren't they wearing PPE?* Dr. McKenna asked himself.

The patient started to move. The paralytic was wearing off. He was gagging with the tube in his throat. Dr. McKenna screamed as loud as he could: "Help! I need help in here." He was alone in the room with the patient and the door was closed to contain the spread of the coronavirus that was overwhelming ER's and ICU's in New York City.

The man was huge. He probably weighed 250lbs. Maybe 300. He was reaching for the tube and trying to pull it out.

"Help!" Dr. McKenna screamed out. "I need help now!"

One of the EKG techs looked through the window. He

was also wearing a mask. Dr. McKenna couldn't hear what he was saying but his eyebrows were peaked which translated into: "What's up?" Dr. McKenna pointed to the door so that the tech could at least open the door that had large signs indicating that this was a Covid-19 patient and no one should enter without appropriate PPE. The tech disappeared.

What the fuck? He said to himself, now overwhelmed and frustrated. If he stayed to secure the tube, the patient could very well jump off the bed. If he ran to stick his head out of the room to call for help, the patient would likely pull the tube out and damage his airway. Not a pretty sight either way. Emergency medicine training and 30 years of experience in hard-core inner-city ER's didn't prepare him for this situation.

At that moment, the charge nurse walked into the room with an EMT. She looked at Dr. McKenna struggling to hold both of the patient's arms down to prevent him from pulling out the tube that was dangling from his mouth. The patient was bucking and turning from side to side, each time gaining momentum causing the gurney to almost tip over.

The charge nurse's first words: "What the fuck?"

"100mg of Roc stat!" Dr. McKenna ordered. He looked at the EMT who was just standing in the corner and whose eyes peering above the face mask revealed shock at what was going on. "Can you please come over here and bag?" Dr. McKenna asked, his eyes screaming "Go build a bridge, get over yourself, and get your ass over here!"

Only 23 days had passed since the beginning of the pandemic and a new norm had already been established. Dr. McKenna laid across the patient's chest and arms to restrain him. The sweat was pouring down his forehead and filling his N95 mask. *What a pathetic way to die,* He thought. He wondered whether death by drowning in one's N95 mask would become a thing.

The charge nurse barged in with the Roc. She moved around the bed looking for the IV line. She traced it down from the bag and noted that the tip was on floor surrounded by a puddle of IV fluid.

"Fuck!" she said. "We lost the IV." She looked at his other arm for another IV.

"He was a tough stick," Dr. McKenna said. He was now blinking excessively because of the salty sweat pouring into his eyes. "Get someone to hold his arms and I'll look in his neck." She ran to the door and yelled for help." One of the techs came to the door. He started to put on his PPE.

"Hurry up!" the charge nurse screamed, which didn't seem to have any noticeable effect on the speed of the tech donning the PPE. He finally came into the room and the charge nurse directed him to restrain the patient. She looked for IV access in the patient's arm while Dr. McKenna looked at his neck. The good news was that the patient was gagging and straining that caused his jugular veins to pop out despite the fact that he was morbidly obese. The bad news was that the patient was gagging, straining, and morbidly obese. He wouldn't stay still. The charge nurse found a vein but the patient was moving too much and the line blew.

Dr. McKenna placed his left forearm across the patient's face and miraculously popped the IV into his right external jugular vein. "Push the Roc now!" he ordered. The charge nurse pushed the Roc. One minute later, the patient was paralyzed. They secured the IV line. Dr. McKenna made sure the endotracheal tube was still in place. The oxygen saturation was still 88%. The likelihood that this patient would walk out of the hospital alive was negligible. He was morbidly obese, had Type II Diabetes and COPD from years of smoking tobacco. That was the reality. Dr. McKenna wondered if they'd have to start black tagging people when the vents became critically low.

Emergency physicians were trained to do this - but few had the experience or psychological fortitude to deal with the likes of wartime medicine with knee-deep casualties. During the past few weeks, they were always on the verge of going into full disaster mode and having to black tag patients.

Dr. McKenna ran the following scenario in his mind:

"Bodhi," the ER clerk calls out. "There's a call for you. The patient that was in 13's family has been calling nonstop. Line 2."

"Hi," Bodhi picks up and responds. "This is Dr. McKenna. How may I help you?"

"I'm calling about the patient Mary Smith," the voice says. "I'm Mr. Smith, her son. I've been trying to get in to see her but security won't let us in."

"I'm really sorry about that Mr. Smith," Bodhi says. "It's every hospital's policy during the pandemic that no visitors are allowed. That's to protect you and prevent the spread of illness."

"I understand Dr. McKenna. How is she?"

"I'm sorry to be the bearer of bad news," Bodhi said, "but she died."

"What?" Mr. Smith exclaimed. "How is that possible? She wasn't that sick."

"She unfortunately deteriorated very quickly," Bodhi explained.

"Did you put her on a vent?" Mr. Smith asked.

"No," Bodhi responded.

"But why?"

"As you're aware," Bodhi explained. "The system has been stretched thin and we have very limited ventilators and ICU beds. Consequently, we're forced to perform medical triage when patients arrive."

"What does that mean Dr. McKenna?"

"Well," Bodhi said more hesitantly. "We try to use our limited resources on patients we think have the best chances of surviving. Your mother was old and she had diabetes so her chances of survival..."

"You black-tagged her? You let her die."

"Well," Bodhi said. "I wouldn't put it like..."

"Dr. McKenna," Mr. Smith said. "I'm a former vet and EMT. Did you black tag my mother?"

Bodhi hesitated before answering: "Yes!" CLICK! Mucho

dial tone! Mr. Smith hangs up.

Bodhi prepared himself for this situation every day before starting his shift because there was always a point during a shift that bordered on implementing the disaster plan. In disaster mode with limited resources, the goal is to maximize the number of lives saved, so a triage officer is assigned. The triage officer's job is to quickly evaluate patients and determine who has the greatest likelihood of surviving with the least intervention. Those are green tag patients. If a patient has a low probability of survival because of the severity of the illness, their age and other illnesses they have, then they are given a black tag. This means that those delegated to treat patients will bypass those patients and allow them to die so that they can treat other patients who have a higher chance of survival.

This is emergency medicine. This is what emergency physicians are trained to do. However, few have ever had to black tag a patient in their entire careers, and nobody ever expected that they'd be in a situation where they'd have do it. Disaster triage is relegated to a hypothetical construct that emergency physicians brush up on every four years when taking the Advanced Trauma Life Support recertification course. But here they were, way beyond their comfort zone and practical expertise. Furthermore, it was one thing to black tag a patient. It was altogether something else to relay to their family how you as the emergency physician allowed their loved one to just die.

"What do I do now?" the EMT asked in that "this is my first week out of training " voice that at any other time would have prompted boat loads of empathy. Now it was the charge nurse's cold, matter-of-fact voice giving him the wake-up call.

"Just keep bagging till respiratory shows up with a vent."

Bodhi doffed his PPE and stepped out of the room. His scrubs were soaked from sweat. He made eye contact with George and Ileana, both advanced practitioners. Their eyes said it all: "Yeah baby. We're in it!" Bodhi ran to the sink behind the charge nurse's desk, washed his hands and rinsed his face.

"What room was the other patient in?" Bodhi asked.

"No worries," Ileana said. "The EM resident just arrived and took care of it."

"Great!" Bodhi sighed in relief.

"There's another patient who's crashing in hallway 8," the charge nurse said. "We're moving the patient in 8 to a non-negative pressure room and moving the new patient in there."

"I can take it," George said.

"I've got it," Bodhi said. "Thanks."

"How many is that for you today?" Ileana asked.

"Nine," Bodhi said. "How about you?"

"Six," Ileana said.

"Hah!" George exclaimed. "Eleven. I win!"

"That's crazy!" Bodhi exclaimed. "We've intubated 26 Covid patients in the first six hours of this shift."

"Barbara intubated 15 in the first three hours of her shift the other night," George added. "By the way, respiratory said we only have a few vents left."

"How are the ICU beds?" Bodhi asked.

"So far we're okay," The charge nurse overheard and responded. "They just closed another unit and converted it to another ICU. Beds aren't the problem. It's the number of vents."

"Please call respiratory and tell her that we're going to need another vent in 8," Bodhi said.

"Already did," the charge nurse replied. This was the beginning.

THE ONSET

There had been talk in the news that there was some virus in China and that lots of people were sick and dying, but that was on the other side of the world. Then it moved to Italy, much closer to home. Despite the large number of deaths, discussions still focused on how it was just another Avian flu-like virus and nothing to worry about. Then it was declared a pandemic.

The reports from Italy were staggering. It spread over the country like wildfire. Doctors were overwhelmed and many of them died. That was when the alarms started ringing. Italy was a hop and a skip away from the United States. For some reason however, very little preparations were made.

Dr. Bodhi McKenna was an emergency physician who had just completed thirty years of practice in some of the toughest inner-city emergency departments (ER's). He had spent most of his career in academics and then as a Locums emergency physician.

Bodhi was back working in New York City when the first cases started arriving at the end of February of 2020. The first few cases were the "worried well" who presented to ER's stating that they had just been in Italy, China or Korea and although asymptomatic, were concerned. They wanted to be tested but there were so few tests at the time that ER's were telling them to go home and self-quarantine. The next ripples were the symptomatic ones, the so-called "walking dead." Their presentation was unlike anything they had ever seen. The patients complained of typical flu-like symptoms such as cough, runny nose, sneezing, body aches and malaise however, there were two major differences: First, they were short of breath and breathing very fast with severe hypoxia. Their oxygen saturations were in the low to mid-eighties. What was strange was that they didn't appear as short of breath as would be expected for their degree of hypoxia. Hence the moniker "walking dead." Many required intubation and ventilation with a respirator almost immediately. Second, relatively young patients were dying. The typical pattern during viral epidemics was that the very old and the very young tended to have higher mortalities.

It was at this stage that the panic started. Everyone wanted to be tested because they believed that they were exposed to someone with Covid-19. In many cases, especially the patients who had just returned from Italy or Korea, where many of the infected Chinese patients were seeking care, their concerns were justified. It was frustrating for patients and providers alike to tell them that the ER did not have the tests to confirm or exclude the diagnosis and that the only thing to do was to go home, self-quarantine, and only return if they developed severe difficulty breathing. In the meantime, many of those patients who were never tested were likely positive and infecting everyone else.

Many of the patients presenting to ER's did so based on panic. Bodhi evaluated a patient early on who demanded to be tested because he was an Uber driver and there were Chinese people in his car who were coughing. He had already been to his primary care doctor and two other ER's wanting to be tested. It was evident that with each encounter he picked up some more lingo that would in normal circumstances prompt a test. He said he was severely short of breath, had fever and had chest pain but his vital signs were normal. He begged and pleaded stating that he did not want to infect his wife and child. There was definitely a heavy layer of anxiety but some of it was definitely appropriate. After spending a lot of time trying to reassure him that he was fine at the moment, the patient finally said indignantly: "So you're sending me home to die." Bodhi lost his patience at this point and told him that it wasn't him, but rather the CDC, the Department of Health and the President of the United States who were sending him home to die. He was just Death's messenger. Later when the shit literally hit the fan and the ER and hospital were completely overwhelmed with extremely ill Covid patients who often required intubation as soon as they walked in because of respiratory failure, Bodhi often wondered how that patient fared. Did he actually send him home to die?

This change for the worse happened in the course of one week. 90% of all the ER visits were then Covid related and at times one-third to one-half of those patients were intubated and on ventilators. The hospital, as did most of the hospitals in New York City, shut down almost all of their services and converted most wards to Intensive Care Units (ICU's) for the overflowing Covid patients on ventilators.

There was a fear in the air of the ER that reminded Bodhi of the rancid air that filled transatlantic flights when cigarette smoking was still allowed. It filled the air and was almost palpable. No one in his ER had yet been diagnosed with Covid. Nonetheless, there were those original reports from China and Italy where many young, dedicated frontline healthcare providers contracted the virus and required intubation due to respiratory failure. Many of them died. Despite all their precautions, the PPE- Personal Protective Equipment- that was often McGiver'ed because of its lack, they waited with bated breath for the same to happen to them. Then it did. There were reports of ER staff in nearby hospitals who got Covid-19- some of whom became very sick, required intubation and were fighting for their lives. Some lost that fight and died all alone in the hospital without friends or family to comfort them. The anxiety level in the ER increased. Everyone knew directly of someone who suffered respiratory failure requiring intubation and then died. The circle was getting smaller and smaller.

The fear was in their eyes peering over their masks. This was something that caught Bodhi's eyes, quite literally. Everyone was now wearing masks and all one could see was their eyes. Bodhi never really noticed people's eyes before. Sure, he would notice and comment if someone really had spectacular eyes that stood out, but in general they were just eyeballs in sockets. All of a sudden, he began to notice the not-so-subtle differences between people's eyes, as different as their personalities, and the universes they contained. The eyes were a world unto themselves that were thrust onto the stage by these masks worn as protection against Covid-19.

Bodhi realized for the first time how much humans relied on facial expressions to decipher what the other person was communicating. Often times, the mouth was saying one thing but the facial expressions were saying something altogether different. He considered that this situation might be similar to adults who lost their vision and then reported that the acuity of their other senses increased tremendously. He wondered if one's sense of discerning what others were really communicating would be enhanced once we learned the subtle art of interpreting the eyes? Would we then rely less on words and ultimately abandon their use except to communicate specific instructions and for literary and entertainment purposes? Would the vocal cords become a vestigial organ once other more efficient means of communication were developed utilizing the portal of the eyes?

Bodhi evaluated a patient with a history of psychiatric illness who presented with a high level of anxiety and a myriad of complaints. After some testing and a large dose of reassurance that he wasn't going to die from Covid, he was able to discharge the patient home. Five days later the same patient returned stating that he couldn't taste or smell. Bodhi attributed his symptoms to anxiety. He explained that there weren't any illnesses that caused the isolated loss of taste and smell and that there wasn't anything to worry about. Bodhi subsequently had many friends who had lost their sense of taste and smell and were otherwise asymptomatic. This was later found to be an early symptom of Covid-19.

One such case was a close friend of Bodhi's. He had a great passion for art and culture, and one of his great pleasures in life was wine. He had just renovated his brownstone and included a 1,500 bottle, temperature-controlled wine cellar. He frequented wine auctions and would never go to a friend's home for dinner or a restaurant without his little leather satchel to transport two to three vintage wines that were worth at least $1,000 each as an offering. A testament of his goodwill and generosity, if that weren't enough, was that he would always have an extra bottle so that the sommeliers and waiters could taste these extraordinary, rare, and ridiculously expensive wines. So, imagine the irony that such a connoisseur and purveyor of wine should be struck with "the Rona" and his only symptom was the loss of taste and smell. The horror! On the bright side, he could have died or become very sick but his overwhelming abundance of collected good karma likely protected him. After a few weeks, his sense of taste and smell returned, which was promptly and ceremoniously celebrated with a bottle of great wine.

Every doctor over the past 2,500 years learned during their training the importance of the history and physical exam. They learned that 90% of making the correct diagnosis and developing a treatment plan derived from a good history and physical exam. Consequently, it was deemed an extremely important skill to master. Covid-19 flushed this 2,500-year wisdom down the toilet. There was no longer any mystery. Every patient presenting to the ER during what would later be called the First Wave, and later sarcastically referred to as the appetizer or foreplay, was identical. They presented with worsening and severe shortness of breath associated with hypoxia. Their lab tests were identical with elevations of liver enzymes, C-reactive protein, lactate dehydrogenase, ferritin, and an elevated D-dimer that was associated with higher rates of death. Their chest x-rays were remarkably similar as well.

What was most remarkable was the level of hypoxia. Normal oxygen saturations ranged from 95% to 100%. Prior to the pandemic, oxygen saturations below 90% would have been of concern and patients typically felt short of breath at these levels. In these Covid-19 patients, their saturations were in the mid-80's and sometimes worse, and their breathing very rapid. They were called the "walking dead" because physicians expected patients with oxygen saturations in the low eighties to appear much worse. These patients didn't present in the same way as patients with severe influenza typically presented. They looked more like patients who suffered from carbon monoxide or methemoglobin poisoning where the oxygen was in good supply but the blood couldn't use it. In these cases, the carbon monoxide or methemoglobin blocked the sites onto which the oxygen was supposed to bind and be useful.

Consequently, the history and physical examination were not helpful because the diagnosis was obvious. Furthermore, the massive numbers of these patients that were bombarding the ER and the rapidity of their deterioration did not lend itself to communication and pleasantries utilized for patient satisfaction scores. The ER had been reduced to a factory line. Staff went from room to room as quickly as possible and repeated the same exact procedure: Don PPE, secure intravenous access, push sedative and paralytic agents, intubate, secure the endotracheal tube, push sedation, doff PPE, wash hands, go to the next room, repeat. The notion that physicians were nothing more than glorified and well-paid factory workers was realized in no uncertain terms.

Bodhi was in the throes of one of those crazy shifts that had now become par for the course. It may very well have just been a welcomed distraction from the stifling fear and anxiety that was spreading through the ER like wildfire. Nonetheless, Bodhi had a realization. He pondered if the loss of smell and taste that was characteristic of Covid-19, and then the PPE covering everything except the eyes, were perhaps an invitation for us to use our eyes for the first time and really see what we had collectively gotten ourselves into. He would later come to believe that "the Rona" took so much away, but gave us one thing: Sight. 20/20 vision in fact. He considered how later generations, if they managed to survive, would teach that hindsight was always 20/20 but too little too late to change the course of the high-speed train that we had set in motion that was headed directly into an impenetrable wall.

Now with everyone's faces covered, leaving their eyes to bear their souls, the fear beamed out of them and cut through the dense fog of pleasantries expressed through words attempting to regain their rapidly fading status quo. It was a revisionist memory that things before were good, work was great, the patients were delightful and appreciative. Those false memories were now overlaid with fear and anxiety of an uncertain future that promised death to everyone who touched it. Regardless of the verbal yarns they were weaving to distract and comfort themselves, the fear spoke clearly through the eyes peering above their surgical masks. It asked what they dared not vocalize under those masks that gagged them: *"Is this what I signed up for?"*

DISASTERS &
CANARIES

Earlier in his career, Bodhi had been the Chair of Emergency Preparedness at Lincoln Medical and Mental Health Center in the South Bronx of New York City, where every day seemed like an unfolding disaster. But it wasn't until after the tragedy of 9/11 that Emergency Preparedness became relevant and actual energy and resources allocated to it.

Bodhi had just resigned from his position at Lincoln after twelve years and on the morning of 9/11, his start date at St. Luke's-Roosevelt Medical Center, went back to Lincoln to say goodbye. Everyone bid him farewell and stated that he would be so bored at St. Luke's-Roosevelt and miss the excitement so much that he would return in no time at all. Bodhi then took the subway to his office at Roosevelt Hospital on Tenth Avenue between 58th and 59th streets to start the next phase of his career. As he entered through the emergency department waiting room, he noticed that everyone was standing in front of the television that showed an airplane crashing into the World Trade Center. He asked the people who were captivated by what was being shown what movie was playing. At that moment, a news commentator came on indicating that this was happening real-time.

Fortunately, or rather unfortunately, there were only two major outcomes of what would become known as the largest terrorist attack on American soil: People either died, or they had a lot of dust in their eyes from the collapse of the buildings. Hospitals close to ground zero were overwhelmed with patients known as the walking wounded but there weren't large numbers of severely injured patients from this mass casualty incident.

One thing learned from that day in 2001 was how poorly prepared New York City hospitals were for such events despite Disaster Preparedness being a requirement of the Joint Commission on Accreditation of Healthcare Organizations. This was not at all surprising for Bodhi because he understood clearly that the only people really prepared for disasters were people who faced disasters frequently enough to give preparedness more than lip service. Consequently, Californians were always prepared because they had experienced enough earthquakes and forest fires to know that another one was imminent. The Israelis were another example because of the frequent mass casualty incidents they faced because of terrorist attacks.

A basic premise in emergency medicine disaster management is that once a disaster with the risk of contamination occurs, the area outside of the ER is treated as a "hot" zone, the ER itself a "cold" zone, and a decontamination area established in between. The hot zone is where people are likely infected and have the potential to contaminate others and the cold zone is technically a safe area. The decontamination area is where patients undergo decontamination procedures before they enter the safe or cold zone in order to minimize the spread of the illness or toxin. Even so, staff in the cold zone would still wear personal protective equipment (PPE) to protect themselves.

This simple and common-sense approach dictated that emergency medicine staff wear full PPE during their entire shift in the ER regardless of the patient's history and presentation. What in fact happened was that the recommendations from the CDC and hospital administration changed daily. At first, PPE was recommended only for "persons of interest," who had just returned from an endemic area such as Wuhan China or Italy, and were symptomatic. Then it was expanded to include patients who had been in contact with "persons of interest." It was obvious to Bodhi and anyone else with a background in Disaster Preparedness that this left the frontline ER staff completely exposed and at risk. It was not only putting them in danger but also increased the risk of spreading the disease to other staff, their families, and to the population in general. Without such a comprehensive approach they consistently found themselves behind the so-called eight-ball and the approach had to constantly be adjusted to become more inclusive. This approach left the frontline providers in a perpetual "too little, too late" scenario.

Bodhi had a great deal of respect for his boss, who he not only considered a friend, but a highly intelligent, seasoned emergency physician and leader. So he couldn't help but wonder why the man had not proposed and implemented such a basic common-sense approach that was listed in every outdated emergency medicine textbook. When Bodhi posed this question, the answer was quite simple and direct: Hospitals across the United States did not have enough PPE to implement this Disaster Management plan that was mandated by the Joint Commission on Accreditation of Healthcare Organizations in order to protect its staff. It now made sense that they were being asked to reuse their PPE and that the PPE was being stored in locked rooms and rationed.

When a canary dies in a goldmine, it is a clear indication that everyone else should get the hell out of there and save themselves. Their sacrifice is for the greater good. Bodhi learned early on in his training that emergency medicine staff were akin to the canaries in goldmines. In the event of a terrorist attack utilizing biologic weapons or an infectious disease pandemic such as Covid, emergency medicine staff, similar to the canaries, would die first and serve as a warning to everyone else. This was always an academic talking point. Now, for the first time in his career, Bodhi recognized that he and his colleagues were in fact glorified canaries who were applauded around the world for their bravery and sacrifice. This created a sense of camaraderie amongst the ER staff and other frontline providers at the hospital and across the world- a coalition of canaries if you will.

There was certainly an endless supply of partisan finger pointing about why the United States was not fully prepared for this pandemic when we clearly witnessed the devastation first in China and then Italy. A line could even be drawn further back to warnings to prepare for inevitable future pandemics that were ushered after the Severe Acute Respiratory Syndrome (SARS) occurred in 2003, Swine Flu (H1N1) in 2009, and Middle East Respiratory Syndrome (MERS) in 2012. Leaving the partisan shit-throwing contest aside, the lack of preparedness in the United States during the first few months after the arrival of the Covid pandemic was not very surprising at all to Bodhi. What was surprising and unacceptable to him was the lack of PPE for frontline staff- the canaries- four months after the pandemic was declared. It was a pathetic and unacceptable response, especially in light of the fact that no one knew at the time the trajectory of the pandemic. The obvious fear was whether the Covid pandemic would follow the course of the 1918 Spanish Flu Pandemic where the first round in 1917 was definitely worse than prior flu seasons but the second round the following fall killed more than 50 million people worldwide.

It was expected that a small subset of canaries would be sacrificed for the greater good and their deaths would warn of the danger and save large numbers of people. Aside from the opinions of those first canaries and their families, it certainly could be argued that the ends in this case justified the means. It was at the very least an occupational hazard. However, it was clear to Bodhi that to then place subsequent canaries in such a situation was pure callousness, stupidity and incompetence.

THE HEROES

There was a lot of talk then about emergency medicine and ICU staff, the frontline providers, being heroes. This notion set off the worldwide phenomenon of people applauding them for their dedication, courage, self-sacrifice and heroism. This occurred every day precisely at 7 O'clock. From the inside however, the fear and anxiety oozed copiously out of the eyes that peered above those masks. The first canary didn't know its fate, but after the 30th canary died horribly from asphyxiation and multiple organ failure all alone in a make-shift ICU, it was no longer a surprise. No one dared verbalize it because the wave of appreciation and applause held frontline providers up on pedestals for the first time in decades. No one wanted to slander this fallacious facade of heroism, but it was obvious. The unvoiced running commentary was as clear on everyone's foreheads as the teleprompters on the back seats in Opera Houses. They read: "What is my life worth? Why should I sacrifice my life and family for some other poor schmuck who was unfortunately at the wrong place at the wrong time? I have a family to take care of, a life to live. Why me? This is not the job I signed up for!"

Most ER staff and other frontline providers didn't have a choice. Like everyone else, they had to work because of financial constraints. Many of them had huge amounts of medical school debt now compounded by interest, in addition to the debt accrued in pursuit of the American Dream, such as buying a home and car. This was layered with the rising cost of living, children's education and for some, divorce debt. The American Dream, as was becoming more and more clear to everyone even before Covid-19, was being recognized for what it always was, a nightmare.

The world around them was experiencing financial devastation and economic uncertainty. They still had jobs and were being paid handsomely. Why complain? Why rock the boat? Those that did were questioned about their loyalty, commitment, sense of service. The unasked questions that resounded loudly were: "Why did you want to be a doctor? Don't you want to help people?" These questions were simultaneously translated as: "Don't you want to save the world?"

For those to whom these questions did not arise spontaneously, there were constant reminders. By then, everyone knew someone who had died secondary to Covid-19. Every healthcare provider knew of a young doctor, nurse, an advanced practitioner without any co-morbid illness who died secondary to contracting Covid-19 while working.

Healthcare providers, especially those on the frontline such as in the ER and Intensive Care Units started to ask themselves more frequently and more openly: "Why not quit? Why serve and sacrifice my life?" "Why take the risk and expose my family?" Some realized that they weren't necessarily seeking answers but rather thrust into a deep and provocative contemplation.

By the end of April, the number of sick Covid-19 patients had drastically decreased. The pandemic in New York City was definitely slowing down. The census in emergency departments and urgent care centers in New York City had decreased by 40%. The number of Covid patients that overwhelmed emergency departments in New York City suddenly decreased significantly and all the other patients with their stubbed toes, upper respiratory infections, acute gastritis, low back pain, abdominal pain and constipation were nowhere to be found. This was not a surprise in light of the widespread anxiety and calls for shelter-in-place and social distancing. What puzzled hospital administrators and leadership was what happened to the heart attacks, strokes, small bowel obstructions, acute appendicitis and diverticulitis patients? What happened to all the patients with acute asthma, COPD exacerbations, and aortic dissections? Were they staying home and dying? This didn't make sense.

It was the beginning of May 2020 and Bodhi was in the middle of another dead shift. Bodhi and his colleagues were now each only evaluating eight to ten patients per shift compared to the twenty-five patients they would have typically evaluated prior to the Covid pandemic. The 40% drop in patient census that was being reported by emergency departments across the United States was palpable. Interestingly, despite the drop in overall cases, there were still about 60 patients with Covid who were still intubated in the makeshift ICU's in the hospital.

Hospitals across the country were now facing a financial crunch and some were facing financial ruin. Their message very quickly changed from "we're a team and in this together," to "we have to protect our bottom line." Hospitals started to reduce salaries by 30% and sending many on furloughs. After all, the integrity of the hospitals had to be maintained at all costs. The perspective that was offered was that salary reductions and furloughs were preferable to terminations.

Physicians, nurses and Advanced Practice Professionals, such as nurse practitioners and physician assistants, had thus far been protected from the financial devastation felt by most of the country because they still had jobs. They quickly discovered that they were now a vulnerable population. They were now reduced from their glorified status that was applauded, thanked and cheered for, to simple factory workers who could face cuts in salary and possible termination depending on the factory's bottom line. This was a wake-up call for everyone.

Despite the best rationales offered, this left a bitter taste in the mouths of frontline providers. They were being asked to sacrifice their lives and to risk infecting their families by working in ER's and ICU's without adequate PPE, when all that mattered to the hospitals was their bottom line. Frontline workers came to understand that they were in fact nothing more than glorified factory workers fulfilling their quotas of widgets. They now felt the tightness of the long leash that was tied around their necks being reeled in. Moreover, they had no choice. Other hospitals were undergoing the same adjustments to protect themselves until there was a return to some semblance of normalcy.

Recognizing for the first time the lack of control in their professional lives was overwhelming. At a superficial level, there was the stress of the daily barrage of critically ill patients. At a slightly deeper level, there was the economic uncertainty. At a much deeper and more pervasive level, there was the anxiety of whether or not they would be next to contract Covid-19 and die.

Healthcare providers of this generation had never experienced such levels of stress. They were now wading in uncharted territory. They were surrounded by death or the possibility of death on a daily basis. They acknowledged their roles as frontline providers but were not prepared or trained for this. Imagine taking the most seasoned emergency physicians and nurses working in the most hardcore inner-city hospitals and teleporting them to a Vietnam War scenario where they were up to their ears in dying soldiers all saying "please don't let me die!" This type of endeavor requires psychological fortitude that can only be obtained from a combination of preparation and experience, neither of which were available up to that point.

It was consequently trial by fire to suddenly experience patients rapidly deteriorate and require aggressive, life-saving measures with the knowledge that there was a high likelihood of death. What made matters worse was the fact that visitors were no longer allowed in the ER and hospital. The patients were all alone. All their needs, something as simple as passing them a tissue or a glass of water, or keeping them company now had to be fulfilled by the staff. It was heartbreaking to witness patients taking their last breaths all alone without any loved ones to hold their hands, thank them for their presence and bid them farewell. This weighed on many of the front-line providers who felt compelled to fill this void. Although overwhelmed by the onslaught of new Covid-19 patients, they were compelled to provide the same comfort and attention they all would want and expect for themselves and their loved ones in that same situation. This took a toll.

Consequently, it wasn't surprising to anyone that there were increasing reports of physician suicides. The first one reported was an emergency physician Bodhi knew. Despite working in New York City, a huge metropolitan area, the emergency medicine community was like a large extended family where everyone was in some way or another connected. The news report confirmed that after interviews with colleagues, family members and friends, there was no prior history of psychiatric illness or depression. The reasons for his suicide were accepted to have been because of the level of stress and the psychological trauma of working in the ER with so many sick patients. This didn't sit well with Bodhi. This very crisis was why physicians chose careers in emergency medicine. It was the adrenaline rush, the rollercoaster ride that attracted them to the profession of emergency medicine. It was the relatively young patient with cardiac arrest, the acute trauma, heart attacks, and disasters big and small. It was the anxious patient with chest pain insisting that this episode was different and that they were going to die. It was holding a child's hand and comforting them before administering local anesthesia to suture their wound in one room, and then in the next room having to tell a patient who had never smoked a day in their lives, was a vegan and exercised daily that they had Stage IV Cancer knowing that they would be dead within one year regardless of all treatment. All in one shift!

Although thrown into a wartime situation and confronted with massive morbidity and casualties was very different than the typical experience of emergency physicians, it was in fact what they were trained for. Consequently, it was difficult for Bodhi to accept that the Covid pandemic, at least at that early stage, was the cause of his colleague's suicide. Emergency physicians were certainly out of their comfort zones and practicing very differently. They had to wear PPE at all times, which was uncomfortable and exhausting. They were afraid for their own safety and that of their families. Many were intubating up to ten patients per shift and witnessing an uptick of the number of deaths in the ER. Nonetheless Bodhi thought it was too facile to attribute that suicide to that early stage of the Covid pandemic.

The number of suicides amongst emergency medicine providers and then ICU staff slowly increased. The pattern was consistent: a frontline provider would suddenly and unexpectedly commit suicide. There were no suicide notes and no discussions with friends or loved ones to provide even a hint of depression. The speculation crystallized that the suicides were mainly due to the stress of managing so many extremely sick patients at the same time, and knowing that no matter what you did, they would likely die. Some would die while in the ER, most of the others would later die in the ICU. The psychological trauma of these deaths was sublimated by a host of rationalizations and inadequate coping mechanisms. The toll was monumental. The humanity of frontline providers had already been sucked out, chewed and spit out by the healthcare system that relegated patients to statistics and billing "relative value units," and rewarded "treat 'em and street 'em" attitudes and practices. Whatever hope and humanity were left in their hearts disintegrated a bit more every day after an increasing number of patients requiring immediate intubation and dying all alone to the rhythmic drone of ventilators and incessantly beeping monitors. These practitioners were emotionally, physically and psychologically bankrupt. Their currency, their humanity checking accounts were rapidly dwindling in the form of checks written as death certificates.

Second was the corroboration that they were in fact the canaries in the goldmines who had little value to the system and were dispensable. They always suspected this but only as a hypothetical construct because it only came to mind every four years during discussions on Disaster Management when taking the Advanced Trauma Life Support Recertification. This realization led to another profound truth that further advanced the sword cutting through them: They had no stock in the goldmines!

Another significant factor was to learn that they were in fact nothing more than glorified factory workers. Their perch on their appointed pedestals of being highly valued professionals was already precarious and had been slowly eroded over time. The applause at 7 O'clock every day started in China and migrated along with the virus to Italy, Spain, Paris, and then to New York City as an expression of gratitude to healthcare workers. It was very moving for emergency medicine physicians and frontline providers but created a cognitive dissonance. Physicians and healthcare providers in general had lost so much respect over the years. There was a time when the general population used to have a high degree of respect for doctors and healthcare providers. Marcus Welby, MD, a popular television series immediately came to mind. People revered and trusted him. Bodhi's generation never experienced this level of trust or respect. The level of trust and respect for doctors was reduced to the same as for car mechanics. The general consensus being that when someone took their car to a mechanic there was a high likelihood that they were going to get robbed. In addition to the general public, hospital administrators demonstrated absolutely no respect for doctors. Their attitudes towards the lowly physician class were at best veiled disdain. For them, doctors were nothing more than functionaries. It was certainly in their realm of consciousness, but the pandemic made it clear exactly how far down they had sunk.

For these frontline providers, it was indeed moving to see the daily outpouring of gratitude from the general public at 7 O'clock. It was a clear indication that people finally realized that consulting google for their medical problems was not the equivalent of the care of a real doctor and more so, couldn't save them from the coronavirus. The applause gave them hope that perhaps people now recognized and appreciated the sacrifices that doctors made in regards to their years of education, training and personal sacrifice. It was perhaps an acknowledgement of how much they had to give up in regards to socialization and family to practice medicine. This was all somewhat reassuring, but the writing had long since been on the wall- the days of Marcus Welby, MD were over!

What made matters infinitely worse was the common misconception amongst frontline providers that they were impervious to psychologic trauma by dint of their profession. They believed that admitting to anyone, even to themselves, that they were overwhelmed or depressed would be perceived as a sign of weakness. They couldn't reconcile these feelings with the image of themselves as saviors, frontline warriors and the heroes for whom the world was clapping and celebrating every day at 7 O'clock. More cognitive dissonance.

Bodhi was well aware that he and his colleagues were lying to themselves. It was becoming more evident to him that he and his colleagues were creating a facade of invincibility through which Covid-19 was so easily blowing holes. Nonetheless, he and many of his colleagues felt that it was better for them to leave it a mystery and continue their charade. These suicides were too close to home. They subconsciously feared that honestly assessing themselves at this juncture would leave them vulnerable to the possibility of contracting not only Covid, but the suicide bug.

SOCIAL DISTANCING

Bodhi had been divorced for many years. He and his ex-wife had three children. His two older children were living in Spain and his eighteen-year-old daughter attended the American University of Paris. Bodhi's sister and nephew lived in the building adjacent to his, and his mother lived in the building after that one.

Bodhi was concerned about his three children living in Europe, but it was a consolation that France and Spain were on strict lockdown. It was also a great relief to know that if things worsened there, they would be able to shelter in their grandparents' farm in Brittany, France. Their grandparents lived in the countryside and were organic dairy farmers. They also grew their own food, so they at least wouldn't starve. In addition to their safety, the move to Brittany would also ensure that their grandparents had help, support, and wouldn't be alone.

Bodhi recognized that his kids were now adults and would make their own decisions. He only hoped that he and their mother had provided them with enough intelligence, resourcefulness and wisdom to survive and navigate this brave new world. Bodhi also recognized that they were in fact in a much better position than he was in New York City and would be far better off if things took a turn for the worse. The bottom-line was that there was absolutely nothing he could do for his kids except to pray for their safety. What remained in his control was to protect his family in New York City. He obviously did not want to get sick and die, but he was working in an extremely high-risk environment and was well-aware of his role as a canary. All he could do to protect himself and his family was to aggressively wear PPE. His biggest fear, shared by all frontline providers, was to have an asymptomatic infection and transmit the disease to someone in his family who would then become deathly ill and die.

This concern was pressed home by his daily experience in the ER and two anecdotes. He heard the first from his sister, who was a former ICU nurse. One of her friends from elementary school was an ultra-rightwing Trump worshiper who followed Trump's original claim that the Covid pandemic was a hoax. She had just completed nursing school and was posting all over Facebook that the pandemic was a hoax and that wearing face masks was not necessary. She offered to work in any hospital without a face mask. My sister and many of her friends strongly advised her to take this Covid-19 situation more seriously, especially in light of the fact that her husband had just underwent cardiac surgery and that she had an elderly mother. She placed politics first and ignored everyone's advice and consequently was infected with Covid-19 and subsequently infected both her mother and husband. Her mother died.

The second was shared by one of his colleagues and close friends who was also an emergency physician. Bodhi's friend was in his early sixties and his wife was almost seventy and had some co-morbid illnesses. Because of his high-risk status, he decided to sleep in a separate bedroom to avoid the possibility of infecting her. This level of sacrifice greatly impressed Bodhi and brought the idea of infecting his family much closer to home. This made the concept of the PPE that he wore in the hospital and how he decontaminated all the more relevant.

DECONTAMINATION

odhi always wore his own scrubs. He tried a variety of brands over the years but really liked the "Aviator Scrubs" because the material was very comfortable and they had many pockets everywhere that always came in handy. He purchased them in a variety of colors and had his name embroidered on them. When the pandemic hit New York City, he initiated a decontamination procedure to avoid bringing the virus home to infect his 91-year-old mother, sister and nephew who he visited frequently. He would at first remove the scrubs in the hallway of his apartment, put them into a bag and then immediately take a shower.

As the number of Covid cases in New York City increased, the patients presented to the ER with increasing severity. More and more of the hospital was being converted to ICU's to manage these patients. Bodhi very quickly made a stronger demarcation between the "hot zone" of the hospital and "cold zone" of his apartment by starting the decontamination procedure in the hospital. For the first time in 25 years, Bodhi used the scrubs provided by the hospital. He found this particularly annoying because there was only one shirt pocket over the chest and one back-pant pocket. This made carrying his smartphone quite difficult.

Putting the smartphone in the breast shirt pocket pulled the shirt down and placed stress on his neck. In addition, this breast pocket was rendered useless and inaccessible by the fact that he now always wore a PPE gown, which made it impossible to get to. Placing the phone in his back-pant pocket pulled the scrubs down and he would often forget and sit on it. He was already seeing so many horrible casualties in the ER, he could not accept allowing his newly purchased iPhone 11, with the best camera he had ever experienced in a smartphone, to become another casualty - crushed in his back pocket with no hope of resuscitation or reimbursement. Bodhi had already broken a number of pens that way, another tool previously taken for granted was now both indispensable and impossible to carry around.

To an outsider this may have seemed petty and trivial but physicians relied more and more on their smartphones. First, it was the major form of communication in the hospital where "Tiger Text" was utilized. It was encrypted and allowed free communication between the various services of the hospital. Second, physicians relied on their smartphones when they weren't sitting at a desk to obtain medical information on the internet.

Another important use of smartphones that emerged in those times of Covid was communicating with the patients. Patients who were suspected of Covid were placed under droplet, contact and airborne precautions and ideally isolated in a room that had negative pressure. The door had very clear signage indicating that this was a Covid patient and the mandatory isolation precautions. These procedures were implemented to maintain a strict demarcation between the "hot zone" of the patient's room and the "cold zone" of the rest of the ER. Similar procedures were instituted all over the hospital. Wards and ICU's were specifically designated as Covid wards in order to prevent the spread of the disease.

Any staff entering the room would have to don PPE- cap, gown, shoe covers, gloves, and N95 mask- and then doff the PPE in a specific manner, leaving them in a bin in the room to be collected and cleaned later. This was a time-consuming procedure for the technician, nursing and physician staff. Furthermore, it was recognized that every contact with such a patient increased the risk of spreading the disease so the leadership instituted policies to limit the contact as much as possible. The staff would coordinate prior to entering the room as to what was required and who would accomplish those tasks. If something was neglected it would wait until someone had to go in for another reason rather than just for the neglected task. Since most patients had mobile phones, further communication with the patient after the initial interview and examination was performed by calling the patient's mobile phone in order to minimize unnecessary and direct face-to-face contact with the patient.

Consequently, Bodhi constantly had to use his smartphone and not having the multiple pockets that were available in his own Aviator Scrubs was another nuisance that he had to accustom himself in this brave new Covid world. Another nuisance that wasn't as major was having to wear a face mask at all times in the ER, even when seated at a desk away from patients. The rationale was that a colleague may have an asymptomatic Covid infection and could potentially infect the rest of the staff sitting next to them.

The only issue with all of these precautions was the shortage of PPE and N95 masks in particular, which were the only masks documented to prevent contamination with airborne pathogens. They were intended to be used once and then discarded in between patients. Now because of the shortage, the staff was asked to wear surgical masks over the N95 masks, discard the surgical masks in between Covid patients and to reuse the N95 masks. This didn't make sense to Bodhi, but this was the reality and everyone had to do the best they could with the limited resources.

There were so many things that were now out of Bodhi's control. He did however find the solution for carrying his smartphone and pen. It was the old school fanny pack that he had abandoned years ago when he started wearing the Aviator Scrubs. He was not pleased with the idea of the fanny pack but it really was the perfect solution. It was easily accessible under the PPE gown, did not give him neck pain from the weight of the phone in his breast scrub pocket, and there was no risk of precipitously destroying his phone by accidentally sitting on it while in his back pocket. Lastly, wearing a PPE gown at all times saved Bodhi's vanity from the fashion faux-pas of wearing a fanny back. It was just another layer of protection worn at all times and he would simply don another gown over it when entering a potential Covid patient's room and doff the outer layer. He was at first criticized for always wearing a PPE gown but as he explained his rationale, more and more of the staff started to do the same.

Bodhi's decontamination procedure was straight forward. He would wear his own scrubs to work, use his ID badge to obtain a pair of clean scrubs in the "scrubs dispensary," change into the hospital scrubs and put on his fanny pack. At the end of his shift, he would take a shower in the hospital, place the hospital scrubs in the dispensary to be cleaned, and then wear his own scrubs home. He would then take off the sneakers he had worn during his shift and leave them at the entrance of his apartment. He considered leaving those sneakers at the hospital and using another pair to commute back and forth, but for some reason that defied logic even to himself, this seemed excessive.

THE PROPHECY

Bodhi had just finished a grueling shift in the ER. What made this particular shift very emotional and traumatic was a seven-year-old girl with a history of asthma who presented with fever, cough and moderate shortness of breath. Nebulizer treatments and steroids were administered immediately without any improvement. The chest x-ray displayed the typical findings of Covid-19 and the rapid test for Covid-19 was positive. The child very quickly deteriorated and required intubation.

Kids with Covid-19 tended to present with mild flu-like symptoms and sent home. As a matter of fact, the census in the Pediatric ER dropped by 80% since the start of the Covid pandemic. It appeared for a time that kids were immune from the devastation that Covid-19 was wreaking on adults. Consequently, it caught everyone by surprise to witness a child circle the drain so rapidly.

Despite everything they did, the child's condition worsened. She became more and more hypoxic and her blood pressure tanked. They started vasopressors and then broad-spectrum antibiotics for presumptive sepsis. Bodhi was on the phone with the pediatric intensivist arranging for transfer to the ICU when the nurse screamed out that the little girl was coding. Her heart stopped beating and she didn't have a blood pressure. Bodhi dropped the phone and ran to her bedside. They immediately started CPR and administered doses of epinephrine.

Although Death had become a fixture in the adult ER by that time, it was still uncommon for children to get Death's attention in such a manner. There was a stark difference in the manner in which pediatric and adult codes were run. The medical management was the same but the difference was the emotions everyone wore on their sleeves. Although everything was done to prevent it, it was nonetheless understood that adults had the habit of dying, and it occurred with increasing frequency as people got older. The reality was that kids sometimes died as well, but it was not acceptable.

Emotions were running high and bouncing off the walls in the room. The pediatric intensivist showed up in the ER in no time, which was extremely rare. The ER staff did their jobs, stabilized the patients and if they survived, the intensivist would wait for them in the ICU. These were different times and having a child present with Covid in such a manner was a relatively rare event that caught everyone's attention. The intensivist didn't have much to contribute as everything that could be done was in fact being done.

It didn't look good. They were already into their third round of CPR and epinephrine. Adult resuscitations were often called and the patient pronounced dead after 20 minutes. The science was the same- no one survived resuscitation after 20 minutes and if they did, they would suffer severe brain damage from the lack of oxygen to their brains. But despite the science, pediatric resuscitations tended to go on and on. Tears started to well in the eyes of everyone in the room.

Bodhi was running the resuscitation and asked one of the technicians to bring the child's parents into the room. Everyone stopped and stared at Bodhi. The charge nurse broke the silence and said: "Bodhi. No visitors. You know that." Since the pandemic started, patients were not allowed to have any visitors anywhere in the hospital in order to limit the spread of the disease.

"Yes," Bodhi stated matter-of-factly. "But I want the parents in here now. Give them PPE and get them in here now." The nurse stared into Bodhi's teary eyes that peered out over the mask and under his cap. His request was not up for discussion. The charge nurse turned to the tech and instructed him to bring in the parents with PPE.

Bodhi met them in front of the room and explained what had happened. He explained that they had done and were doing everything possible. He was brutally honest and told them that their child's chance for survival was slim. He invited them into the room and instructed them to stand at the level of her knees so that they wouldn't get in the way of the resuscitation. He told them that they should hold onto their daughter's legs and pray.

They were well beyond 20 minutes of active resuscitation. Almost everyone in the room was now crying. Except for the parents, everyone knew the ultimate outcome but it was therapeutic for the staff and parents to know that every chance of survival was given. There was silence in the room except for the nurse calling out the time and Bodhi ordering medications. Bodhi was standing at the head of the bed and noticed that some of the nurses were leaving the room. They could no longer hold back their tears. Bodhi could see them embrace each other just outside the room.

They were now going on 35 minutes. The charge nurse walked up to Bodhi and stood directly in front of him. She stared into his eyes without saying a word. Bodhi pulled over the ultrasound machine, placed the probe just below the sternum where the ribs meet and asked them to stop CPR. He asked the parents to look at the screen and pointed to their child's heart that wasn't beating. Bodhi didn't use any euphemisms or sugarcoating. He put the probe down, put his hands on their shoulders and said: "I'm so sorry, but your child is dead. We did everything we could." His comment was factual, straightforward and to the point. His years of experience taught him that parents who had the opportunity to witness the resuscitation, the teamwork, professionalism, empathy and effort made, knew the outcome deep in their hearts. Any words before stating the word "dead" were ignored in anticipation and subsequent words muddled in their loss.

Bodhi pronounced her dead. The parents then did what parents do in that situation. They threw their bodies over their dead child, cried, screamed, and cursed. Despite their screams, there was a silence in the room, as though their cries were being sucked into a vacuum. The staff just stood there or did whatever they were supposed to do, but were visibly shaken. No matter how many years of experience they had, no one gets used to a child dying. It's just not supposed to happen. Some of them were crying and hugging each other. The charge nurse approached Bodhi with tears in her eyes and looked into his teary eyes. He was expecting her to give him shit about breaking the hospital's strict policy of not allowing visitors, but she just stood there, nodded her head yes, and then gave him a big hug. She understood.

Bodhi walked over to the parents and again put his hands on their shoulders. They were leaning over their dead child and perhaps pleading with God to bring her back. He told them that they could stay for as long as they needed to and he would be available for them when they were ready.

This tragedy occurred towards the very end of their shift. Some of the nurses came to Bodhi, embraced and thanked him. Aside from these exchanges, the tone in the ER was subdued. Everyone was deep in their inner journeys. Some thought about their own mortality or that of their loved ones. Others were just angry about how unfair it was that such a young innocent child should die, and empathized with how they themselves would deal with such a loss. Events such as this brought it all home.

Bodhi ended his shift with his typical decontamination procedure. The adrenaline was still flowing high in his body. He drove home and felt proud of the way he handled the situation. He clearly understood the rational for the "no visitor" policy but in this particular instance, he had no doubt that bringing the parents in wearing PPE was absolutely the right thing to do.

Bodhi parked the car and was walking home when the desire for a cold beer hit him. He wasn't much of a drinker and didn't have any at home so he decided to stop by the supermarket. Then the thought of a walnut hamantash cookie suddenly popped into his mind. This was so bizarre because he had not had one for over 20 years and the only place that they were sold in the neighborhood was the Hungarian Pastry Shop on 111th street and Amsterdam Avenue. He was already at the supermarket on 110th street and Broadway so he decided to indulge his sweet tooth. He rationalized that after what had happened that day, he certainly deserved it.

Bodhi spent the large part of his youth at the Hungarian because he was enamored with the idea of the café society he read so much about in Paris. Bodhi did much of his studying as an undergraduate at the Hungarian and when he had kids, would bring them there as well. When the weather was nice, he sat at the tables outside. Unlike many outdoor cafés that only provided a view to passing cars and flat buildings across the street, the Hungarian was just catercorner to St. John the Divine Cathedral, the sixth largest gothic cathedral in the world. Its grounds extended south to 110th street and were very green and spacious. Beautiful peacocks took leisurely strolls on the grounds. On the cathedral grounds and directly in front of the Hungarian was the Peace Fountain. Bodhi remembered the outcry from the community when it was built in 1985 by Greg Wyatt to depict the struggle of good and evil, shown by the archangel Michael vanquishing Satan. Many felt that it was horrid. For Bodhi, it was a grand and remarkable statue. He thought it was fascinating because it appeared to contain every bit of religious imagery known to humankind. Before entering the Hungarian, he stared at the Peace Fountain and wondered if Satan was making a comeback and what the world was now experiencing was his vengeance.

Bodhi entered the Hungarian and the smell of the place

immediately brought to mind so many fond memories of his youth. He couldn't believe that he had not stepped foot in this place that held such an important place in his youth for over 10 years. What was eerily different was the fact that it was completely empty because of Covid-19 restrictions. The place was typically jam-packed. He bought the walnut hamantash and couldn't wait to get home to bite into it and jump onto some Proustian rollercoaster ride.

On his way into the Hungarian, Bodhi had noted a large crowd on the steps of the cathedral. On his way out, he noticed that it was even larger. He walked over to see what was going on. As he got closer, he noticed that everyone was gathered around a man standing higher on the steps. As soon as Bodhi approached the crowd, he recognized the man. Bodhi was shocked.

Bodhi didn't know the man's name but knew him since his childhood in the neighborhood. The man was an Upper West Side fixture as much as he and his own family were. The man was Haitian and must have been by now in his late 80's. He looked a lot thinner and was wearing a worn brown suit that was much too big for him. He was well-known but completely ignored because for as long as Bodhi could remember, the man would walk up and down Broadway waving a Bible over his head and repeating in a high voice: "Jesus loves you! Jesus loves you! Jesus loves you!" This went on all day, every day, for at least forty years. No one had ever heard him utter another word except for "Jesus loves you!" This is what shocked Bodhi. The man was now speaking intelligently and coherently. What also shocked Bodhi was the fact that this same man who everyone in the neighborhood ignored for so many decades, now had captivated the attention of these people and mesmerized them with his words. Bodhi got closer.

The man was holding the same worn Bible and gesticulating as though it were a conductor's baton. He spoke passionately, clearly and in the manner of a preacher. He said:

"This is the big reset. The age of Aquarius is coming. The

end of the madness we created as modern society. The slate will be wiped clean and some will have another chance to set things right. Many will disappear along with every facet of the madness we created. Can you see it?

"Everything will burn to the ground. You'll disintegrate without even a flicker or flash because you were always duds that threatened to explode, but now your impotence is clear. Your only glory was that you drove humanity to the brink of destruction and through your self-immolation you held a mirror for the rest of us to see ourselves. You projected your ridiculousness and showed us how not to be, how the world should be without your selfishness, cruelty, self-righteousness and cowardice. We thank you and will honor thee for your blindness and confer upon thee the Darwin award.

"Nothing will be the same: Amen! Like butterflies, we'll be condemned to evolve into another species. While flying in the air, we will see the rivers, the earth, the trees for the first time without your eyes and see ourselves in the reflection, in its grandeur. Covid-19 has held a mirror large enough for us to see our wings! I'm in! Are you? Will we miss the money, smart phones, slaving at 9-to-5 jobs in order to feed our mortgages, car loans and debt? Will we miss the cigarettes and other tools of self-destruction? With our new eyes, we'll see a reflection in the earth and see that we were destroying it and ourselves. So easy to do when we view ourselves as separate. Ha ha! Do you get it now? The body is a temple, as is the earth. All that it requires is care and gratitude, and abundance follows. How many will see this? It doesn't matter because the earth and almost everyone will be scorched.

"An alternative vision will arise and it won't just be the small minority of tree huggers. Pockets of the earth will breed bearers of the light and create a shift that will be so obvious that people will follow. The others- the haters will be irrelevant. They will create ever deeper and sinister levels of hell for themselves. There are no locks in this hell and everyone will be free to leave whenever they choose. This has always been the case but in this new world it will be more obvious because another way of being, another way of breathing and associating with the self, others and the earth will be evident. It will be so beautiful to see it all burn. Ha ha! Our strings that have always been controlled by the puppet masters will burn away. Pinocchio liberated! 'I used to have strings on me but have no more. I am free!'

"What a privilege to live in this time and recognize what is happening. It seems so clear. Embrace it! Prepare yourself! How you ask? Begin to let go of everything! Recognize everything you presently cherish and worship will burn and fall to the wayside. All that will be left is you! Ha ha! Say hello, I don't think you've ever met! Ha ha! Don't be left behind. This is the time to grow your wings, set your sails so that when the wind comes, you'll be ready to fly. Will you be ready?"

At that moment it started to rain. The crowd started to disperse. The man continued in a more subdued tone:

"It's raining! So beautiful! The earth is cleansing itself. Finally! Thank you! The earth will reclaim itself! It's started! The fungi will then rise from the chaos and recycle the ashes into something new. A new age. One of wisdom. There will be leaders who will rise to the occasion and set the example for the others. Some, or many, will be reluctant to follow and leave what they were accustomed to. Have patience, have faith. They just need examples, leaders to show them the way. And if they don't, they can re-create their own hell societies in the memory of the shit that led to its own destruction."

It started to pour. The crowd thinned even more. The man tucked his Bible under his jacket and continued: "People will learn to feel the earth again. Communicate with plants and ubiquitous energies that have been ignored for so long. Their guides will surface to show them the way out of this confusion and bring together people of spirit. The New Age will dawn."

Then, just as suddenly as the rain came and went, a transformation took place. The man looked out blankly over the crowd and started to walk down the steps and towards Broadway. He took his Bible from under his jacket, started to wave it over his head and repeated over and over again: "Jesus loves you! Jesus loves you! Jesus loves you!"

Bodhi couldn't believe what he had just witnessed and was too exhausted to try to figure it out. *Damn peculiar!* He thought to himself.

QUIET DESPERATION

T he First Wave of Covid-19 wreaked havoc on a world-wide scale. The world was in a frying pan on simmer, slowly getting hotter and the discomfort slowly increasing. What Henry David Thoreau described as the 'quiet desperation' in which humankind lives was now transformed into a witch's cauldron that was almost at a boiling point.

There was fear. Fear of exposure to Covid-19. Fear that nothing would ever be the same. Social distancing, wearing masks, shelter-at-home, working from home, closed restaurants, businesses, gyms, cinemas and theaters- all of these forced upon the masses a new way of being, new ways of thinking and seeing themselves, their families, partners, children and the world. There was fear of dying alone in an overwhelmed hospital without visitors. Fear of the building concerns over not having an income and unable to pay one's bills compounded by pundits on every screen talking about the global economic crash that would lead to full-blown societal panic attack over what the future would bring. Sports teams across the country were shut down. Broadway shows closed until further notice. Tourism was dead. The flow of dollars came to a screeching halt. Driving through Times Square or SoHo became an eerie tourist attraction for New Yorkers who were dumbfounded to witness a ghost town without cars or human beings. All the typical distractions removed except for the ubiquitous screens of mobile phones, televisions and computers. People were left face-to-face with their pets, families, partners and themselves.

The news was old news in that every day brought the same headlines: The number of cases of Covid-19 and the death count were increasing; and the global economy was on the verge of collapse. This was then followed by the never-ending stream of pundits discussing the lack of PPE, test kits, the benefits or folly of social distancing and wearing masks followed by heaps of partisan attacks and blame. Everything was politicized and polarized from a Left or Right bias. Pundits did what pundits did best, they spouted opinions that filled the imaginations of whoever cared to listen and provided distractions to everyone's shelter-in-home sensory deprivation tanks, where constant adjustments were made to the new level of discomfort and angst.

OUT OF THE
FRYING PAN

T hey were three months into the pandemic and the applause for frontline providers feverishly increased with
vigor and enthusiasm. Like clockwork, it would start
all over the world at 7 O'clock. Bodhi wondered what the
effect of clapping at precisely the same time regardless of time
zone would have. There was a belief in spiritual circles that a
large enough group of people meditating with the same intent,
such as world peace or feeding everyone on the planet, would
manifest those changes. If there was the slightest chance that
this could happen, this was the time to try it. It would be
the equivalent of a Hail Mary pass during a professional sport
contest. Well, it hadn't happened yet, perhaps due to a lack of
imagination preoccupied with self-preservation. His thoughts
then turned to whether or not such coordinated clapping
worldwide could be heard out in space?

It was at this time that Bodhi was serendipitously
offered a consulting position. This consulting gig was the ideal
job for many reasons: It provided him and his family with
safety from infection with Covid. Moreover, it was much easier
than working in the ER in every regard: Fewer hours, and less
psychological, emotional and physical stress. Another blessing
was that it allowed him to work from home and finally have

time to pursue some of his personal interests that had long since fallen by the wayside.

Bodhi was at first torn between taking this position that clearly was in his best interest versus the self-sacrifice to "fight the good fight" against Covid for the common good. Bodhi sat with his boss to openly discuss his dilemma. His boss was very understanding and their conversation waxed philosophical. His boss mentioned that the decision was his to make but emphasized the system's need for experienced physicians in this crisis situation. He also made the point that it was unethical for the wealthy to take much needed physicians out of the system to serve their personal needs. It was a genuine ethical dilemma for Bodhi as many of the points that his boss was making resonated with him.

Bodhi questioned himself, his ethics and morals. He wondered where this ethical sense of self-sacrifice originated in the first place. What was the source of this moral imperative that suggested that physicians and other healthcare providers place the lives of their patients before their own? He saw the parallel between his dilemma and soldiers who offered their lives for God and country. He personally believed that such blind loyalty to one's country was anachronistic in the age of the internet where information about the corruption of governments and the real motives behind most modern wars had long since percolated to the surface. He wondered if the United States went into a full-scale war at that moment in time if the American youth would rally behind the flag and offer their lives now that alternate versions of the true motives behind both Gulf Wars and the War on Terror in the Middle East were widely available? It seemed to Bodhi that there was widespread skepticism and suspected that there were many people who now understood that such conflicts had nefarious motives behind them or were false flags to propagate hidden agendas.

This dilemma was not set in Bodhi's mind in isolation. There was the reality of practicing medicine in the United States, which was first and foremost a profit driven business and a mechanism to promote health a distant second. The role of the physician that was once exalted and respected had been reduced to that of a distrusted functionary whose primary function was to serve its primary motive to gain profit. Physicians became mere cogs in the wheel. They lost more and more control of their profession, earning power, while simultaneously losing the respect of the public. There were numerous articles, podcasts and YouTube videos describing the decline of the medical profession. They pointed out the decline in medical school enrollment and increased drug dependency, depression, mental illness, divorce rates and suicide amongst physicians.

The average physician graduated from medical school with a debt of $232,000, and then faced three to six years of residency training depending on the specialty and a few more if further specialization was desired. Bodhi recalled the grueling hours, strain and personal sacrifice he and his colleagues experienced during residency training. What debt did he and his colleagues owe society? They paid up front for their privilege to earn higher than average salaries. After taking into account their personal and financial sacrifices, and the slowly diminishing respect they garnered, what was it exactly that they owed society that warranted sacrificing their own lives and putting the lives of their families at risk?

Bodhi could only rationalize that it was a form of brainwashing or self-hypnosis in order to perhaps convince themselves of their importance to society. The mental wrangling was wearing Bodhi down and he acknowledged that he was not a philosopher and didn't have the tools to wrestle with such profound questions. He discussed his dilemma with some of his trusted colleagues and everyone pointed out that there was in fact no dilemma. Physicians were nothing more than glorified factory workers with higher salaries and better working conditions, and despite their so-called "glorified" status, the vast majority of them were disgruntled.

They provided Bodhi with the analogy of a prisoner

with a life sentence who had managed to ingratiate himself with the warden and guards. This prisoner was treated extremely well, received much better benefits than the other inmates and was quite happy with his circumstances. Then one day the warden retires and a new warden takes his place. New rules are implemented to suit the new warden's point of view and all of a sudden, the prisoner loses all the benefits of the favoritism that he cultivated. He was now demoted to the level of common prisoner. In other words, the glorified factory worker, despite all of his or her benefits, sooner or later learns that they are in fact just a factory worker.

In addition to the decreased salaries and furloughs, the PPE shortage appeared to worsen and hospitals were now rationing PPE. By the end of April, the hospital provided only one N95 mask to each practitioner per week. Bodhi knew that it was not any particular institution's fault that there was a shortage of PPE in the United States at the beginning of the pandemic. However, this shortage was inexcusable five months later.

Bodhi might not have been a philosopher, but he was smart enough to see the writing on the wall. With all of the distressing factors that placed frontline providers in uncharted territory and out of their comfort zones, and now suddenly a significant decrease in patient census, what should have been a relief had become an adrenaline crash. This provided physicians more time to nourish their subconscious fears. Those same heartstrings that pulled frontline providers to sacrifice themselves for the greater good, now tugged back ever so slightly the other way with a faint whisper in their ears that repeated: "This is bullshit!"

The pay cut that came with the adrenaline crash was the final bitch-slap to open Bodhi's eyes. He realized that the risk of being the first canary to die in the coal mine was an occupational hazard he had willingly signed up for and accepted for the 30 years he practiced emergency medicine. What was unacceptable to him was to be the next in line after the ninety-ninth canary died, and expected to do so with a 30% decrease in salary and lack of PPE.

If James Bond did not expect his career and lifespan to be very long, he probably accepted that risk because he had an unlimited credit card to live that short life extravagantly. The system had just taken Bodhi's credit card away and tore it up in front of his face. Hence the emergency medicine adage that provided solace to emergency physicians- "If I'm going to get fucked like a whore, I expect to get paid like one!"- was thrown out the window.

It was at this juncture that Bodhi promptly submitted his resignation letter. He thought it would have been more difficult because his contract stipulated that he provide three months' notice. But since the hospital was in a financial crisis, Bodhi's resignation was received as a gift. From that sober perspective of having already submitted his resignation, a question popped up in Bodhi's head that he wanted to pose to his boss, but never did. The question was: So, if you had significant personal financial resources and faced with a severe pandemic that could potentially kill you and your family, would you first utilize your significant resources to ensure the safety and well-being of you and your family, or would you first think of what was best for the system?

From this perspective, Bodhi realized that there was never in fact a true dilemma. The decision was quite simple but complicated by the heartstrings and guilt nourished by society to serve its own ends. Bodhi was relieved by his decision but still experienced doubt and guilt surrounding the idea that he was abandoning patients and his colleagues who needed him more than ever. He resolved himself to follow an ex-girlfriend's advice: "Go build a bridge and get over yourself!" He recognized those heartstrings that filled him and his colleagues with the ideas of being superheroes and indispensable. Those were the same heartstrings that led young soldiers to war and firemen into burning buildings. Those heartstrings were now slowly being undone and Bodhi felt as though he was waking up from a dream. Something told him that he was not in fact waking up but circumstances had pushed him out of that dream and he was now walking into another.

PART 2: THE APOCALYPSE

THE DOUBLE
WHAMMY

B y September 2020, the pandemic had become predictable. The death toll in the United States was 194,000,
and the number of cases steadily increased. Many states
that had been devastated by Covid-19 had for the most part
recovered, or in the vernacular of the time, had flattened
the curve. Simultaneously however, the inexorable wave of
destruction continued to move on to other states. This was
especially the case in states where Covid-19 was treated as a
mere political talking point. When Covid-19 first hit New York,
this perspective could have been attributed to short-sighted-
ness. However, after witnessing first-hand the devastation in
California, Michigan, Florida, Texas, and Arizona, the outcome
was predictable and such political grandstanding bordered on
the absurd and created stiff competition for the 2020 Darwin
Awards.

The number of cases continued to increase at a steady
rate. By mid-October the death toll in the United States had
increased to 218,000, and to 1.1 million worldwide. By the end
of December 2020, there were 326,000 deaths in the United
States and 1.7 million deaths worldwide. The fear at the fore-
front of everyone's mind was another raging pandemic on the
scale of the 1918 Spanish Flu. What mitigated this fear was

that highly anticipated Covid vaccines were developed and distribution initiated. An end to the madness was in sight. There were reports of a new strain of Covid that emerged in the UK, and other strains developed from other places, but the consensus was that these strains were susceptible to the vaccine.

There were issues with distribution of the vaccine in regards to the number of vaccine doses available, insufficient centers for vaccine distribution, as well as the reluctance of a significant percentage of healthcare providers and the general population who declined vaccination. Nonetheless, a significant percentage of the world population was vaccinated against Covid-19 by June 2021, and the number of cases and Covid-related deaths worldwide markedly declined.

People went back to work. Restaurants, gyms, theaters and cinemas re-opened. Countries that had banned travel to tourists opened their borders. Airlines and hotels offered special deals to promote travel. There was still an air of caution and people worldwide for the most part continued to wear masks. Nonetheless, the optimism was out of the gates creating a wave of elation throughout the world.

The summer of 2021 was exuberant and full of energy. Life had returned to a recognizable normal. The number of cases continued to decline and by October 2021 was negligible. There was some apprehension about the winter months but there was no resurgence as yet. Moreover, influenza was almost nonexistent. The news spread rapidly that the world was victorious in its battle against the coronavirus.

By December 2021, it was as though Covid-19 never happened. It was placed in the same box in the attic where memories of the 2003 SARS, the 2009 H1N1, the 2012 MERS epidemics, and the 1918 Spanish Flu pandemic were stored away.

Then in January 2022, there was a sudden large spike in the total number of Covid cases and simultaneously, a tremendous spike in the number of deaths. It started in Hawaii. Newsrooms across the world reported on this event. For the first time in modern history, there was no spin, no partisan bias. There was just information with a tinge of anxiety in the voices of the newscasters. People were glued to their screens. Interestingly, without the sensationalism and partisan shit-throwing, the reports worldwide were essentially the same.

Bodhi, his mother and sister had just finished dinner and sat to watch the news on CNN:

"Good evening. This is Brian McNeally reporting from CNN World News Tonight with breaking news. There were a large number of people in Hawaii diagnosed with what is believed to be a variant of Covid-19. Dr. Karla Escher, one of the foremost Infectious Disease specialists from Harvard is here to shed some light on this new development."

"Thank you for having me, Brian. Good evening everyone. This is truly shocking news. It appears that Covid-19 is back but on steroids. The Covid-19 that plagued us last year by filling our ICU beds and pushing our medical system to its limits now seems rather tame when compared to this variant."

"What makes it different?" Mr. McNeally asked.

"First," Dr. Escher explained. "This variant is clearly more contagious and with a higher mortality rate. We don't have exact numbers yet, but it appears that at least 34,000 people in Hawaii have been infected with 22,780 dead. This puts the mortality at 67%; and it all happened in one week! To put that number in perspective, the mortality of last year's Covid-19 pandemic was 2.2%."

"That's unbelievable!" Exclaimed Mr. McNeally. "We've heard news that there were some differences in presentation. What can you tell us?"

"Well, the moderate and severe cases of Covid-19 during the First Wave were characterized by hypoxia- not enough oxygen getting to the lungs. This resulted in respiratory difficulty and failure. These were the patients who had filled the ICU beds across the country. Intubating these patients and placing them on a ventilator could at least forestall their deaths and in some cases kept them alive long enough to recover and sometimes leave the hospital. Especially in patients older than 65, the mortality was overwhelmingly due to respiratory failure. What's happening now in Hawaii is a drastic departure."

"How so?" asked Mr. McNeally.

"These patients are now presenting similarly with hypoxia but then very rapidly develop Disseminated Intravascular Coagulation, known as DIC. These patients rapidly progress from walkie-talkie patients to severe shortness of breath, bruises all over their bodies, low blood pressure and bleeding to death from every orifice in their body. It's a double whammy: Respiratory failure and DIC."

"This is beginning to sound like a horror movie," Mr. McNeally interrupted. "What's DIC? Is it a new disease? Is there a treatment?"

"No, it's not a new disease. DIC is a well-known disorder that results in overactive blood clotting."

"Overactive?" asked Mr. McNeally. "Then why are these patients bleeding out?"

"DIC is complicated," explained Dr. Escher. "When someone is injured or sick, proteins in the blood that form blood clots travel to the injury site to help stop bleeding. If these proteins become abnormally active throughout the body, they could cause DIC. In some cases of DIC, small blood clots form in the blood vessels that can clog the vessels and cut off the normal blood supply to organs such as the liver, brain, or kidneys. This results in major injury to the organs, leading to multisystem organ failure. In other cases of DIC, the clotting proteins in the blood are consumed, which results in serious bleeding."

"Is there a treatment?" asked Mr. McNeally.

"Unfortunately not, because DIC isn't the primary disease. It's a reaction to something else, such as inflammation, infection, or cancer. Consequently, treatments are directed to the disease process that activated the DIC."

"So, in this case, the DIC is caused by the Covid infection?"

"Exactly!" Exclaimed Dr. Escher.

Mr. McNeally paused for a second and then stated the obvious: "But there's no treatment for Covid."

"No, there isn't."

"Then what can we do?" Mr. McNeally asked with a slight bit of anxiety in his voice, fearing that Dr. Escher would reply: "Pray!"

"Well," Dr. Escher replied. "Although there isn't specific treatment for DIC, there are supportive treatments. If a large amount of bleeding is occurring, we can give plasma transfusions to replace blood clotting factors. Sometimes we have to transfuse platelets. If a large amount of clotting is occurring, we can give blood thinner medicine, such as heparin, to prevent blood clotting."

"Are these treatments effective?"

Dr. Escher raised her eyebrows, grimaced, and moved her head from side to side. "20%-50% of people with DIC die regardless of treatment."

"Well, that's a bummer!" Mr. McNeally was noticeably shaken. He looked down at his desk. He putzed around with some papers and then looked over at Dr. Escher. "Is there anything that you'd like to share with the audience before we sign off?"

"Sure," she nodded. "At the risk of sounding like Captain Obvious, I want to emphasize that this is serious business like nothing we've ever seen before. Until we get a handle on this, everyone should shelter-in-place and if you have to go out for any reason, absolutely wear a mask. Don't travel. This is a highly contagious and deadly variation of Covid-19. Keep safe."

"Thank you very much for your insights on the resurgence of Covid-19. Our hearts go out to the families in Hawaii who are suffering such losses. This is Brian McNeally with *CNN World News Tonight* saying good night for now. Stay tuned for updates. Stay safe. God Bless!"

Bodhi, his mother and his sister stared back and forth at each other for a long time without saying a word. The television was still playing in the background.

"So, this is it?" Bodhi's mother asked in a flat, matter-of-fact tone of voice. They continued to exchange stares.

"Could be," Bodhi said.

"Yes, it could be," his sister, the ever-practical former ICU nurse said sharply. "But in the meantime, we need to prepare. Let's take inventory of our food supplies and stock up. Same types of food we stored last time." Her tone of voice was a call to arms. Bodhi and their mother both snapped to attention and went into planning mode.

"I agree," Bodhi added. "But I think we should have enough to last for one year."

"One year!" His mother exclaimed.

"Bodhi's right," his sister nodded. "This situation is going to get bad really fast. We need to be prepared to stay home for the long haul."

"If that's the case," his mother added. "I'll need another refrigerator."

"That's actually a great idea," Bodhi said. "Let's get an extra fridge and stand-alone freezers for each apartment. I'll take care of that."

"What about the kids?" His mother asked. They looked at each other for a second in silence.

"There's nothing we can do," Bodhi said. "They're adults now. I don't think traveling is safe and the fact is, they're probably safer in Europe."

"I agree," his sister said.

"I'll give them a call to let them know what's going on. Worst case scenario, they'll go to the farm and shelter-in-place there." There was another moment of silent reckoning of their situation. The preparations they had made during the First Wave was a drill for a hypothetical disaster. Although still on the other side of the country, this Second Wave seemed like the real deal.

"Let's go to Costco first thing in the morning," his sister suggested in a tone that was clearly a command.

Bodhi nodded and added: "We can buy the refrigerators and freezers there too." Bodhi was preoccupied with the thought of his kids in Europe and started to get up to leave. His sister interrupted his thoughts with the following question:

"So, we shelter-in-place starting tomorrow. Right?" It seemed obvious enough but Bodhi wasn't thinking that far ahead. His initial thought was that this was a bit drastic, but then immediately reconsidered with the reality of the 67% mortality of this new Covid variant and the image of people bleeding to death from every orifice. *Covid-19 and DIC*, he thought to himself. *A double-whammy indeed!*

"Absolutely!" Bodhi replied. "Let's get everything we need and watch the end of the world on television."

THE SECOND WAVE

T he entire island of Hawaii was immediately quarantined by the military but it was too late. People with the disease had already traveled to other states and countries. The cat was out of the bag. The spread of this new variant of Covid-19 spread at a blistering rate. Plasma, cryoprecipitate and platelets transfusions were often used as a last resort to treat the DIC, but the patients would bleed to death before these products could be thawed in the blood bank and delivered.

There was little that the medical system could offer patients with the first iteration of Covid-19, and absolutely nothing to offer this Godzilla variation. By way of comparison, it was a drastic mutation akin to a monkey evolving into a modern-day iPhone carrying hipster in one generation. This baffled scientists across the world.

By the third week of January, 37% of Hawaii's population was decimated. The apocalypse had begun and the deaths were piling up very rapidly. By the end of March, the number of deaths in the United states had increased to 57 million.

Suddenly there was silence. The politicians who survived up until this point were mute. The skeptics and conspiracy buffs who had granted themselves overnight doctorates in Epidemiology and fellowships in Infectious Disease were nowhere to be found. The streets were empty and no one was clamoring for bars, churches and gyms to reopen. No one questioned the mandatory use of masks and quarantine rules that were now stricter than those imposed by countries with totalitarian governments. Everyone now rallied behind the scientists but it was too late. They had nothing to offer except shelter-in-home and to pray.

By June 2022, the worldwide death toll was 2.5 billion. Hospitals were filled to capacity and could offer nothing except comfort care and an avenue to spread the disease. As more doctors, nurses, advanced practitioners and ancillary staff died, most of the survivors abandoned their posts and stayed home with their families. It was no longer a moral dilemma but a practical one. It was a simple risk-benefit analysis that clearly showed that there was nothing to offer these patients, therefore little benefit, while placing themselves and their families at great risk. The healthcare system collapsed. People were advised to stay home regardless of symptoms. Being a good citizen was to die at home rather than spread the disease to anyone else.

Ambulances were converted into hearses. The EMT's were geared with high-tech PPE that looked like space suits. Their jobs were now to place the dead in medical grade bags and transport them to mass graves where their bodies were immediately incinerated. They reported the horror of finding the dead bodies that were completely black and blue and covered with dry blood. What was worse according to them were the tears in the eyes of the families of the dead. They were not tears for their dead loved one, but of fear. They knew that they would likely be placed in a similar bag within one or two weeks.

The EMT's learned to avoid any eye contact with family members. They came in, loaded the dead bodies into the bags, put them into the truck and then to the mass graves. It was not a sign of disrespect or a lack of empathy. It was a total loss of faith in humanity. Humanity was losing and they could not look it in the eye for fear of seeing themselves in those eyes reflecting humanity in a body bag. The rate of severe depression, drug and alcohol use, and suicide in these EMT's increased exponentially. Many of them quit their jobs because they could no longer shoulder the burden of carrying the dead. They became EMT's for the adrenaline rush of saving lives, not to bear witness to piles and piles of dead bodies, and those left alive as soon to be additions to the ever-growing pile of ashes.

Severe depression, drug and alcohol use, and suicide rates also increased dramatically in the general population. Suicide and assisted suicide became "a thing." The idea of dying in such a horrific manner- the pain, bleeding from every orifice, drowning in blood pooling in their lungs- was too much to bear. Increasing numbers of people took the cue from vampire and werewolf movies to kill themselves and their loved ones before they "turned." Finding a friend or family member to assist in a suicide became increasingly easier because no one wanted to witness such a slow, agonizing and visually horrific death. It was one thing to watch someone die peacefully or even with distress. It was an altogether different matter to see the red dots all over their bodies then convert to black and blue blotches, followed by the spewing of blood from every bodily orifice. This was too much of a shitshow to bear. They were consequently happy to enter into a Ponzi-like scheme of you do me and then find someone to commit to doing you when you began to turn. Everyone was "passing it forward."

There was total radio silence. The news had become a broken record that repeated itself and had nothing new to add. One could argue that even before Covid-19 the news was a broken record that was on a 24-hour cycle. They did however, offer hope along partisan lines, and there was certainly enough blame to throw around. This at the very least fanned the flames of distrust and discontent enough to distract the masses from the profound misery they sought to hide from. Now there was just the repetition of the increasing numbers of deaths and suicides. There was no hope to offer and no one to blame.

The clear sign that humankind was in deep shit was the fact that the politicians, who had always found a way to spin any event and keep the dialogue amped up to distract from the real issues, fell silent. Democrats, Republicans, Right, Left, Neo-this or that, were now convenient clichés. They were puppets from a forgotten era that no longer served any purpose. Governments all over the world proved ineffectual. There was nothing they could offer their citizenry. No prophetic leaders emerged. The only voices that resounded were the evangelicals who with glee reminded the world that they had told us so. They shook their fingers while spewing venom that we brought all of this upon humankind with our embrace of LGBTQIA+, abortion rights, and liberalism. But no one listened.

Everyone looked to the one group that could possibly save them- scientists. This was the same group they cursed and spit at when they warned us of climate change and the relation between factory farmed meat and the increasing number of pandemics in general. The same scientists they maligned and discredited over almost every warning and guidance on this very pandemic. The masses now begged and pleaded for their guidance, a glimmer of hope. The scientists were silent. It wasn't because they were being cruel and punishing the masses for their past insults, but rather because they literally had nothing to offer. The evidence was incontrovertible- humankind was on the verge of a mass extinction event.

Services had collapsed by June 2022. Garbage piled up on the streets and rats flourished. Dead decaying bodies lay on the streets partially eaten by rats and stray dogs. There were so many rats on the streets that it appeared that they were destined to be the inheritors of the earth. It was a miracle that another calamity such as the Bubonic Plague did not bear its ugly head. Such a calamity certainly would have given credulity to what the evangelicals were spewing. But at this point, it was irrelevant. The "Rona" was quite competent at bringing humankind to its knees all by itself.

By July the worldwide death toll was 3.2 billion. There was no end in sight. The idea of the end of humankind was on everyone's mind and the only thing one could do was to make peace with one's maker. A transformation had occurred by this time. The fear had transformed to acceptance. There was the same learned helplessness across the world that one saw when rats in a cage were shocked again and again. At first, they jumped around and tried vigorously to escape. After a while, they just sat there and accepted the shocks. There was nothing they could do so they did nothing. People said whatever they had to say to loved ones and just waited for the inevitable visit that Death would pay.

It was perhaps at that moment when the shift occurred. Some of the remaining survivors changed. The learned helplessness now transmuted to a deep inner peace. This was the same peace that would sometimes manifest soon before someone dies. Everything they had been carrying just dropped. They just let it all go. It was a grand "I don't give a fuck!" moment that allows the peace to move and settle in. Through the spectacles of peace, they were able to see who they really were and see everyone else and everything for what they were. There was no more struggle. They arrived at a profound understanding of "it is what it is" and it was all good. Now with 20/20 vision they were able to see through all the gobbledygook that moved and controlled them with invisible strings. They were now singing Pinocchio's song: "I had strings but now I'm free. I have no strings on me." With this newfound freedom, they waited for Death.

By November 2022, the worldwide death toll was 4 billion. Half of the world's population was dead. Then, just as suddenly as this mutated Godzilla Covid-19 appeared and swept the globe, it disappeared. The event was immediately palpable. No one needed to tune in to the now silent newsrooms to know that the march of the disease had slowed down. Now those same people they saw a few days ago were still alive. People in their households were still alive. The news spread on the internet in the form of questions about the last time someone saw or heard of someone dying from blood pouring out of what was once a human being.

By December 2022, people all over the world started to cautiously go out again. They explored the ruins and took account of what remained. For the first time, they wondered to themselves what they would do tomorrow and the day after. Where would they get food? They now had the luxury to ask themselves: *What's the plan?*

Once it settled in that the danger had passed and that they wouldn't die a horrid Covid death, they began to ask: *But How? Why?* How could a disease that killed 4 billion people suddenly just stop? Some hypothesized that just as it so rapidly mutated into a Godzilla virus, it mutated to a benign form. Others considered the possibility that those who had survived had some specific DNA sequence that conferred immunity. They reasoned that since the virus couldn't find any new hosts, it died. The survivors were overwhelmed with feelings of guilt combined with elation. These feelings thoroughly dominated their psychologic state of being, rendering those intellectual curiosities of why or how they survived irrelevant.

NEW BEGINNINGS

The world had very rapidly changed for the remaining survivors. The world as they knew it vanished into thin air. They suddenly found themselves in a world without recognizable foundations. Government at the highest and lowest levels was decimated. The global economy evaporated. The supply chain was nonexistent. The healthcare system had dissolved. The survivors had to rely on themselves to survive.

Bodhi remembered an Instagram post of a poem he saw during the First Wave that seemed so prophetic at the time and so quaint now from his 20/20 perspective. The poem "And the People Stayed Home" was written and posted on the internet by Kitty O'Meara in March 2020. It went viral. Bodhi had saved the poem and read it to himself whenever looking for hope and inspiration. The poem read:

And the people stayed home. And read books, and listened, and rested, and exercised, and made art, and played games, and learned new ways of being, and were still. And listened more deeply. Some meditated, some prayed, some danced. Some met their shadows. And the people began to think differently.

And the people healed. And, in the absence of people living in ignorant, dangerous, mindless, and heartless ways, the earth began to heal.

And when the danger passed, and the people joined together again, they grieved their losses, and made new choices, and dreamed new images, and created new ways to live and heal the earth fully, as they had been healed.

Bodhi wondered if she was still alive. If so, he wanted to ask her two questions: How did she know? And was she still so optimistic?

PART 3: POST-APOCALYPSE NYC

THE SURVIVORS

Bodhi received the news that his youngest daughter made it to their maternal grandparents' farm in the northwest of France, but his two older children had died in Spain. He was devastated. After 30 years of working in busy emergency departments, Bodhi was quite familiar with the many faces of Death, but nothing could prepare him for the death of his children.

It was a period of deep mourning. Bodhi joined in with the collective depression of survivors that was prompted by the death of almost everyone they knew, cared for and loved, and survivor guilt. Bodhi thought of his children as he vividly imagined the fear in their eyes just before they exploded and splattered blood in every direction. He bawled as he visualized their hands desperately reaching out for help, for the comfort of a loving embrace. He was devastated with an overwhelming feeling of nausea realizing that what they likely found was the look of even greater fear that rejected their plea for help and consolation. They were left to die ignoble deaths all alone. Along with the other survivors, Bodhi was overwhelmed with guilt and ran those scenarios again and again in his mind.

Bodhi and the survivors were also grieving for themselves. Grieving that they did not die, asking themselves, *what is there to live for?* They grieved for a way of life that had been erased along with 4 billion people. They now realized that all their pre-Covid worries and complaints were truly trivial and irrelevant. They were now stranded in an unknown world where everything that was previously taken for granted was no longer a reality. The buildings, restaurants, and storefronts now appeared as props for an elaborate set that just filmed a B-list zombie apocalypse movie and were then abandoned. The city was just a shell.

To make matters worse, the winter of 2023 was brutal. The northeast was overwhelmed with heavy snowfall starting in January 2023 and persisted throughout the winter. There were no street-cleaning services so the snow just piled up. The cars on the streets were completely covered. The temperature dropped to below zero and remained there for the entire winter. It seemed as though Mother Nature and Covid-19 had conspired to purge humanity from the face of the earth.

In addition, there was the harsh reality of diminishing food supplies, and the lingering fear that Covid-19 was on holiday and would return with a vengeance. The industrial world was ravaged and translocated to a bygone era where food was not a given. There were many poor countries in the world where perhaps this was nothing new, but for countries where food could be ordered online and half of it thrown away, this was devastating. The juxtaposition of food shortages against the backdrop of skyscrapers, cars and asphalt was shocking to anyone who could think of anything else except where their next meal would come from. Supermarkets and restaurants were already looted and no further deliveries could be counted on.

It was mid-January, snowing, and the temperature below freezing. People were sinking deeper into their misery and self-imposed isolation when the oil that provided heat in the buildings ran out and many of the water pipes froze. They were hungry, cold and filled with the fear of freezing or starving to death. They had already broken into empty apartments of the dead and ransacked whatever food, blankets and comforters they could find. They then broke into sporting goods and appliance stores for tents, sleeping bags and space heaters.

There was nothing else they could do at that point about food except to go door to door and beg. Most people didn't open their doors because they didn't want to share their limited supply of food. There was also the fear of being robbed. Gangs, and even neighbors, were breaking into apartments and stealing whatever food people had saved, leaving them to starve to death.

Bodhi's mother, sister and nephew had survived and provided him with tremendous support during these difficult times. They pushed him to focus on the survival issues facing them. Fortunately, they had enough food. They had stockpiled quinoa, faro, pasta, rice, various dried beans, lentils and pasta sauce. Bodhi remembered thinking that the quantity of food they had stockpiled was overkill but was now thankful they did. They had also purchased additional refrigerators and freezers for perishables. They calculated that if rationed, they had enough food for almost a year.

Bodhi's apartment building was relatively newer than his mother's and sister's. It had better insulation, so they all moved into his place. They consolidated their food and comforters. Bodhi used to take the kids camping and still had two tents. He set up the larger one for his mother, sister and nephew, and he slept in the smaller one. He followed the advice of someone in his building to leave his water running at a low rate to prevent the pipes from freezing, so he still had water.

His building still had electricity and they had electrical burners for cooking. His mother's building had had some issue with the gas lines many years prior and the management provided them with electric burners while they were being repaired. Bodhi and his sister had always criticized their mother for being a hoarder, but in this case, it was a blessing that she held on to them. They expected the electricity to fail at any moment, so they used the refrigerated and frozen food first. They kept one week's supply in the freezer and another in the fridge for future use.

People in the neighborhood knew Bodhi was a doctor so

he was frequently asked to consult on medical problems. He was able to help with some issues but was helpless when confronted with people who were having heart attacks, strokes, and severe complications of diabetes, such as diabetic ketoacidosis or hyperglycemic hyperosmolar non-ketotic coma. Hypothermia was extremely common amongst the elderly and young children. There were several times he was called and found someone who had frozen to death or died from likely starvation. He didn't present it as a barter, but offered his services for contributions of food and blankets that he shared with the neediest in his community.

It was a long winter. Keeping track of how many people died at that point was irrelevant. People stopped counting after 4 billion people died from the Second Wave of the pandemic. By the time the snow thawed however, it was evident that a significant number had died from the cold and starvation.

In contrast, the spring of 2023 was glorious. The days were getting longer and warmer. Everything that spring had ever represented to humankind that had been forgotten in the metro-boulot-dodo hypnosis of modern pre-Covid life, exploded into the consciousness of the survivors. It was like they were seeing, hearing and smelling for the first time. Every little expression of nature was like a July 4th fireworks display- the budding flowers and leaves, and their rich colors and aromas, the sound of birds chirping and the warm breezes that kissed their cheeks. They had miraculously survived the near mass extinction of humankind, freezing and starving to death. They now more than ever needed human contact and wanted to share their stories, to commiserate.

People slowly came out of their mental shelters-in-place and embraced each other as though they were long lost friends. As they met and introduced themselves, they realized that these were the same people with whom they had passed by every day for years and for whom they had devised elaborate mechanisms to avoid eye contact at all cost and never say hello. They now enthusiastically embraced each other because they were now a community with something in common-they were survivors.

There was also the realization that their food supply was rapidly dwindling. They knew that they had to quickly find an alternative food supply to avoid resorting to hunting for the plump New York City rats that were now in abundant supply. That thought was disturbing to Bodhi not so much because it was so disgusting, but gagged with the thought of chefs charging exorbitant amounts of coin for their nouveau cuisine specialties "Rat au Vin" and "Rat Wellington."

His sister had even taken into account the fact that they would have to share some of their food with friends and those in severe need who had not prepared. This consequently left Bodhi and his family with enough food to last for another few months. Nonetheless, planning for a future supply was paramount on everyone's mind. Bodhi's first thought was a natural extension of an idea he had many years before. Since he grew up in the city, he had been oblivious about where food came from other than the supermarket. It was an eye-opener for him to spend time on his ex-in-laws farm in France where he learned that potatoes came from the ground. He also loved all the flowers they planted in the garden. His ex-wife inherited this love of gardening and participated in the nurture of a few neighborhood flower gardens that were planted in empty building lots. She had always planned to ask their landlord to use the roof to plant a garden but never did because they traveled so much.

Bodhi was not at all mechanically inclined but managed to find wood, a hammer and nails to build planting containers on the roof. He raided the local flower shops for soil. Someone on his block saw him making frequent trips carrying the soil.

"Hey!" The man called. He was in his seventies, pale and gaunt. "You're the doctor, right?" Bodhi nodded yes.

"How's your mom? Still alive?"

"Yeah," Bodhi said. "She's a survivor."

"I've seen you go back and forth with that soil. What are you doing?"

"I'm making planting boxes to grow food on the roof."

"That's a great idea," the man said. "Can I take a look?"

"Sure. I'm Bodhi. What's your name?"

"Peter," the man replied. "I used to sing in the church choir with your mom." They went to the roof of Bodhi's building. Peter walked around the boxes without saying a word. Bodhi was stacking the bags of soil. Peter then knelt down in front of one of the boxes. "Nice idea Bodhi. But this won't work."

"What do you mean? Why not?"

"How's the water going to drain? The water will accumulate and kill the seeds."

"I didn't think of that," Bodhi said. "I've never done this before. Do you have experience?"

"Just a bit," Peter said. "I grew up on a farm in Pennsylvania and had to help out as a kid, so I know my way around. I had other plans for my life so I got the hell out of there as soon as I could, but it's in my blood."

"Can you help me?" Bodhi asked.

"Absolutely!" Peter exclaimed. "There are other people in the neighborhood who have lots of experience with growing food. I used to work with them in the community gardens on 111th and Amsterdam. I don't know if they survived, but if they did, I'm sure they'd be willing to help. Hell, it's either that or starve."

Bodhi was thrilled to hear the news because he acknowledged that he didn't have a clue about growing food. There were indeed a few survivors with experience. Many of them were diehard survivalists who had prepared themselves for exactly this situation. After being criticized for so long about their so-called crazy ideas, they were finally vindicated and consequently eager to share their knowledge and provide guidance.

One of the people Peter introduced to Bodhi was Karl. He

and his wife Abigail moved to New York City in 2015 with their daughter Nancy, who was now nine years old. He had been the CEO of a large company in California and was promoted to head the company's larger affiliate branch in New York City. Karl was intelligent, insightful, and a great organizer. He had the uncanny ability to hear an idea and organize the right people and materials required to get the job done. They quickly became friends and made a great team together.

Bodhi and Karl organized groups to secure the materials and plan how to most efficiently grow food on the rooftops. They constructed wooden supports to avoid damaging the rooftops, built planter boxes in the correct way, and re-purposed wooden containers for their rooftop farms. They also constructed walls for implementing vertical gardens and had the foresight to plan for large greenhouses for the winter months. Soil was obtained from looting flower shops and then from the parks. They had unlimited rooftop terrain on which to plant and an apparent abundance of seeds. They were acutely aware of the dwindling food supply and first planted fast growing vegetables. These included sunflower shoots, scallions, radishes, spinach, lettuce, turnips, zucchini, beets, broccoli, baby carrots, and cucumbers, which would produce a harvest in 30 to 60 days. They also planted potatoes that would yield a harvest in 70 to 120 days.

Their group started with 37 people who were interested in participating in growing food as a community. They formed a cooperative where their labor gave them access to food. What was amazing to Bodhi was that within a five-block radius they were able to find experts in a wide variety of subjects and people with amazing skills that contributed in varying ways. For instance, there were a large number of carpenters that built the foundations on the roof and the plant boxes. Five rooftops were sufficient for the needs of their small group but Bodhi had the insight that more people would inevitably join. So as long as they could find wood, soil and seeds, and had the carpenters on hand, he created planting areas on almost every rooftop in his neighborhood.

The quality of the soil that they were able to obtain in the parks wasn't that great so they traveled outside of the city for better soil. Gas was still available but limited, so people with access to electric cars made the trips. As news traveled more people did in fact join their group, which quickly grew to over 150 people. More people brought more local expertise that guided what they grew and how best to grow it. They were watering the soil with hoses that they ran from the top floor apartments. This was certainly adequate but a bunch of plumbers obtained all the hardware necessary from local hardware stores and created dedicated water lines for the rooftops.

Once they planted their seeds, it was now out of their hands. All they could do was to pray, as people had done for millennia, for a successful harvest. The backup plan was hunting and fishing. Since there were less boats and traffic in the Hudson River since the First Wave, the Hudson River now abounded with fish. Avid fisherman who did so previously for sport, now taught many others how to fish for their survival.

The large number of people with fishing rods did not greatly surprise Bodhi. What surprised him was the large number of people in their ever-expanding group with guns. They hunted deer, caribou, wild boar, turkey, bear, moose, wild hogs, rabbits, raccoons, opossums, coyotes and beavers. These animal populations had markedly increased after the first Covid wave and were plentiful. Bodhi imagined the new television ads for Tesla and other electric cars showing them with these dead animals tied across their rooftops with people standing in front of them with rifles. It was at the very least reassuring to know that they were unlikely to die from starvation.

PRACTICAL ISSUES

There were other issues that took priority once their food supply was assured. They had run out of oil in January and a significant number of people froze to death during the winter. They still did not have hot running water. The winter months were seven months away but without the supply chain, there was no hope of obtaining oil to run the boilers. Burning wood was not an option because there wasn't enough wood and the likelihood of burning buildings to the ground was quite high. They had already raided stores for electric heaters but they were insufficient in number and it was uncertain if the already weakened electrical power grid could support such an energy requirement.

Bodhi and Karl reached out to a few people in the community who worked with renewable energy. They then drew upon their network of colleagues in the renewable energy field. They worked together and proposed solar energy as a primary source and using hydropower derived from the Hudson River as a backup. Their group expanded to experts all over the city, New Jersey and Connecticut who had the knowledge and technical skills to plan and install the solar panels and hydropower. They pillaged existing materials from wherever they could to build them. There were hundreds of people in the community, including teenagers, who were interested in learning how to build and install them. They converted many of the storefronts no longer in use into factories to build the equipment.

Those who had the know-how then installed them on top of every building and along the Hudson River shoreline.

The plan was to install solar panels, river turbines as well as a grid to store and conduct the harvested energy by the end of October 2023. Their calculations indicated that they would be able to store enough energy in the intervening three months to get them through the winter. The concern however, was what would happen when the community plugged in, en masse, with their electric cooktops, appliances, computers and televisions. There were a lot of meetings discussing the importance of limiting the use of electrical appliances during the winter months to avoid a complete shutdown. They were all hoping that everyone would understand the gravity of the situation and do their part to conserve energy. The goal was not to make the living spaces cozy and toasty, but livable.

They also simultaneously implemented another strategy. They selected a few high-rise buildings that were modern, well-insulated and could accommodate large numbers of families. The energy grid was directed at these few buildings that would be better able to conserve and distribute energy. There was little resistance as these were for the most part luxury buildings and only small numbers of people chose to stay in their homes. If their plan failed, they had already raided the sporting goods stores and warehouses and had a stockpile of tents, sleeping bags, coats, hats, gloves, and comforters designed for extreme cold weather. In the worst-case scenario, they really only needed a minimum of heat in each building to prevent the water pipes from freezing. They ultimately reasoned that Eskimos and indigenous people lived outdoors in the bitter cold for millennia. They consequently should be able to survive the two to three harsh winter months since they had shelter.

The only concern about moving everyone into a few buildings was the possibility of a Third Wave of Covid-19 that could then again spread like wildfire with so many people in close proximity. There weren't any new reported deaths related to Covid-19 but the fear of a Third Wave hung over their heads like a guillotine. All they could do was exactly what they were doing and pray for the best. It was a calculated risk that they were willing to take rather than freeze to death.

COMMUNITY HEALTH

Bodhi was up to his ears in tapioca. In addition to his leadership role and participation with the food gardens and energy supply, he was working long hours at the medical clinic he had established at the neighborhood urgent care center. He found himself running around nonstop and stretched paper thin between the work and attention demanded by the three projects. He was exhausted and knew that what he was doing was not sustainable. Moreover, he was aware that it was more than the survival issues that were driving him. He still had not come to terms with the death of his two older children and was subconsciously jumping into projects to avoid confronting the void they left in his heart. But no matter how much work he piled on to distract himself, the abyss was always there.

Bodhi was rushing home from the medical clinic in the middle of the day to shower and then run to another meeting about the energy supply. His eyes were bloodshot and had dark circles under them. He was looking at the ground and mumbling to himself, rehearsing what he planned to say at the meeting. As he was turning around the corner of 107th street, he literally bumped into Karl, who was walking towards him. Bodhi was thrown off-balance and was about to fall.

"Whoa man!" Karl just barely caught the unsteady Bodhi. He took a look at the dark bags under his friend's eyes. "Dude, are you okay? You look like shit!" Karl exclaimed.

"I feel like shit," Bodhi smiled. "I really need to sleep."

"What's going on?"

"Just getting pulled in too many directions," Bodhi replied. "The clinic is killing me."

"Are you being pulled, or are you throwing yourself in too many directions?" Bodhi just looked down and shook his head. Karl held Bodhi's shoulders firmly. Tears welled in Bodhi's eyes. Karl gave him a hug for a long time. He could feel Bodhi sobbing. Karl whispered in his ear:

"I can't begin to imagine what it's like to lose a child, let alone two," Karl whispered in his ear. "But burying yourself in work isn't the answer." Bodhi tried to separate himself but Karl held Bodhi's shoulders tight and stared into his eyes. There was so much more he wanted to say but didn't think it was the right moment. He nodded and smiled at Bodhi.

"I've really got to getting going," Bodhi said as he wiped his tears. "I have a meeting in a few minutes."

Karl smiled, let go of Bodhi's shoulders and offered to walk with him. They walked in silence for half the block. Karl then interjected:

"So what's going on at the clinic?"

"The patients are so needy and we just don't have the resources."

"What do you mean by needy?" Karl asked.

"They want a quick-fix pill to solve all their problems and aren't invested in their own health. Same as before. It didn't matter so much before the pandemic because there was a lot of buffer. But now with our limited resources, it just doesn't make any sense."

"But I've heard you talk about how people have to take personal responsibility for their health. Are you sharing that message to them?"

"Yeah," Bodhi replied. "They just don't seem to care or get it."

"Dude," Karl said. "It's not your problem. It's theirs 100%. Can I make a suggestion?"

"Sure."

"First of all," Karl said. "You're not a martyr. There are plenty of doctors around here. Let's get them together and organize them to divide the responsibility. Then we'll set up a series of community meetings where you can talk about health issues."

"But it's nothing new," Bodhi objected. "They've heard this so many times that they're numb to it."

"The difference now is that they are the survivors of a near mass extinction event. Just like I've heard you say so many times, the job of doctors in this reality is to support and help with real medical conditions that they can't take care of themselves. You're the one who keeps saying that we don't have the resources to carry dead wood. If they can't take care of themselves, then fuck 'em!"

"Yeah," Bodhi nodded. "Sounds familiar."

"Then hold them accountable. Everyone who can has to carry their own weight. Listen, go get some rest and let's meet tomorrow to get this ball rolling. Are you in?"

Karl was a mover and a shaker. Within a week, he got the word out and set up a series of meetings with groups of doctors and nurses. Bodhi set the meeting priorities and together they formed clinics. Some were based in the former Urgent Care centers and others were established in the abandoned hospitals. There were enough doctors, nurses and ancillary staff in the area from a variety of specialties that allowed them to even deal with major cases of acute appendicitis, general surgeries and the vast majority of ailments. There were, however, harsh realities to face in their post-Covid reality. Patients with major heart attacks previously had access to catheterization labs to break up the blood clots in the coronary vessels or place stents, as well as open heart surgery and life-saving medications. This was no longer the case. Even during the best of times pre-Covid, there was little to offer patients with catastrophic strokes and now there was nothing except aspirin.

Karl then set up a series of community meetings where

Bodhi presented the reality of what medical capabilities could be offered and what couldn't. He pointed out that many of their illnesses were self-induced and related to life-style choices. Consequently, they could be controlled or altogether avoided with a better diet, smoking cessation and exercise. Unlike his pre-Covid presentations on this subject, Bodhi presented the cold reality that there was no longer a system to deal with their self-imposed medical disasters. In their present predicament, they would just be left to suffer and die.

Bodhi's message did not fall on deaf ears this time. People asked questions and appeared genuinely motivated to learn how to lead healthier lives. Bodhi offered regular lectures on health-related issues. As the word spread and the crowds grew larger and larger, he organized experts to teach about diet, exercise, yoga and meditation. Bodhi was then invited to present these lectures all over the city. People were genuinely interested in a way rarely seen pre-Covid. Perhaps it was the realization of how pathetic it would be to now die from an obesity or smoking-related cause after the miracle of having survived a near extinction event.

Bodhi's presentations were harsh and laid the responsibility of health squarely on every individual's shoulders. He explained that everyone of course had the right to smoke and eat garbage, but now there was no safety net and they only had a small and finite supply of medications. It was consequently everyone's responsibility to be as healthy as possible.

Bodhi's message resonated with the community. It was certainly easier to eat healthier because of the paucity of industrially produced meat, processed foods and the supply of Hostess Twinky-like sugar products that were limited and diminishing. Exercise was now facilitated by the fact that people were working outdoors to farm and playing with the kids.

Bodhi's message spread widely. Trainers who lived in the community opened the gyms and offered free classes. People participated because they recognized that obesity and being out of shape was now a survival issue rather than simply a fad.

There were yoga and meditation classes and people arrived *en masse*. Bodhi was at first surprised and believed that this was simply a coping mechanism to keep themselves busy. He was even more surprised when the numbers continued to increase and the adults started to bring their kids.

There was a lot of talk during the First Wave of how the pandemic was an opportunity for growth and change. Well, the First Wave was equivalent to a small tremor that everyone felt but were used to and ignored. Many, however, knew that the small tremors were warnings of the larger earthquake that would subsequently follow. In hindsight, the First Wave was insufficient to emotionally or psychologically move people out of their petrified habits. The Second Wave washed everything away and now there was little choice. It was change or die a pathetic death. Pathetic because it was akin to performing Hara-kiri outside of the cultural imperatives of an act of honor and simply an act of suicide. Pathetic because life had suddenly been placed on a pedestal above the rotting corpses of 4 billion people worldwide who had died from Covid. Consequently, such a suicide by smoking or engorging oneself with Hostess Twinkies, which was stupid before, was now absurd.

POST-APOCALYPSE
NEW YORK CITY

D espite the horror of the Second Wave, it was a very special time to be in New York City. The streets were desolate. Most people died and of those who survived, many of them fled the city. It was beautiful and majestic as it had always been but now even more so without the hordes of people. It was magical to bike all over the city and witness empty streets for miles and miles. Bodhi wondered if those same buildings would be discovered under a thick overgrown jungle in 1,000 years.

Many years before Bodhi and his ex-wife had children, they witnessed that many friends in their peer group moved out of the city once they had children. This was especially the case if they had two or three children because large apartments were ridiculously expensive and finding a decent public school almost impossible.

They had friends who lived in the Berkshires of Massachusetts, which was beautiful. They spent a lot of time there and loved their friends' community. They even considered moving there and started to look at homes. It wasn't until one of their friends died that reality hit home. Most of their friends in the Berkshires were amazing and inspiring human beings. They were for the most part artists and intellectuals who grew up in the sixties. For some reason, it never clicked that most of them were their parent's age. It was shocking to them when this became apparent. Since they were considering moving there, they started to actively seek out people their age. They were very disappointed. What they found was that their Berkshire peers were the polar opposites of their friends. This shouldn't have been surprising at all because it is relatively common that one generation rebels against the standards set by the previous one. Consequently, once they started to look beyond their friends' community, they found xenophobia, extreme Right perspectives and racism. They at first rationalized that they would find a house in the country with lots of land and insulate themselves from those types of people, but then always asked themselves if these were the types of people they wanted their kids associating with. Even worse was the possibility of really disliking their kids for who they would grow up to be because of those associations. They opted to stay in the city.

Bodhi and his ex-wife both grew up in large, cosmopolitan cities and thrived in the cultural paella that they had learned to navigate in New York City and Paris. They loved the fact that in a jaunt down the street they would nonchalantly pass a Hassidic Jew, a black person with dyed pink hair, and then a gay couple walking hand in hand, and not really even notice or care. In addition, they lived on the Upper West Side near both Riverside Park and Central Park, and lots of activities with which to engage children. They were also blessed to have Bodhi's mother and sister in the neighborhood who were always willing to take the kids. This allowed them to fully enjoy the nightlife and all the culture New York City had to offer. This was exactly the environment that they both wanted to live and raise their kids.

When they had their first child, they started to explore the possibilities for schools and explored the private schools as well. It was the mid-1990's and annual tuition for elementary schools was about $25,000. This was not possible on his salary of an academic emergency physician. The vast majority of public schools in New York City were simply terrible, which left about 15 of them that were in the acceptable to great category. Now they understood why so many people left New York City when they had kids. They were fortunate to get their kids into a great public school so they stayed in the city.

Bodhi jokingly reasoned to himself that if they managed to thrive in New York City with three kids, then the Covid-19 pandemic certainly would not drive him out. In fact, he couldn't understand why people were leaving in droves. The only advantages he could think of to leave were living in a house where a family could grow their own food, and less risk of infection because shelter-in-home and social distancing were facilitated.

Bodhi countered to himself that the advantages of staying in New York City far outweighed these few advantages. First, 53% of the world population just died. Consequently, the city was desolate. It was almost a ghost town that retained its shell, its superficial veneer and consequently was more beautiful and glorious than ever. Yes, there was a risk of contracting Covid-19 from others but that risk was greatly reduced by the diminished numbers of people who survived, the mass exodus, and the fact that the coronavirus appeared to have mutated and disappeared.

Second, the infrastructure- buildings, restaurants, stores, parks, gyms, movie theaters and performance halls- was still in place. Sure, they were all closed but provided all imaginable supplies and resources that one could possibly imagine except for food.

There was also the possibility of human contact that provided an escape from loneliness, depression and provided the hope of rebuilding. This became evident after the First Wave when people first started to shelter-in-place. The psychologic toll it exacted was tremendous despite the fact that everyone still had their circle of friends and family with whom to either call or Zoom. Some were still working from home and consequently still had to communicate with their colleagues.

Most rational people never considered that life would return to normal, but it was expected that there would at least be some semblance. There was still food. There was still enough distraction to wax political and engage in what now was recognized to be mental masturbation. Life as it was or imagined had disintegrated along with half of the human population. Human contact was now medicine. A human voice that had previously been taken for granted was now a reference point, a beacon, a compass.

In the city, people were not isolated. They were not solitary islands counting on themselves to survive. It wasn't only a question of physical survival, but psychological and spiritual survival. There were other people with whom to commune and commiserate. This provided the opportunity for survivors to crawl out of their learned helplessness, depression and the psychic trauma of what had occurred. At the very least, the others served as a distraction from the pain and provided another outlook rather than staring into their own inner abyss.

Out of the rubble and piles of the ashes of the dead, there were people who provided inspiration. They had brilliant ideas, enthusiasm, and skills. They were willing to share and rebuild a new society. Sure, there were still the assholes, but most of them managed to recognize that this was not the time to flaunt that aspect of their personality. Perhaps because it was genuinely a life, starve or death situation, people were making a genuine effort to work with each other. This was in fact one of the many beautiful outcomes of this worldwide catastrophe. The beauty of the human spirit was clearly on display and when placed against the backdrop of the New York City skyline, it was a peak experience, a sight to behold.

There were unimaginable human resources. Who would have imagined that within a five-block radius that one could find a group of experts in any field required? Everyone contributed what they could and large or small contributions were equally appreciated and applauded. Whatever one required could be found in the community.

One surprising outcome was the number of elderly people who survived. Prior to Covid-19 they were rotting in nursing homes and considered little more than burdens to their families and society. They were lonely and idling their time while patiently waiting for death to relieve them of their boredom. They were now needed again. They had purpose in their lives and resurrected long put away skills and experience they had accumulated over a lifetime. It gave them a new lease on life. The survivors gained a new perspective on who the elderly really represented in society and in their lives. Of course, this was nothing new for the indigenous peoples who had always revered their elderly. Things had come full circle in many regards now that the blinders of a modern society gone wild were lifted.

One of the most important benefits was to be in a community of people working towards the same goal: Survival. There were clearly disagreements but very few petty fights. Everyone brought their best game and the community was consequently lifted to a much higher level than any individual could ever achieve. This provided hope and during this near mass extinction event, hope was what got them through the day.

There were also minor benefits of remaining in the city once the bitter pill of what Covid-19 unleashed upon them was digested. Once the issue of having enough food was resolved, there was time for contemplation and leisure. They now had the freedom to consider educational and recreational activities.

Someone in the community that formerly worked in the local movie theater opened it up and played movies for the community on a regular basis. They formed a group of projectionists and shared movies amongst themselves so that each community could have access to an unlimited supply of movies. The experience was replete with popcorn but without the butter, candy and soda whose supply was out.

Performers gathered and opened performance spaces such as Symphony Space, the Metro Theatre, the Beacon Theater, Lincoln Center and put on theatrical plays, operas, ballets and musicals. There were book readings that took place on a regular basis, which rarely occurred in the pre-Covid world.

It was a great time for children. There was certainly a lot of suffering amongst the kids who had lost parents and siblings, but kids were resilient. They were now given the attention that children naturally craved for. Parents weren't rushing off to work and leaving their kids to be raised by babysitters and nannies. Without any intellectual wrangling or explicit plans, people went back to the old ways of the indigenous peoples where children were placed under the care of their revered community elders while parents worked. Parents also spent much more time with their children because there was no "workplace." The concept of workplace had already started to unravel during the First Wave and people worked from home. This started to rebuild the concept of a family that just spent time together rather than "quality time." The family unit was further reenforced because parents now did whatever they had to do with their kids, and the kids participated whenever they could. This was akin to a real-life Montessori or Steiner school. For the kids there was now little distinction between work and play. It was all part of their normal day spent with their parents, other kids, elders and community. They were learning valuable skills during the course of their day without anyone ever having to indicate that they had to learn anything.

Despite the mayhem, chaos, death and fear of death, another positive that emerged from the Covid-19 pandemic was a sense of community. People had to become more resilient and self-reliant but the importance of community was never more evident. Everyone was willing to share what they had and they learned to freely ask for help when needed. Everyone just tried to live as well as one could. Bodhi thought of Elbert Hubbard's phrase made popular by Dale Carnegie: "If you have a lemon, make lemonade." They had survived a catastrophic event and after the anxiety, fear, grief, they had nothing else to do but to get on with it.

There were impromptu gatherings on the rooftops, in the streets and on stoops. The kids filled the streets and were playing all sorts of games. It reminded Bodhi of his own childhood on the Upper West Side. Back then, there were so many kids just hanging around outside with the invisible eyes of parents who would report on any misdeed that had occurred during the day. There was an undeclared understanding that the kids were the community's responsibility. Every adult who was in the area or looking out their windows naturally watched the kids, and the kids were respectful and obedient when adults reprimanded them.

The kids played stoop ball, stickball, Chinese handball, a variation of tag called ringolevio, touch football, Scully, sometimes called skelzy depending on the neighborhood, two-hand touch football, jump rope, Double Dutch, running bases, spinning tops, or play under a running fire hydrant. A lot of time would just be spent sitting on building stoops. These games were often played in the middle of the street and kids would scatter when cars would pass. There were rarely if ever any car accidents because there were less cars in New York City at the time, car drivers understood that kids were at play, and kids had a sixth sense about how to navigate traffic. It was one of the early senses that developed when growing in the city.

The older kids were free to wander to the parks to play basketball and other neighborhoods to play with other kids. Bodhi recalled his youth when kids from all over New York City would come to the wall of the public school on 108th street between Amsterdam and Broadway to play Chinese Handball. This was where the best handball players would meet to be declared "King." The wall was particularly long and allowed 20-30 kids to play. Sometimes they played "Booties up," where whoever lost would have to lean against the wall with their butt sticking out and everyone would line up and throw the rubber "Spalding" ball to hit them on the butt. "Spaldings" were ubiquitous and could be found in any corner store or *bodega*. With one "Spalding" a bunch of kids could keep themselves busy all day long playing a variety of street games.

It was a marvelous way to grow up. There was community. Then came the advent of cable TV, the internet and Nintendo type games. All the kids disappeared. The parents no longer sat in front of their windows. The streets were now quiet. That sense of community that was so strong receded in the same way that the desert advances when top soil erodes after generations of abuse.

Bodhi was thrilled to see kids back on the streets playing. He and some others of his generation showed them how to play those games that occupied much of their childhoods. Bodhi and those adults knew that these games weren't just a way in which to keep the kids occupied while the adults took care of the business of survival. Those games taught kids how to communicate, negotiate, aspire to be the best, deal with defeat, and were important lessons in how to deal with others in the sandbox called life. Bodhi wondered if they would be in the mess they found themselves in if there was no cable TV and Nintendo games.

They still had cable TV, internet, Xbox and PlayStation, but yet the kids were out on the street. The mental health lectures provided to the community emphasized the negative consequences of these activities on people in general, but especially on kids. It was understood that they served a purpose. They kept the kids busy and served as alternate babysitters while parents were at work and came home physically, psychologically and emotionally bankrupt from long days of unfulfilling and soul-crushing work. Times had changed. Parents knew but had suppressed the knowledge that spending hours in front of a screen was not conducive to being human. The message sunk in at this time. Parents for the most part severely restricted or just cut off their children's access to these activities. Education was no longer just an occupation to pass the day. Learning now became very practical to ensure survival and participation in the community. Playing was also recognized as an important endeavor that taught kids essential skills that ultimately contributed to both community and survival.

PART 4: THE GANGS

THE GANGS

Bodhi's community was doing well. Their pre-Covid world was still prominent on their minds, but they were thrust into a new reality that offered no option of return. This was their life now and although it was filled with uncertainty, there was a great sense of relief. It was hard to pinpoint the reason but it was as though a weight had been lifted from their shoulders. They had been somehow excused from Thoreau's life "of quiet desperation." There was a peace that came with living in the present and doing what was being done at that moment. There was food, family, friends and community. Everything else was extraneous in their post-Covid reality.

People from other communities heard by word of mouth how well Bodhi's Upper West Side community was doing. They came in groups to see with their own eyes what was going on and were amazed by what had been accomplished in such a short time. Bodhi and the leaders of his community met with the leaders of the other communities to discuss and share ideas, accomplishments, and challenges. The challenges they faced were identical but the solutions they came up with were very different. Their intention was to develop best practices that would facilitate their post-Covid journey.

The communities began to coalesce along lines of shared vision rather than geography. Their little community shortly developed into a small city-state. Their first harvest was in sight, they had shelter, healthcare, and the excitement of a developing society and bright future. Far from a utopian society but overall, life was good.

Looking back as some struggled to do, they recognized that the so-called American Dream- work, buy more, own more, accumulate more and more debt, work more than ever before, make longer and longer commutes to work- was really the last level of Dante Alighieri's hell depicted in his "Divine Comedy" that he dared not describe for fear of mass suicide. It paled in comparison to the French vision of the dystopian society embodied in the simple phrase *métro-boulot-dodo*, which boils a life down to wake up every day, take the train to work, come back home and go to sleep.

Some now recognized that even George Orwell's dystopian "1984" was a Disneyland vacation in comparison to their pre-Covid world. In Orwell's vision as described by the character Wilson, the future is a boot stomping on a human face- forever. Their reality was infinitely worse because the boot was mechanical and they themselves repeatedly pushed the button that activated the boot to stomp their faces. It was ritual Hara-kiri without the ritual or meaning. It was doing this without meaning for the sole purpose of getting more likes on Instagram.

Yes. 20/20 in 2020. The apparent horror of the First Wave of Covid-19 was an insufficient bitch-slap to awaken humanity from their collective Ambien-like induced somnambulism. It was the gentle coddling and jostling of a loving parent trying to awaken their child to get ready for school with soft touches, back rubs and endearments. They still held on to their dream as though it were the greatest gift. This was exactly what made it the very last level of hell: It was completely self-imposed.

The Second Wave was the cold splash of ice water that awakened humanity from its deep slumber and ripped off its eye shields that kept it in the dark. It was clear now to the vast majority. Despite their present reality and teetering on the edge of the abyss of death along with the 4 billion souls that had just been pushed over the edge, very few, even if they could, would have chosen to return to that pre-Covid world. The button and the giant bloody boot immediately over their heads were now squarely in their sites and the wiring connecting them no longer a mystery. The future was uncertain but better to forge ahead toward the unknown than be the author of one's own suffering.

The first sign of trouble began in June 2023. A group of thugs started hanging around the neighborhood openly wielding knives and bats. They just loitered in front of buildings playing handball, stickball and craps. They kept to themselves but their presence was acutely palpable because of their thuggish demeanor and the loud music they blasted from a boombox. The community brought them up at their meeting. They learned that other groups of men were doing the same on almost every block in their neighborhood as well as other neighborhoods throughout the city. They acknowledged that the gang wasn't explicitly confronting anyone but their presence was intimidating and their loud music disruptive.

Karl approached the gang to find out what was going on.

"Hi," Karl said with a big smile and extended his hand warmly. "My name is Karl and this is Chuck and Albert. Karl and his two companions were quickly surrounded by the gang. One of the men stepped forward.

"Yo," the man said and shook Karl's hand. "Pleased to meet you Karl, Chuck and Albert. My name is Max, and these are my people." The men greeted them with smiles and tapped Karl, Chuck and Albert on their shoulders and arms. "What can we do you for?"

"Well, we actually came over to ask you the very same question."

"Ahhh!" Max exclaimed with a laugh. His crew followed his lead and laughed. Max stepped closer to Karl. "Well, we were just checking out the real estate."

"What do you mean?"

"Exactly what I said. We've been checking out your 'hood and like it. So we're taking it."

"Taking it?" Karl asked. "Taking what? What do you mean?"

"Well," Max said. "You're growing all that food on the rooftops. That's a commodity. I'm sure you've heard about all these bad guys that are all over the city. They're doing some really sick shit that we don't approve of. As you've seen, we're the good guys."

"I have the feeling you're going to make us an offer we can't refuse."

"You're a smart guy, Karl."

"No Max. It's just that I've seen a lot of bad gangster movies."

"Okay wise guy," Max said as he stepped a little closer to Karl. He stared him down, as though trying to figure out if Karl had just insulted him. "Here's the deal. Straight up. You give us 10% of your food every month and in return, we make sure the bad guys don't bother you. You good with that?" Karl was silent and simply stared back at Max. Karl looked at Chuck and Albert. They all raised their eyebrows simultaneously. Max's crew tightened the circle around them. There was complete silence except for the polyrhythmic tapping of the bats on the concrete.

"We'll have to present your gracious offer to the community board," Karl replied. "Or do you need an answer right now?"

"Nah man. You go ahead and talk about it. We'll be here. Just make sure you look at what your people on other blocks are going through. You let them know that we'll take good care of them. Cool?" Max extended his hand. Karl just stood there and stared at Max's hand for a moment. He then half-smiled and shook it.

"You tell your people that we're really looking forward to doing business with them. Okay?" Max's crew opened the circle, patting their shoulders politely to say goodbye and then quickly disbanded. Some returned to play stoop ball while others walked over to the wall of the next building to play Chinese handball.

Karl, Chuck and Albert were about ten feet away when they turned around and came back.

"What's up?" Max asked.

"Well," Karl said. "Since we're going to be doing business together and sharing this lovely block, would it be too much to ask you to turn down the music?" Max smiled broadly.

"You got it homey. No problem. Anything else?"

"That's it for now," Karl said. "Thank you."

"No. Thank you!" Max replied. "We're in this together, right?" Karl paused for a second, smiled, and walked away.

Karl called an emergency community meeting. Karl seated himself at a desk in front of the room. Nancy, his nine-year-old daughter, sat beside him and next to Bodhi. She was playing out a scene from *Beauty and the Beast* with some dolls. She was the only one in the room who was smiling and happily waving at everyone as they entered the room and took their seats. Once everyone had arrived and was seated, and the general murmur of people finishing their conversations died down, Karl told Nancy to join the other children in the back of the room. She pouted, crossed her arms and shook her head no. Karl smiled warmly, gave her a hug and whispered something in her ear. Nancy smiled broadly. She stood up, gave Bodhi a kiss on the cheek, hugged Karl, and skipped to the back of the room.

"It looks like everyone's here," Karl said slowly. The tension in the room had risen as the noise had quieted down, and now he could have cut it with a knife. Karl looked around at the dark faces of the people around him before clearing his voice and continuing. "Let's get started. Everyone's aware of the situation. Gangs have popped up all over the city and are making demands. Max' gang wants 10% of our food in return for protection against the..."

"That's bullshit!" Mark exclaimed, interrupting Karl.

Mark was a big burly guy who was often outspoken at meetings. "We worked hard to grow that food. I say we don't give them shit. We stand and fight!"

Some of his friends who were standing with him clapped and cheered. Others mumbled amongst themselves, less sure.

Karl recognized Max' demands to be anachronistic, short-sighted and small-minded, but he didn't see any alternative. This situation was certainly not new in the history of humanity, but a completely novel and frightening experience for those living in New York City in modern times. It was the age-old protection racket. Max, despite his friendly demeanor, made it clear that the community had only two choices: Comply or suffer dire consequences.

"I agree," Karl continued. "It's all of our hard work that they're asking a piece of. But we have to look at our options."

"What options?" Mark blurted out. "It's a racket! Today they want 10% and tomorrow it'll be 20%."

"We have to draw a line in the sand now!" Another of Mark's friends, an older man named Sam, agreed. "If we show weakness, they'll take everything we have." More people clapped and cheered. Amanda, a young mother who had lost her husband to Covid and had wandered into their community looking for help stood up and waited for everyone to calm down.

"Are you guys crazy?" She asked. "Have you heard about what's going on all over the city? Just yesterday, a gang nearly beat a man to death for standing up to them. We just survived a pandemic and you macho guys want to start a war. Really? Are you willing to fight and get your teeth kicked in, and maybe get killed for 10% of our food?"

"Amanda's right," Old Man Joe chimed in. "Even if we wanted to, I don't think we could defend ourselves. I say we go along with them. Hopefully they'll keep their word and protect us from some of the other more cutthroat gangs."

Mark was standing up impatiently waiting to speak. He

jumped in as soon as Joe finished: "But you know that if we give them an inch, they'll take and take and take."

"Actually, we don't know that," Chuck said. "I get what you're saying, but are you really willing to stand up to those guys?"

"Listen," Mark replied. "If we all stand together and fight, we'd have a chance."

"A chance for what?" Amanda asked. "Let's play this out. So, we all hypothetically stand up and fight. Let's imagine that we manage to survive. How many casualties would there be? Then the other gangs would come after us because they certainly couldn't allow for a rebellion next door. Do we then fight them too?"

"I'm definitely not up for constant war," Old Man Joe butted in. "It's not worth it."

Bishop stood up. "I agree. I mean, does anyone here even know how to fight or use a weapon." Everyone sat silent except for the kids playing in the back. Bodhi raised his hand to speak.

"We're in a tough situation but it's not all or nothing," Bodhi said. "The fact is that giving them 10% of our food is really not a hardship. Especially if they protect us from the other gangs. But if Mark is right and they try to take more and more, then we'll have to draw a line in the sand. But for now, I don't think it's worth sacrificing our lives for 10% of our food." Mark stood up suddenly and stormed out of the room.

"Does anyone else have anything else to add?" Karl asked. Everyone silently looked around. "Okay then, let's vote. Raise your hand if you agree to give Max and his gang 10% of our food."

"Wait!" Barbara blurted out. "It may be too much to ask, but it would be great if they could behave like good neighbors... I'm kind of scared to have the kids around them when they're brandishing weapons and behaving like thugs."

"Karl asked them to turn down the music, and they did," Albert replied. "I don't think they'll have a problem with us asking them to be more civil."

"I'll bring this up to Max." Karl said. "He's been reasonable so far. Are we ready to vote?" Everyone in the room except for Sam raised their hand in agreement. "Done then. I'll let Max know and we'll see how things go."

Despite the majority vote for giving up 10% of their food, many in the community were upset. They were upset because it forced them to confront their fear. They recognized their former privilege of living in an area of New York City at a time where they rarely had to deal with violence, self-defense and a you versus me mentality. It wasn't only because they had just survived a near extinction event that claimed 4 billion people worldwide and couldn't face the idea of risking their lives to fight for food when they in fact had plenty. What prompted them to vote yes was the fear of entering into a violence begets violence scenario that would devolve into all the horrors that humanity had set upon itself before the Covid pandemic. It was the fear of recreating that hell from which they thought they were liberated. It wasn't about the 10% but the fact that they were bullied into giving it away. This created inner turmoil, anger, self-loathing and shame.

Fortunately, these feelings were quickly sublimated because once the agreement was made with Max's gang, life remarkably returned to normal. Max and his gang had a very strong presence on the block but were indeed good neighbors. They no longer blasted their boomboxes and abandoned their intimidating demeanor. They were polite and helpful. They slowly formed relationships with the community and by August, managed to integrate themselves into community life. What broke the ice was the relationship they developed with the kids. They played street games with the kids and kept them occupied for hours. Parents were at first hesitant to allow the kids to play with Max's gang but over time, learned to trust them. After a while, it wasn't such a strange sight to see the gang helping out with the harvest and participating in other community-building activities. They even had some members show up to the community meetings on a rotation. It was a symbiotic relationship.

The heavy lifting in preparation for the winter, which included food, alternative energy supplies and backups, was already accomplished. The harvest was good enough to give them hope and ensure that they would not starve during the winter months. They had gradually set up more rooftops for planting and constructed greenhouses that would permit them to continue growing food during the winter months. Their only concern at that moment was a Third Wave of Covid-19, but there were no reports of any recurrences. For the first time since the Second Wave, they were able to breathe, appreciate their good fortune that they survived and their many blessings that allowed them to get over what they thought was the worst. Life was good.

The gangs had become part of the fabric of New York City and each gang attached themselves to particular blocks. Each gang remained in their territories and rarely crossed neighborhood lines. Some, like Max' gang, were quite nice and integrated into their communities. Others had no presence whatsoever and only showed up to collect whatever they negotiated or demanded. There were other gangs however, that were brutal and terrorized their neighborhoods. They made frequent and increasing demands on their communities. They appeared to relish in meting out punishment for the slightest perceived infraction, but in reality, it was all about control and indulging their sadistic tendencies. Just as people learned to weather the near mass extinction of the human race due to Covid, and then almost dying from starvation and freezing cold, they managed to adapt to co-existence with the gangs.

In mid-October however, news started circulated about violent conflicts that were taking place between the gangs. It turned out that the protection racket was quite lucrative. Rival gangs had already claimed their territories and the only way to expand was to move into another gang's territory. This led to violent battles, drive-by shootings and innocent bystanders who were accidentally caught in the crossfire. It was reminiscent of the crack wars that took place in the early 1990's where drug dealers battled over particular street corners. The word on the street was that there was one particular gang led by a murderous psychopath that was rapidly taking over larger and larger swathes of the city. Karl and other community leaders asked Max about this news, but he downplayed their concerns. They could only cross their fingers and hope that their little community wouldn't draw any attention.

Unfortunately, their hopes didn't hold up. On the last weekend of October, gun shots were fired and a voice projected over a bullhorn demanded that everyone come out. They came out to find Max and his gang lined up on their knees in the middle of the street with their hands tied behind their backs. Their faces were swollen and bloody. The man with the bullhorn paced in front of them and spoke through the bullhorn. He was very tall, thin, and had his dark, curly hair pulled back into a ponytail. His arms were covered with tattoos, as was his entire neck. There were tattoos of tears appearing to flow from both his eyes and some of his front teeth were gold-plated. He wore a holster on both hips. He had a gun in one hand and the other in the holster.

"Yo people!" he shouted. "There's a new sheriff in town. Name is Junior. Whatevah deal youz had with these punk-ass mothafuckas is done. Youz ansa to me now. Dig?" Junior paced back and forth in front of Max and his gang and then continued. "These punk-ass bitches tried to organize against me and now they gonna pay."

Junior's men lined up behind Max and his gang. They cocked and aimed their pistols to the back of their heads. The women turned in front of their children and held them tight. Chuck stepped forward.

"Junior," Chuck said. "Is there any way we can resolve this peacefully?"

"Yeah, homey," Junior said as he quickly pulled out his gun and shot Chuck right between the eyes. Chuck dropped to the floor. Some screamed. Some gasped. Others stood quietly in horror and disbelief. Chuck's wife Margaret ran over to his body and held it tight in her arms as she cried. Bodhi knelt next to Chuck's wife and held her in his arms. Sam and Mark stood silently and looked at the ground.

"Rule number one," Junior said as he waived his gun over the crowd. "Don't dare say a fucking word to me 'less I ask you to speak. Got that?" Junior turned back to Max and his gang.

"So youz here to proteck these fools?" Junior asked Max. "Well, do sumthin' bitch!" Max looked down at the ground. "You ain't got nothin' to say? I didn't think so." Junior raised his gun to Max's head and fired. Max fell sideways to the ground. Junior turned back to the crowd.

"Dig this," he said. "There ain't nobody to protek you 'cause there ain't nobody but me now that's gonna fuck you up. I'm it." Junior snapped his finger and his men simultaneously shot everyone in Max's gang in the back of the head. They collapsed onto their splattered brain matter. The crowd was silent. They were numbed by that level of extreme violence that made the near mass extinction seem quaint. Junior approached the crowd.

"Whose yo leader?" he asked. Karl stepped forward. Junior walked over to him with two of his thugs. The two thugs stood behind Karl and kicked the back of his knees. He fell directly forward onto his hands and knees. Junior pulled him up by his hair and pointed his gun to the side of his head.

"Listen up bitch," Junior said. "I'm only gonna say this once. Y'all got a sweet operation here. Now it's mine. We'll be here every two weeks to pick up 30% of your food. Then we set up a factory and you provide the labor. Kids, women, fags- I don't give a shit. You pick 'em. Got it?" Karl nodded yes. Junior paused and stared at Karl to let his message sink in. He then turned away from Karl and the community. While walking past the dead bodies he made a circular gesture with index finger in the air that his gang immediately understood. They mobilized and dragged all the bodies together and piled them onto each other. They walked toward Chuck's body. Margaret through herself over it, screaming "No! No! Please!" The gang looked at Junior who waived his hand dismissively. The gang returned to the pile of bodies, picked up a jerrycan and poured gasoline over them.

"Y'all got any words for these sorry-ass muthafuckas?" Junior asked. No one moved. "I didn't think so." He lit a match and threw it at the pile. A fire started immediately followed by the unmistakable stench of burning flesh. Bodhi looked up at the sky and it occurred to him that their bright future had just gone up in that dark, black smoke.

KIDNAPPINGS

December this year was relatively mild. Bodhi and many friends from the community gathered in Riverside Park to relax and breathe the cool crisp air. They walked downtown along the Hudson River, which was almost crystal clear now that boat traffic had markedly diminished. Its surface radiantly reflected the beams of light from the sun and tall buildings. There were musicians scattered throughout the park playing different types of music to entertain themselves and the strollers. Kids were playing various games as parents and caregivers chatted and strolled.

They turned east on 72nd street and entered Central Park to have a picnic. They saw with new eyes the majesty of this grand park in the middle of their urban landscape. They were in awe of and felt a kinship with the magnificent trees that had already shed their leaves and had no doubt that their leaves would return in the spring.

Bodhi was sitting on the rim of Bethesda Fountain in Central Park with some friends. There were many people rowing canoes in the lake, others sipping drinks, and kids and dogs running and playing. Although no one dared to say it aloud after their experience with Junior, many were thinking that such a gorgeous and propitious day heralded the bright future that was to come.

One of the kids jumped on the rim of the fountain and pointed to the steps on the right of the overpass. Everyone near the fountain looked over as others who were closer ran over to a man stumbling down the steps as though severely intoxicated.

"What's going on?" Bodhi asked. He was facing the lake and didn't see the man at first.

"It's Karl!" A voice screamed out.

"Oh my God!" A woman exclaimed covering her mouth with one hand while pressing her child against her.

Bodhi ran over to find Karl on the floor. His face was bloody and swollen, and some teeth were missing.

"What happened?" Bodhi asked as he supported Karl's head on his lap. A woman handed Bodhi a wet cloth with which he wiped the blood from Karl's mouth and tried to control the bleeding from a cut on his temple.

"Nancy. My baby. They took my baby!" Karl muttered.

"What?!" Bodhi asked. "Who took Nancy?"

Karl was having a hard time talking with all the blood pouring out of his nose. He was holding the right side of his chest and appeared to be in a lot of pain. Bodhi ran his hand across Karl's ribs and when he touched a particular spot, Karl cried out in pain.

"A bunch of guys wearing bandanas across their faces grabbed her and ran off. I ran after them, got into a scuffle but there were too many of them." Karl started to cry. "They beat me with rocks and a bat, and then ran off with Nancy."

They had heard through the grapevine about a rash of child abductions throughout the city. The reports were from distant areas of the city, but they were concerned enough to take precautions to keep the kids in their sights and travel in groups. Their biggest fear was now at their doorstep.

"What the fuck?" Someone in the crowd shouted.

Another voice in the crowd yelled out: "Let's get on our bikes and look for her before it gets dark."

"Let's go." Bodhi said. "Let's divide up and check..." Karl pulled on Bodhi's shirt.

"I saw one of them." Karl mumbled.

"Who was it?" Bodhi asked.

"A guy from Junior's gang." Karl said.

"Are you sure?" Bodhi asked.

"Absolutely." Karl replied. "I remember him clearly."

"Those fuckers!" Someone exclaimed. Bodhi stood up. Everyone gathered around him.

"Call everyone you know and tell them to meet us on the block with whatever weapons they have. Let's get Nancy back."

By the time they arrived at the block, there were already about 20 people from the community standing around waiting for them. There was a lot of talk and the emotions were echoing off the building walls. Some of them had bats and knives. Bodhi went upstairs to his apartment to get a bat. He was sweating profusely and could feel his heart beating in his temples. Rage filled him. He washed his face and drank some water.

MURDER BY DEATH

Bodhi walked slowly down the stairs gathering his focus. As soon as he stepped out of the building, he saw that Junior and his gang were standing there waiting for him. People from the community were still in the streets but were now dispersed and silent. The bats and knives were no longer visible.

"Whaddup?" Junior asked. "Heard you be looking for me. You the boss now?"

Bodhi walked down the steps, faced Junior and looked directly into his eyes. "Where's Nancy?"

Junior shoved Bodhi forcefully. "Yo! Why you be frontin' me like that? Who you be?"

Bodhi raised his bat and Junior and his gang members pulled out guns. Bodhi dropped the bat.

"Now you a tough guy?" Junior said in a mocking voice. "That's the way you wanna to play it, huh?" Junior turned around and paced around the crowd with a menacing demeanor and taunted them.

Junior shouted out: "Let's get somphin straight." He then pointed his gun at random people. "I own you people." Junior continued to strut around the crowd waving his gun. "I do what I want and I take what I want. You my bitches!" Junior started to laugh and his gang did the same.

Junior walked back to Bodhi. "So, you think you a tough guy? A boss? That's bullshit because there's only one boss and that be me." Junior pushed the muzzle of the gun against Bodhi's forehead. "You feel me?"

Bodhi just stared into Junior's eyes. He was sweating profusely but felt no fear or anger. After everything that had happened since the First Wave, after all the deaths he witnessed while working in the ER, his children dying all alone in Spain, and the news of all the deaths around the world, he was just numb.

"You wanna set an example for these people?" Junior asked. "You a docta, right? Let's make you an example." A bunch of the gang grabbed Bodhi and tied his hands behind his back. Junior walked away from Bodhi and told one of his minions to get the rope. The guy ran to a car and returned with a long rope. Junior took the rope and threw one end over a light post and tied a noose at the other end. Another goon drove the car directly under the noose.

"You ready to be a hero homey?" Junior asked mockingly. His minions brought Bodhi to the front of the car.

Junior looked over at Bodhi. "What you waitin' fo'? Get yo ass up there. It's almost 7 O'clock and everyone's gonna be clapping for you." The goons shoved Bodhi towards the car and helped him onto the hood of the car and then the roof.

"Now they'll have somphin to clap about." Junior looked around the crowd who were staring in disbelief.

"Wait a minute. Where's everybody? I need everybody down here now." Junior opened the trunk of the car and pulled out a bullhorn.

"Yo!" He pulled out his gun and waved it at the crowd. "Call everyone you know and tell 'em to get their asses down here now or we gonna drag 'em out. Fast. Do it fast. I wanna do this at exactly 7 O'Clock." Everyone pulled out their phones and started making calls.

Bodhi was standing on top of the car looking down at everyone. They all turned their backs or put their heads down as soon as they saw him looking their way. They had guilt and shame in their eyes. Bodhi realized that he was alone. No one was going to step up for him.

Junior stepped into the middle of the street and shouted into the bullhorn: "Yo! I need y'all to get down here now for the main event. You got 3 minutes or I'm coming up and draggin' yo ass down here to join your leader. Clocks ticking!"

Bodhi felt more abandoned now than how he had felt when he was a numbered canary working on the factory line for the hospital. He had worked with these people tirelessly for the past eight months. Mark, Sam and the others who wanted so badly to fight Max because he demanded their food, just stood there. Now they wouldn't even stand up for him, or at least look at him sympathetically. *How pathetic!* Bodhi thought to himself. *Before Covid. After Covid. Same old shit.*

"It's almost 7 O'clock homey," Junior said with a huge smile. "Do you want'em to clap for you before or after you hang? Your call." Bodhi remained silent and looked straight ahead.

"No last words?" Junior asked. Bodhi remained silent. He stared out into the crowd of people he thought he knew so well who wouldn't even look at him now. He wondered if this was how Jesus Christ felt: Alone and abandoned. *Yes*, Bodhi thought to himself. *He finally had his flock and it wasn't all it was cracked up to be.*

Junior looked at his phone and spoke to the crowd. "Two minutes to go. Get ready to clap like crazy. Let's make Bodhi feel like he was the most important person in the world." There was complete silence. One of the gangsters got into the car and turned on the engine.

"One minute to go." Junior announced. "Get ready to show Bodhi some love." Some of the people in the crowd were now crying. Bodhi wondered if they were really crying because he was going to die a slow, horrible death by asphyxiation, would drool all over himself, turn blue, and start to convulse before it was all over; or was it because they were looking deep inside of themselves and were confronted by their hypocrisy, self-loathing and cowardice?

"Okay now. Get ready. Let's make some noise! 10, 9, 8..." Junior counted and gesticulated wildly with his arms. "7, 6, 5..." The driver revved the car's engine. Bodhi now closed his eyes and put his head down.

Junior continued: "4, 3, 2..."

"BANG! BANG!" The front window of the car shattered and the driver's head suddenly flopped to the side, clearly showing the top of his forehead blown off. There was a mixture of blood and brain dripping from the headrest. Junior and his goons took out their guns looking for where the shots were being fired from. The crowd dispersed.

"BANG! BANG! BANG!" Three of the gang members standing right next to Junior dropped to the floor with pools of blood pouring from their heads. Junior ducked behind the car. His other gangsters were running for cover when more shots were fired. They dropped to the floor, landing in bizarre configurations. Only Junior and one minion were left. Bodhi looked up at the rooftops but couldn't see anyone. There was only dead silence punctuated by Junior and his minion's heavy breathing.

"Okay! Okay!" Junior screams as he threw his guns out to the middle of the street. His minion followed suit.

A woman's voice commanded from a rooftop: "Crawl out on your hands and knees to the middle of the street and then lie on you stomachs with your hands stretched out." Both Junior and his minion start to crawl out to the middle of the street. The silence was now interlaced with Junior repeating, as though it were a mantra: "Fuck me. Fuck me. Fuck me."

A woman came out of one of the buildings and walked out to the middle of the street. She had olive skin and dark wavy hair pulled back in a bun. She wore black leather pants and jacket with a bullet proof vest. She had an assault rifle strapped across her shoulder, a utility belt with a handgun, two grenades and a hunting knife strapped to her thigh. She was followed by one man and a woman wearing the same outfits and gear. She looked up at Bodhi and smiled. She then gave a signal to the man, who climbed up on the car, took the noose off Bodhi's neck and cut his hands free.

Junior pushed himself up to his knees, put his hands back behind his head and asked: "Who the fuck are you?"

Just as he finished his question, the woman threw a violent side-kick to the side of his head that lifted him off his knees and hurled him to the ground. His mouth was bloody and he spit out some teeth as he rolled onto his back.

The woman stood over him and replied: "I'm your Beatrice, bitch!"

The remaining thug who was still behind the car very quietly pulled out a gun that was tucked into the small of his back. He took aim at the woman.

"BANG!" A shot hit the thug's hand and the gun dropped. The other woman ran over and kicked the thug in his flank. He fell to his side panting. The woman picked up his handgun and searched him for any other weapons.

The woman in leather looked up to the rooftop and gave a thumbs-up. She walked over to Junior and kicked him again and again in the torso. The crowd had now returned and filled the sidewalk. They looked on silently. Beatrice turned and addressed the crowd.

"What the fuck is wrong with you people?" The woman asked as she approached them. She pointed to Bodhi and continued: "This guy has been your savior. They're talking about him all over the city. He's given you peace, security and a hope for the future...and you stand there to watch him hang by these lowlife scumbags." The woman walked back to Junior and kicked him again in the head. Blood poured from his nose. The crowd looked down in shame.

"We've been following and admiring the amazing work and progress that's being made by your community." She continued. "You've become the model that the rest of us follow, that we look to for guidance...and it's all because of him... his vision and leadership... and you pathetic people were ready to watch him die without even an objection. Shame on you!"

A voice spoke up from the crowd. "What could we do? They had guns."

Another voice: "They would have killed us for sure."

The woman in leather raised her hand indicating they should shut up.

"That's bullshit...and you know it." The woman said calmly. "Times have changed." She walked over to Junior who was still rolled over on his side and rocking. She pointed at him. "We can no longer tolerate dark, evil forces to prey on us." She walked amongst them while continuing to speak. "The weak shall not inherit the earth but rather take it. This is a new era, a new age of cooperation, community, sharing, light and well-being. Just look at what you've created here."

The woman walked back to Junior and stood over him. "We cannot allow people like this scumbag to prey on us and our children. We have to stand strong together and show them we aren't afraid to fight to defend what is rightfully ours."

Amanda stepped up from the crowd: "But violence begets violence. We're not fighters."

The woman in leather looked down at the ground and shook her head. "Violence is the last resort. We show them love, acceptance and a bright new future, such as the one you created here. But as you've now experienced, there are people who cannot accept this new world..." She paused and pointed her assault rifle at Junior's head. "...and they must be annihilated. They must learn that we are a peaceful people but are not weak. We must not sacrifice our hard-earned gains. Who among you would accept losing your children and loved ones, your young men and women raped and then sold to the slave trade?" She paused, took the rifle away from Junior's head and stood in front of him. "What would your community do without Bodhi? He's a gift not only to you but to all of us. After surviving Covid, how do you survive the loss of your children to thieves knowing that they are still alive serving as slaves, abused and mutilated. We must stand tall."

Junior was now behind her and sheltered from the view

of her people. He reached into his boot, quietly pulled out a knife and was about to stab her in the back. Bodhi noticed this and screamed out: "Watch out!" Just as the woman turned to see what was going on, Junior lunged at her with his knife. She quickly moved away. Junior missed her back but managed to slash through her leather pants and into her left thigh. She fell to the ground and immediately spun around, kicked Junior across the chest and rendered his knife-wielding hand in an arm bar. She thrust her hips upward and a large pop was heard from his elbow. Junior screamed out in pain. She then wrestled the knife from this hand and cut deeply across his forearm, almost amputating it. She got up and examined her left thigh and noted a deep laceration. She limped towards to crowd. Junior was crying in pain.

"People like him must embrace love and the gifts we offer, or die. No exceptions. She held out her hand and one of the women in her group handed her a samurai sword. She slowly unsheathed it revealing a shiny long blade that reflected the streetlight that was directly above her. Junior was still crying. He saw the sword and attempted to crawl away. She stood over him and stomped his knee. She grabbed him by his ponytail and dragged him to face the crowd. Blood was dripping down her leg and her black leather pants were now maroon colored. Parents grabbed their kids, turned them around and pressed them against their stomachs to prevent them from seeing.

"No!" She shouted. "In this post-Covid world, there's no time for blind youth and fairytales. This is reality. In the same way that Covid took away their loved ones and friends, kids need to understand that there are evil people in the world that will harm, rape, take them away from their remaining loved ones, and kill them. When we can't bring them over to the light with love and a better way of life, then they choose death." The parents held onto their children even tighter.

"Children! Open your eyes and understand that every day you make a choice to be on the side of the Light or the

Dark. You never bow down to the Dark." She yanked on Junior's ponytail and hyperextended his neck. She placed the sword under his neck and pressed it hard enough that blood was dripping from his neck.

"Where's Nancy?" The woman demanded. She yanked harder on his ponytail and presses the blade deeper into his neck. "I'm only going to ask once."

"Fuck you bitch!" Junior shouted. "You ain't shit!"

The woman threw his head onto the concrete and stood to his side while one of the women pulled on his ponytail to extend his neck.

"Fuck you!" Junior shouted. "Fuck all of you!" The woman raised the sword over her head and without any hesitation brought the sword down in one swift and direct blow. Junior fell silent at that precise moment and his head was now swinging freely from his ponytail in the other woman's hand. No one turned away. There was complete silence. The woman that was holding the ponytail then impaled Junior's head on a broomstick and held it up for everyone to see.

The woman wiped the sword clean on Junior's headless body. She limped over to the last surviving member who was seated on the floor and pressed against a car. He was whimpering. The woman stood over him. Her thigh wound was now bleeding profusely.

"Where's Nancy?" She asked.

"I don't know who Nancy is," the guy answered while sniffling and crying.

The woman smacked the guy's head. "Dude! The little girl you kidnapped earlier. Where is she?"

The guy looked up at the woman. "I don't know where she is. I don't know." He then looked over at Junior's head on the stake dripping blood. "I swear I don't know. Please. I don't want to die."

"Get up!" The woman commanded. The guy got up slowly covering his head. The woman handed him the stake with Junior's head. "You go back to your hangout and tell your crew we want the girl back in one hour or we're coming to get them. You understand. They have one hour to bring the girl here or they're all dead."

The guy was trembling and hunched over as Junior's blood dripped down the stake and onto his hand.

"Now go!" The woman commanded. The guy started running down the street.

A man from the crowd stepped forward. "You think they'll bring Nancy back?"

"Of course not," the woman replied. "But my people are following him right now. He'll lead us to their hangout and then we'll ambush them."

"But how will that get Nancy back?" Another woman from the crowd nervously asked.

The leader put her hand on the woman's shoulder. "It's not just about Nancy. They've kidnapped a bunch of women and children. We have to get them all back."

Another man spoke up: "How will you do that?"

"I don't think you want to know that." The woman responded. "This is the first time that we have the opportunity to find their hideout. Once we get them, I guarantee that they'll tell us everything we want to know."

"Will you put them in prison?" Someone else asked.

"Prison?" The leader laughed. "No more prisons. You're either in or out, with us or against us. If you're not with us and can't live in peace, then you die." Everyone was silent.

Bodhi, moving completely on instinct, stepped up and opened his arms to hug the leader. She faced him, smiled and he hugged her tightly.

"Beatrice. Thank you for saving my life." Bodhi said. "Thank you for showing us that we can take a stand." They remained in each other's embrace and breathed deeply.

"Thank you, Bodhi, for being you." The leader responded. She separated from their embrace and held his shoulders trying to stay steady on her wounded leg. "Thank you for showing us that we can thrive in the post-Covid world."

The leader hopped away and struggled to support herself. She slowly lowered herself to the sidewalk edge and held her leg.

"That's a really bad wound." Bodhi said. "Let me take care of it."

"No time now," the leader responded. "We can't afford to lose the gang this time."

"Let me at least dress it so you don't bleed to death," Bodhi replied. She smiled at him and nodded yes. Bodhi ran into his building and returned a few minutes later with a backpack. He opened it and took out a water bottle, hydrogen peroxide and gauze. He cleaned the wound and applied a pressure dressing.

One of the woman's men leaned over her. "The lowlife is headed to the east side."

"Let's roll," the woman said as she stood up. "Let's get those fuckers and find those kids."

"You'll come back so I can fix that properly?" Bodhi asked.

"Are you asking me out on a date, Dr. Bodhi?" The woman asked.

Bodhi was caught unprepared and smiled nervously. "Yeah, I'm asking you on a date."

"Then I'd better get going so I don't come back too late."

"Thank you, Beatrice," Bodhi said again.

"No problem dude," she replied. "That just how I roll." They laughed.

She started to limp away and then turned around. "By the way, my name isn't Beatrice."

"I thought you told Junior that was your name."

"No," she replied. "I told him that I was his Beatrice."

"Who's Beatrice?"

"Are you kidding me?" She mocked him. "You have two possibilities and you don't know?"

"I really don't," Bodhi replied. "I wasn't ever any good with trivia."

"Too busy saving the world one patient at a time I guess."

"Something like that," Bodhi said. "Who's Beatrice?"

"There's Beatrice from 'Dante's Inferno,' who gives Dante a tour of Hell."

"Okay, and the other one?" Bodhi asked.

"This one you should know," she said. "It's Beatrix Kiddo from 'Kill Bill.'"

"Ahhh," Bodhi said as he nodded his head. "That right."

"So, do you want to know my name?"

"Please."

"Adya."

"It's a pleasure to meet you Adya," Bodhi said as he bowed and kissed her hand. "Thank you very much for saving my life."

"The pleasure was all mine, Bodhi," she replied. "All mine."

"When can I expect you back?" Bodhi asked, still holding her hand.

"Soon," Adya replied. "As soon as I can." Adya slowly let go of his hand and limped away. Her group followed her.

PART 5: ADYA

ADYA'S MILITIA

Adya's thigh was killing her but this was the closest she had come to catching a predator, understanding their supply chain and hopefully acquiring their list of buyers. She knew that there were several operation headquarters scattered throughout the city and in other states. Buyers were located all over the map. This wasn't only about Nancy but an increasing number of women and kids that were abducted and never seen again. First and foremost, Adya's priority was to get the women and kids back. A close second was to catch the predators and make them pay in such a way that others would think twice about repeating those actions. She definitely considered the possibility that the predators would simply take their operations further underground. What she was betting on was catching enough of them and their buyers before they scattered. This would render their formal operations anemic and the risk of being a buyer too treacherous.

Adya had been amassing a large army. It was at first a small group dedicated to protecting their neighborhood from the gangs. As the gangs grew, so did Adya's militia. Word of mouth brought many uprooted, disenfranchised and mad-as-hell people to her doorstep willing to dedicate and sacrifice themselves to a cause. It started as a frustration they felt under the surface of their everyday lives even before the Covid pandemic. It was an incessant rumbling inside that reminded them every day that something was wrong with their lives and with the world. They sensed it in others. It was a smell that oozed from the pores of their colleagues at work, their families and children. It was so ubiquitous that they dared not speak of it fearing that everyone would point their fingers at them indicating that they themselves were the problem. They were afraid of the underlying truth that was just below the surface that there was something inherently wrong with them. So, they remained silent and learned to live with that gnawing feeling inside that never subsided. They rationalized that it was a deep abscess buried inside an area of their brain that couldn't be reached. Consequently, they learned to live with it. They feigned smiles at home and at work, took their kids to soccer, the men went bowling with the boys, watched sports on TV, and the women went to yoga and spin classes.

Then Covid changed everything. It allowed them to see that what was rotting their insides also resided in everyone else. It was the world itself. The Second Wave liberated them from their deep-seated angst but they then suddenly found themselves alone. Their colleagues, friends and families were thrown into the Covid Vitamix and pureed into oblivion. They were lost and didn't know what to do with themselves.

These were people who had nothing to lose. They asked themselves if surviving Covid-19 was a blessing or a curse in light of the fact that the vast majority of their friends and family had perished. Why were they condemned to survive when everything and everyone they knew vanished? They had no raison d'être to justify their existence, no purpose to get them out of bed and do something. Do what? It was all gone and to create something new required a vision, a purpose.

Adya recognized their suffering and desperation. She gave them a purpose to move forward in their post-Covid reality. They were at first very pleased with their role to uphold law and order, facilitate community projects and give a helping hand to those in need. Then as the news spread about the abduction of women and children, it triggered a deep anger. The news reminded them that there was indeed something terribly wrong with the world. The pre-Covid criminal justice system had failed and it was clear to them that Covid wasn't enough to cleanse it. They now felt that it was up to them. It was their responsibility. This was their purpose, the reason for which they were spared from Covid. Adya gave them a rallying cry, a purpose, a cause to justify their survival: Kill the bad guys!

After the initial excitement of joining Adya's cause, many challenged her saying that "killing the bad guys" was too vague. She met this challenge pointing out that Covid-19 provided the world with the opportunity of doing everything differently, abandoning the old ways and getting it right. Adya held the belief, as many people had expressed even as early as the First Wave, that Covid-19 was the earth's way of cleansing itself. It was the breaker of worlds. It was the big reset. It was in her eyes the greatest gift given to humankind: A means of changing course and avoid extinction.

"What a blessing!" Adya would shout. "Are we going to allow the bad guys to blow it for the rest of us? Are we going to allow them to do so in the name of greed, selfishness and total disregard for this beautiful blue planet hurtling through the infinity of dark space?" This became her rallying cry to which her loyal followers would cry back: "Fuck no!"

Adya would continue: "Are we better than that? Stronger than that? Do we have more heart and love for humanity and this beautiful planet that graces us all with our existence and given us a second chance to get it right?"

Their enthusiastic response was followed by cheers: "Fuck yeah!" They found their purpose, their raison d'être. They trained endlessly with grueling workouts consisting of improving mixed martial arts techniques, strength and conditioning, sparring, and then mastering weapons such as knives, swords, and guns.

Adya's background was in Krav Maga. Her father was a brilliant university professor who raised her as a single parent after her mother died of cancer. He raised her to be independent, intelligent, confident, fiercely competitive, and able to protect herself. He would always remind her of the rampant date rapes that occurred on college campuses. His purpose wasn't to inspire fear, but to provide her with a motivation to prepare herself. He enrolled her in Krav Maga classes when she was ten years old and joined her to motivate her. In addition to pursuing highly intellectual activities in order to develop her critical thinking skills, he fed her a steady stream of popular movies with strong female leads kicking everyone's ass. Their favorites were "Kill Bill," "Atomic Blonde," "Stick it," "La Femme Nikita" and "Avatar." They would spend hours exercising and sparring together.

As Adya's group grew, it spread and absorbed some of the communities around her. She now had a militia. This then spread to other states. She sent out ambassadors from her group to train interested parties, ensure that they shared the same goals and modus operandi. The ambassadors also inventoried their weapons and developed a means to communicate on the dark web and help each other when necessary.

THE HUNT

They followed Junior's minion through East Harlem. What was once a vibrant and thriving Hispanic community was now a desolate wasteland. Covid-19 didn't have any preferences about its victims, but perhaps because of a predilection to Cuchifritos and Salsa music, it ravaged "El Barrio" and certain other areas and populations more brutally than others. The streets were empty except for the ghosts of the souls lost to Covid-19 still hanging in front of the Cuchifritos places blasting Eddie Palmieri's "Puerto Rico" on their boomboxes. Those guaguanco rhythms competed with the rumberos in front of the other Cuchifritos place across the street who were chanting to their Orishas. They chanted feverishly in attempts to summon their Orishas, who appeared to have abandoned "El Barrio." Only Elegua, the trickster deity who maintained the illusion that they were still alive, heeded their call. Occasional old souls would wander from the old "Marqueta" on 116th street and Park Avenue to join them. They used to try to inform these new souls that they were in fact dead, but were ignored. After a while, they gave up and simply joined in on one side of the street to dance to the Salsadura or Mambo rhythms the DJ spun, or the other to chill into the trance-inducing rumbas and chants on the other.

The minion was still carrying the stake with Junior's head as he rushed towards the East River. Blood was still dripping down the stake, onto his hands and the pavement. Even if the militia had lost him, finding him would have been ridiculously easy because there was a trail of blood behind him. They stayed far away behind him and trailed on the other side of the street. Despite doing their best to remain inconspicuous wearing their bulletproof vests packed with grenades and carrying assault rifles, people on the streets scattered as they passed by. Only the men playing Dominoes on their tiny table sitting on the sidewalk seemed unperturbed by their presence. They cursed a flurry of Boriquen epithets to those who were distracted and turned their heads towards the minion carrying Junior's severed head and then more emphatically when the militia passed.

When Junior's minion arrived at the Wilson projects at 106th street and First Avenue, a few of them followed the minion closely while the remainder of the militia regrouped at the gas station that was across the street. Adya hand-signaled that they should put up their guard and expect a confrontation as they entered.

They split up into four groups and entered the Wilson Projects from the entrances on First Avenue, the FDR Drive, 105th and 106th Streets. They were immediately surprised that Junior's gang didn't even bother to have lookouts. The projects had been a bustling place filled with kids and a cacophony of noise that included loud music spanning the gamut from hip-hop to boleros, children playing, their parents screaming at them out from their windows, and shouting matches from adolescents just hanging out. Now, the streets and project grounds were deserted. There was the sound of some kids playing basketball in the playground, the pigeons that were flying all over the place, and the few cars driving on First Avenue. The gangs obviously felt they were invincible since no one had ever challenged them.

This was good news for Adya because they still had the element of surprise on their side. She knew that subsequent raids would become more difficult without this element of surprise. They had to hit as many cells as possible simultaneously and get everything they needed before the word could spread that they were being hunted.

This was their first big break. They called in all their resources who were within three hours driving distance. They wanted to enter Junior's headquarters with overwhelming force to minimize effort and possible injury, ensure that no one escaped, and to deter resistance.

As soon as the minion was about to enter the building, Tristan, one of Adya's men, grabbed him in a neck hold and pushed him against the wall. The minion dropped Junior's head on the pavement and it rolled onto his foot.

"Here's the deal," Tristan said. "Open the door and tell us which apartments they're in and where they're holding the kids and maybe you'll get out of this alive."

The minion whined in fear: "B-but I'm just a runner! I don't know-"

"Cut the bullshit!" Tristan smashed his head against the wall. "You get one more chance or you'll end up like Junior. Open the door and lead the way."

He opened the door. Tristan kept the gun to the minion's head as he led him inside. "Okay. I need apartment numbers for headquarters, your buddies, computers, databases, and the kids." The thug gave him what he wanted without any resistance.

"Do Johns come here to do the kids?" Adya asked, limping beside them. He nodded yes. More and more of her team entered the building and climbed the stairway. The others spread out in groups of five, covering the building entrance, back, rooftop, and basement exits.

"Which apartments?" Adya asked.

The minion quickly replied and then said: "I told you everything I know. Please let me go. Please. I got kids."

"Sorry buddy." Tristan said. "That's not the way it works. Hang tough."

They spread out to mount an attack simultaneously. The largest groups went to the headquarters and business office.

This was where their client databases and listings of their other businesses were kept. Smaller groups of two or three were assigned to find the kids.

Fifteen of them walked up to the third floor and gathered around the door of the headquarters. The remainder took the minion to lead them up to the other apartments where the kids were located. They set a timer on their watches for 15 minutes so that they could attack simultaneously to make sure no one escaped. They set a plastic bomb and detonator on the door lock and donned gas masks. As soon as the timer buzzed, they exploded the bomb and the door flung open. They immediately threw in tear gas and stormed the apartment.

It was a quick and effortless takedown. The gang was quickly overwhelmed by the tear gas and never had time to get their guns out. It was just as Adya had suspected: They were the only major gang in town, had no competition, and there wasn't any law enforcement to harass them. Consequently, they let their defenses down.

There were only 11 of them in the apartment. Adya instructed her team to tie them up with zip ties and line them up against the wall. In about 15 minutes, the team brought down nine men who were raping kids in various apartments in the buildings. Some were in their underwear and a few were naked. They were zip tied and placed standing along the wall as well. The good news was that they were able to find 14 kids. There were nine girls and five boys with ages ranging from six years old to thirteen. Adya instructed her team to bring them downstair to the van that would be arriving shortly. They opened the windows wide to air out the tear gas. The gang and sexual predators were still very uncomfortable because of the tear gas and more so because they couldn't wipe their eyes since their hands were tied.

Adya's militia brought out a desk to the center of the room and one chair on either side of the desk. Some of them immediately went to the laptops and computers that were in the apartment and started to look through them and copy the hard drives for any useful information. Adya walked in front of them slowly.

"Here's what happens next. We're going to bring you up to the table one by one and ask you a series of questions. We're only going to ask once. You have five seconds to answer or we cut something off. Are we clear?"

The gang member immediately in front of Adya spit in her face.

"We ain't telling you shit bitch!"

Adya wiped the spit from her face. "Thanks for volunteering. You're first." Her men dragged him to the chair, forced him to sit down and strapped him to the chair.

"There's nothing you can do to make me talk. You're wasting your time."

"You show 'em G," one of the gang members shouted out. "Don't tell 'em shit. You ain't no pussy!"

Adya signaled to Nico, her torture specialist. He had once run a butcher shop in Soho, and discovered a new and better use for his talents in the militia. He walked up and put a tool box on the table, opening it quickly and spreading the tools out one by one. After lining them up, he chose a pair of heavy-duty scissors and stood behind G's chair.

"Okay then. Let's get started." Adya sat in the seat in front of the gang member. "I want the databases of every gang that you're in touch with and every buyer you deal with. Where do you keep that info?"

"Bitch. You be smoking that dope if you think I'm going to tell you that."

Adya nodded to Nico. One of the militia members held G down, and another one held his arms behind his back. Nico pulled on his pinky and cut it off at the knuckle. G screamed out in pain. The man put the pinky down on the table in front of G.

"Ouch!" Adya deadpanned. "That must have hurt."

"FUUCKKKK YOU CUNT!" G snarled, his face warped

with pain.

Adya ignored him. "I'm going to ask again, and every time you don't answer, you lose a finger. If that's not enough, then we'll cut off all your toes. If that's still not enough, we'll take more, you feel me? So, think hard this time. Where are the databases?"

Everyone in the room was now dead silent except for G who was crying in pain.

Adya counted: "Five, four, three..." She nodded to Nico who grabbed the finger next to his still bleeding stump.

"Wait! Wait!" G screamed.

"Too late." Adya said. The man cut off his fourth finger and placed on the table.

"Arrgh!" G screamed out even louder and rocked his body back and forth. "You fucking crazy!"

"I told you the rules G," Adya said smiling. "You have five seconds to answer. You blew it. Don't worry, I'll ask again." She nodded. Nico tried to pull on his third digit but had difficulty holding it down because his fingers were slippery from the blood dripping from the amputated digits.

"I'll talk! I'll talk!" G screamed out while crying.

"Great!" Adya said. "I thought you would." Adya looked over to her crew and instructed them to take him to another room to get the information. They released him from the chair and took him to the other room.

Adya stood up and walked toward the gang. "Okay," Adya said. "Who's next?" The men stared silently down at the floor, each trying to shrink themselves as much as possible. "How about one of you short-eyes?" Her crew grabbed one of the men who was naked and threw him onto his back on the table. They tied his wrists and ankles with a rope and tied those ropes tightly under the table.

"I-I I don't know an-nything," the naked man protested in fear, his eyes wide with panic. "I'm j-just here t-to..." He dared not finish his sentence.

"From you, lowlife scumbag," Adya spoke matter-of-factly. "I want to know every single place where you have access to kids, who your connections are, and then every single person you know who screws little kids." Adya took out her knife and makes a superficial incision from his sternum down to his pubis. "I guess you know which part we're going to cut off first. Feel free to start whenever you'd like."

The man started to whimper. "I don't know anyone else and..."

Nico loudly put on a pair of gloves, letting them snap against his wrist, before he reached out and stretched the short-eye's penis straight up in the air.

The short-eye pleaded. "No. Please. Don't!"

Adya slammed her hand on the desk. "Listen you fuckers," she shouted. "I don't have time for this. It's simple. I ask a question and you have five seconds to answer. You answer and we go on to the next question. You don't answer, then chop-chop. Got it!" Adya nodded and one of her men held the large sharp knife against the base of the man's stretched penis.

"Please. Please don't." The man begged. "I beg you!"

Nico hesitated and looked at Adya for confirmation.

"Would you prefer me to do it?" Adya asked.

Nico took a deep breath and cut, immediately dropping the bleeding penis onto the short-eye's chest in disgust. The man screamed out loudly. Adya sat down behind him with her arms crossed.

"Let me know when you're ready," Adya said. "We have all the time in the world." She looked over at the gang and looked at the guy who was cheering G on. "You're next homey. Get ready." The guy looked down, his face blue.

"Okay. Tell me every single place where you have access to kids, who your connections are, and then every single person you know who screws little kids. I think we'll cut your hands off next to make sure you never touch a child again." The man was twisting his body back and forth in pain and moaning.

"Five, four..." Adya counted. Nico took out a drill and attached a circular saw while two other men held his arm down.

"Okay. I'll talk." the man said whimpering. All the information is in my phone." Her men had the predators' clothing lined up in piles. They asked the predators who were standing to identify their own clothing, picked up the remaining pile and took out the phone.

"Are you sure everything I asked for is in your phone?" Adya asked.

"Y-yeah," the man blubbered. "It's all there."

"Okay," said Adya. "If you disappoint us, we'll bring you back and cut off two parts off the bat. Do you understand that?" The man nodded and sobbed. The militia untied him and sat him up. His penis fell to the floor and a pool of blood collected under the table. They walked him to another room and brought the next guy up. He was very skinny, wore a durag and had his pants below his ass.

"Yo," he said. "That was some cold-blooded gangsta shit."

"We're just getting started," Adya replied. "What's your name?"

"Eric."

"So, what can you tell me Eric?"

"Yo, I'll tell you whatever you want to know," Eric answered, grinning nervously. "I wanna walk out of here with my Johnson, ya feel?"

"You're a smart man Eric," Adya smiled. "The computers are password protected. Who's the tech guy here?"

"I am."

"Awesome," Adya beamed. "Then you also know about the databases, right?"

"I know everything," Eric responded. "Just don't cut me."

"Okay then. It looks like you're the man." Adya looked at the gang and predators along the wall and addressed her crew. "All the computers and laptops are here. Take them to one of the empty apartments and continue the interrogation. You know what we need." The men led the gang and predators out of the apartment along with the tool box.

"Eric," Adya clapped her hand. "Let's get started." Eric stood up and sat down in front of the desktop.

"I'd like to introduce you to Mark. He's our tech guy. He's going to ask you questions along the way." Adya placed her hand on Eric's shoulder. "Any funny business and I'm going to show you what gangsta is all about. Understand?" Eric nodded.

UNINTENDED REPERCUSSIONS

A dya's first raid was by all accounts a great success. First, she succeeded in obtaining the databases of the headquarters of all the other gangs associated with Junior's. She was at first surprised and horrified that there were so many of them located almost everywhere in the United States and Europe, and that they were connected. She then understood that there was absolutely nothing to be surprised about because there have always been lowlife-scumbag-short-eyes who've preyed on children from time immemorial. These lowlifes included high-ranking politicians and very wealthy, important people. They've always been part of the fabric of humankind. Perhaps what surprised her was their ability to reorganize so quickly after what many predicted and feared to be an extinction event. The gangs knew the awful truth about human nature and capitalized on the fact that up until the last flicker of the last breath that humans take prior to extinction, there will be short-eyes looking for fresh meat.

Second, the databases contained the locations and the predators to whom the kids were sold. Third, the databases contained the contact information of every short-eyes that they ever did business with. This in and of itself was gold. Adya figured that as they busted more gangs, they'd obtain more databases of other gangs and short-eyes; and as they busted the short-eyes, they'd find out about more gangs and other short-eyes. Time however, was of the essence. She had a small window to round up as many of them as possible before they went underground.

Adya was not naive and had no delusions about eliminating the child sex trade or vanquishing bad guys from the new post-Covid world. That would be like amputating a limb to cure a cancer that had already spread throughout the body. Rather, she was adopting a similar strategy she mastered when playing the game Go: Collect smaller territories, sometimes at opposite ends of the board, and then connect them. This left her with more territory to win the game but also kept opponents out of those territories.

Adya's goal was simply to tilt the balance in the favor of the good guys while they got their bearings. Covid-19 had provided the world with what many considered and hoped for to be a reset. It was an opportunity to see oneself, humanity and the world in a different light and consequently, do things differently. There were many who always accused humankind of "destroying the planet" and that we had to change our course in order to "save the planet." Adya appreciated the people who felt this way but ultimately felt that their viewpoints were misguided and short-sighted. The planet did not need to be saved at all. Our pre-Covid actions simply would have led us to an extinction event and made us the laughing stock of the universe.

Adya always considered it absurd and quite arrogant to believe that we were the only forms of intelligent life in the universe. She believed that other sentient beings in the universe were far too advanced, intelligent and wise to engage with such primitive beings like us and stayed away quite content to observe our progress. They understood the natural life cycles of planets all over the universe. They would consequently double over in laughter over the fact that we would be the first recipients of the "Intergalactic Darwin Awards." This was the prize for being gifted the blessing of living on such a beautiful planet flying through dark space and yet actively managing to destroy it, and hence ourselves. She imagined that these beings were at this very moment placing bets on whether we would take this eye-opening opportunity, this gift of receiving 20/20 vision after a lifetime of being totally blind and change course, or just restart the process towards mass extinction.

Adya had no delusions about humankind. She simply wanted to take this moment to tip the scales as much as possible by decreasing the number of scumbag providers and predators, and disrupt their supply chains. She wanted to inspire fear in their hearts about what would happen when they were caught, which was now a real possibility. She was counting on the fact that once they got word about the atrocities that she was inflicting upon their buddies before she granted them mercy and killed them, they would reconsider whether or not they should act on their demonic impulses.

Adya acknowledged that she was sinking to the age-old prison philosophy of how not to become someone's prison bitch. She was demonstrating extreme force to show the bad guys that they would not be taken advantage of. She wanted to show in no uncertain terms that the bad guys would not have their day in court. There would be no plea bargaining. In comparison to the justice she was meting out, prison would be a vacation for the wicked. Adya made it clear that what they should expect was a vicious, extremely dehumanizing, painful and slow death during which useful information would be extracted. They needed to know that her basic guiding principle was to not take any prisoners. She would make them suffer in ways that were unimaginable while extracting useful information before granting them death.

Adya's tactics were quite simple. Step one: Capture the bad guys and predators, torture them, secure databases of other headquarters, centers of activity, and then kill them. Step two: Find the kids, bring them home, and with the information about other bad guys, repeat step one.

This first bust provided them with a tremendous amount of useful information. Adya immediately mobilized her militias all over the country and Europe and dispatched them on similar raids. She made it a point of always having men and women who had trained directly under her to lead these groups. This ensured success, measured by the number of bad guys, headquarters, and kids that could be retrieved. It also ensured that the same actions would be carried out. She didn't want any improvisation where someone would decide to not torture a bad guy or kill them once the information was extracted. There would inevitably be someone with a highly developed sense of justice and morality that would consider taking the bad guys into custody. This was unacceptable to Adya.

Improvisation was acceptable for beer microbreweries that could afford to experiment with their beer. This was the great pleasure in finding such microbreweries, to find great beer that was original. The major brands such as Heineken or Coors however, absolutely had to have the same exact taste. They already made their mark and had to lock into that reality, and this was great if you liked Heineken or Coors.

Adya was in the process of developing a brand that she wanted to be immediately and unquestionably recognizable. She wanted that brand on every billboard, website and television screen that popped up with every click and channel in blinking, bold and unavoidable lights: If you're a bad guy, we're coming for you and will make you suffer until you beg for death. She didn't want her brand to be altered in anyway by someone who signed up and then later discovered that they didn't have the stomach for torture and killing scumbags. This was the reason for always having one of her people present at all times.

Within six hours of obtaining the databases, they had raided all the headquarters in the United States and exacted her brand of justice to both the providers and predators. Most importantly, they were able to retrieve the children. Once the kids were safe, they continued their mission to "kill the bad buys." They planned on reuniting the kids with their loved ones and communities once their primary mission as accomplished. They still had time on their side but didn't want to squander this benefit and allow the bad guys to go underground.

This second round of raids secured further databases that included mostly the same information, but did in fact provide additional names of centers of activity and predators. Adya feared that her militia would tire for lack of sleep and the psychological strain of torture and killing. She knew that each raid would result in diminishing numbers of scumbag providers and predators but wanted to weed out the very last one while she still had the opportunity. She developed the strategy of breaking her militia into shifts so that one team could rest while the others went out on raids. This was feasible because of the number of headquarters with armed gangs were significantly less and did not require the big guns. Interestingly the number of predators remained fairly steady. Their names weren't found on the databases since they had the good sense to falsify their identities. What they couldn't hide was that one friend who either got them in touch with the networks, or for whom they themselves made the introduction. These predators were less likely to be armed and dangerous. When confronted with the reality of being tortured, they readily ratted out all their so-called friends and contacts before joining those before them who Adya put on Kharon's ferry to make their journey across the Acheron to the underworld.

They finally thought that they were done and were just about to celebrate when they learned of another a cell in New Orleans. The word was already out that there was a militia coming after them and their businesses so they were prepared and heavily armed.

It was that militia's sixth raid and they were physically, emotionally and psychologically bankrupt. Someone proposed

bombing the building but they had no idea of how many innocent people lived in the building or how many children were
in there. Killing innocent people even for the benefit of "killing
the bad guys," the age-old "ends justifies the means" did not sit
well with the leader of that militia who opted to hold back and
call in reinforcements.

While waiting for reinforcements, a few predators tried
to escape but were immediately apprehended for later interrogation and extermination. They attempted to extract information from the predators while in the field but were un-
successful without the visual demonstration of the atrocities
they were willing to exact for that information. They opted to
postpone the inevitable.

It took exactly three hours and seventeen minutes for
reinforcements to arrive. This cell was prepared for an attack
and were heavily armed. The element of surprise that gave
them such an advantage during the prior raids had vanished.
They knew they had a fight ahead of them and that there
would likely be casualties. This however, was not a deterrent.
This was in fact exactly what they signed up for. It was the
adrenaline rush. It gave them a purpose to justify their existence when everyone they loved vanished in hospitals all alone
without anyone to comfort them. Moreover, they needed a
more concrete justification for the torture, murder, and atrocities they were committing in the name of the higher good. "Kill
the bad guys" was their rallying cry but seemed insufficient
a justification for plucking a man's eyeball out or amputating
all their extremities and auto-transfusing them to keep them
alive for more torture. What they were doing was beyond the
pale. It was disproportionate to even the most heinous crimes
conceivable. Yet this is exactly what Adya demanded.

The cries of joy of the women and children when released was overwhelming to them. Their gratitude and that
expressed by their families and loved ones almost justified
everything. However, there was that bit of humanity that remained even after the Covid-19 pandemic and the graphic de-

scriptions of what the women and kids suffered. They were still human and no matter how they intellectually tried to justify, consciously or subconsciously, the atrocities that they were inflicting on other human beings, it gnawed on them. After the original cathartic release of the first few waves, their hearts secretly wished that each subsequent one were the last. They feared deep down inside that they would slowly begin to actually enjoy what they were doing and would subsequently lose the small bit of humanity left to them.

This raid was different. There would be a fight. A true battle between Good and Evil where Evil did not wear a human mask. Its ugliness, holding an AR-15 to their heads or to the head of a helpless and innocent child, was bare, unadulterated, and unapologetic. Evil in its pure form and without a mask did not plead for mercy or cry like a baby as its testicles were removed, chopped up and fed to him or to his colleagues. It spit in your eye as you peeled off its skin and screamed out: "Fuck you, fuck your mother, and *fuck* everyone you know." It laughed aloud as you cut off its ears and taunted: "Do what you will motherfucker. I'll be back because I am human. I'll find another body to inhabit and continue my work. I am you. We are two sides of the same coin. Ha ha ha!"

This was concrete. When Evil personified had an AK-47 pointed at their hearts offering to liberate their souls to join the other 4 billion people's lives that were snuffed out by Covid-19, there was no little bastard inside questioning how or why they could set someone on fire and watch them burn to death. There was just the inner and outer voice screaming out: "Fuck yeah! Kill the bad guys!" They found that raison d'être that was washed away with the Second Wave. The flame that Adya provided them that was slowly dwindling with each subsequent raid was now reignited and burning strong.

By the time the other twenty-three reinforcements arrived with heavy artillery and equipment, they were antsy to see Evil's true face and dance the dance. Their plan was simple: Attack from all sides. Three men would rappel down the building and simultaneously break through each window of the apartment with their automatic rifles blasting. Simultaneously, another group breaking through the front door with all their firepower. The only caution was to avoid shooting each other in the crossfire.

The siege was ultimately unsatisfactory. They expected a lot from Evil who didn't hold up his end of the bargain. The so-called battle lasted less than three minutes and there was only one casualty and three injured. The bad guys had deleted most of their databases but the information Eric provided them before they killed him allowed them to hack their system and download the hidden backups. The bad guys were very sophisticated but Eric gave them the keys to get into their network. They had already downloaded most of the information they required. The torture they inflicted on these representatives of Evil didn't have anything to do with the women, children or their cause. They had crossed the line they always feared they would and relished in the pain they were inflicting.

The mission was a success. What would later become known as the "24-Hour war on Evil" was over. It was the last holdout of the providers and now their supply chain in the United States and Europe was completely disrupted. They had shown for the very first time in the history of humankind that the good would no longer take shit from the bad guys. They preferred peace and love but after the loss of so many loved ones and even those they didn't know from Covid-19, they would no longer turn the other cheek. Covid-19 had given them another opportunity to get humanity on another track that was not self-destructive and destructive to the planet. They now recognized this clearly with 20/20 vision and were willing to fight for it. Many of them feared the implications of having crossed that line. They rationalized that this was their sacrifice to humanity and hoped they would be remembered. In the meantime, they still had a handful of predators to eliminate and a world to rebuild.

Adya had an intuition about what had happened immediately after looking into the eyes of each of her militia that returned. She embraced them all firmly. Some cried and she cried with them. She cried even harder because she knew that she had in fact served as Dante's Beatrice. She guided them through hell and brought them back knowing that their lives would never be the same. Intellectually she knew that in their post-Covid world no one's lives would ever be the same. She wanted to ensure that at least in certain respects, certain things such as the struggle between Good and Evil that always seemed to fall in the favor of Evil, would never be the same either. It was a calculated risk for which she was willing to sacrifice herself and her militia. She had crossed that line long before ever going into battle and only now, seeing the reflection of herself in their teary eyes, did she recognize the magnitude of what she had done.

She cried long into the night, long after her militia's wounds were tended to. It gnawed on her from the inside.

PART 6: ADYA
AND BODHI

SEPTIC SHOCK

It was now 48 hours after Adya had been stabbed and as much pus was oozing out of the wound as the tears that flowed from her eyes. She began to sweat profusely. Late in the wee hours, she began to vomit green material from what seemed like a bottomless pit. She was delirious and too weak to call for help. Luckily someone knocked on her door early that morning with the excuse of some procedural question but in fact needed comfort. When Adya didn't answer her smartphone or the banging on the door, and no one had seen her leave the building, they broke her door down. They found her on the floor next to the toilet covered in vomit and barely breathing. There was the strong stench of vomit that was overwhelmed by the putrid and foul odor emanating from the pus that was oozing from her left thigh. Her pulse was rapid but very faint. She was barely responsive to pain. They didn't need to have any medical training or background to know that she was in trouble. They carried her to a car and drove her to Bodhi.

Bodhi was sleeping when they rang his bell. They told him that Adya was sick. He ran downstairs and immediately felt her pulse and touched her forehead. She was drenched in sweat.

"Adya! Adya!" Bodhi called out as he shook her. She only moaned. He then looked at the wound that was leaking a thick, foul-smelling, purulent liquid.

"She's in septic shock," Bodhi said. He handed them a set

of keys. "Get her upstairs to apartment 2C and lay her on the bed on the right. I'm going to take a scooter to the hospital and get some more fluids and antibiotics. A nurse will meet you there in a few minutes." They took her out of the car. Her body was limp as a noodle and she was drooling on herself. It took three of them to carry her dead weight into the building and upstairs.

Bodhi took out his smartphone to make a call. "Bri. It's Bodhi...I need you right now at my clinic...Yeah, septic shock... Great! Please start two lines and give her 4 liters of Ringer's Lactate...No, I ran out of antibiotics and know where to find some...I'll be back in 20 minutes. Thank you!"

Bodhi scrolled through his contacts and made another call. "Sheila. I need your help...Remember the woman that saved my life...Yeah, I have her upstairs. She's in septic shock...She doesn't look good. I need seven days of vancomycin and zosyn...Shit! What have you got?...That's fine. Can I come over now?...Great! I'll be there in 10 minutes."

Bodhi jumped on the electric scooter that was parked near his building and drove off in a hurry. He arrived on 69th and Columbus Avenue in no time. He parked right in front of Magnolia Bakery where he for so many years bought the exact same things: German chocolate cake and banana pudding. For him it was a match made in heaven, like peanut butter and jelly or peanut butter and chocolate. Magnolia unfortunately didn't survive the Second Wave. Some local bakers reopened it, but it wasn't the same.

Bodhi ran into the doorman building that no longer had a doorman. Sheila was waiting for him in the lobby and gave him a big hug.

"Thank you so much," Bodhi said.

"No worries, brother," Sheila responded. "She saved your life. Go save hers. Let me know if you need anything else." They embraced again and Bodhi sped off.

Bodhi made it back to 107th Street in record time and didn't bother waiting for the elevator. He sprinted up the stairs and burst into the apartment panting.

"How is she?" Bodhi asked in between breaths.

"Not good," Bri responded. "She's still hypotensive after the first 2 liters and she's getting the second two right now."

Bodhi put his hand on her forehead and looked at her pale face. He recalled her smile when he first saw her while strung up with the noose around his neck. "Let's hang the Cefepime first and then the Vanc." At that moment, Adya started to dry heave. Bodhi immediately turned her towards him and she promptly vomited all over him.

"Do we have any IV Zofran," Bodhi asked.

"No," Bri replied. "We ran out. I'll get the sublingual." Bodhi maintained her on her side and she again vomited all over him. He could now feel the moist vomit seep through his jeans onto his legs. Bri returned. She placed the tablet under her tongue and smeared it against her parchment-dry mucosa. After another minute, Bodhi set Adya down. He looked at his vomit infused jeans and sneakers.

"I'm going next door to change," Bodhi said. "Let's get her undressed, cleaned up as best as you can, into a gown and then place a foley."

Bri put her arms across her chest and the smirk on her face didn't need an interpreter to say: "Those days are over bitch." But her voice wasn't as direct and said: "And am I supposed to do all of this by myself?" Bodhi looked at her and smiled. He picked up the shears on the table and cut off her T-shirt and leather pants. He helped to roll her while Bri pulled the vomit, urine and diarrhea impregnated clothing from under her. They then covered her with a sheet and blanket. Her body felt cold and her temperature was 94°F. Bri filled up a bucket with soap and water, threw a sponge in it and handed it to Bodhi.

"I'll be back in a few minutes," Bri said. "I've got to check on the kids. I'll put the foley in when I get back." She started to walk out but turned around. "That's the third liter. Don't forget to put up the fourth." Bodhi breathed a sigh of relief. Her blood pressure had stabilized after receiving almost three liters of Lactated Ringer's fluid and her heart rate decreased from the 150's to 117. She was moving in the right direction.

VOYEURISM

Bodhi started to sponge her face. Even when he was on top of that car with the noose around his neck waiting for Death to take him, he couldn't help to notice how beautiful she was. It was one of those strange moments when two completely contradictory thoughts collided. The first thought was: Yup. I'm going to die a horrible death by asphyxiation because these morons didn't put the knot of the noose to the side of my neck so that my neck would snap and gift me a swift and painless death. The second thought was: Damn! She's hot. He couldn't appreciate the humor at that time but it made him smile now as he gently washed the caked vomit from her face. Even in her state of septic shock, covered with puke, and dry, scaly lips, she was still outrageously beautiful.

Adya's lips were full with high cheek bones and a broader than average nose. She had multiple earrings on each ear and a tiny nose stud on the left. Based on her full lips, broad nose, wavy hair and olive skin, he guessed that her parents must have been biracial. Bodhi noticed that the third bag of fluids was now empty and in the other arm, the antibiotic was just finishing. Her heart rate was now 109 and she had bounding pulses. She started to groan a bit louder and was starting to move around. Bodhi hung the fourth bag of fluid.

Adya had numerous tattoos on her arms and torso. He noted that many of them had spiritual connotations, most of which he didn't understand. He lifted her left arm up and washed her inner arm, armpits, and left flank. Her shoulders and arms were quite muscular. She had a tattoo of the "Om" symbol on her left shoulder. This one he recognized. A recent girlfriend who adopted the name Kali, was a yoga teacher who introduced him to both yoga and Tantra. She changed his life. They would begin every yoga class chanting "Om." Kali explained to him that Om was a foundation of Hinduism, where it was considered the very first sound of the universe and one of the most important spiritual symbols.

Bodhi remembered how Kali defined "Om": "It signifies the essence of the ultimate reality, consciousness. It's all-encompassing. The whole universe joined into a single sound. It represents the union of the mind, body, and the spirit. The vibrations that the Om sound creates energize the chakras throughout the body, especially the third eye and crown chakras, which help us connect with our Divine selves."

Kali's yoga classes were brutal and would often bring him to tears. He appreciated that Kali was indeed a yoga master but felt quite strongly that she had missed her calling as a dominatrix. He would often joke with her that she put him in touch with his inner "sub." Kali would sometimes have him hold a difficult yoga posture for what seemed like an eternity. He asked friends and colleagues who were avid yoga practitioners if they ever had to hold a posture for as long as 30 minutes in a yoga class and they universally condemned it as insane and even harmful.

Bodhi remembered vividly how Kali would stand over him while he was in excruciating pain holding a pose. She would slowly circle around him and speak in a deep, sultry but professorial tone. All that was missing was leather. He was always on the verge of breaking out of the pose and collapsing. He imagined himself cursing her out and telling her he never wanted to see her again. But he never did. It was a perfect dominatrix-submissive relationship. Despite the strong BDSM undercurrent, Bodhi rationalized that the difference was that this was spiritually oriented.

Kali seemed to know when Bodhi was just about to give up and break from the posture. She would bend over and whisper in his ear, the equivalent at those moments of a cold slap of her hand on his butt cheek that was already raw from the paddle.

Kali would whisper: "Imagine that I am God and tell you that for every second beyond this moment that I would allow one child in Africa to live who was about to die from starvation." Bodhi imagined another violent slap on the same raw, red buttock followed immediately with one turn on the metal nipple clamp. The pain was unbearable. He was sweating profusely. His breathing was short and staccato-like. Kali would continue: "How long would you hold the pose knowing that you could save so many children?"

"Bitch!" Bodhi would think to himself.

"This is the very essence of life," Kali would say as she wiped the sweat off his brow. He imagined how she would sink her teeth deeply into his inner thigh causing him to cringe in pain.

"This is where you leave the pedestrian behind," Kali continued, "and enter into the sacred realms. It all begins just when you thought you could no longer go on for another second." Bodhi imagined Kali's sharp nails digging into his back as she made tracks from his neck down to his lower back. The sharp pain was immediately followed by intense burning from the sweat pooling in those tracks.

"Everything," Kali would continue. "All the pain, suffering is all for the purpose of arriving at this moment of truth. It all begins now. This is life without the filters, the illusion. How many children will you save?" Bodhi would imagine her licking the side of this face, his neck as she squeezed and twisted the flesh on his flank between her fingers. He hated her so much at those moments but it was interlaced with so much passion and lust. Bodhi had never explored sexuality beyond the vanilla but he was now addicted. He wasn't sure if it was the sexual energy or the deeper meaning, the truth she presented to him that kept him in those postures. It was exhilarating!

Something happened in that eternity measured in seconds between the *I can't anymore. I have to stop. I can't,* to when he actually collapsed out of the posture. Bodhi found that he transcended the pain and entered into another realm beyond himself. There was no ego. There were no limitations and he could no longer detect the boundary between himself and everything else. It was so powerful that everything and anything was worthwhile to get there.

Bodhi continued to gently bathe Adya. Another tattoo on the volar surface of the left forearm read: "Memento Mori!" Deciphering her tattoos felt like a trivia game and he was losing. He did however know that "Memento Mori" meant "remember your death." He had come across this Latin phrase after starting his emergency medicine training at Lincoln Medical Center. "Memento Mori" was a reminder that you are not immortal. You will die and you don't know when you're going to die. So, don't take life for granted and live it to the fullest. This was at least Bodhi's understanding at that time. It was certainly appropriate when he started his training at Bellevue where patients were dropping like flies to the AID's epidemic. It made even more sense at Lincoln where "death by lead poisoning," an euphemism for being shot on Saturday night while minding your own business and waiting for the church to open. It took on even greater significance in their post-Covid world.

Adya had a tattoo with three parallel lines going across the volar aspect of her wrist with a dot in the middle of the space closest to her hand. Bodhi had no idea what that stood for. After scrubbing her arms down, Bodhi pulled down the sheet to clean her torso. He couldn't help but to notice Adya's lovely medium-sized, firm breasts and large, dark, pierced nipples contrasted against her olive skin. Even her chest muscles were well-defined. He gently washed her breasts with tenderness and care. He noted her belly-button ring and thought what a nightmare it would be to have her as a patient in the trauma bay. They would have had to painstakingly remove all her earrings, studs, and piercings before taking her to CT. By the time he arrived at her shaved pubic hair and was patting her breasts and washboard six-pack abdomen dry, he felt a burning in his loin and an uncomfortable erection pushing against his wet, vomit-laden jeans. It was physically uncomfortable but psychologically disturbing as well.

Bodhi had practiced emergency medicine for 30 years. He had seen countless naked bodies and performed innumerable breast and pelvic exams. He approached these encounters with deep respect and extreme professionalism. The only time he experienced such an ethical and psychological conflict was during his third-year obstetric rotation in medical school. It was then that he discovered that he had a thing for pregnant women, especially at about their sixth month. Their breasts, lips and vulvas were plump and he imagined how soft their bodies must have been. They glowed. He remembered how embarrassed he was to have an erection during the entire six weeks of his rotation. He felt like a horny school boy. Since then, he had learned to shut off that switch that allowed him to see the most beautiful women naked in the professional setting and simply view them as patients. There was never another thought. He was extremely professional and would ensure that even during trauma resuscitations that women were exposed only as much as was necessary to perform a thorough examination. Here he found himself, 30 years later, less than a year after the Second Wave, and just two days after almost being hanged, sexually aroused washing this vomit and pus-laden body of the woman who saved his life.

How pathetic! Bodhi thought to himself. This thought was then immediately followed by the same thought he had when he had the noose around his head: *Damn! She's hot.* Bodhi thought of a story he read in Anaïs Nin's collection of short stories "Delta of Venus." Anaïs Nin described a man walking on the docks where there were many crates and shipping containers. He noticed a foot sticking from behind one of the crates. He went to investigate and found the dead and naked body of an absolutely gorgeous woman. Bodhi had read this story in his teens and didn't remember the details but remembered that the man noted the woman must have just died or been killed because her skin was still warm. He also noted her voluptuous body. She so aroused him that he couldn't control himself and made love to her dead body!

This story disturbed Bodhi's teenage mind, but it stuck with him in a big way. His friends would complain after scoring a one-night stand with a woman who "just lay there like a dead fish." This was not Bodhi's preference but whenever in that situation, he would think of Anaïs Nin's story. He would fantasize that the woman in his bed, who happened to "just lay there like a dead fish," was actually dead and he was making love to her dead body.

How fucked up is that? Bodhi thought to himself. It was at that precise moment that Bri walked back into the apartment.

"Perfect timing!" Bodhi exclaimed. "Let's wash her back and get all this poop off her. Then we'll do her legs and change the sheets."

"Sure," Bri replied. "Maybe debride the wound first since the sheet's already dirty?"

"Great idea," Bodhi said. "The Cefepime just finished. Can you get the vanc while I debride?" Bri nodded yes.

MY ANGEL

Bodhi dumped his gloves in the garbage, washed his hands, and then got a disposable 11-blade. He didn't bother to use a chuck under her leg since the bed was already wet and dirty. Bodhi first exposed her left lower extremity. There was still pus draining from the wound. It was an 8-inch laceration that ran diagonally down the anterolateral aspect of her left thigh.

"Is it deep?" Bri asked.

"Just the upper part," Bodhi replied. "Lucky it wasn't on the medial side. It would've been just deep enough to sever the femoral artery or vein."

"That would've been a disaster," Bodhi said. "She would've bled to death on the street."

"She's lucky," Bri said.

"No," Bodhi replied. "I'm lucky. I would've been dead if it weren't for her."

"Well then," Bri added. "It looks like you're both lucky to have found each other."

"Yup," Bodhi nodded. "Damn lucky." Bodhi started to manipulate and palpate Adya's thigh around the wound, which increased the flow of pus pouring from the wound.

"I think she has an abscess," Bodhi said. "Could you please bring over the ultrasound machine? I think it's in the next room." Bodhi continued to softly palpate the rest of her thigh. Bri returned with the ultrasound machine, put it next to him and plugged it in.

"Help me to roll her to her side," Bodhi asked. Once Adya was on her side, he palpated the back of her thigh. "At least there's no crepitus or skin changes to suggest Nec Fasc. That would've killed her too."

"She's lucky," Bri repeated as she rolled Adya onto her back. Bodhi didn't respond but thought to himself: *We're lucky!*

Bodhi squirted the ultrasound gel near the wound and almost as soon as he placed the probe on her skin, he said: "Yup. She's got an abscess." Bodhi pointed out the abscess to Bri and continued to scan the area to determine its extent. He wiped the probe down, put it back in place and looked at Bri smiling. "That I can take care of!"

"Is that why she's so sick?" Bri asked.

"Not at all," Bodhi said. "She's septic. The infection started in her thigh but got into her blood stream. The antibiotics will take care of that."

"Her vitals are improving," Bri said. "Heart rates down to 103, respirations 24 and her systolic is up to 94. Are you going to I&D the abscess now?"

"Yeah," Bodhi replied. "Why?"

"The boys were acting up this morning," Bri replied. "I have to go back to make sure they're not killing each other."

"Can you give me 10 minutes?" Bodhi asked. Once I drain the abscess, you can help me clean her back and then place the foley. I can stay and watch her after that."

"Sure," Bri said. "I'll call Angela to check in on them."

"Great!" He exclaimed. "Let's do this!"

Bodhi drew up some local anesthesia and injected deeply into the wound. He again applied the ultrasound probe to measure the depth of the abscess from the skin and where there was the most amount of pus. He inserted the 11-blade scalpel into the wound and made a deep stab and then cut. A river of even worse smelling pus poured out of the wound. The stench filled the room. Bri opened the windows and placed a fan blowing over Adya's thigh towards the window. Bodhi then milked her thigh from different directions around the wound extruding even more pus. Adya groaned in pain.

"Well, that's a good sign!" Bodhi exclaimed. When Bodhi wasn't able to extrude any more pus, he filled a bulb syringe with tap water and irrigated the wound until the water coming out was clear. He dressed the wound.

"Do you want to roll her or wash?" Bri asked.

"I'll wash," Bodhi replied. "I'm already soaked from before." Bodhi dumped the dirty water he was washing her with before and filled the basin with clean water and soap. Bri rolled her over to reveal a large tattoo of wings that started from the upper part of her lower back to her shoulders. It was incredibly detailed and colorful.

"Wow!" Bri said. "That's impressive!" Bodhi washed her back very gently and thoroughly. She also had a small tattoo on the back of her neck. It was a smaller set of wings connected by a heart that had a quarter moon and a star in it. It looked familiar but Bodhi couldn't think of where he had seen it before.

He spread her buttocks that he didn't fail to notice were full and muscular, and scrubbed the dried and caked diarrhea. He then dried her with soft dabs. He rolled the sheet under her, placed a clean one on that side and they turned Adya the other way to clean her other side. Once they turned and cleaned the other side, they removed the dirty sheet and unrolled the clean one.

There was a moment that lasted an eternity for Bodhi. Time was frozen. Bri was getting the foley catheter and Bodhi was just about to cover Adya's torso with a sheet. Adya was flat on her back and completely naked. It was just a moment but Bodhi's eyes couldn't help to notice that Adya was the most beautiful woman he had ever seen. She had the body of a goddess. She was perfect. He wondered if in fact she was a goddess or an angel. After all, she had those wings tattooed on her back and saved his life in such a dramatic way. That split second was enough time for his eyes to capture a photograph of this exquisite woman before him and his body to register the cascade of endorphins and testosterone that immediately resulted in another erection. Bodhi quickly covered her just before Bri returned and pressed his body against the gurney to hide his embarrassment.

They both lifted her butt off the gurney by her knees and tucked a chuck underneath her and on top of the clean sheets. Bri brought a new bucket of water and soap and asked Bodhi to spread her legs. Bri gently washed her perineum. Bodhi stared as though he were teleported back in time to the first time he had seen a vagina. Adya had piercings with rings on each vulva. He observed with excitement how the sponge pushed her full vulva from one side to the other and how they separated as the sponge left a wake of sudsy soap as it made its way through the valley between them.

"Dude!" Bri scolded and snapped Bodhi out of his reverie. "Stop drooling and give me a towel." Bodhi felt his face flush and handed her the towel. He turned away and did some busy work while she dried Adya's perineum. Bodhi cleaned the ultrasound probe and wheeled the ultrasound machine back to the other room. When he returned Bri was opening the foley catheter tray and signaled him to come over and hold her other leg to maintain a frog-leg position.

Bri put on a pair of sterile gloves, cleaned Adya's perineum with betadine and with her left hand spread Adya's vulva wide. Bri spent a few seconds searching for the urethra and then inserted the foley catheter. 70ml of dark urine filled the bag.

"Well," Bodhi said. "At least she's making urine. Let's hang another two liters." They put Adya's legs down, taped the foley to her leg and covered her up. Bodhi raised the head of the gurney about 30 degrees and stroked Adya's head. *My angel*, he thought to himself.

Bodhi's smartphone rang at the same time that Bri was leaving to tend to her kids. "Hello...Yeah...She's doing okay...Absolutely. Stop by whenever you want...You're downstairs? Great! Just ring 2C. I'll buzz you up."

INSTRUMENT OF
THE DEVIL

A s Bodhi was waiting for Adya's friends to come up, he couldn't help but to notice the stark contrast between the medical care he was rendering before he quit working as a canary in the ER and after. The singular most important difference was the fact that he didn't have to spend hours documenting everything he did in some electronic medical record or signing charts that medical scribes entered based on his interactions with patients and consultants. Bodhi had figured out early on that these electronic medical records had very little to do with improving medical care and everything to do extracting the maximum payment from insurance companies and governmental agencies.

Bodhi remembered the joy he experienced the first time he worked with an electronic medical record. Yes, it was easier to type than write. Yes, it was absolutely true that it was extremely beneficial to read someone's note for quality improvement or continuity of care. There were other clear benefits to the electronic medical record, but there were so many impositions placed on providers that turned them into crosses for them to bear rather than facilitate or improve the care they were rendering to patients. Bodhi at first naively thought that scribes, who were trained to transcribe their history and physicals into a medical record, were hired to facilitate care and allow healthcare providers to evaluate more patients rather than spend the time documenting. This was in fact true, but the overriding reason was that scribes documented much better than physicians and consequently, improved billing.

It was never that much of a burden for Bodhi to use an electronic medical record and learn to document in an efficient manner that was satisfactory to the hospital billers. It was just annoying that every year the amount of trivial and irrelevant data they were required to document increased. It will be recorded in the history of medicine that the doctor-patient relationship in primary care offices was singlehandedly destroyed by the electronic medical record and the amount of information that primary care physicians had to document. Rather than actually spend time with their patients, they were busy documenting. Moreover, since their reimbursement was diminishing on an almost monthly basis, they had to evaluate impossible numbers of patients. To make a living, they were forced to reduce the amount of time spent with each patient, and in the name of efficiency, had their attention focused on the computer screen rather than the patient.

There was a joy, satisfaction, reward and gratitude that both the patient and physician derived from a practice honed over millennia. It was now being sucked away by these electronic medical records leaving a vapid and bankrupt interaction that left everyone dissatisfied and frustrated. One of Bodhi's greatest joys and one of his personal measures of success as an emergency physician, was when a patient asked him to be their primary care provider. Bodhi would then ask them why, out of genuine curiosity and also to milk the compliment for as much as it was worth. Patients would often say that he had spent more time with them in the ER and made them feel that they were being listened to and acknowledged more than their primary care provider. This did bring Bodhi great satisfaction but he also recognized that this was a warning sign of the decline and possible death of the doctor-patient relationship and likely the entire healthcare system. How could it be possible that in a busy ER, he was spending more clock time and giving a patient more attention than their primary care physician? The bells tolled!

Since leaving the system behind, there were no obstacles between him and his patients. They came to him with their pain and suffering, and he offered some remedies and potions wrapped in love. He listened to them, expressed empathy, and taught them how to care for themselves. As he had always done before, he touched his patients as much as possible and allowed healing energy to flow through him and into his patients. Bodhi understood the basic principles of energetic healing and knew that no intention had to be set. He only had to remain open in order for the energy to flow and bring the patient whatever they needed. If the patient was amenable, he always ended every encounter with a hug.

For the first time in years, he began to fall in love again with patient care. He always loved emergency medicine in the way that an old couple loved each other. Now in his post-Covid practice, it was the falling in love between that same couple when they had first met and had the hots for each other. Bodhi was experiencing the practice of medicine with new eyes.

Bodhi was startled by the ringing doorbell. He opened the door and there were three women and a man at the door. He recognized the man and the woman who had brought Adya. Bodhi extended his hand to the first woman who came in but she threw herself into his arms and gave him a big hug. The other three did the same.

"Thank you so much," the first woman said. "We don't know how we could ever repay you."

"Repay me?" Bodhi exclaimed. "Adya saved my life. I owe her."

"Thank you, brother," the man said as he put one hand on his heart and the other on Bodhi's shoulder. "My name is Tristan, and this is Giovanna, Hanna, Kenzie and Nico."

"My pleasure," Bodhi said. "Please come in. Adya is over

there. Just keep in mind that she's still very sick and isn't really responding yet."

"What was the problem?" Hanna asked.

Bodhi walked them into Adya's room. He started to explain but they all ran to her bedside and embraced her. They stood at both sides of the gurney, held Adya's hands and stroked her hair.

"It started out as a simple infection from the stab wound," Bodhi started, "but then developed into an abscess and then seeded her bloodstream."

"Is she going to get better?" Hanna asked as she stroked Adya's hair.

"Sure," Bodhi replied. I already drained the abscess and she's definitely gotten better with the antibiotics and fluids. She should..."

"We just met and you're already talking behind my back," Adya whispered.

"Adya!" Giovanna embraced her as Kenzie silently clapped her hands in joy. Nico and Hanna beamed. "You're awake." Adya opened her eyes very slightly and struggled to smile.

"Can you guys stay with her?" Bodhi asked. "I desperately need a shower." They all nodded yes. Bodhi started to walk out when he barely heard his name being called.

"Bodhi," Adya whispered again. Bodhi walked over. Adya looked at him and smiled. Adya was trying to say something but Bodhi couldn't make it out. He placed his head next to her mouth.

"Bodhi," Adya repeated. "I told you I'd come back." She gently kissed his cheek and whispered. "Thank you." Bodhi lifted his head and was almost moved to tears by the emotions that ricocheted in his brain, heart and abdomen.

"Don't think you're getting off that easy," Bodhi whispered in her ear. "You still owe me a date." Adya smiled. "I'll be back. Bri, the nurse, will be in shortly to give her another dose of antibiotics." They all thanked Bodhi as he walked out. Bodhi was so filled with joy he was just about to jump up and click his heels when he saw Bri coming up the stairs.

"You seem happy," Bri remarked. "Is she better?"

"Yeah," Bodhi smiled. "She's just starting to wake up. Five of her friends are with her right now. I told them they could stay and I'm sure they'll be willing to help.

"Where are you going?" Bri asked.

"Shower and change."

"Well, that's nice," Bri said with a wry smile. "The way you were looking at her I thought you were going to keep those clothes on for the rest of the week!"

"Ha ha!" Bodhi responded. "That's disgusting!"

THE INVITATION

By the time Bodhi returned, Adya's friends were still standing around the bed just as he left them. They were holding her hands and stroking her hair. Adya smiled when she saw Bodhi come in.

"Hey," Adya whispered.

"Hey!" Bodhi exclaimed. "How do you feel?"

"Blah!" Adya answered.

Bodhi picked up and started to speak while writing in a notepad: "Patient's medical condition is 'blah'." They both laughed.

"I won't disturb you too much," Bodhi said. "I just wanted to check your vitals." He checked the vital signs that Bri recorded and everything had normalized. They had gotten to her with fluids and antibiotics just in time.

"Tell it to me straight doc," Adya asked. "Will I be able to dance ballet again?"

"Absolutely!" Bodhi exclaimed.

"You see," Adya told her friends. "I told you he was a great doctor."

"What makes you say that?" Bodhi asked.

"Well, I never danced ballet before and now I can." Adya said. "You're amazing!" They all laughed.

"I'll give you some time with your friends," Bodhi told her and was about to leave. "I'll check the wound later."

"No." Adya said. "Please stay. They were just telling me

about the raids."

Hanna jumped in. "After getting the database from Junior's gang, we were able to get information on gangs throughout the United States and Europe. We also got lists of predators who dabbled, bought the women and kids, and locations of the kids."

"That's great news!" Bodhi exclaimed.

"We weren't expecting that," Kenzie chimed in. "We were able to get to each group, get more information and databases each time and eliminate them before they were able to warn anyone and go into hiding."

"We crushed them!" Giovanni added.

"You got them all?" Adya asked surprisingly.

"Unlikely," Hanna replied. "But we took out the major providers and have their databases." Adya raised both hands in the air and they all high-fived.

Hanna continued: "I'm sure there are a bunch of predators that were off the grid but without a supply chain, they'll have to lay low for a while."

"What's important," Kenzie chimed in, "Is that they know that there's a heavy price to pay now and that we're not fucking around." They all high-fived again. "We're hoping that our overwhelming response teaches the remaining lowlife scumbags to think twice."

"Hopefully what just happened," Giovanna added, "will wake up and energize people to not take shit anymore. This is the dawn of a new age and the bad guys need to know that we're no longer going to pathetically stand by and watch them walk all over us."

"Word!" Kenzie exclaimed.

"Where are the women and children?" Adya asked.

"They're safe," Hanna replied. "We've got them in our hood, well-fed and cleaned up."

"Did you find Nancy?" Bodhi asked, entering the conversation for the first time.

"Yeah," Giovanna smiled. "She was one of the lucky ones.

We found her with about 20 little kids that were on the launching pad for distribution to other areas outside of New York. They hadn't been assaulted yet."

"Thank you!" Bodhi exclaimed, a heavy weight falling off his chest. "She's like family."

"Like Giovanna said," Nico added. "She was one of the lucky ones. We found so many kids. The next step is to find out who they are and to reunite them with their families."

"Those families will be so happy and grateful," Bodhi said. Everyone nodded in agreement.

"By the way," Bodhi commented. "They'll need medical evaluations. Psychological counseling too."

"We didn't think of that." Kenzie acknowledged. "Can you do that?"

"Not me personally," Bodhi replied. "But we've got a network of all kinds of doctors, psychologists and psychiatrists that can help."

"That's great!" Adya said. "Those poor women and kids."

"You saved them," Bodhi clapped. "And you saved me. Thank you!" They all started to clap.

"And you saved Adya!" Giovanni added and they all clapped for Bodhi.

"I guess we're all doing our bit in this brave new world," Bodhi added. "You know. Even though I'm an ER doctor, I really didn't get what the clapping at 7 O'clock was all about."

"You were this close," Kenzie interrupted as she held her hand up and placed her fingers really close together in front of her eye, "to finding out the meaning with that rope around your neck." They all laughed.

"Right," Bodhi agreed and then continued. "I guess I was cynical about the whole thing but I get it now. We're clapping for each other to celebrate another day of life, for what each one of us brings to the community, and to encourage those that haven't gotten the idea yet. I get it now."

"Bravo!" Adya said. She smiled at him warmly. "Hey. Can you do me a big favor?"

"Sure," Bodhi answered. "What's up?"

Adya signaled Bodhi to come closer so she could whisper in his ear. "You know that thing you put in my coochie? Can you please take it out?"

Bodhi leaned back and smiled at her. "Yeah," Bodhi answered. "I don't think we need it anymore. I'll ask Bri to take it out when she gets back."

Adya again signaled him to come closer and whispered in his ear: "I want you to take it out. Only you."

Bodhi sat back and felt his face flushed. They stared into each other's eyes for a moment but Bodhi felt nervous and broke his gaze.

"Sure," Bodhi said. "It'll be my pleasure..." Bodhi paused. "Well, that didn't come out right." They both laughed. The others looked at each other confused and left out of their inside joke.

"You know," Kenzie said sarcastically, "we can leave you two alone if you'd like."

"No," Adya responded while still staring at Bodhi. "Please stay. I love you guys. Bodhi and I have a date later." She raised her eyebrows and head towards Bodhi. "Right?"

Bodhi smiled shyly. "Absolutely. Candles, Champagne. The whole shebang."

"Cool," Adya smiled. They all spent a few hours chatting and sharing stories about the raid and future plans. Adya then began to look visibly tired. She then looked to her friends and said: "I love you guys so much. I'm so happy you're here with me but I'm starting to fade. Can you come back later?"

"No problema!" Hanna exclaimed. "We'll stop by tomorrow. Rest." They each hugged Adya and Bodhi for a long time.

"*Hasta pronto amiga*," Tristan said cheerfully. "*Cuidate bien.*"

"Thank you, Bodhi," Tristan said as he placed his hand on his chest. "We love you. Welcome to the family."

"Thank you," Bodhi responded. "That means a lot to me." Bodhi then looked over to Adya, put his hand on hers and said:

"I'm happy to see that you're better. I'll stop by later."

"Don't forget the candles and Champagne!" Adya smiled.

THE SEDUCTION

L ater that day, Bodhi opened the door very quietly in case Adya was still sleeping. As soon as he opened the door, he heard Adya's voice: "Bodhi. Is that you?"

"Yes," Bodhi replied. He was surprised to see her sitting at the side of the bed. "How are you feeling?"

"Much better," Adya said. "Bri was here and took out the foley. I asked her to wait to let you take it out and she thought I was crazy. Where were you?"

"I had to help a colleague out with a sick patient," Bodhi replied.

"Well, you don't know what you just missed," Adya smiled.

"I have to admit," Bodhi said, "that I was really looking forward to taking out your foley."

"Really?" Adya asked.

"I fantasized putting candles all over the room with some nice sexy music..."

"Like what?" Adya asked as she leaned forward.

"I was thinking D'Angelo's 'How does it feel?' "

"Okay," Adya nodded.

Bodhi hesitated. He pulled a chair in front of her and just smiled. They stared into each other's eyes.

"Please go on," Adya insisted.

Bodhi blushed and continued. "So, while D'Angelo is playing, I'd dim the lights and light the candles. Then I was

planning on unwrapping a 10cc syringe while kissing your
face softly."

"Ummm," Adya purred.

"Then I'd start kissing your neck while gently running
the syringe down your back..." Bodhi leaned in and took her
hand. "...and stealthily undo the ties to your gown."

"Frisky, are we?" Adya said as she sat at the edge of the
bed. Bodhi was now running the tips of his fingers lightly over
her arm. Adya leaned over and kissed his cheek.

"Don't stop now," Adya said. "I want all the juicy details."

"Then I'd rip the gown off you..." Bodhi said as he moved
his lips across her cheek just stopping shy of the side of her
lips.

"Oh yeah," Adya whispered as she threw her head back. "I
like a strong man who's in charge."

"I'd then just step back and circle the bed looking at you,"
Bodhi said as he kissed her eyes, nose, chin and ran his lips
along the front of her neck. "I'd stare at you naked on the white
sheets of the gurney with the sexy foley and IV coming out of
you....Ummm."

"I'd be trembling by then," Adya held Bodhi's head pressing his lips on her neck. "Begging you to take it out."

"That's right baby," Bodhi added. "You'd be writhing in
that gurney, breathing really deeply and begging for it."

"I can hear D'Angelo right now," Adya sighed. "Don't
stop!"

"I'd pry your legs open and go nuts seeing that beige
catheter in your urethra...undulating like a snake as your hips
moved back and forth." Adya now pulled Bodhi's head to the
side and she kissed his neck and licked the back of his ear.

"Go on. Go on," Adya pleaded.

"Well," Bodhi murmured as he groaned to her deep kisses
on his neck. "I could tell how badly you wanted it but I'd keep
you waiting...keep teasing you."

"That's terrible," Adya said. "Who would have known
that you could be such a naughty boy?"

"Then I'd run my fingers gently over your body," Bodhi kissed her lips gently..."and squeeze your nipple hard."

"I like it rough," Adya said, now licking his lips.

"I know," Bodhi replied.

"Really?" Adya asked surprised. "What gave it away?" Adya now kissed him more deeply.

"Well..." Bodhi said as he sat back, took both her hands and kissed them as he looked into her eyes. "It came to mind when I saw you so elegantly chop Junior's head off."

"Shit!" Adya said as she took one hand and covered her eye and one side of her face while simultaneously raising her knee up to her chest. "I was really trying to be subtle!"

"But the dead giveaway was..." Bodhi now sat squarely in front of her on the edge of his seat and placed both hands on her knees.

"The suspense is killing me," Adya smiled. "What gave my BDSM tendencies away?"

"The piercings," Bodhi said as he ran his hands along the outside of her thighs until he reached the dressing on her left thigh.

"Hmmm," Adya sounded. "And how did you know about my piercings?"

Bodhi instantly felt very awkward and sat back in his chair. "Well, as you can see, we're a little short-staffed around here and I had to help Bri bathe you." Bodhi started to blush and stutter. "You were covered in a mixture of pus, caked and fresh vomit. It's not that I was looking...but...we had to clean you, right." Adya just stared at him with a straight face. Bodhi continued: "I didn't do anything wrong...or unethical...and Bri was there...well...most of the time." Adya started to laugh hysterically. She reached out and took Bodhi's hand.

"Bodhi," she said. "It's alright. Really. I appreciate everything you did for me. No worries." Bodhi smiled. "Did you say pus, caked and fresh vomit?" Bodhi nodded yes.

"Yuk!" she exclaimed.

"I thought it was kinda sexy," Bodhi said. "But Bri insisted that I clean you up. So, I gave you a luxurious bath."

"And did you like what you saw?" Adya asked as she placed his hands back on her knees and guided them slowly over the inner aspect of her thighs.

"I was awestruck," Bodhi responded.

"Did you like the way I felt?" Adya asked.

"Like heaven," Bodhi replied as he dropped to his knees between her legs and put his arms around her waist. She embraced him and rocked her body back and forth.

"Bodhi," Adya said still holding him tightly.

"Yeah."

"I think this is the start of a beautiful friendship." They separated from their embrace, stared into each other's eyes and kissed deeply. They were orbiting another planet in another dimension when Bri entered. They didn't even notice her. Bri purposely made noise and they still didn't notice her. She stood behind them.

"Bodhi!" Bri called out loudly. She finally stood right behind him and shouted "Dr. McKenna!"

Bodhi and Adya were startled and he jumped up to his feet. He was obviously flustered. Adya smiled.

"Dude!" Bri said firmly. "Isn't there something ethically wrong with this picture?'"

Bodhi smiled. "I'm not sure. Let's get the ethics committee together and discuss it."

Bri smirked. "Listen, I've got to take inventory. Do you think you can wait till I'm done?"

"Absolutely!" Bodhi responded. Both he and Adya laughed.

Bri rolled her eyes, but couldn't hide the big smile threatening to break out. "I'm really happy for the both of you. I won't be long."

"While we're talking about business," Adya said. "Can we take the IV out?"

"Unfortunately not," Bodhi replied. "You were in septic shock..." Adya had a puzzled look on her face. Bodhi continued:

"Bacteria in your blood stream. It could've killed you. You're better but will need another seven days of antibiotics."

"What?!" Adya exclaimed. "You mean I have to stay here for another week."

"Yes."

"That's ridiculous," Adya continued. "I've got important things to do. Can I sign out against medical advice?"

"I won't let you," Bodhi replied firmly.

"What do you mean you won't let me?" Adya asked.

"Exactly what I said," Bodhi answered. "I won't let you out of here. I'll tie you up if I have to."

Adya smiled. "Does that mean that you like me?"

"I know it sounds silly to say such a ridiculous thing," Bodhi said. "But we're living in ridiculous times."

"What do you want to say that's so silly?"

"I just met you," Bodhi said, "and I'm already madly in love with you."

"That is really, really the silliest thing I've heard since the First Wave," she countered, "but you know what, I'm already madly in love with you too."

"I have an idea," Bodhi said as he pulled her up to her feet and hugged her.

"Shoot!"

"Why don't you move in with me?" Bodhi asked.

"Well, that's moving kinda fast."

"Ridiculous times. Ridiculous love. Ridiculous gestures." Bodhi said. "I live right next door. We'll leave the IV in and give you antibiotics for the next week."

"And then what?"

"Que sera, sera!" Bodhi said. "Who knows? We'll cross that bridge when we get to it."

"Okay then," Adya slapped both hands on the side of her thighs. "I'll start packing!"

They both laughed and hugged.

LIGHT MY FIRE

A week had passed since moving into Bodhi's apartment. Adya took her last bite of food and closed her eyes as she allowed the various flavors to burst into her palate. Some of them exploded individually, while others did so sequentially, building up to final burst of flavors that was much stronger than the individual ones. The most amazing and unexpected was when the flavors exploded simultaneously and transcended the carnival that was taking place in her mouth into her entire body. They erupted into one emotion that led to another and then another. They were like ripples in a crystalline lake initiated with that single bite of deliciousness that grew into bigger ripples and then waves and then into a veritable tsunami.

Adya tried to explain what she was experiencing with words. She was the hapless enthusiast insisting on finding ways to describe colors to a blind person. Bodhi loved her more and more for her boundless enthusiasm. Adya explained: "It's like a very brief and intense flight from reality into this strange place filled with a type of ringing in one's ears that occurs while taking whippets."

"I hate whippets!" Bodhi exclaimed. "But what you're describing sounds like a total body orgasm."

"What's that?" Adya asked. Bodhi nodded and smiled in amazement and awe of her beauty.

"It's an orgasm that's not based in your genitals," Bodhi

explained. "It builds up from the flow of energy that you channel up your chakras and explodes all over your body. They can last a really long time."

"I want one of those!" Adya exclaimed excitedly as she wildly waved her glass of wine. "Did they teach you this in medical school?" They laughed. Bodhi told Adya about his ex-girlfriend Kali who introduced him to yoga, Tantra and BDSM.

"I'd love to meet her!" Adya said. Bodhi smiled.

"Another amazing meal," Adya added. "I never got off on food like this even before Covid!"

"So, you'll stay?" Bodhi asked.

"Hmmm," Adya sounded as she finished her glass of wine. Bodhi reached and grabbed the wine bottle to pour her another glass but the bottle was empty. He put the empty bottle next to the other two empty bottles on the table, stumbled over to the cabinet and brought another bottle. He could barely stand straight but held the bottle in front of her waiting for her approval.

"St. Émilion. Grand Cru. 1992," Bodhi said in a terrible, affected French accent. She nodded yes and he sat to open the bottle.

"Where did you get the wine?" Adya asked. It's very hard to come by these days."

Bodhi poured the wine into their glasses. "I'm actually not much of a drinker but I had a few great bottles like this one that I was saving for a special occasion."

"Are you saying I'm special, Bodhi?"

Bodhi looked at her, raised his eyebrows and said: "Yeah. Big time."

"Right back atcha, Dr. McKenna."

Bodhi poured the wine into their glasses. "By the way, this was my very last bottle."

"No worries," Adya said with a big smile. "The apartment I moved into has a 2,000-bottle wine cellar. I was waiting for a special occasion to crack it."

"Cheers to special occasions!"

"Cheers!"

There was a moment of silence. They both looked into their wine glasses, perhaps looking for words that weren't necessary. Adya looked up from her glass, smiled and said: "You know, my father always warned me to never stay in a relationship with a one-trick pony."

"Ouch!" Bodhi exclaimed as he allowed himself to fall to one side and knocking down a few of the candles he had set all over the dining room. One of the candles fell directly on the cloth napkin he was using and it caught on fire. They both jumped up excitedly and were screaming, telling each other what to do while laughing out of control.

The fire rapidly spread to the tablecloth and even in their drunken stupor, they stopped dead in their tracks and had a "Holy Shit! The house is on fire" moment. They stopped laughing simultaneously. Adya poured their glasses of water onto the fire without any demonstrable result. Bodhi ran into the bathroom, grabbed a few towels and soaked them in water. The dining room and kitchen were now filling up with smoke. The fire alarm was ringing and Adya started to cough uncontrollably.

Bodhi put on the oven gloves and dropped the soaked towels directly onto the fire and patted the area down. This helped a little but the fire was still spreading over the entire tablecloth. Bodhi pulled the tablecloth off the table causing the plates, cutlery, and glasses to fly in all directions onto the floor. The glasses shattered. Bodhi now ran back into the bathroom with a bundle of fire between both hands threw it into the tub. He turned on the faucet full blast and doused the fire.

"Holy shit!" Bodhi exclaimed.

"That was insane!" Adya stated as she walked over to him. She turned him around and gave him a big hug. Bodhi was still wearing the oven gloves that were now covered with soot and dripping black mud onto Adya's back down to the floor. The fire alarm was still ringing. Adya opened the door and windows to air out. Bodhi climbed onto a chair to silence the alarm.

"Whoa!" Bodhi blurted out as he held Adya's hand and led her to the living room. Adya sat on the couch and Bodhi stood in front of her. "I can see the headlines," Bodhi said as he drew a horizontal line in front of him with his hands. "Girl saves ER doctor from horrific death by hanging. ER doctor then saves girl from death by septic shock. They fall madly in love and then set each other on fire." Bodhi sat down next to her. He put his arm around her and gave her soft kisses. He again drew a horizontal line in front of them. "Their ashes were found in an Upper West Side apartment where their burnt corpses were found lying next to each other wrapped in each other's arms. It's not clear what really happened but authorities suspect a double suicide." They both laugh.

"That's so sick!" Adya said while slightly pulling away from him.

"Not bad for a one-trick pony huh?" Bodhi asked.

"Ohhh," Adya exclaimed. "Did I hurt the big doctor's enormous ego?" Bodhi responded by simultaneously raising his eyebrows, pouting, turning his head to the side and shrugging his shoulders.

"By the way," Bodhi asked. "What my one trick?"

"Your mastery in the kitchen, silly." Bodhi looked disappointed.

"Would it make you feel better if I admitted that you're a two-trick pony?" Adya asked while stroking his cheek.

"Depends on what you see as my second trick," Bodhi smiled.

"I think you're a really great lover," Adya said. "Better?"

"Yes love," Bodhi beamed. "Much better."

Adya pushed him away forcefully. "You're such a little boy," Adya said as she got up to go to the bathroom. Just as she was leaving the living room Adya turned around and drew an enormous circle with both hands and said: "All ego." They laughed.

MOVING OUT

Adya returned from the bathroom with a big smile on her face.

"What's so funny?" Bodhi asked.

"You are, of course," Adya replied.

"Okay," Bodhi said. "A two-trick pony who also happens to be funny. I'll take that." Bodhi took her hand and pulled her down onto his lap. "You just received your last dose of IV antibiotics. You're a free woman. Will you stay with me?" Adya gave him a big hug, a kiss, and then buried her head in his neck.

"No," Adya replied. Silence. Adya got up, walked to the kitchen and returned with two glasses of water. She sat next to him but left a little distance between them. Bodhi stared at her leaving the obvious question of "why" screaming out in that space between them.

"Bodhi." Adya took his hand into hers and stared into his eyes. "Do you want to be with me?"

"Obviously," Bodhi replied. "That's why I asked you to stay with me. How come you don't want to be with me?"

"That's silly," Adya replied.

"Silly?" Bodhi asked. "Then why..."

"I never said that I didn't want to be with you." Adya interrupted. "Wasn't it obvious that even after the first time we met that there was a strong connection between us? Isn't it obvious that I love you now?"

Bodhi shook his head. "I really don't understand."

"I want us to be together Bodhi. I just don't want to stay here."

"Why?" Bodhi asked.

"My community needs me," Adya said. "And I need them. We're doing a lot of important things."

"I get that," Bodhi said. "My community needs me too."

"Bullshit!" Adya exclaimed. "Is this an ego thing?" They were going to watch you hang without even having the guts to look you in the eye to say goodbye." Bodhi remained silent and looked down. He slipped his hand out of hers and held them with his fingers interlaced between his legs.

"I don't understand how they dare even look at you now," Adya added. "I honestly don't know how you can bear to look at them with any sense of respect. I couldn't even if I tried. I won't try." Bodhi was obviously very uncomfortable and didn't know what to do with his hands. He grabbed the glass of water and took a sip.

Adya continued: "I know about everything you've done here. Everyone's been following your lead, Bodhi. But what are they bringing to the table?"

"They're doing the best they can," Bodhi whispered while still looking at the ground.

"Community is about sharing, Bodhi. They're just going along for the ride." Adya took the glass out of Bodhi's hand and straddled him with her knees on the couch. She kissed his face gently.

"I love you!" Adya whispered as she kissed him. She then suddenly pulled away from him and said: "I want you to come live with me. Let's do it right now." Bodhi looked at her and smiled.

"I need you," Adya added. "My community needs you and they'll show you real appreciation. Like me, they'd die before letting anyone harm you. Have you ever experienced that kind of community love?" Bodhi shook his head no.

"It's so powerful!" Adya continued. "Have you ever been to Burning Man?" Bodhi again nodded no.

"Well, Burning Man is all about community. It's a festival that takes place in the Nevada desert. They literally build a city and about 70,000 people show up in crazy costumes to party, share, dance, and be part of a community. Sure, there's a lot of drugs. I'm sure that all the MDMA has a lot to do with all that love that's being projected out of everyone's eyes and received through every pour of their skin. But it's transformational."

"I've heard so much about it and always wanted to go," Bodhi said.

"Well, if it ever starts up again," Adya said, "You can be my virgin."

"Virgin?" Bodhi asked.

"Newbies are called virgins," Adya explained, "So you'll be mine."

"I'd love to be your virgin!" Bodhi beamed.

"But the crazy thing," Adya said enthusiastically, "is that we're somehow managing to create that same kind of community here based on the '10 Burning Man Principles.'"

"I always thought that Burning Man was a free-for-all," Bodhi interjected.

"They're more guidelines than rules," Adya explained, "But they define the community's ethos and culture. I actually declared them the principles of our community."

"You could do that?" Bodhi asked.

"Fuck yeah, brother," Adya exclaimed. "I'm the boss!" They laughed. She got up and went to the bedroom for her smartphone.

"I have them right here," Adya said. "May I read them to you?"

"Absolutely," Bodhi replied. "Before you start, do you feel like a Brandy or some Cognac?"

"Dude!" Adya exclaimed. "We just almost burnt the house down! I think we should stick to water, no?" Bodhi nodded in agreement. "So here are the 10 Principles for Burning Man and Adya's hood." First is radical inclusion. Anyone can join the community without any prerequisites. We welcome everyone with open arms. Second. The community is devoted to acts of gift giving without anticipation of getting anything in return or exchange."

"So, no money?" Bodhi asked.

"Nope," Adya replied and continued. Third is decommodification."

"What?"

"That means creating a social environment that's unmediated by commercial sponsorship, transactions, or advertising. That's what preserves the spirit of gifting. Think about it Bodhi. This is exactly what paralyzes society. You think we would have all those mass shootings in the pre-Covid era if it weren't for the powerful lobbies paying millions of dollars to congress and the senate to prevent sensible gun-control legislation. Same is true for healthcare reform and the agricultural subsidies that keeps high-fructose corn syrup on the tables of so many people who don't know better and poison themselves. I don't want to go back to that. Do you?"

"No way," Bodhi said. "You know, a lot of people were saying after the First Wave that Covid-19 gave us such an opportunity to reflect on who we were as a society and really see and understand what we were doing to ourselves and to the planet."

"Yeah," Adya agreed. "It was a wake-up call, but too late. May I continue?" Bodhi nodded and took a sip of water. "Fourth is radical self-reliance. Everyone has to discover, exercise and rely on his or her inner resources. Are you getting the idea that when Larry Harvey wrote..."

"Who's Larry Harvey?" Bodhi asked.

"He started Burning Man and wrote these principles," Adya answered. "It's like he was able to see into the future and was letting us know what we needed to do to survive in this post-Covid world."

"It's a bit creepy." Bodhi agreed.

"Wait till you hear the rest," Adya continued. "Fifth is radical self-expression that arises from the unique gifts of the individual. Harvey wrote that 'No one other than the individual or a collaborating group can determine its content. It is offered as a gift to others. In this spirit, the giver should respect the rights and liberties of the recipient'."

"How many times did you go to Burning Man?" Bodhi asked.

"Eighteen years in a row," Adya said proudly. "I missed my first 'Burn' three years ago. They had some really ridiculous reason to cancel...something about a pandemic. What bullshit!" They laughed.

"In your experience," Bodhi asked. "Did people abide by these principles?"

"For the most part yes," Adya replied. "You're talking about 70,000 people in crazy costumes and at least two-thirds on them rolling on 'E' or something else. It's incredible that mostly everyone was with the program. If a stray did something that wasn't cool, the community would let them know immediately."

"That's a truly amazing feat," Bodhi said. "Go on."

"Sixth is communal effort," Adya continued. "There's a premium placed on cooperation and collaboration. The goal is to produce, promote and protect social networks, public spaces, works of art, and methods of communication that support such interaction." Adya looked up from her phone. "It's like he's describing our present situation."

"Crazy!" Bodhi nodded.

"Seventh is civic responsibility. Harvey placed a high value on civil society where 'community members who organized events should assume responsibility for public welfare and endeavor to communicate civic responsibilities to participants. They must also assume responsibility for conducting events in accordance with local, state and federal laws.'" Adya looked up from her phone to check Bodhi out. "I at first just wanted to share this with you for fun, but I'm realizing how important this is. We're almost done."

"I'm crazy about you," Bodhi said. Adya looked up and

smiled.

"Eighth is 'Leaving No Trace'," Adya continued. "This one is all about common sense and respect for the environment. Harvey wrote that 'We are committed to leaving no physical trace of our activities wherever we gather. We clean up after ourselves and endeavor, whenever possible, to leave such places in a better state than when we found them.'"

"Sounds like common sense advice that parents should have taught all of us," Bodhi added.

"You'd be surprised," Adya responded. "This goes a little further. Imagine living in a vast desert for seven days. Leaving no trace means that you can't piss on the ground."

"What?"

"Yeah," Adya continued. "It means that you collect the water you showered or cooked with. It's called 'brown water.' We collect it in containers and let it evaporate in the sun."

"Wow!"

"Like I said, Adya responded. "It gets deep. Imagine the effect that living like this would have on the planet? It's a sign of ultimate respect for the planet and everyone you share it with."

"I think I'll adopt these principles here," Bodhi said.

"No love," Adya said firmly. "You're packing your shit and moving in with me where you don't have to be everything to everyone all the time. You can leave them these principles in your goodbye note and let them decide if they want to adopt them." Bodhi stared back into her eyes without saying a word.

"Are you with me?" Adya asked.

"Yes," Bodhi answered.

"Good to hear," Adya said. "In any case, it's not like you had a choice." She smiled, leaned over and kissed him hard on the lips. "Ninth is Participation," Adya continued. "This one's really important. Harvey wrote that "Our community is committed to a radically participatory ethic. We believe that transformative change, whether in the individual or in society, can occur only through the medium of deeply personal participation. We achieve being through doing. Everyone is invited to work. Everyone is invited to play. We make the world real through actions that open the heart.' "

"That's really deep!" Bodhi exclaimed.

"Harvey was brilliant!" Adya added. "Last was 'Immediacy'. Harvey wrote that 'Immediate experience is, in many ways, the most important touchstone of value in our culture. We seek to overcome barriers that stand between us and a recognition of our inner selves, the reality of those around us, participation in society, and contact with a natural world exceeding human powers. No idea can substitute for this experience.' "

"Brilliant!" Bodhi exclaimed. "What a visionary! You know I've been playing with this thought in my head since this all started."

"What's that?" Adya asked.

"The idea that hindsight is 20/20," Bodhi started.

"Well, that's not very original, is it?" Adya asked sarcastically.

"Not at all," Bodhi responded. "The idea is that Covid-19 gave us 20/20 vision."

"That's cool and so true," Adya agreed.

"Wait. That's not it," Bodhi said as he held his finger up.

"Okay," Adya said smiling. "I'm ready."

"And we got it in 2020," Bodhi said excitedly. "Get it? 20/20 in 2020."

"That's brilliant!" Adya clapped and then gave Bodhi a high five.

"What's amazing is that Harvey had 20/20 way before," Bodhi said. "That's genius!"

"Yup," Adya added. She then put her arm around him and squeezed him tight.

"Do you trust me?" Adya asked. Bodhi looked into her eyes and nodded yes. "I mean, do you really trust me at a deep level?" Bodhi was about to answer but she put her index finger across his lips.

She added: "I don't want a mind answer. I want to hear it from your heart. I'm talking about a trust that goes beyond our crazy attraction to each other and the dramatic way that we were brought together." Adya paused. Bodhi again was about to say something and she now put her entire hand across his mouth.

She continued: "I'm asking you to feel. Don't think. Words aren't necessary. Can you feel that there's something really powerful between you and me that goes far beyond us? Far beyond our wants, needs, desires and dreams?" Adya moved her hand over his eyes and closed them. She then placed the palm of her hand over the center of his forehead and held it there. Bodhi breathed deeply. Adya then placed her hand over the center of his chest.

"Try to feel that," Adya whispered. "It's so strong." Adya adjusted her position to sit perpendicular to him. She took his hand and held it squarely on the center of her chest while she kept her other hand on his. They both breathed deeply with their eyes closed.

Adya spoke very clearly: "I want you in my life Bodhi." She pressed firmly on his chest. "I want you to live with me in Williamsburg and be part of something really special. Be part of creating something really powerful." Bodhi opened his eyes and started to reply. Adya again put her hand across his mouth. "Just say yes."

"Yes! Yes!" Bodhi exclaimed. "Yes!" They kissed deeply.

"How much time do you need to pack?" Adya asked while kissing his neck.

"I've lived here for over 20 years," Bodhi said. "But I'm ready for a new life with you. I'll take the bare minimum and start fresh."

"Great!" Adya exclaimed. "I'll have my people bring a truck to pick you up in the afternoon. That'll also give you time to say goodbye to everyone and find someone to take over the clinic." Bodhi pulled away and stared at her.

"Why can't I continue to work here?" he asked.

Adya smirked. "Exactly. Why? There are plenty of docs to run the clinic here. Why commute?"

Bodhi threw his head back and sighed.

"Babe," Adya added. "Think of it like a vacation. Give it 30 days and if you really want to you can come back then."

"Hah!" Bodhi exclaimed with a big smile. "I just had this vision of you in black leather standing over me and I'm all tied up."

"I can do that if it turns you on," Adya beamed.

"I don't think I'll have the choice to ever come back," Bodhi said.

"That's beside the point," Adya responded. "What's important is that I'm giving you the illusion of free will." She took his chin and lifted it so that they were eye to eye.

"New life, Bodhi. New possibilities. Are you ready to let go?"

Bodhi paused, looked at her and smiled. "Yes."

PART 7: NEW TRIBE

THE LONG GOODBYE

odhi was conflicted about leaving his community. He
lived there since childhood, was married and raised
his children there, and his mother and sister still lived
there. The roots were strong. But he also knew that all his hem-
ming and hawing was a waste of time because Adya was just
too compelling a human being to part from. Bodhi announced
his plan to move to Williamsburg with Adya at a community
meeting.

"Wow!" Karl said. "That's a surprise."

"Yeah," Amanda agreed. "You barely know Adya and
you're moving in with her?"

"I find it hard to believe myself," Bodhi said. "But
if there's anything that Covid taught us, it's *Carpe Diem*. I'm
doing this." Everyone cheered.

"You'll continue to work here, right?" Joe asked.
Bodhi was silent and looked out at his friends and neighbors with whom he lived for so many years. All of a sudden,
the entire room fell silent. They were thrilled that Bodhi had
found love and were willing to accept that he was moving to
Williamsburg, but they assumed that he would maintain his
leadership role in the community. They had come to depend on
Bodhi. Rather than insisting they take responsibility for themselves, he was more than happy to do things that they should
have been doing themselves. He was their enabler. For every
second that passed with Bodhi's silence, a weight pulled every-

one deeper into feelings of loss, anger, and panic.

"No," Bodhi said matter-of-factly. "I want to start a new life and dividing myself between here and Brooklyn wouldn't do justice to either.

"So, you're leaving us just like that?" Joe asked.

"What do you mean by 'just like that'?" Bodhi asked. He looked deep inside himself and tried to find any surviving remnants of that bond he had with these people, his community, but it was gone. A wall had erupted between them.

"It feels like you're abandoning us." Joe blurted out. Bodhi considered that they had survived a near mass-extinction, death by starvation and freezing, and then the gangs. Yet, the connection was gone.

"How am I abandoning you?" Bodhi was visibly upset. "I've been a part of this community all my life and contributed in whatever way I could. But it's not a responsibility. There are so many great people here to take my place and continue building on what we've accomplished. Bodhi at first thought that his raging love for Adya blinded him, but knew that Adya was right. That bond was severed when Junior put that noose around his neck and no one lifted an eyelash to save him.

"Of course it's not your responsibility, Bodhi," Albert added. "What we're trying to say is that we don't want you to go. You're family."

"Is there anything we can do to convince you to stay?" Karl asked. Nancy ran over to Bodhi and hugged him. She started to cry, which opened a floodgate of emotions. Tears started to well in his eyes.

Bodhi already acknowledged to himself that there was absolutely nothing that they could have done in that situation against a psychopathic killer and his armed goons. He had no illusions that he would have done anything differently if the noose were around someone else's neck and he were watching. But at that moment, everything had changed.

"How can we dare ask him to stay?" Bri, who had been thoughtfully silent since Bodhi announced his decision, interjected, "when we just stood there to watch him hang?" Silence fell on the room suddenly.

"What were we supposed to do?" Mark angrily blustered. "They had guns."

"From the macho guy who always wanted to stand up and fight," Old Man Joe pointed out sarcastically.

Bodhi stood up and put up both of his hands. "Please stop! That's not the reason I'm leaving. Mark is right. There's nothing you could have done." As Adya had said, he could no longer look them in the eye. Moreover, they now looked at him differently. Perhaps it was because he now served as a mirror that reminded them of their fear, shame and cowardice. Bodhi continued: "Listen. Let's not make this complicated. It's very simple. I met the woman of my dreams, fell head over heels in love with her, and I'm ready to follow her to the ends of the earth." The tension in the room diffused partially.

"You said that right," Karl finally joked. "Williamsburg is pretty close to the ends of the earth." Everyone laughed.

"Well," Amanda said, "we're going to miss you." She walked over to him and hugged him. Everyone lined up to give him a hug and say their goodbyes. Those long, firm and sincere hugs were to the closest Bodhi came to that feeling of connection and belonging since Adya saved him from death by hanging. It was a lovely feeling for which he was grateful, but it was time to move on.

What Bodhi thought would have been more difficult was to share the news with his mother and sister. They had met Adya, loved her, and were both very happy for him. They just reminded him to visit often. The year 2023 was coming to a close. With their blessing, Bodhi was ready to start a new life.

NEW LIFE

"**W**hat do you think of my crib?" Adya asked as they walked into a very spacious, bright luxury apartment.

"Wow!" Bodhi exclaimed. "This is amazing."

"Yeah," Adya smiled as she nodded. "I figured I'd go large in light of all the craziness out there." Bodhi stood frozen as he scanned the floor-to-ceiling windows, ultra-high ceilings, the curved staircase leading to a second floor on one side of the spacious living area and a spiral staircase on the other side. Adya took his hand and led him out to a large balcony that had glorious views over the East River and the Manhattan, Brooklyn and Williamsburg bridges.

"What a view!" Bodhi remarked.

"Wait till you see it at night," Adya said as she put her arms around him and kissed his cheeks gently. "Do you feel like a drink to celebrate?"

"Absolutely!" Bodhi replied.

"How about an Aperol Spritz?" Adya asked as she led him back inside. She sat him at the white marble-topped island separating the state-of-the-art kitchen from the living room and opened the fridge.

"How large is this apartment?" Bodhi asked still in awe of the grandeur of the apartment.

"Something like 4000 square feet," Adya replied as she filled two large spritzer glasses with ice and poured in some

Aperol. "You could get used to this, right?"

Bodhi just nodded his head yes as he continued to look around. Adya took a bottle of Prosecco out of the fridge, popped the cork and poured it over the Aperol, followed by a dash of sparkling water. She stirred each glass with her finger and licked her finger.

"Needs more Prosecco." She poured a bit more into both glasses, stirred again with her finger, and tasted. "Perfect!" Adya stepped around the island and handed Bodhi the glass. She squeezed in between his legs, put an arm around his neck and gave him a deep wet kiss. Adya stepped back, raised her glass while looking into his eyes.

"Here's to love in the time of Coronavirus," Adya toasted.

Bodhi raised his glass and repeated: "Love in the time of Coronavirus." They clinked their glasses and drank.

"That's one my favorites," Adya said.

"Aperol Spritzes?" Bodhi asked.

"No," Adya smiled. "Gabriel García Márquez' 'Love in the Time of Cholera.' Have you read it?"

"No," Bodhi replied, "but it sounds relevant." They drank some more.

"Wanna see the bedroom?" Adya asked with a bright smile, reaching the bottom of her glass.

"That sounds like a proposition," Bodhi replied, putting his own finished glass beside hers.

"I didn't know I was so transparent," Adya laughed, standing up and offering him her hand. She pulled him up and led him up the curved staircase to the second floor. She led him into a bedroom that was larger than his former apartment on the Upper West Side. The room was filled with a large bed, Art Deco end tables, randomly placed white marble statues of a nude men and women in interesting poses, and a round table and two chairs in the corner of the room. The ceilings were about 15 feet high and there were floor-to-ceiling windows on three sides of the rectangular bedroom. The windows on the long and north side of the bedroom had spectacular views of the Manhattan skyline, the Brooklyn and Manhattan bridges and East River. The window on the west side of the bedroom had a picturesque view of the Hudson River and Verrazano Bridge. Bodhi walked over to the window and stared out.

"Bodhi!" Adya called out, startling him. Bodhi turned around to find her standing completely naked in front of the bed. "So, what's a girl gotta do to get your attention?"

RISE AND SHINE

"Rise and shine, gorgeous." Adya said as she shook Bodhi. The sun was still shining through the windows on the West over the Hudson River. It had a beautiful red and orange hue that contrasted against the bright blue New York City sky.

Bodhi awakened in a confused state. "Is it already morning?"

"No," Adya responded with a smile and still jostling him. "It's 3:30 in the afternoon. Dinner's at five."

"Why so early?" Bodhi asked.

"We're broadcasting live to the rest of the world where they'll be having lunch or a late dinner."

"Cool," Bodhi said.

"Yeah," Adya continued. "It's pretty amazing how we're so connected now. Our community is literally all over the world. We're all sharing ideas, best practices, and growing so rapidly."

"That is amazing," Bodhi said. "You're amazing!"

Bodhi stretched, rubbed his eyes and then sat up. He leaned over to Adya and kissed her. "Can't we take a raincheck and stay in bed."

"Don't you wish," Adya jested. "We have to go because we are the guests of honor. They're celebrating our return home."

"What?" Bodhi asked. "I know why you're a guest of honor, but why me?"

"Well," Adya said "First because you saved my life." Bodhi was about to interrupt but she put her finger up to stop him. "Second, you may not realize it but you're quite famous."

"Are you kidding me?" Bodhi asked in a surprised tone.

Adya gave him a perplexed look. "Are you kidding me? Do you realize that everyone in the city and by now, most of the country has followed your lead on rooftop farming, green energy, healthcare, optimal health, community organization and leadership?" Bodhi looked surprised. "That's huge," Adya continued. "Everyone knows your name." Bodhi still had a look of surprise on his face and raised his eyebrows. Adya pushed him down onto the bed and straddled him. She kissed his face gently while running her fingers through his hair. "You're a hero, Bodhi." Adya then laughed. "I've got a hero in my bed and he's mine."

Bodhi pulled her down to him and kissed her passionately. He then looked into her eyes, smiled, and then flipped her onto her back and placed himself between her legs. He began to kiss her neck. She closed her eyes and purred. Bodhi then kissed her chest and then subtlety flicked her nipple with the tip of his tongue while running his nails gently from the medial aspect of her knee to her inner thighs, making a small circle around her navel and then larger and larger circles over her abdomen.

"Hmmm," she sounded as she threw her head back. "I'm really loving this but we have to get ready. They're picking us up at 4:30." Bodhi now moved his head down and alternated between soft kisses and licking the midline of her abdomen. Adya was now breathing heavier while trying to push his head away.

"Bodhi!" Adya half-pleaded. "We have to get ready." Bodhi forcefully spread her thighs and pressed his entire tongue on her vagina and gave one hard lick. Adya sighed and arched her back.

"Bodhi!" Adya insisted. "Stop!" Adya closed her legs and turned to her side away from him. He immediately pushed her onto her stomach and gave her a firm open-handed slap on her buttock.

"Ouch!" Adya screamed. Bodhi gave her another firm slap on her other buttock.

Adya let out a slow, throaty, guttural sound. "Argh."

Bodhi gently moved his hand over her buttocks that were now red with his handprints.

"Ow!" Adya murmured.

Bodhi climbed on top of her and whispered in her ear, "Now you're mine. You have my mark."

"Hmmm," Adya smiled and sounded. Bodhi sucked the back of her neck as though he were a cat trying to pick up her kitten by the back of the neck. Adya moaned. He quickly made a line with his tongue down her spine and gently kissed her buttocks. Adya took a deep breath and blew it out as she raised her hips higher. Bodhi moved his mouth down and allowed his tongue to explore her vagina and play with her vulva piercings. Adya pressed her pelvis against the bed and Bodhi's tongue returned to her anus causing her to bounce her pelvis rhythmically against the bed and his mouth.

Bodhi climbed back on top of her and was about to enter her from behind when in a bat of an eye Adya did some Jiu Jitsu move that landed Bodhi flat on the bed with her on top him and holding his arms down.

"Whoa!" Bodhi exclaimed as he moved her up and down by thrusting his pelvis.

"You're very convincing," Adya said, "but we really have to get ready."

"Okay," Bodhi replied as he leaned forward and kissed her breasts. Adya allowed herself to fall onto him. He ravished her neck as he moved his hands down and guided himself into her. At this moment, Adya propped herself up, looked at him and smiled. She then took both sides of his face into her hands and kissed him passionately as she vigorously moved over him, grinding herself against his pubis. She then suddenly slowed down and transmitted deep guttural sounds with her tongue into his mouth. Just as suddenly she stopped, propped herself up again, looked into his eyes, smiled and said: "As much as I'm loving this, we really need to get going."

Adya kissed him on the cheek and got up. She extended her hand and when he gave her his, she pulled him up. "Let's take a shower."

"Is this a fancy dinner?" Bodhi asked.

"Yeah," Adya replied. "Black tie."

"But I don't have anything to wear," Bodhi said.

"No worries," Adya smiled. "I sized you up and sent someone to hook you up. Let's move it. We've got 20 minutes before they pick us up."

Adya led him around the wall that the bed was against. It opened to a corridor leading to a huge walk-in closet and bathroom. The bathroom was magnificent. Everything was in white marble. She walked him into a large Turkish hammam shower and water jets massaged their bodies from all directions and created steam. Adya soaped a large sponge and quickly scrubbed Bodhi's body and she then handed him the sponge. Bodhi started to gently scrub and massage her body, careful to get into every crevice. Adya suddenly grabbed the sponge from his hand surprising him.

"Not now love," Adya said as she rinsed herself. "We really have to run." Adya stepped out of the hammam and threw him a towel. After drying, she took him to the walk-in closet that was about the size of a small studio apartment. Bodhi noticed immediately that the room was almost empty with a few articles of clothing scattered about.

"That one's yours," Adya said pointing to a hanging garment bag on one side of the room. She continued: "By the way, that's your side of the closet."

Bodhi opened the garment bag to find a black Versace tuxedo. "Whoa!" Bodhi exclaimed. "This is completely over the top. Where'd you get it?" Adya smiled as she slipped into a gorgeous silver gown with a very provocative low back.

"You look spectacular!" Bodhi exclaimed again. Adya

blew him a kiss and signaled him to stop gawking and to get dressed. She walked over to a cabinet and opened a draw filled with jewelry. She picked up a few earrings and held them to her ear before settling on a pair of simple diamond earrings that matched a butterfly pendant studded with diamonds on a gold chain. She then selected a beautiful gold ring that twisted on itself and formed a sort of pedestal for a large flat diamond. By the time she finished Bodhi was fully dressed and putzing with his bowtie. Adya walked over to him, untied it and bowed a beautiful tie. Bodhi was impressed.

"My father taught me how to do that."

"Is he alive?" Bodhi asked.

"He died in the First Wave," she replied.

"He must've been a good guy," Bodhi added.

"He was the best," Adya said with a big smile. "I'll tell you all about him sometime."

"What about your mom?" Bodhi asked.

"She died when I was a little girl," Adya answered. "I really don't have too many memories of her. It was just me and my dad." Bodhi put his hand on her shoulder and maintained eye contact to get a feel for how she was handling the conversation. The doorbell rang a few times.

"Perfect timing. Let's go. The shoes are downstairs." They walked down the spiral staircase that left them closer to the entrance. Adya answered the intercom saying that they'd be right down. She walked into the closet near the entrance and came out with a pair of shoes for each of them. There was a bench on either side of the entrance and they both sat to put on their shoes. Bodhi first sat down and stared at her.

"What?" Adya asked.

"You are outrageously beautiful," Bodhi beamed.

Adya got up, leaned over and gave him a big kiss. "You're not too bad yourself Dr. Bodhi."

"The shoes are perfect," Bodhi said. "How did you know my size?"

"That was easy," Adya replied. "I just checked your

sneakers. The suit was more of a guesstimate. Are you ready?"

"Ready, Freddy," Bodhi said, smiling.

"Let's roll then," Adya said.

THE RIVER CAFÉ

The sun was still high in the sky. There was also a very faint chill in the air that was very comfortable.

"Where's the dinner?" Bodhi asked.

"The River Café," Adya said as she looked around and then at her smartphone. "Have you been there?"

"Long time ago," Bodhi replied. "How are we going to get there?

Adya smiled and pointed to the Porsche Taycan that pulled up to the curb.

"Really?" Bodhi asked in a surprised tone.

"Why not?" Adya said. "These are the perks of being a survivor of a near mass extinction event. Do you like it?"

"It's lovely," Bodhi replied. A man got out, greeted them and opened the back door for them.

"This is Gabe," Adya said. "Gabe, this is Bodhi."

"I've heard so much about you," Gabe said as they shook hands. "It's such a pleasure to finally meet you."

There was acid jazz playing softly on the system when they got into the car. Gabe turned down the music as he drove off and asked if they wanted to hear something else. They both said that what he was playing was fine. They remained silent during the entire ride and held hands. Their only communication was in the form of tracings, pressure, scratches and taps they were making in each other's palms and applied to different parts of their fingers that they hadn't as yet learned to decipher.

Adya broke their silence as they approached the Brooklyn Bridge. "I love bridges."

"Why?" Bodhi asked while holding one hand and stroking the inner part of her forearm.

"They go somewhere," she replied. "It's not that I want to go anywhere but they remind me of the possibility that there are so many places to explore. More importantly, they connect. They're portals."

"Portals?" Bodhi asked, now gently squeezing different parts of her thigh. Adya smiled and took his hand that was on her thigh with her free hand.

"Portals are everywhere," she replied. "They're everywhere and can present in many different ways."

"What do you mean?" Bodhi asked.

"An open window is the most obvious." Adya began. "You look out and see something. Sometimes you're transported to somewhere other than what you're looking at. Inside yourself if you're lucky. Words in a poem, a beautiful flower, a homeless person, sex, an emotion, a picture of a starving child in Africa, a beautiful symphony or a rap beat. They're all potential portals. Proust's Madeleine moment was a portal."

"I get it," Bodhi said. "Basically, anything that transcends your everyday reality."

"Yeah," Adya nodded. "That's exactly it. Covid-19 is a portal. Right?"

"Sure," Bodhi replied. "Like getting thrown out of a plane at 13,000 feet without a parachute." Bodhi paused to look out the window. "Transcendence on steroids." The car pulled in front of the River Café where a large crowd of people were waiting. Many had Champagne glasses in their hands. Gabe came around to Adya's side and opened the door for her. He followed. As soon as she got out, everyone started to clap and cheer. What surprised Bodhi, however, was that the clapping and cheering got louder when he got out. He was genuinely moved. Everyone gathered around them and gave them both hugs. Adya tried to introduce everyone but Bodhi couldn't keep up. He just smiled a lot.

Champagne glasses were placed in their hands and someone raised their glass and toasted: "To Adya and Bodhi. The future." Everyone raised their glasses and repeated: "The future." Bodhi took a sip from his glass after the toast and was caught off guard. It wasn't Champagne or even sparkling wine. It was beer.

Adya saw the look on his face and clinked his glass. "Champagne was one of the casualties of the pandemic," she said. "We make our own beer."

They went inside and mingled. Their glasses were never empty for more than a minute. What immediately caught Bodhi's attention was the incongruence of their post-apocalyptic world and the mood and setting of the evening. It reminded him of the first time he was in Mumbai, one of the most populous cities in the world.

He had traveled the world and was used to seeing poverty, but nothing prepared him for Mumbai. He was amazed at being in a bar or restaurant that was world-class in every way. For a moment, he often had to think twice because the setting was identical to being in any modern and rich city in the world. What then shocked him was the juxtaposition, the incongruence of that experience and stepping out to find entire families begging, sleeping, eating and shitting on the sidewalk immediately in front of the place.

The contrast between Mumbai and his present experience was nowhere near as stark, but it was remarkable to have survived the near mass extinction of the human race and then stand in the River Café drinking beer out of a Champagne glass. Unlike those venues in Mumbai where it would have been impossible for someone who had been brought there with a blindfold to guess if they were in Paris, Rome, or New York, there were some giveaways in Bodhi's reality. Everyone was well-dressed but in an incomplete and almost comic, tongue-in-cheek manner. Men wore tuxedo jackets with jeans or a T-shirt. Some had formal shirts and pants, but wore sneakers. Very few had formal ties or bowties, and when they did, they often clashed with whatever else they were wearing. Some women had formal gowns but also wore sneakers, while others wore summer dresses. It was impossible to differentiate between the servers and the guests because they dressed exactly the same. Bodhi later learned that the servers were part of their overall tribe who volunteered to serve and contribute to making the evening special. Everyone's clothing was a hodge-podge based on whatever people could find to simulate a black-tie affair. There were no airs of pretension.

Adya and Bodhi were separated by the crowd forming circles around them. Everyone was ecstatic to see Adya alive and a line formed to hug her. Some people had tears. The crowd around Bodhi was very excited to meet him and bombarded him with questions: "How long have you been a doctor? How did you get into farming? Where did you get the idea for the power grid? Do you really think people will embrace the optimal health model you're promoting?" The questions came faster than Bodhi could come up with answers. He never realized that his ideas were known and appreciated to this extent outside of his community. It filled him with pride and joy to be praised and appreciated. Bodhi felt welcomed.

Bodhi and Adya's eyes met for a moment. They just smiled and winked at each other. The conversation and questions continued and many people expressed sincere interest in meeting with him to further discuss and explore his ideas and vision for the future. Bodhi was equally interested in seeing how they were able to take his ideas and build on them. There was excitement in the air.

A woman stood up in front of a microphone that was set up against the backdrop of the large windows facing the Manhattan skyline. She clinked her glass to get everyone's attention and asked everyone to be seated. Gabe, who was now wearing a tuxedo, greeted Bodhi and walked him over to Adya. Bodhi was so overwhelmed with joy to be with her. He gave her a big hug just as everyone was sitting, so they stood out. Everyone clapped. He blushed. Gabe led them to a table that was just to the right of the microphone. There were six of them at the table.

"These are members of the core leadership," Adya started as she introduced them to Bodhi. "The others are scattered around. You'll meet them soon enough. Bodhi shook everyone's hand and took his seat next to Adya.

Bodhi leaned over and whispered: "You look stunning."

Adya smiled and kissed his cheek.

The same woman addressed the guests as the last of them took their seats.

"That's Ramona." Adya leaned over and whispered. "She's been a guiding light in our group." There was a large screen strategically placed just to the right of the microphone so that it didn't obstruct the view of the windows, and a projector six feet in front of it. Images of crowds in "black tie" from all over the world were projected onto the screen. Every few seconds the images changed and appeared to be in a different setting.

"Good evening everyone," Ramona announced. "Wow! Everyone looks so beautiful." She clapped and everyone followed suit and clapped as well.

Romana continued: "This is the first time since the Second Wave hit that we've gathered to celebrate...and what an occasion. We have so much to be thankful for. We shut down the pedophile sex trade operation, and sent a resounding message to the world that such practices will not be tolerated." Everyone clapped vigorously. A waiter came to the table and filled everyone's glass with more beer.

Ramona continued: "We almost lost our precious Adya, but not only did we get her back safe and sound, but she brought back with her the man who saved her and to whom we owe so much, Dr. Bodhi McKenna." Everyone stood up and applauded. Bodhi blushed. Adya nudged him to stand up. Bodhi stood up, bowed and waved to everyone.

Ramona looked around the audience and announced: "We're here tonight to celebrate, not to make long speeches. I'd like to invite our great leader to say a few words." Everyone started clapping. The people on the screen were also clapping.

Bodhi looked around to see who the leader was. Bodhi leaned over and asked Adya to point out the leader. She took both his cheeks into her hands and kissed him deeply. Everyone clapped even more vigorously.

Adya stood up and then bent down to whisper in his ear: "You just fucked her." She smiled at him and then turned to walk to the microphone. When she arrived at the microphone everyone stood up, whistled, made cheering noises and clapped excitedly. Adya stood to the side of the microphone, put her hands over her heart and nodded. People clapped even more vigorously. She kept her eyes closed and then put her hands in prayer position over her forehead and slightly bowed. The clapping continued. Bodhi was now standing and clapping wildly. He was genuinely moved. Adya then lowered her hands to the front of her forehead. The clapping continued. Tears were flowing down Adya's eyes. She then moved her hands over her heart, took a deep breath and opened her eyes. She looked around for a tissue to wipe her eyes and a few of the guests in front of her handed her a napkin. She wiped her tears and moved in front of the microphone.

"Thank you!" Adya exclaimed. "Thank you! Thank you!" She started clapping back at the audience. Finally, the guests started to sit down. The screen continued to show other guests sitting in different restaurants slowly sitting down after clapping enthusiastically. Everyone appeared so happy.

"There's so much to be thankful for," Adya began. "Who would have thought that after a near mass extinction event that we'd be sitting here in the River Café and other great restaurants all over the country, all over the world! And all dressed to kill. We survived and we're killing it!" Everyone again started to clap loudly. Adya looked over at Bodhi and winked.

"I certainly have a lot to be thankful for," Adya continued. "Thanks to Bodhi I'm alive. Thanks to all of you we have a growing community that's creating a beautiful world." Everyone clapped.

"*Koyaanisquatsi*," Adya said and then paused. "It's a Hopi term that means crazy life, life in turmoil, life disintegrating, and life out of balance." There was silence in the room. "This is the life we lived prior to the Second Wave- *Koyaanisquatsi*. It's a state that was screaming out for another way of living but we were all so deep into it that it permeated our every breath, our thoughts, our very being. Covid-19 took off the veils and allowed us see clearly and gave us the opportunity to create a better life, a better world. Even when I was on death's bed and really thought I was going to die, I was happy and expressed gratitude to have caught a glimpse of that life, of that world, and to have known all of you who accepted this challenge of leaving the old ways behind and creating a better future." Adya paused and looked over the crowd. There was silence.

"We've accomplished so much, but there's so much more to do," Adya continued. "This is just the beginning. Let's raise our glasses and give thanks and gratitude to each other, and to have the vision, conviction and inspiration to forge ahead. Cheers!" Everyone stood up, raised their glasses and drank. They then applauded even more enthusiastically. Adya bowed and she blew kisses to everyone as she made her way back to the table. Bodhi stood up and met her with open arms. They embraced.

"I bet you thought I was just another pretty face," Adya said as they sat down. Bodhi raised his Champagne glass and replied:

"No. I thought you were a total badass with a pretty face and a really hot body who went around chopping bad guys' heads off. Cheers!"

"I'll drink to that," Adya said with a chuckle. "Cheers!"

It was a long and fun night. The dinner was spectacular. They cleared the tables after dinner and a DJ who was located in San Francisco spun music that kept them dancing until the early morning. Everyone made Bodhi feel welcomed. His pockets were filled with business cards of people who wanted to talk to him about this or that idea that he had implemented or to explore new ideas. It didn't take long for Bodhi to realize that Adya was right and that he would never return to his Upper West Side Community. He had found his tribe. Bodhi looked at Adya as she mingled, chatted, hugged and moved through the world. He knew that he had found his life partner and would never leave her side. Adya's words about *Koyaanisqatsi* resonated deep within him. Up until that moment, despite all his knowledge of medicine, and living a lifestyle to promote optimal health, he recognized that his life had in fact been out of balance. There was an inner turmoil that gnawed at him but was too deep to identify and cleanse. At that moment, Bodhi answered the call for another way of life that would lead him to tranquility, peace and authenticity.

Adya looked over and saw that Bodhi was lost in his thoughts. She walked over and stood directly in front of him. The music was blaring and the bass felt as though it was driving their heartbeats. People had doffed their jackets and high-heeled shoes and were dancing wildly. They held hands but didn't say a word as they stared into each other's eyes. They had no idea how long that moment lasted but were aware that the music had changed twice. The only movement between them was an occasional squeezing of a hand and changing the position of their heads to perhaps find a better angle to access the portal of their eyes.

"Are you ready to go home?" Adya broke their silence.

"Home is being with you wherever you are." Bodhi answered.

"Okay. Now you're getting mushy on me," Adya smiled and stepped closer to him. "Let me rephrase the question. Are you ready to jump into bed with me?"

Bodhi just smiled and gently nodded his head yes. Adya took Bodhi's hand and led him out where Gabe was waiting with the car in front of the building. It was already in the wee hours. It was a clear evening, no clouds in the sky. And with the reduction in air and light pollution since Covid, the stars were brilliantly visible, making the New York City skyline even more spectacular. They again crossed the Brooklyn Bridge that was now spectacularly lit against the backdrop of that skyline and the now dark, star-filled sky.

THE VENUS

I t was almost dawn by the time they arrived home.

"Are you tired?" Adya asked.

"Exhausted!" Bodhi replied.

"Let's sit on the roof and have some tea," Adya suggested.

"Sure," Bodhi replied. Adya walked over to the kitchen cabinet and pulled out a tray with various teas.

"My favorite is the Rooibos Cinnamon Chai," Adya said. "Want to try it?"

"Sure," Bodhi replied again. Adya boiled some water and poured some loose tea in a pot.

"Biscotti?" Adya asked.

"Sure," Bodhi replied again, now smiling.

Adya turned to face him and smirked: "Feel like a 12-inch dildo up your ass this morning Bodhi?" Bodhi looked surprised and didn't answer.

"Well," Adya said in a provocative tone. "I'm waiting for your 'sure'."

"Sure...I think...maybe," Bodhi replied, grimacing. They laughed. The water boiled and Adya poured it into the pot. She pointed to the overhead cabinet and he got the mugs. She put the pot, biscotti and mugs on a tray. She was about to pick it up when he insisted on carrying it.

"Honey or sugar?" Adya asked.

"Shu..." Bodhi was about to say and stopped immediately when she gave him a sharp look. "Yes please. I'd love some honey. Thanks." They laughed again. Bodhi followed Adya up the spiral staircase. At the other end of the hallway from the bedroom, she climbed another spiral staircase that led to the rooftop.

Bodhi's first words when he stood on the roof was "Wow!" He spun around to take in the 360-degree view. The rooftop was sprawling with different sitting areas, lounge chairs, shade area, trees, a jacuzzi and a bar.

"So, this is the way rich people live," Bodhi said.

"No," Adya said. "It's the way rich people used to live, and the way we live now. It's the right of survival."

"I love it!" Bodhi exclaimed.

They sat in an area where there were a few café tables. The sun was just coming up and the sky was very expressive. Its yellow and orange hues pushing through the darkness and giving birth to a dark blue sky that was slowing morphing into lighter shades of blue. There was a chill in the air that made the tea even more delicious and promised that the biscotti in Bodhi's hand would perhaps rise to the majesty of Proust's Madeleine. The birds were just waking up and even on the top floor of this isolated high-rise building, they were rehearsing their symphonies. They poured more tea and ate their biscotti in silence trying to decipher what the birds augured for the future. The sun rose higher and was now just on top of buildings. Bodhi ran his hand over Adya's left thigh and gently applied pressure as his hands wandered aimlessly. He accidentally pressed on her wound and she winced.

"So sorry," Bodhi said. "Remind me to take a look at it later and change the bandage."

"Yes, doctor," Adya agreed. "First thing in the morning. By the way, do you make house calls?"

"I do," Bodhi said. "How about I come over to your place later this afternoon?"

"That's perfect," Adya mused. "I'll look forward to your visit." Bodhi leaned over and kissed her. The sun was a bit higher now and getting hot.

"Shall we head down?" Adya asked.

"Yeah," Bodhi said as he squeezed her hand. "I'm crashing."

"Me too," Adya said.

"Any plans later?" Bodhi asked.

"Big plans" Adya replied.

"Like what?" Bodhi asked.

"I'm going to lounge around in bed with you all day and make up for all the lifetimes we missed each other."

"Sounds like a plan," Bodhi said. They gathered the pot, cups and biscotti onto the tray and went downstairs. They jumped into the hammam and washed each other with care and attention. They then dried each other meticulously as though trying to memorize every detail of each other's bodies. The bedroom was drizzled with indirect sunlight. Once in bed, Adya flicked a switch and all the windows became opaque and the room was pitch dark. They tied themselves up into a knot and immediately fell asleep in each other's arms without a word. Everything had been said with their furtive glances and embraces. It was now only necessary to let it all sink in.

They woke up a few times and observed the other sleeping until they each were called back to their dreams. If they awakened simultaneously, they exchanged pleasantries and endearments. They gave each other soft kisses and touches seeking to find the ignition switch to passionate play, but the alcohol and fatigue summoned them back to their dreams where they made love again and again.

They awakened in the same interlaced position in which they crashed. Bodhi gently pulled his left arm from under Adya and tried to shake out the numbness from having Adya's weight on it. Adya rolled away to shake out the numbness of her right arm from having slept on it all night. Their eyes met as they were reviving their limbs and they burst out laughing.

"Doctor! Doctor!" Adya yelled. "My arm is dead. Help me! Help me!"

"Calm down, ma'am," Bodhi said in a very professional

voice. "Let me take a look at it." Bodhi started kissing her right hand, forearm, front and back of her arm, then her shoulder and neck.

"But Doctor, what are you doing to my neck?" Adya asked. "It's only my arm that's dead."

"I'm just being thorough ma'am," Bodhi replied. He continued to kiss and lick the side and back of her neck. "You see," he continued, "the nerves that innervate your arm all come from the neck and I'm trying to diagnose the problem." Bodhi then moved down her back and flank with soft wet kisses. He rolled her over onto her back and licked the area just medial to the iliac crest and lateral to her pubis. Adya shuddered.

"But Doctor," Adya said as she breathed more deeply. "It's only my arm that hurts. What are you doing...." Bodhi then licked across her vagina and continued to repeat that exact same motion, licking from her inner thigh across her vagina to the other side. Adya moaned.

"Ma'am, I'm afraid I have some really bad news for you," Bodhi said in between the journey from one inner thigh to the next. "I'm afraid that your arm is dying and its only hope is advanced resuscitation. This is a special technique I've developed over many years of practice and I've had very good results."

"Okay then Doctor," Adya moaned. "I trust you. Please save my arm. Please." Bodhi patiently explored Adya's external parts to determine how they reacted to his tongue, how much they liked soft versus hard pressure, pulling versus pushing, licking versus sucking, fast versus slow, and how they reacted to long pauses. Adya was flying when Bodhi suddenly stopped. He grabbed her ankles and violently pulled her to the edge of the bed. He bent under and placed his shoulders under her knees and lifted her bottom off the bed while stuffing two pillows under her bottom. Bodhi set her down. Her legs were pointed straight up against his torso.

"But Doctor," Adya started to say.

"Shhhh," Bodhi sounded as he leaned forward and put his hand over her mouth. "This is the most important part. I have to concentrate." Bodhi entered her very slightly. She was very moist and eager for him. He moved making very delicate circles with his penis just barely inside of her. Adya sighed. Bodhi entered just a bit more still making circles. Adya was about to say something else when he thrust himself deep inside her cutting her off at mid-breath. He pulled out just to the entrance of paradise and drew sand mandalas with his penis. Bodhi let Adya's legs drop to the side and placed one hand on the middle of her chest and the other just above her pubis. They stared into each other's eyes and breathed deeply together. He then started to probe a little deeper and faster until they were flying together. They had found a portal and had transcended the in and out body fuck. They were now surfing the energy waves flowing through the both of them. Bodhi squeezed her nipples hard and was now making those same mandalas deep inside of her. Slowly. Then more rapidly. Like a syncopated Latin rhythm punctuated by a slap on the skin of her buttock.

Adya came again and again- some hard, some subtle, some accompanied with cries and others with just a tremble or murmur. Inner journeys. She left him in those moments to explore her inner continents and universes. It made Bodhi happy that Adya was multi-orgasmic. It wasn't an ego-macho-I'm-a-mac-daddy satisfaction. He knew better. It was just a joy to know that Adya was in touch with her inner bliss and trusted him with the privilege of sharing it with him.

"I want you to come inside me." Adya said. "I want to feel you inside me." Bodhi shook his head no.

"Why?" Adya asked.

"I'm moving the energy," Bodhi responded. "Saving it for the next time. Letting it grow."

"Tantra?" Adya asked. Bodhi smiled and nodded yes.

"I have the feeling that I'm going to fall madly in love with you," Adya said, almost inaudibly.

"I'm disappointed," Bodhi remarked.

"Really?" Adya remarked with a puzzled look on her face.

"Why?"

"That it's taking you so long," Bodhi responded. "I fell head over heels in love with you a long time ago."

"When you were checking out my body when I was in a coma?" Adya jested. Bodhi chuckled.

"Almost," Bodhi replied. Adya frowned and slapped his arm.

"No," Bodhi continued. "I fell madly in love with you the moment you chopped Junior's head off and was holding it up for everyone to see. That was soooo sexy." Adya pulled him down onto her and hugged him. They were silent for a long moment.

When they were done, she held both of his cheeks in her hand.

"I love you Bodhi McKenna."

"I love you Adya."

"Great!" Adya exclaimed. "Now that that's settled, are you hungry?"

"Famished."

"How about some French toast?" Adya offered. "I make killer French toast."

"I'll be your sous-chef so I can learn your secrets."

"No secrets love," Adya said in a serious tone. "I'm yours." They looked into each other's eyes and both subtly nodded yes.

"Make me your master," Bodhi quoted a David Bowie line from one of his favorite movies, "Labyrinth", "and I'll be your slave forever."

"Humm," Adya sounded. "Now you're pushing it." They laughed together, and Bodhi promised to himself to show her the movie someday. She pushed him off her and they hugged side-to-side.

Finally, Adya couldn't bear her hunger anymore and sighed, moving out of his arms.

"French toast?"

"Let's do it!"

They showered quickly, brushed their teeth and got

dressed. Bodhi's stuff was still in his suitcase. He started to unpack but didn't feel like it. He took out a pair of his favorite skyblue fisherman's pants from Thailand and a T-shirt. Adya put on a loose pair of thin cotton shorts and tank top. They walked down the curved staircase hand in hand and were greeted by the soft sunlight beaming through the wall of windows.

"Can you wait or would you like coffee now?" Adya asked.

"Decisions, decisions." Bodhi said. He was leaning against the island with his chin supported by his hand, and continued: "Let's do coffee first with a biscotti. Are there any left?"

"So decadent," Adya responded. "Yes, we have biscotti. Would you like an espresso? Wait! Let me guess." She crossed one arm and supported the other arm that was holding her chin. "You seem like a Macchiato kind of guy. Am I right?" He just smiled suggesting she take another guess.

"Don't tell me you're one of those 'Can I please have a 'Cinnamon dulce mocha latte with whip cream' hipsters," Adya said placing both hands on her hips. "Please not that."

Finally, Bodhi responded: "I love Americanos."

"Perfect!" Adya exclaimed. "That's what I drink. See. We were destined for each other." They gave each other a high five. Adya walked over to the a large, gorgeous, brass espresso machine that was the centerpiece of the counter. Bodhi couldn't believe he didn't notice it before but then again, he was quite intoxicated with both the alcohol and more so with Adya.

"What is that thing?" Bodhi asked.

"It is..." Adya said as she turned it on. "...a Victoria Arduino Venus Bar Semiautomatic Espresso Maker. Handmade."

"It looks like a work of art," Bodhi said.

"It is a work of art," Adya added as she ground the coffee beans and pressed the coffee in the portafilter. "More importantly, it makes really great coffee." The rich aroma of the coffee as it dripped into the cups was heavenly. She then added the

RICHARD LANOIX M.D.

boiling water. Adya put the mugs and biscotti on the same tray she used last night and led Bodhi out to the terrace.

They sat next to each other at a marble-topped table that was under a large umbrella and looked out onto the Hudson River as it meandered under the Verrazano Bridge. The Hudson River was calm with a few sailboats leisurely pushed along by the gentle wind. There was a cool breeze on the terrace that suffused the indirect light.

"Oh my God!" Bodhi exclaimed. "This coffee is amazing. Where do you get it from? We ran out months ago and haven't been able to find any."

"Connections, my love," Adya said with smile. "It's all about who you know."

"Sounds good to me."

"The reality is that we have a very limited supply and no one, as far as we know, is growing coffee right now. So, enjoy it."

"Yumm!" Bodhi sounded as he nibbled on the biscotti and followed with another sip of the Americano. "The only thing that's missing is a piece of dark chocolate." Adya started to get up stating that she in fact had some chocolate but Bodhi held her arm and said that it would really be too much. Especially since they were going to have French toast.

"Are you ready then?" Adya asked.

"Absolutely." Bodhi said taking the last sip of coffee. "You tell me what to do." They went back to the kitchen and Adya started pulling things out of the pantry and fridge.

"You can start by chopping up these bananas, blueberries and strawberries," Adya said. "Put all of the berries together in that bowl over there and then crush them."

"Where did you get berries?" Bodhi asked.

"We grew them on the rooftops following your lead. The harvest was so good in July that I froze a bunch and take out a bit at a time. They're delicious." Bodhi tasted a blueberry and strawberry and said: "They are delicious. So sweet. We never planted any berries or fruits."

"You're kidding me, right?" Adya asked in a surprised tone. "We've planted everything you can imagine. The apple, pear, peach orchards won't give fruit until next year. We even planted nuts. I can't wait." Adya beat 2 eggs in a large bowl and added two teaspoons of vanilla extract, some almond milk, and a lot of cinnamon.

"Now here's the secret ingredient," Adya said. She pulled out a bottle of Grand Marnier and poured a bit into the mixture without any particular measurement. She also poured a bit of the Grand Marnier into the crushed banana and berry mixture along with a small amount of maple syrup.

"Taste the berry mixture and let me know if you'd like more maple syrup," Adya asked. "I don't like it too sweet and prefer to taste the berries.

Bodhi took a taste with a teaspoon. "It's perfect." Adya now cut some Challah bread into thick slices and soaked them into the almond milk batter and then put them in a casserole. She then poured the remaining batter into the casserole. She then put a large frying pan on the electric range and when it was hot, put in a generous amount of butter. She was able to put all four slices of bread into the frying pan simultaneously. After a few minutes, she flipped them over and they were golden yellow and brown.

"Here's the other trick," Adya said. "Shortly after flipping them, you take them out, add more butter, and then put them back in. This is what gives them that rich color." After they were cooked, she them laid them on a buttered baking pan and put them in the oven.

"So, the outside is cooked on the frying pan," Adya continued, "but the soggy inside with all that flavor needs to cook in the oven. More coffee?"

"Please," Bodhi said. "Can you show me how to use the Venus?"

"Sure," Adya said. "The French toast will be ready in about 30 minutes." Adya waited until the French toast was almost ready. She then heated the berry mixture and then showed Bodhi how to use the Venus. They loaded the tray and went back out on the terrace. It was hotter now but was still comfortable because of the cool breeze coming off the river. When they were seated, Adya placed a dollop of the berry mixture on Bodhi's French toast and waited for him to taste it. He took a bite and closed his eyes while chewing slowly.

"What do you think?" Adya asked. Bodhi remained with his eyes closed and continued to chew.

"Well?" Adya asked impatiently. Bodhi finally opened his eyes and nodded his head yes.

"This is the best French toast I've ever had," Bodhi said.

"Serious," Adya asked as she now placed a dollop of the berry-banana mixture on her French toast.

"Serious," Bodhi replied. "It's outstanding."

"My father used to make them for me just like this and showed me how to make them." Adya paused. "I miss him."

"You mentioned that he died," Bodhi said. "Tell me about him."

"He was a truly remarkable human being," Adya started. She was about to continue when her smartphone rang. She had left it on the counter in the kitchen and ran inside to get it. It was still ringing when she returned.

"It's Nico," Adya said. "I'm sorry but I have to answer." She took her seat.

"Hey, Nico," Adya said, "What's up?" Bodhi continued to savor every bite of the French toast and sipped his coffee slowly.

"I was hoping for a quiet evening at home with Bodhi," Adya spoke into the phone.

"I know," Adya answered. "It has been a long time since we shared time. I promise we'll hang soon and you'll have a chance to get to know Bodhi." Bodhi heard his name and smiled at her. Adya raised her hand to her forehead, put the phone away from her head and mouthed that he wouldn't take no for answer.

"You'll cook?" Adya repeated. "That sounds really great

but..." She listened to whatever Nico was saying on the phone for a while and then finally said: "Okay. Okay. Seven O'clock. See you then."

"I hope you don't mind," Adya said. "He's a really good friend from the old days and he can be really pushy."

"*No problema!*" Bodhi said. "I want to meet your friends."

"I want you to meet them too." Adya said, "But just not today. I was so looking forward to lounging around with you all day."

"It's only two O'clock so we still have all day," Bodhi said.

"Yeah," she said. "You're right. Where were we?"

"You were about to tell me about your father."

ADYA'S FATHER

Adya suddenly became very enthusiastic.

"He was my hero," Adya said.

"Tell me more," Bodhi prodded.

"He was an economics professor at Columbia," Adya continued. "Basically, a family man who really loved teaching. But when my mother died, he was destroyed and went into a deep depression. It was so bad that I had to live with my aunt for a while. He loved my mother so much that he couldn't cope with the idea of living without her and being a single dad."

"Then what happened?" Bodhi asked.

"About seven months later," Adya continue, "everything changed. He told me when I got older that he had a sort of epiphany. He understood that if my mother died then she was supposed to have died and he was supposed to be a single dad. He embraced that idea, picked me up from my aunt's place, and dedicated himself to being the best person and father that he could be."

"So, he embraced that idea?" Bodhi mirrored.

"Yeah," Adya said. "All of a sudden he had a purpose in life. He became super present with everything he was doing. He was already a well-respected teacher before that but afterwards became a sort of superstar. His academic output increased and he wrote a couple of books that were well-received. But what I really remember was how I became the jewel in his eye. I could feel it and it made me feel so special."

"He made you feel special," Bodhi added.

"He was so present with me," Adya said. "He always found ways for me to push my boundaries, to grow."

"Did he push you a lot?" Bodhi asked.

"No. Not at all," Adya answered. "Looking back at it, he inspired me to push myself. He inspired me to be curious, to love to learn and to grow."

"Sounds like he was a great dad with a vision," Bodhi said.

"You know," Adya said. "I didn't realize it when I was younger but everything that he did with me had a larger meaning, an underlying purpose."

"What do you mean?"

"For instance, he taught me how to play chess to teach me how to think, how to strategize," she said. "He loved chess but he didn't spend all those hours playing with a little kid just for fun. He wanted me to learn how to think in a certain way. When he felt that I got that, we dropped chess and moved on to the game Go."

"Go?" Bodhi asked. "Never heard of it."

"Oh my God!" Adya exclaimed. "Go is so deep. It's the world's oldest board game. It originated in China. Just to give you an idea of its complexity, the crowning achievement of artificial intelligence was when the Google computer AlphaGo beat Lee Sedol, a world-renowned Go Master in 2016. It then beat the world Go champion Ke Jie in 2019." Adya was very excited now. She continued: "There's something you have to understand, Go seems on the surface to be such a simple game but it is infinitely more complex than chess. The number of possible moves from each position is exponentially greater in Go than in chess. That's why it took so long to build a computer that could beat a Go master."

"Are you sure about that?" Bodhi challenged. "I play chess and can't believe that Go can be that much more complex."

"You don't have to take my word for it," Adya said. "Just

google it and see for yourself." Bodhi raised his eyebrow in disbelief. "Chess is a tactical game that only requires a moderate amount of general strategy, and consequently mostly uses the analytic part of the brain. Go is all about strategy as well as complex tactics. It uses both the analytic left side and pattern matching right side of the brain. The thing is that the game seems so simple," Adya said. "But once you get into it, you begin to get an idea of the depths of it. Fascinating!"

"I'll have to check this out," Bodhi said.

"Anyway," Adya continued. "Go went beyond just being a game that my father and I loved playing together. It was a way of life. Even now, my entire approach has been to capture territories and coalesce them just as I would in the game. It's beautiful.

"Tell me more about your dad," Bodhi said.

"Hey!" Adya exclaimed. "That's not fair. I'm doing all the talking. It's your turn to tell me about yourself."

"But your father sounds like such an interesting man," Bodhi protested. "I'll tell you all my dark, dirty secrets afterwards."

"Promise?" Adya said as she extended her pinky finger.

Bodhi crossed his pinky fingers with hers and responded: "Promise. Before you start, I'm going to make another Americano," Bodhi added. "Would you like another one?"

"Yeah," Adya replied. "I only ate one of my French Toast. Wanna share it?" Bodhi bit his lip with a broad smile, raised his eyebrows and nodded his head up and down very rapidly."

"I'll heat it up while you make the Americanos." Adya followed him into the kitchen.

"My dad was a very interesting man. He...

"Sorry to interrupt," Bodhi interjected. "But what was his name?"

"Horatio."

"Horatio?" Bodhi exclaimed. "Interesting man. Interesting name." They laughed.

"He was lovely. The most important thing he taught me

was a fierce love of learning for no other purpose than to learn. Even on vacations, we would set a certain amount of time to read together and practice something. It taught me the power of discipline."

"How so?" Bodhi asked.

"I learned that by doing something a little bit every day added up to an accomplishment that I could be proud of," Adya answered. "It showed me that I could do things, accomplish whatever I wanted to by doing it consistently. So, I naturally wanted more. It was addictive." Bodhi cleaned out the portafilter, packed in some more coffee and let the Venus do its magic.

"What did you do for fun with him?" Bodhi asked.

"You know," Adya answered. "My dad had a way of making everything fun. That was his gift. I never felt like anything, even studying or doing Krav Maga was work. It was all fun."

"What's Krav Maga?"

"It's a combat form developed by the Israeli Defense Force," Adya replied.

"How'd you get into that?"

"My father got me started when I was really young," Adya replied. "When I was older, he told me that there were so many reports of women being raped in universities. He never wanted me to be in a situation where I couldn't defend myself. Actually, he couldn't care less about self-defense. He wanted me to kill and maim the bastard that ever tried to harm me."

"That's a little much, no?" Bodhi asked.

"You think?" Adya asked. "How many of those fuckers that hurt and raped women did the justice system let go with just a slap on the wrist, who then did it again or worse?"

"You're certainly right about that," Bodhi admitted.

"In any case," Adya said. "It gave me an incredible amount of confidence." They spread the berry-banana mix on the French toast and each took bites.

"Yumm!" Bodhi sounded. "This really is the best French toast I've ever had."

"Flattery will get you everywhere," Adya mused. Suddenly there was a strong cool breeze that interrupted the sun that was now over them.

"You know what was crazy?" Adya asked. "It was as though my dad had everything planned out in his head. Nothing was random."

"What do you mean?" Bodhi asked.

"The chess, Go, introducing me to all kinds of literature, martial arts," Adya rattle on. "They were all pieces of a puzzle that he gave me and knew that one day I'd put together." She paused and looked into her coffee mug as though looking for something. "I realized later that even the movies he turned me on to had an underlying purpose."

"Like what?" Bodhi asked.

"So many of the movies had really strong women leads," Adya said. "When I was really young, we'd watch Disney movies like 'Brave,' 'Pocahontas,' 'Mulan.' When I got a little older, he turned me on to movies like 'Lara Croft,' 'Kill Bill' and 'La Femme Nikita.' The thing is that he enjoyed them as much as I did. We were just hanging together. That was fun."

"He had great taste in movies." Bodhi said.

"Yeah," Adya responded again looking into her mug. "I really miss him."

"I'm sure he was really proud of you," Bodhi added. He stood up, pulled her up to her feet and gave her a big hug. "I wish I could have met him."

The foreplay started while they did the dishes. Adya ran her fingers up and down his back and then hugged him from behind, feeling his chest and abdomen. She held his thighs just where they met his groin and pressed herself against him. When they were walking up the stairs Bodhi palmed her buttocks and gently ran his hand against her inner thighs synchronously with her steps. They stopped at the middle of the staircase and kissed passionately. They both took off their T-shirts and Bodhi kissed her neck and shoulders. She pulled off his pants as she licked his flanks up to his nipples. She teased him with her mouth getting closer and closer to his penis and then retreating to find other triggers, zones of pleasure. He slid from under her and kissed her face, neck and the middle of her chest while pulling on her nipple piercing. He then took off her pants and gently nibbled on her anterior and middle thighs. He alternated soft kisses, gently bites and firm licks just up to point where her firm muscular thighs met her vagina, but careful to avoid that pink, engorged area pleading for attention.

Adya pushed him away and they made the rest of the journey up the stairs naked leaving their clothes behind like casualties of a confrontation that found its resolution. They dove directly into the bed and into each other's arms. The pace was now less frenetic. They meticulously measured their volleys and the responses they engendered, deciphering their subliminal codes. There was a precious moment after circling each other playfully that demanded a definitive action to take their ravenous intention to fruition, but the call was not answered. They settled into each other's arms and promptly fell into a glorious sleep understanding that the embers were lit and a bonfire could be started at any time.

ADYA'S CREW

They were both abruptly awakened by the intercom ringing very loudly. They were completely disoriented and had no idea what time it was because the windows were in dark mode. Adya looked at the clock. It was 5:45 PM.

"Who the fuck could that be?" Adya asked herself in an annoyed tone. She picked up the intercom device: "Who is it?"

"Nico," the voice responded.

"But we said..." Adya started to speak but was interrupted.

"Just open the door, bitch," Nico interjected. "Hurry up!"

"Fuck!" Adya exclaimed as she buzzed him in.

"Nico's really great," Adya said, "but he can be a bit over the top. Fasten your seatbelt."

"Quick shower?" Bodhi asked, still somewhat groggy.

"Definitely," Adya responded. "He'll let himself him."

They showered quickly and got dressed. As soon as they arrived at the top of the curved staircase, they were greeted with "Surprise!"

There were a large group of her friends at the bottom of the stairs clapping. Nico held up each of their underwear that he found on the stairs in both hands: "I hope we didn't interrupt anything?" Everyone laughed.

"What the fuck?" Adya exclaimed as she and Bodhi walked down the stairs.

"I know. I know." Nico said still holding both of his hands

up at his sides with their underwear dangling from his fingers. "I know you wanted to have a quiet day at home and I felt so privileged that you let me invite myself. But then I felt so selfish keeping you all to myself so I invited a few of your best friends who were dying to see you and meet your man."

Adya got to the bottom of the stairs, walked over to Nico and stood in front of him.

"You forgive me?" Nico asked innocently as he placed their underwear on top of her head.

She took the underwear off her head and replied: "I'll have to think about it." Everyone laughed. Adya gave Nico a big hug. They all gathered and gave Adya and Bodhi hugs.

"You remember Tristan, Giovanna, Kenzie and Hanna," Adya said.

"Definitely!" Bodhi exclaimed. They gave him hugs.

"You probably met everyone else last night," Adya added. "This is Phineas, Seraphina, Margot, Theo, Dahlia, Inez, Kai and Dante." They each gave Bodhi a warm hug.

"You don't have to lift a finger. Okay?" Nico said. "We're going to make a big salad and a kick-ass venison paella. We also brought lots of booze. You both just relax."

Adya looked at Bodhi and they both smiled.

"So, here's the deal," Nico said. "Tristan's going to empty the bags and organize everything on the counter. Phineas is going to chop garlic and onions. Kenzie the peppers and string beans. Kai's going to open the cans of green beans, Hanna can wash the rice, and Theo can cut the venison. Got it?"

"Do you need pans?" Adya asked. Nico gave her a look indicating that he couldn't believe she could possibly ask such as silly question.

"You know how I roll girl!" Nico exclaimed as he pulled out two large paella pans. "Now go to the terrace and entertain your guests!"

"I'll make the drinks," Dante offered. "Listen up. We brought rum, gin, vodka, lime, mint, scotch and lots of home-made ginger beer. I can make Moscow or Kentucky mules, Dark and Stormies, and mojitos. What do you want?"

"I also have some Prosecco and Aperol for spritzes," Adya added.

"I want a spritz," Inez said.

"Me too," Kai said.

"I'll take a Kentucky mule," Margot said. Everyone else told Dante what they wanted to drink.

"Why don't I make the spritzes and you can make the others?" Seraphina offered.

"Sweet!" Dante exclaimed. Everyone had a drink in their hand in no time and was sitting on the terrace. It was a gorgeous evening. The sun was gracefully making its way down over the horizon and was bright orange and yellow, blending into the darkening blue sky.

"How do you like it here so far?" Dahlia asked Bodhi.

At that moment, Nico came out and yelled: "How am I supposed to cook without music? I need music!"

"You got it mister," Adya exclaimed and turned on the stereo. She put on one of her favorite playlists on shuffle and the first song that played was "Malamente" by Rosalia. Now there was a groove.

Dahlia's attention went back to Bodhi. "Do you miss the Upper West Side?" She asked.

"Surprisingly not," Bodhi answered. "I love it here."

"What's not to love?" Hanna exclaimed. "And you're with Adya. She's been by herself for a long time now. It's really great to see her happy."

"Have you known her for a long time?" Bodhi asked.

"Yeah," Hanna replied. "A bunch of us here met at Burning Man eleven years ago and we've been tight since then."

"We're really excited that you're here," Phineas said enthusiastically. "You're a bit of a legend you know."

Bodhi nodded his head no incredulously.

"Dude," Phineas continued counting off on his fingers. "You were the first to successful farm on rooftops, convert living spaces to green energy using solar and hydroelectric power, developed an entire healthcare system when everyone else was scrambling around aimlessly, and motivating people to live healthy lives."

"But those weren't my ideas," Bodhi said as he finished his drink. "I just got the right people together."

Margot took his glass and asked: "What were you drinking?"

"A Kentucky Mule," Bodhi replied.

"Same?" Margot asked.

"Please," Bodhi answered. "Thank you."

"That's leadership, Bodhi," Phineas stressed. "You're way too modest. No one else was doing it. We were all following your lead. Especially your ideas about optimal health and living." Phineas gave him a fist bump and said: "It's like gospel to us. Thank you." Bodhi looked surprised.

"You are welcome my friend," Bodhi replied.

"Wait till you see all the great stuff we're doing," Seraphina chimed in. "It all started local and before we knew it, our community spread all over the United States and now includes most of Europe, South America, and parts of Africa."

"Adya's a visionary," Tristan added. "She's pulling it all together."

"She's a great fucking leader," Margot chimed in. "We're blessed to have her."

"And now we're blessed to have you," Kai said as he raised his glass to make a toast. "Here's to incredible people coming together!" Everyone raised their glasses, clinked them and cheered.

"Where's Adya?" Giovanna asked.

"She's going over some business with Nico while he's doing his paella magic," Tristan answered.

"Really?" Giovanna added. ""I'm going to get her and bring her over."

"Great idea!" Margot said. Margot then grabbed Bodhi's hand and put it in between hers. She looked at him very sincerely and told him: "I just want to tell you that I personally

RICHARD LANOIX M.D.

don't give a shit about everything you've accomplished. The fact that you saved Adya is enough to make you my hero. Thank you!" She stood up, pulled him up and gave him a hug. Kai raised his glass and cheered: "To our hero!" Everyone clinked their glasses.

"Isn't the ER crazy intense?" Theo asked. "Even before Covid!" Bodhi smiled and nodded yes.

"I can't even begin to imagine what it's like to be knee-deep in death and dying all the time," Dante said.

"Dude!" Tristan chimed in. "Did you just miss the pandemic? We were all knee-deep in death and dying." Everyone laughed.

"Yeah," Dante retorted with a smirk on his face and giving Tristan the finger. "But it's a little different being in the position where you're responsible for saving lives and putting yourself in the line of fire. We were just spectators." Dante looked over to Bodhi and asked: "How did you deal with it?"

"It was intense," Bodhi said. "But it's the same for me and all other ER docs and frontline providers. We do what we do. It becomes a reflex."

"But doesn't all the death get to you?" Dahlia asked.

"I can't speak for anyone else," Bodhi replied. "But I just see everything happening and I'm just a witness. I'm doing my best to help people but at the end of the day, people die. My job is to do the best I can to save them and accompany them on their journey."

"It doesn't bother you?" Kai asked in a surprised tone.

"Only when kids get really sick and die. That's a tough pill to swallow. We get used to everything else and take it in stride, but it gets really emotional for everyone when a kid dies in the ER."

"So, what's the craziest thing you've seen in the ER?" Theo asked.

"Give him a break," Seraphina said. "I'm sure he doesn't want to talk about work."

"I really don't mind," Bodhi said. "I've seen so much over

these past 30 years. It's all a blur now."

"Come on," Theo prodded. "Just one."

"Okay," Bodhi said, "It's not the craziest, but it was kind of funny." Everyone's attention focused on Bodhi. "It's the end of March 2020 and the First Wave of Covid-19 was at its peak. EMS brings in a nursing home patient who was 101 years old and had severe dementia."

"101 years old. Wow!" Kai exclaimed.

Bodhi continued: "Her presentation was classic for Covid-19. She was severely hypoxic to 82% and her breathing was very rapid and labored. If any of you came in like that you'd get tired with such respiratory effort and spiral into respiratory failure and death. So, you can imagine that at her age, she had little reserve. The only hope to keep her alive was to intubate her and place her on a ventilator to breathe for her." Bodhi had everyone's attention. "I was just about to prepare to intubate her when the nurse tells me that the old lady has a living will stating that she was DNR/DNI."

"What's that?" Inez asked.

"It means Do not resuscitate/ Do not intubate. It's a decision, an advanced directive that a patient would make while they still had their mental faculties or by their health care proxy. It simply means that when it's time for them to die, they should be allowed to do so with dignity and without any heroic measures, like tubes in every orifice and a machine breathing for them."

"My mother had a DNR order," Hanna said. "But when she died they did all that stuff anyway. We were pissed."

"I get it," Bodhi said. "Sometimes if the proper documentation of these DNR/DNI orders aren't immediately available, some doctors feel obligated, morally and medico-legally to ignore the pleas of loved ones and initiate resuscitation and intubate the patient against their wishes."

"But that's ridiculous," Hanna said. She was noticeably upset. "My mother had end-stage ovarian cancer and was suffering. She just wanted to die in peace. That's what we all

231

wanted." Hanna had tears in her eyes.

Bodhi leaned forward and put his hand on her shoulder, simply nodding in agreement. Margot passed Hanna a tissue. Bodhi stood up, pulled Hanna up and gave her a big hug. After a few moments, he let her go. She sat down and wiped her tears. Bodhi was still standing and put his hand on her shoulder.

"Are you okay?" he asked. Hanna blew her nose and nodded yes. He continued: "You know, after seeing this happen again and again, I decided that at a certain age I would get a tattoo." Everyone looked puzzled since his comment came out of the blue. Bodhi lifted his sleeves, picked up his T-shirt, and continued: "I never liked tattoos and don't have any. But when I'm 70, I'm getting a large tattoo, in bright colors across my chest clearly stating DNR/DNI, and underneath it, the words: 'Don't you fucking dare try to bring me back to this hellhole!'" Everyone cracked up.

"What happened to the old lady?" Theo asked.

"Well," Bodhi said. "It was obvious that it was her time to die. The patient's daughter kept on calling to find out how the old lady was doing. Every hospital at that time had a no visitor policy because of Covid. I remember that it was busy as hell, but I answered every time because it was the right thing to do."

Margot interrupted him: "That was so nice of you Bodhi."

"It's not just being nice. I'd want and expect the same attention if my mother were on death's doorstep and all alone. In any case, I was always very patient with her and answered all her questions. She expressed her gratitude to him after every call. During one of the calls, the daughter asked him to be honest and tell her if this was a 'terminal event.' I wasn't even thinking and immediately responded: "With all due respect Ma'am, at your mother's age and even without the Covid-19 infection, a fart could represent a terminal event." Everyone cracked up again. After their fit of laughter, Bodhi continued. "I caught myself as soon as I said it, and realized that it definitely wasn't very professional of me to say that. There was a dead silence on the line, and I could already envision my boss calling me into his office with a complaint from her. Then all of a sudden, the daughter starting laughing hysterically. I'll never forget that moment in all the craziness that was going on."

"That's hilarious!" Dante said. "Give us one more."

"Dante!" Seraphina exclaimed. "Give the guy a break!"

"It's really fine," Bodhi said. "One more."

"What's the scariest experience you've had?"

"Well," Bodhi said. That's easy. This happened in April 2020. We were still getting killed with the First Wave. My mother was 91 years old at the time and quite healthy."

"God bless her!" Margot said. Adya walked over from the kitchen with Nico and Giovanna.

"What did I miss?" Adya asked.

"Nothing much," Bodhi said. "They were just warning me that you're an amazing human being but like a black widow spider, you devour your men after having sex with them."

Adya looked at everyone and chided them: "I thought you were my friends. Why would give my secrets away like that?" They all laughed. Adya sat across Bodhi's lap and put her arms around him. "Was Bodhi regaling you with his war stories?"

"He's great!" Dante exclaimed. "He's telling us about his scariest moment in the ER."

"This didn't happen in the ER Dante," Bodhi said. "But it was the scariest experience I've had in my 30 years as a doctor."

"Sorry I interrupted," Adya said. "Go on."

"I was saying that my mother was 91 years old, which put her at high risk of dying if she were to ever get Covid. She wasn't getting out much anyway, and aside from me, everyone in the family was sheltering-in-place except for visiting her to bring her food, necessities, and to keep her company. I knew I was at high risk because of my exposure in the ER, so I didn't kiss or hug her, always wore a mask around her, and as much as possible, maintained a distance of six feet. I was extremely cautious."

"We certainly wouldn't be in our present situation," Dahlia interrupted, "if everyone would have been as cautious!"

"That's 20/20 hindsight!" Theo retorted.

"Let's not go there!" Inez exclaimed. "Let Bodhi finish."

"So, it's 3am, I just got home from a noon to midnight shift, and I'm dead. I just fell asleep and I get a call from my mother. She sounded terrible, and she said that she felt as though she were going to die. She complained of feeling nauseous, extremely weak, shaky, and couldn't even get out of bed to go to the bathroom. I rush over to her place and find her in bed shaking vigorously. She looked awful. I literally had to carry her to the bathroom. She had terrible diarrhea."

"That sounds horrible," Hanna said.

"Now," Bodhi continued. "I'm a doctor, right? I knew my mom was 91 years old and was well aware that her years were numbered. But the reality was that I never considered it because she never behaved like an old lady. This was one of the few times that I could clearly see that she was indeed a frail old lady. I've had many conversations with her about dying and we're both at peace with the idea and its inevitability. But this was different. All of a sudden, the idea pops into my head that she has Covid and I gave it to her. It's one thing for her to die naturally, but it's another thing to know that I infected her with Covid and would be the instrument of her death."

"Oh no!" Adya said as she hugged him. "That must have been awful."

"Let's put this in perspective," Bodhi continued, "I've worked in major inner-city trauma centers and believe me when I tell you that I've seen everything imaginable in the ER. Nothing phases me a bit. But here I am at her bedside and I'm trembling. I'm wondering if I should call the ambulance, but then no one could visit her and she'd die all alone. And if she didn't have Covid, she'd probably catch it there. I have tears in my eyes and can't think straight."

"What happened?" Margot asked.

"My sister shows up," Bodhi said. "She was an ICU nurse for many years. She immediately checks her vital signs, which was the first thing I should have done but didn't because I was in such a panic. She looked at me up and down like I was some pathetic soul. Before I could say anything, she basically gave me a rapid bitch-slap-pimp-slap combination and reminded me that what she needed at that moment was an experienced emergency medicine physician and not a guilty and anxious son."

Hanna shyly raised her hand and asked: "Is she still alive?"

"Yeah. She's 95 now and doing great."

"Thank God!" Hanna blurted out. Her eyes were still red from crying about her mom earlier. "I couldn't handle a sad ending right now." Bodhi stood her up and gave her another hug.

"No worries," Bodhi said. "No sad endings. It wasn't Covid and was most likely food poisoning. She felt much better the next day. So that was the scariest moment I ever had as a doctor."

"I get it!" Dante said. "I would've shit in my pants."

"Me too," Kai said. "Thanks for sharing Bodhi. We've got mad respect for you ER docs and nurses!"

"Thank you, Kai," Bodhi said. "It means a lot to me to hear that." Phineas came out from the kitchen at that moment and relayed the message: "Nico said the Paella will be ready in about 10 minutes and we should set the table."

"Are we eating inside or outside?" Adya asked the group.

"It's such a beautiful night," Tristan said. "I think we should eat out here."

"Okay," Adya said as she jumped off Bodhi's lap. "I'll get the table cloth and napkins. I'll need a bunch of you to bring out the cutlery, glasses and plates." They followed Adya into the kitchen, brought everything out and set the table.

Bodhi walked to the other end of the terrace by himself and stared out. The sun was just over the horizon reflecting on the glass buildings of the New York City skyline. In that light he acknowledged how happy he was for the first time in many years. The soft breeze blew across his face. Whatever burdens he was carrying were blown away by that breeze. He felt an inner peace that he had never experienced before. He was then taken aback, felt guilty and somewhat aghast by the next thought that boldly popped into his head: "Covid was the best thing that ever happened to me!"

The fact is that it indeed was the best thing that happened to him. Bodhi realized at that moment that most of his revered beliefs that he would have previously fought for had since vanished. All that remained was the essential. Moreover, he was seeing that mental marble slab that he had labeled "essential" whittle away slowing leading to the very core of his being. Life was becoming simpler. All he had to do was breathe.

Adya sneaked up behind him and put her arms around him from behind.

"Do you prefer to be alone?" Adya asked.

"No, my love." Bodhi held her arms tight and leaned back into her.

"You seemed to be really deep in thought."

"I just had a bizarre thought," Bodhi said. "I was thinking about my life and it occurred to me that Covid was the best thing that ever happened to me."

"Why is that so bizarre?" Adya asked, hugging him tighter.

"I don't know," Bodhi responded. "With so many people dying and others suffering, I just felt guilty to be so deliriously happy."

"Are you really? She asked. Bodhi turned around and faced her.

"Yeah. I am. It's not only because we're together...I mean to say that meeting you and moving in with you now has allowed me to see how much has changed. I'm lighter now. So much of the bullshit I was carrying around just fell by the wayside.

"That's great!" Adya exclaimed. "I feel the same. It's what I was trying to say at the River Café- *Koyaanisquatsi*. Covid is giving us the possibility of setting things straight, finding balance, another way of living, realigning ourselves with the divine flow." They embraced each other.

"There's nothing to feel guilty about," Adya stated. "You answered that call and are now reaping the benefits." Bodhi nodded yes. They stared into each other's eyes.

"I love you!" Bodhi exclaimed. Adya beamed a smile and hugged him tight.

"I love you more!" She said. They remained in each other's arms for a long time. The sun was now setting and the sky was again crystal clear with highlights of orange and yellow over where the sun dipped below the horizon to continue its task of bringing light to the other side of the planet. The music changed to Chambao singing "!Ahi Estás tu!" This snapped Adya back from sinking deeper into their energy. "Let's go back. Everyone's already seated."

Nico and Tristan brought out the two large steaming hot paella pans and placed them on wooden blocks on the table. Despite being on an open terrace, the delightful aroma filled the terrace as though contained in an enclosed space. The colors of the paella- red peppers, green beans, string beans, yellow artichoke hearts, all set against the bright yellow rice- were brilliant. Nico stood on the side of the table and served everyone. While they were serving, Dante went around the table serving wine.

Once everyone was served, Margot raised her glass and toasted: "To a bright future and to our leader who makes it brighter." Everyone clinked and cheered.

"I love you guys so much," Adya said with great emotion. "There's no one else I'd rather be with during the next near mass extinction event." Everyone clinked and cheered again.

"Nico, tell us about your culinary masterpiece," Kai asked.

"It's a traditional Valencian paella," Nico said, "but not so traditional. It's traditionally made with chicken or seafood. Now in the post-Covid world with the overpopulation of deer, venison is the new chicken!"

"Olé!" Inez exclaimed. "Your father would be turning in his grave right now." They laughed and then clapped for Nico.

"Buon Appetito!" Nico exclaimed. Then there was silence, the greatest gift that can be given to a chef. There were only random sounds expressing great delight.

After their delightful meal, the discussion was raucous, fun and light. Bodhi had graciously been admitted into their circle and he felt at home. He felt so much lighter. No one was depending on him. They lived by the "10 Burning Man Principles," of which the most relevant to Bodhi were: Radical self-reliance, communal effort, and participation." This freed him from the burden of carrying a community. Bodhi thought of Ultron quoting Pinocchio: *I had strings but now I'm free. There are no strings on me.* Adya was 100% correct. He could now respect and fully appreciate everyone at a much deeper level because they were all participating adults sharing their gifts. Bodhi experienced a light buzz throughout his entire body. It was certainly in part due to the quantity of alcohol he consumed, but more so represented the love and gratitude he felt for his newfound friends, home and community. He felt as though he had been traveling all of his life and had now found a home. *Olé!* He thought to himself.

PART 8: THE FUTURE

HEADQUARTERS

Adya guided Bodhi into an apartment that was a few floors below theirs. It was similar in that it was spacious, bright with floor to ceiling windows that rendered spectacular views of New York City. The similarities ended there. The apartment had been converted to what appeared to be a large office. There were computer screens and desks everywhere. One of the walls was completely covered with large screens and the desk in front of it looked like the console of a spaceship. There were many people sitting at desks in front of their computers, and others talking around desks with laptops in front of them.

"This is headquarters," Adya said. "This is where all the magic happens."

"Wow!" Bodhi said. "It feels like we were teleported into the future."

"The best engineers and computer scientists designed everything and reproduced it all over the world." Adya said.

"All over the world?" Bodhi asked.

"Yup," Adya replied. "We've partnered with the best minds we could find all over the world. We share whatever we come up with and they share with us so we all have similar resources. Consequently, there isn't any need to compete, steal, distrust or envy your neighbor."

"That's brilliant!" Bodhi exclaimed.

"It also sets the example," Adya added.

"What do you mean?" Bodhi asked.

"When people across the globe see that we're sharing resources equitably, freely and with good will," Adya replied, "they develop a sense of trust that they're not going to get screwed, so they then turn around and give back and forward. But it's not from a sense of debt, but rather a sense of gratitude and because it's the right thing to do. Take the fear away and people tend to shine."

"That sounds amazing," Bodhi exclaimed.

"Let's sit on the terrace," Adya said. "I'll introduce you to everyone later. "An Americano?"

"Yes please," Bodhi replied. Adya pointed to a table that was under an awning and told him she'd be right back. The sky was somewhat gray. There were heavy clouds in the sky auguring rain. It was still seasonably mild for this time in November. Bodhi suddenly realized that almost two years had passed since the onset of the near extinction event that claimed 4 billion lives. Now they were sitting on a large terrace with gorgeous views of Manhattan and Brooklyn about to luxuriate in their Americano's. *Puta qui pariú!* Bodhi thought. He chuckled to himself that this Brazilian expression popped up in his mind at that moment.

Adya returned with two Americano's and four chunks of dark chocolate.

"Puta qui pariú!" Bodhi exclaimed.

"What?!" Adya asked with a surprised tone.

"It literally translates as the whore who gave birth to you, but it's the Brazilian way of saying 'that looks amazing!'" Bodhi explained.

"I know kiddo," Adya said. "I did Capoeira for years. I was just wondering where you picked it up."

"An old Brazilian girlfriend," Bodhi said.

"Okay Don Juan," Adya mused. Bodhi chuckled.

"I love the way Brazilians use the phrase as an all-purpose expletive that's used when they stub their toe, or see something really great like coffee and chocolate."

"Oooo-kay," Adya said smiling in an exaggerated manner.

"You know," Bodhi said. "Every time I wake up in the middle of the night and I look over at you sleeping, I think *Puta qui pariú!* Every time we look into each other's eyes, I think *Puta qui pariú!* The first thought that comes to my mind after we make love is: *Puta qui pariú!* Whenever I...."

"Okay! okay already!" Adya interrupted with a big smile. She took a piece of chocolate and forced it into his mouth. "*Puta qui pariú!* this!" They laughed.

They sipped their Americanos and nibbled on the chocolate and enjoyed the cool, damp breeze blowing over the terrace.

"I was just thinking that it's been exactly one year since the Second Wave," Bodhi said.

"It's crazy, right?" Adya asked.

"After everything that happened," Bodhi continued. "I can't believe that I'm so lucky to be alive and to be here with you." Adya reached out and took his hand.

"*Puta qui pariú!*" She exclaimed. The both laughed.

"So, tell me more about what you're doing?" Bodhi asked.

"Sure. It all started as a matter of necessity," Adya began. "Same with you, right?" Bodhi nodded. "It was all about survival and the first challenge was food. At first it was every person for themselves and then it just made more sense to work together in small groups. Keep in mind that I already had the Burning Man Principles in mind. Many of us had stored food as soon as the First Wave came and although a lot of people thought we were crazy, we kept on storing. I don't think anyone could explain why we were doing it but it just seemed to make sense."

"I kind of did the same," Bodhi added. "The First Wave was real. I can tell you that in my 30 years of ER experience, I never, ever experienced so many people who were so sick. It made perfect sense to stock up on food. What kind of food did you store?"

"Lots of beans and grains," Adya replied. "Mung beans, lentils, black and red beans, chick peas, quinoa, faro, oatmeal and amaranth."

"I did exactly the same!" Bodhi exclaimed. "But I also stocked up on a lot of pasta and pasta sauce."

"Yumm," Adya sounded. "I didn't even consider pasta. I just wanted to have stuff that was super healthy and wouldn't spoil."

"It's also interesting that you could live on these grains and beans for a year and come out healthier than you did when you started."

"Absolutely!" Adya agreed. "Some of us took inventory of what we had and realized that we'd only be covered for a maximum of six months. We did the rounds of the stores and supermarkets but everything had already been raided. That's when we heard about the work you were doing with the roof farming. We had some connections with people in your group and they shared what you were doing. Then everyone in the city started doing the same. You were definitely ahead of the curve so we kept an eye on what you were doing and borrowed generously."

"You're welcome," Bodhi jested.

"You know," Adya added. "We hadn't even thought about the fact that there might not have been heat in the buildings. We would have frozen to death if we didn't follow your lead and start using solar energy. Thank you!"

"For the record," Bodhi said, "Those weren't my ideas. I just found the right people..." Adya held her finger up to interrupt him.

"There's a great quote by Golda Meier," Adya said. "Don't be humble, you're not that great.'" They both laughed.

PLAYING GO

"**I**t all started locally. Similar to what you were doing," Adya continued. "But then as our community started to get larger, I recognized it was a game of Go on the world stage."

"Really?" Bodhi asked. "You wanted to conquer the world?"

"No, dingleling," Adya said. "The game Go as a means of spreading ideas, new perspectives, aid, hope. A beginner playing Go just tries to accumulate territories that are contiguous. A master however, will do so with territories that don't seem to have anything to do with each other and slowly put them together. That's exactly what I started to do. I gathered more and more territories."

"They're your territories?" Bodhi asked.

"No," Adya said. "What I mean is that there are now islands of people who share similar ideas, looking for a promising future. It's nobody's territory except for those who live there. They decide. But once they see the benefits, the beauty, then it's an easy choice. Those islands surround other ones that still live in fear and have doubt. Once they see how their neighbors have progressed and are benefitting from this new way of life- collaborative, open- they usually join in. There's no coercion. Total freedom to choose. What no one is allowed to do is to force anything onto anyone else. No one can take anything away from anyone else by force or coercion. That's the only time that we would intervene."

"Like you did with the gangs and the predators?" Bodhi asked.

"You got it!" Adya exclaimed.

"That's powerful!" Bodhi added.

"Life is powerful once you let it in. It's nurturing and bountiful. What's interesting is that the indigenous people of the world and every wise soul who walked the face of the earth pointed this out. It just took a near extinction event for people to get the message."

"It seems so obvious now," Bodhi said.

"At first it was about survival so I started to actively spread your ideas and other practices that made sense."

"Without my permission?" Bodhi asked jokingly.

"I gave you full credit my love," Adya replied. "That's why everyone knows and reveres you." Bodhi stood up and took a bow. Adya continued, "As soon as we started, we knew that there would be some bad eggs who would try to steal from us so we developed a small militia to protect ourselves. It started really small but when I started to extrapolate the possible outcomes of having to defend ourselves, it got really deep. By that time, I had formed small communities all over the country. We raided all the gun shops, police stations and then the military bases. We went from small militia to a real army."

"Why?" Bodhi asked.

"It's not that we planned to use those weapons. But I wanted to make sure that the crazies didn't get them. And if we ever needed them, we'd be ready. Then when the gangs started to show up, we were ready for them. We had these Go-like territories that surrounded other territories and slowly they joined us and we got bigger and more powerful."

"That sounds really dangerous." Bodhi said.

"Why?"

"You know," Bodhi said. "Power corrupts. Absolute power absolutely corrupts."

"I see," Adya said. "What you're missing is that this has

nothing to do with power. It's sharing principles, ideas, help and hope. We never force anyone to join us, but they do once they see what we offer. We give them the possibility to grow and thrive. Then if they're interested, they can find further meaning in their lives by helping others. The only rule is that no one forces anyone to do anything for their own benefit." Bodhi was silent and staring at her. He nibbled on a piece of chocolate and took the last sip of his Americano that was now cold.

"I just don't want to go back to the way things were, Bodhi. Covid wiped about 4 billion people off the face of the planet. That was horrible but it's also giving us an opportunity. I just want to make sure that we don't pass it up."

"But aren't you imposing your ideas on everyone else?" Bodhi asked.

"No!" Adya exclaimed. "I'm not. I'm not imposing anything on anyone. I'm showing them examples of what it could be like to live in peace, to share, to love. If they want to join us, they are welcome. Everyone is welcome. If not, they continue doing whatever they want to do just as long as they don't try to take anything from us or impose themselves on us. That's radical inclusivity and acceptance. The reality is that so far, people across the world are completely on board with what we're doing. They don't want to go back to the old ways either. Most are looking for a new way of life that's collaborative and in sync with the planet. We were all blind before and Covid gave us the gift of vision."

"20/20 in 2020," Bodhi said.

"Exactly!" Adya exclaimed. "People are searching for a path to a new way of life but don't have the means. It's just like you paved the way to urban farming, healthy living and clean energy. You gave your community what they were seeking but didn't have the means or resources to do it themselves. I'm just holding out my hand with a gift. It's theirs if they want it."

"I get it now," Bodhi said.

"The only obstacle was fear," Adya continued. "Fear of

being taken advantage of, robbed, imprisoned, put into slavery, always getting the short end of the stick. Once we dealt with the fear, it was easy." Bodhi nodded as he contemplated what she said.

"Are you hungry?" Adya asked.

"I'm famished," Bodhi said.

"Sit tight," Adya said. "I'm going to surprise you." Bodhi walked to the edge of the terrace and looked out in all directions. There was space, possibilities, and few limitations. He wondered if this is what Adya was referring to. *When everything is possible, what do you choose?* He asked himself. He realized that his trepidation about what Adya was presenting was based on his own fear and biases, his limitations that he was imposing on humankind. He asked himself: *What could be achieved if we put our fears aside? Why not dream of a grand future and strive for it? Why not?"*

At that moment Adya tapped him on the shoulder and startled him out of his reverie. She was holding a plate with a lovely pizza that smelled and looked delicious. The tomato sauce was bright red on which the islands of white cheese floated and was decorated with basil and wild mushrooms.

"That looks amazing! Bodhi exclaimed. "Did you make it yourself?"

"Yup," she replied. "Well sort of. Josh made the dough and I think Malia made the marinara sauce."

"How did you get the cheese?" Bodhi asked as they walked back to their table.

"It's cashew cheese," Adya said. "It's actually really easy to make." When they arrived at the table it was already set. Adya added: "I put the venison on the side just in case you wanted some. There's salad and home-brewed beer." Bodhi was obviously impressed.

"Well, we've got to pamper ourselves if we're going to create a new world," Adya said as she raised her glass. "To our future together." Bodhi clinked his beer glass, repeated the toast and leaned over and gave her a big kiss.

"I love you," he told her.

"I love you more," she said.

"You know, changing the world is definitely possible," he said. "But loving me more than I love you, impossible!" They smiled and clinked glasses again. After a brief silence, Bodhi prompted her to continue speaking.

"Where was I before?" Adya asked.

"Playing Go," Bodhi mused.

"Right," Adya said. "As our communities became more widespread and more efficient, we started to send teams to areas in need. We helped in any way we could- farming, teaching, sharing technology, clean energy, water purification, relocating families and communities. Whenever necessary, we protected them with our militias. We then did the same thing all over the world. At first, they wondered what we wanted in return. When we didn't ask for anything, they learned to trust us."

BORDERS

"**D**id anyone ever turn you away?" Bodhi asked.

"Of course," she replied. "Some people wanted to do it their own way, to shut themselves from larger communities. That's fear."

"I'm sure it's fear sometimes, "Bodhi added. "But I'm sure there are others, like the Russians, North Koreans, Chinese and Iranians, that just want to dominate their people and impose their will on others."

"You're right," Adya agreed. "But in all of those cases and others, it's not the people. It's the government. The people want the same things that everyone else wants. Don't you agree?"

"Absolutely!" Bodhi said. "But isn't it a moot point if the government controls the people and prevents them from living their lives freely?"

"In the pre-Covid world," Adya replied. "I'd definitely agree with you. But now there's opportunity. Governments have either been weakened or disintegrated. People now have a chance to express themselves and if they want, the rest of the world can help."

"What do you do in that circumstance when they reject your help?" Bodhi asked.

"We leave," Adya said. "Who are we to judge others? Even when it's apparent that they're struggling and would inevitably fail, it's always their prerogative to choose. We simply point out the communities around them that were prospering based on our collective wisdom and let them know that we as a community would always be there to assist them when and if they were ready."

"Has anyone attacked you?" Bodhi asked.

"In the beginning yes," Adya answered. "We always sought peaceful resolution and would at first retreat. If they continued to attack, we would crush them decisively in order to show that we didn't accept their violence. We would then offer to help them and if they refused, we would leave without taking anything. We wanted to show the world that we were extremely powerful but circulated in the world with love, caring and compassion."

"That's quite an accomplishment," Bodhi stated.

"It's what this time calls for Bodhi," she said. "We've been body slammed into a new paradigm with so much promise. We'd have to be idiots to go back to our old ways."

Bodhi raised his glass and toasted: "20/20 in 2020!"

"20/20 in 2020!" Adya repeated. "Did you like the pizza and the beer?"

"Absolutely delicious!" Bodhi exclaimed. "I was a big beer drinker and for a while and dabbled in home brewing. This is over the top!"

"It's called 'Rise,' " Adya said. "It's probably the first beer brewed post-Covid."

"It's great! Is this the one I had at the River Café?"

Adya nodded yes. "We've also got a darker, hoppier one called 'Boner.' "

"You're kidding right?" Bodhi jested.

"Mass extinction events lend themselves to some weird humor," Adya answered. "Wanna try the 'Boner'?"

"Sure," Bodhi replied. Adya got up and walked inside. She returned immediately with a liter bottle of 'Boner' and a plate with guacamole and pita chips.

"The fact that some people wanted to stake out their own territories led to a discussion about borders," Adya continued as she filled their glasses with the beer. "That was a tough one for us."

"Who's us?" Bodhi asked. He raised his glass, clinked it with hers and took a sip. "Whoa! That's hoppy!"

"That's why it's called 'Boner'!" Adya exclaimed. He tasted the chips and guacamole.

"Yumm!" Bodhi sounded.

"Which do you prefer?" Adya asked.

"I liked the 'Rise' better, but the 'Boner' goes well with the guac and chips."

"I prefer the 'Rise' too," Adya said. She lifted the neck of her T-shirt and looked at her chest. "I always wonder if the 'Boner' put some hair on my chest." They laughed. She continued with their conversation: "See those monitors in there?" Adya pointed inside. "Community leaders from all over the world meet with us. We spend hours sharing ideas, solutions, hashing things out. The concept of borders was a sticky one."

"In what way?" Bodhi asked.

"Some of us asked why we actually needed borders," Adya said. "This led to some pretty heated debates. But what was so beautiful was that at the heart of all these discussions, negotiations, there was the overriding principle that we all wanted to move forward together. It wasn't about what was best for me or this group versus that group. Rather, the focus was always on how we could move forward together."

"But you need borders to define your territory, who you are, what belongs to you, and a line telling others to stay out unless if invited," Bodhi chimed in.

"And where has that gotten us?" she asked. "It creates a them versus us mentality. The haves versus the have nots."

"But wait a minute Adya," Bodhi said. "If we didn't have borders, the United States or Europe would be inundated with immigrants."

"And?" Adya asked.

"Well," Bodhi said. "We wouldn't have enough resources for everyone. It would dilute our culture."

"You really think so?" Adya asked. Bodhi furrowed his eyebrows, smirked and nodded yes vigorously. "Could that be the case because some countries raped and pillaged others for centuries and left them at a disadvantage? Could it be the case because of competing political systems trying to dominate others?"

"Well..." Bodhi started to speak.

"Wait," Adya interjected. "Sorry to cut you off but I just want to make clear that I'm not making any judgement. Countries and people did whatever they did. There was never any forethought or consideration of the long-term outcomes of their actions. We just did what we did and future generations had to deal with the consequences."

"Okay," Bodhi conceded. "You do have a point but it's important for people to have an identity and borders provide that."

"Bodhi," Adya said. "What prevents you from having an identity if there are no borders? That kind of nationalism is a disease. It's born out of fear and a consequence of shit happening."

"What do you mean?" Bodhi asked.

"For example," Adya said. "People in Africa lived in tribes and each had their languages and culture. The imperialists came in, conquered parts of Africa and defined borders based on their own needs and benefits. This separated some tribes who may have loved each other and spoken the same language, and brought together tribes that didn't speak the same language and hated each other. Those people lost some of their culture and were forced to adapt to a new one. This led to violence, war, and sometimes genocide. Sometimes it created poverty and famine. I don't necessarily believe that those imperialists were evil. They were just doing what people did at that time based on their level of consciousness. They never sat to consider what their actions would lead to down the line, such as mass immigration from their former colonies, now requiring fortified borders and more immigration laws."

"Unintended consequences," Bodhi said.

"You got it," Adya said as she raised her glass and gulped down her beer. "One thing led to another haphazardly and we created rationalizations, beliefs and laws after the fact to deal with those unintended consequences." Bodhi reached over for the bottle and filled her glass.

"Listen," Adya said, moving to the edge of her seat. "We have such an opportunity right now. We just lost more than one-half of the world's population and the rigid governmental structures that were tethered to old, antiquated ideas are gone. We're free to create a new world with a new vision. We don't have to just let things evolve haphazardly and end up with more unintended consequences."

"But no one has a crystal ball Adya," Bodhi stated.

"Of course not," Adya agreed. "But we can put our heads together and move forward consciously. Of course we'll make disastrous mistakes. But we'll make them consciously and hopefully acknowledge those mistakes with humility and make corrections. Don't you think that's better than acting on the whims of some dick politicians?" Bodhi sipped his beer and dipped the pita into the guacamole.

"Yes," Bodhi said, raising a piece of pita in the air. "Just as long as you don't later become the dick politician. Isn't that what usually happens?"

"*Touché!*" Adya said and raised her glass to him. "But the big difference here is that we are not creating the revolution. It happened when the Second Wave decimated 4 billion people and washed away all our institutions. We're just rebuilding. The question is whether or not we should go back to our old ways, or try something new for the fuck of it since it wasn't working out so well for the vast majority of people on the planet."

"*Touché!*" Bodhi said.

"Like I said," Adya continued. "We have a great opportunity here in these unprecedented times. This is the thought experiment that we're all working on right now." She paused.

"Think about this based on future possibilities, not past biases." Bodhi nodded yes as he finished nibbling on some guac and chips, and sipped his 'Boner.'

"We pool the world's resources and redistribute it equitably and fairly based on population size, existing natural resources, wealth, technology and infrastructure," Adya said excitedly.

"Will this be limited to those who are part of your communities?" Bodhi asked.

"No!" Adya responded emphatically. She was now standing and gesticulating. "Everyone gets their share of resources, wealth and as much access to technologies, education, human resources as they need. We all start in more or less the same place."

"What about people that live in places that don't have natural resources like water, fertile land and the means to feed themselves?" Bodhi asked.

"That's Phase Two," Adya said. "So now that everyone has equitable resources, why the need for borders? If people in the Middle East or Africa can't feed themselves because of resources, we'll share whatever resources they need. If it's because the land is not fertile, and they're willing, they can relocate wherever they want. Why not?" Adya sat down and filled their glasses with beer and ate some chips.

"That sounds compelling," Bodhi said and seemed to be thinking carefully.

"Isn't it?" Adya added. "They're not hurting anyone or taking anything away from anyone, and will likely contribute to their new community in the same way that immigrants have always contributed. The only rules are first and foremost, not forcing anything upon anyone, and then the main Burning Man principles I mentioned before: radical self-reliance, acceptance, inclusivity, radical self-expression, participation, civic responsibility, and leaving no trace, which basically means that we take into consideration the impact of what we're doing to the planet."

"What if they don't want to contribute or participate?" Bodhi asked.

"But why wouldn't they?" Adya exclaimed. She was now back on her feet. "What they contribute to the community only benefits them. And if a few outliers don't participate, who cares? What's more important is enforcing the cardinal rule of not forcing anything upon anyone. If someone can't abide by that rule despite warnings and education, then they're excommunicated."

"Excommunicated?" Bodhi exclaimed. "Where do you excommunicate them to?"

"To any of the territories that decided not to follow our rules and wanted to do their own thing."

"Isn't that a little drastic?"

"Bullshit!" Adya replied. "This is a new paradigm Bodhi. No time for bullshit. There's a lot of latitude here to express oneself. We only demand that no one forces anything on anyone else. That's it! If they can't roll with that, then there are other places where that rule isn't a big thing." She nonchalantly took a sip of beer and continued: "Ahhh. Now I remember. I wanted to talk about taking care of our planet by making conscious decisions on the impact of our actions. For instance, those areas we discussed in Africa or the Middle East where the earth isn't fertile enough to grow food. We relocate anyone who wants to move but we don't just ignore that earth. We have the technology and know-how to reclaim that earth, the advancing desert and make it fertile again."

"How do you know about all of this?" Bodhi asked.

"Before my so-called liberation," Adya said using her fingers to indicate quotation marks, I wanted to be an environmental lawyer."

"Wow! Environmental lawyer to Burner and Ninja Assassin!" Bodhi exclaimed. "That was a radical change!"

"No shit!" Adya commented. "I was actually in my last year at Harvard Law School."

"Really?" Bodhi asked.

"Why do you look so surprised?" Adya asked.

"Well, my love," Bodhi said leaning forward to kiss her. Adya pulled away. "When you swept in to save me from Junior and had his head on a stake, my first thought wasn't "what an amazing lawyer she would be?"'

"Fair enough," Adya replied, now leaning in and kissing him.

"So, what happened?" Bodhi asked.

"I dropped out," she replied.

"But you only had one year to finish," Bodhi commented.

"No Bodhi," she said. "I had my entire life to finish and that's not what I wanted to do. I was actually killing it," Adya smiled broadly. "I had a 3.8 GPA and my professors pegged me as the rising star in the class with a promising future."

"I really don't get it," Bodhi said. "Law is like medicine in that the field is so broad. Everyone can find a niche that suits them."

"I recognized that the issues were too deep and I didn't want to spend my entire life chipping at a mountain with a nail file. I recognized that it was really important work but that's not how I wanted to spend my life. So, I dropped out, traveled the world, fell in love with Burning Man, did Capoeira, and took a deep dive into myself."

"What did your father have to say?" Bodhi asked.

"He told me that I should follow my heart and that he trusted me. He was the best. In any case, that law degree wouldn't have done me much good now."

"That's not true Adya," Bodhi exclaimed. "Just like playing Go taught you how to strategize and think a certain way, so did those three years at Harvard Law. The degree wouldn't have helped, but I'm sure what you learned has helped you a lot in your ability to reason, communicate and lead. No?"

"*Touché*!" Adya exclaimed. She jumped on his lap and gave him a big hug.

"I really love what you've done," Bodhi said. "It's visionary."

"I didn't do it love," Adya responded. "What's happening to humankind right now is both evolutionary and revolutionary. We just have the blessing to have front row seats."

"Don't be so modest," Bodhi said with a big smile, "you're not that great."

"*Touché!*" She exclaimed as she gave him a gentle push.

"What can I do to help?" Bodhi asked.

"You may not realize it," Adya said, "but you've already done so much. It wasn't so much your particular ideas or specific accomplishments, but how you organized people and brought them together. That was huge and gave us a model to work off of."

"But what can I do now?" Bodhi asked.

"Participate. Contribute. Be part of the conversation." Adya added. "Everyone already knows you and respects you. Just be yourself."

"How do I get started?" Bodhi asked.

"Easy." Adya said. There's a sort of google calendar that's posted daily that has all the group discussions for different levels of participants."

"How does it work?"

"It's like a pyramid," Adya said. "Anyone can participate in any discussion group at the lower levels, and anyone can post an idea and create another group. These groups are not moderated. Each group summarizes their key ideas and kicks them up to the next level. The ideas that stand out are further discussed, revised and developed at that next level with the key people who presented those ideas at the lower level. If the idea takes hold, the idea and the major contributors to that idea continue to rise to the higher levels of the pyramid where other broader factors are taken into account that the lower levels may not have been aware. Since the groups are inclusive, they draw amazing talent and make it easy for great thinkers to rise to the top."

"Is there a body that votes to promote people up the pyramid?" Bodhi asked.

"That hasn't been necessary so far," Adya replied. "The groups have been very dynamic and so far, that's helped to produce dynamic ideas. The focus isn't on climbing the pyramid but rather to participate and contribute. There's no inherent value on being on top of the pyramid except that a particular idea was good enough to warrant more attention and consideration for implementation. The person or group that came up with the idea follows it up the pyramid and is joined by people with more expertise to help them make it happen. In the process, they learn and if interested, they can choose to help other people grow their ideas."

"That sounds great!" Bodhi exclaimed. "Can I look at it now?"

"Sure," Adya said. "But I thought we'd have a quiet day together." She smiled and put her hand on his upper thigh. "You know what I mean?"

Bodhi leaned over and kissed her cheeks. "That sounds like an offer I can't refuse." He suddenly stood up.

"Where are you going?" Adya asked. Bodhi pulled her up to her feet, hugged her and led her towards the exit. "I'm taking you to start our quiet day together."

"Yes!" Adya exclaimed. "I love a man who's knows what he wants and when he wants it."

"And I love a woman who lets me know what I'm supposed to want and when to want it," Bodhi added.

"Sounds like a match made in heaven!" Adya exclaimed.

IN THE MOOD
FOR LOVE

They woke up sprawled on opposite sides of the bed. They forgot to black out the windows so the room was filled with bright sunlight. They reached for each other's hands from across the bed. Just as their index fingers were about to make contact, they suddenly realized that they were reenacting Michelangelo's "The Creation of Adam." They burst out laughing and rolled away from each other. They then rolled back and did the same thing but more seriously. When their index fingers touched, they lay still and just stared into each other's eyes.

"Bodhi," Adya said in a dead serious tone of voice.

"Yeah," Bodhi said trying hard to contain himself from laughing.

"Through these fingers," she continued, "I hereby give you my soul. Do you promise to keep, nurture and cherish it?" Bodhi suddenly became very serious. He propped himself up never losing contact with her finger.

"I do with all my heart Adya." Bodhi continued. "Adya. Through these fingers I give you my soul. Do you promise to keep, nurture and cherish it?"

"You know this is serious right?" Adya asked, again in a dead serious tone of voice. Bodhi never lowered his eyes from hers and nodded yes. Adya continued. "I do Bodhi. With all my heart." They crawled toward each other and fell into each other's embrace. They hugged each other for a long time without exchanging any words.

"I love you!" Bodhi said. Adya leaned back and placed her hand on his cheek.

"I love you!" Adya said.

"Life partners?" Bodhi asked shyly.

"Yes! Adya exclaimed. "And spiritual partners." Bodhi had a puzzled look on his face and asked:

"What's that?"

It's really deep," Adya said as she sat up on the bed. Bodhi did the same. They sat crossed-legged directly in front of each other, held hands and looked into each other's eyes.

"So, what's a spiritual partner?" Bodhi asked again.

"Patience love," Adya said, squeezing his hand. "Do you realize what we just did?" Bodhi smiled and nodded yes. "It was epic, no?" Bodhi continued to smile and again nodded yes. "I just want to close my eyes and let it settle in. Okay?" Bodhi just continued to nod yes. "You're not going to change your mind, right?" Bodhi now frowned and nodded no. "Okay. Let's meditate on that for a few minutes." They both closed their eyes and held hands. They both held a delicate smile on their faces. After a few minutes, their smiles became more pronounced as though they were sharing an inside joke.

Adya opened her eyes first and noticed the smile on Bodhi's face. She always considered herself a happy person. People felt the joy that she exuded and often made note of it. But it wasn't until that moment that she truly experienced bliss. She felt whole. It wasn't in the sense that she needed someone to be complete. Not at all. She was fiercely independent and learned long ago that happiness was always an inside job. But this was something new. Like all the other opportunities that the pandemic so graciously, albeit violently gifted, perhaps this was another offering. An invitation to open her heart and go deeper. To welcome a true partnership. Not just with the words defining spiritual partnership that she picked up somewhere and then repeated so many times, but with an open heart. Adya knew that this would be challenging because it would mean allowing herself to be vulnerable. It would mean that she would leave herself open to let go of her hard-won and earned territories in her inner game of Go.

Do you realize what we just did? Adya mentally repeated to herself. She smiled softly and nodded yes. *It was epic, no?* Adya continued to smile and again nodded yes. *You're not going to change your mind, right?* Adya closed her eyes tight and grimaced, holding her breath. She then let it out, closed her eyes and took another few deep breaths. *Well?* She asked herself. Adya's breathing became shallower and quickened. This was new. A profound challenge. Adya was never one to walk away from anything. *Games on!* She thought to herself and nodded yes.

"What was that about?" Bodhi asked. "You went from a peaceful smile to a look of dread, then a panic attack to deep concentration and back to a peaceful smile."

"Mind games," she replied matter-of-factly.

"Can you share?" Bodhi asked, squeezing her hands.

"Maybe another time," Adya shook his hands. "Want to hear about spiritual partnerships?"

"Yeah," Bodhi replied. "But before you start..." Bodhi leaned over and kissed her cheeks. He then got on his knees and kissed, softly licked and sucked her neck. He then firmly pushed her onto her back and set himself on his knees in between her legs. "...I think we should consummate this thing we just did."

Adya ran her fingers across his chest as he lifted both of her legs to the sides of his head. She asked: "This thing you say?"

Bodhi spit into his hand and wet his erect penis. He just barely entered her with the head of his penis.

"Yeah," he replied. He repeated "this thing" as he penetrated her deeply a few times and then withdrew to her vaginal introitus and explored that area.

"And what is this thing that we need to consummate?" Adya asked as she pressed her calves against his shoulders to raise herself up and down.

Bodhi lowered her hips to the bed, pushed himself inside of her deeply and supported himself on his elbows above her. He moved slowly and rhythmically, and began to sing King Pleasure's "Moody's Mood for Love": "Our souls are bound, come on and take me I'll be what you make me my darling my sweet."

"Oooh baby!" Adya swooned in an exaggerated, hokey manner. "Now you're really turning me on. I didn't know you were such a crooner."

Bodhi smiled. "I didn't want to overwhelm you with the totality of my awesomeness all at once."

"That was very thoughtful of you," Adya said as she flipped him over onto his back and straddled him. She propped herself up with her hands on his chest and pushed herself hard and deep onto him. She then started to slide her pelvis back and forth very rapidly. She closed her eyes and continued this rapid movement that synchronized with her breathing. She stopped suddenly, dug her nails into Bodhi's chest and let out a deep moan, followed by another. Adya dropped her weight onto Bodhi's chest and kissed him deeply. Her pelvis started to move spontaneously and very subtly. Her body started to tremble at first and then shake, followed by more moans into Bodhi's mouth. Bodhi breathed her in, absorbed her and then poured himself back into her mouth. He was completely absorbed by their breathing into each other and the electrical current running up the back of his spine and settling into his head. Each wave getting stronger and stronger and circulating wildly around his head.

Bodhi held Adya tight against his chest and felt the staccato bursts of her chest and abdomen pushing against his. Then stillness. She dropped her head to the side and all her weight pressed against him. He was having a hard time breathing with her weight on his chest but wanted to feel her for as long as he could take it.

Adya whispered in his ear: "So what exactly were we consummating?"

"I honestly don't remember," Bodhi said. He pushed her off to the side. "I'm sure it'll come back to me at some point." They laughed.

"You never come?" she asked.

"Sometimes," he answered.

"Will you come for me once in a while if I ask you to?" She asked.

"It depends," he answered.

Adya propped herself up on her elbow and placed her hand on his chest. "On what?"

"It all depends on whether you're a good girl or not?" Bodhi replied. "Are you going to be a good girl?"

"It'll be a challenge," Adya replied now stroking his still-erect penis. "But I think it'll be worth it." Bodhi smiled.

"Don't you ever miss coming?" Adya asked in a more serious tone.

"Never," Bodhi answered. "I'm having a continuous orgasm that's all over my body. It goes on and on. When I ejaculate, that type of orgasm lasts for 10 seconds and is limited to my cock. Why bother?"

"Good point," Adya agreed.

"Also." Bodhi continued. "If I come, I don't have any real desire to make love again for a while. When I don't ejaculate, I'm always ready, filled with desire, and I conserve all that energy for my body to use in other ways."

"That sounds amazing!" Adya exclaimed. "Is it the same for women? Can you teach me how to do that?"

"I've heard it's pretty amazing for women," Bodhi replied. "But I really don't know enough about it to teach you. What I can teach you is how to move energy up your chakras which is the first step."

"Great!" Adya exclaimed enthusiastically. "When do we start?"

"Soon," Bodhi said. "But first you're going to tell me about spiritual partnerships."

"Sure," Adya said. "Do you want to go for a walk? We can walk across the Brooklyn bridge and have a picnic on the promenade. Are you in?"

"All in my love," Bodhi replied. "All in."

SPIRITUAL PARTNERS

I t was a spectacular day. The sky was bright blue without a cloud in the sky. It was a bit windy out, which became quite prominent as they walked across the Brooklyn Bridge. They huddled against each other, held hands and walked in silence. There was only the sound of the wind, the crashing waves, and the occasional car that passed. They walked back across the bridge and arrived at the Brooklyn Promenade where they marveled at the New York City skyline. They unpacked their picnic and a bottle of wine.

"So, I picked up this idea of spiritual partnerships," Adya started, "from my good friend Rowan who was a Buddhist. He learned it from Geshe Michael Roach, a Tibetan Buddhist teacher who was the first American to receive the Geshe degree at Sera Monastery in Tibet. The basic principle is that each of us creates the entire world around us, and the reality that we perceive and experience is dependent on our past karma. This includes all of our relationships. All our experiences- good, bad or indifferent- are created by us. Therefore, the world, our reality, is merely a reflection of our karma." Bodhi smiled.

"Are you making fun of me," Adya asked somewhat annoyed.

"Not at all!" Bodhi protested. "I'm just smiling."

"I know this sounds far-fetched," Adya continued, "but hear me out. The application of this idea is quite powerful and can be life-transforming."

"Okey-dokey," Bodhi said. "I'm with you."

"When you adopt this perspective," Adya continued. "You recognize your partner to be your spiritual guide, and likewise, you are their spiritual guide." Adya paused and studied Bodhi to gauge how receptive he was to what she was saying. She continued: "Here's where it gets deep. So, if your partner is the spiritual guide who you, or your Higher Self has created, then everything they do is for the purpose of serving your highest best. Even when they appear to be torturing you, you created them to do exactly that - for the purpose of teaching you what you wanted to learn and experience from being tortured. Are you with me so far?"

"Let me repeat it to see if I'm getting it," Bodhi said. Adya nodded yes and sat back on the bench. "I created you as my spiritual guide and everything you do is an expression of exactly what my Higher Self designed for me to experience." Adya was pleased with his summary and nodded yes. "So right now," Bodhi continued. "You are my angel, my savior, my goddess." Adya blew on her fingernails and polished them on her T-shirt smiling. "But later on, when you transform into a complete bitch who is making me miserable, it's still all me. It's my Higher Self that is creating that experience for me through you for my benefit."

"Yes!" Adya exclaimed excitedly. "You're a fast learner." Bodhi now blew on his fingernails and polished them on his T-shirt. "Another way of expressing this is to say that your partner serves as your mirror, allowing you to see yourself as you truly are. All relationships serve this same purpose. This is the reason why many other people can do the same things without it bothering you at all, but when your partner or close relations do the same thing, it triggers you. They are your mirrors and allow you to see parts of yourself that you need to experience."

"That is so right!" Bodhi exclaimed. "Remind me to tell you a related story when you're done."

"You want to tell me now?" Adya asked.

"No," he said. "I really want to hear where you go with

this."

"So, from this perspective," Adya continued, "When I do turn into a royal bitch and do something that triggers a negative emotion in you, take a deep breath, give me a heart-felt hug, bow to me and say thank you."

"Whoa!" Bodhi said. "Have you ever tried this?"

"I haven't been in a relationship for ages," Adya admitted.

"Really?" Bodhi asked in a surprised tone.

"I've been doing the celibacy thing for a long time now," Adya answered. "For years. I've been very conscious about it. Then you came along and ruined everything."

"Ahhh!" Bodhi explained. "So, your Higher Self created me to show you what you needed to experience in a loving relationship and having mind-blowing, tantric, chandelier-monkey-sex."

"Oooo-kay!" Adya said. "Maybe you're learning a little too quickly!"

"This is so fascinating!" Bodhi said. "It goes way beyond relationships and applies to everything we experience and how we relate to it."

"Yup!" Adya smiled. "So, in the example of me being a bitch and torturing you, the reason you express gratitude is because in that situation, I'm showing you something that you, your Higher Self created in order to show you," Adya poked his shoulder, "your present self, what you needed to bring to your awareness, deal with, confront, and address."

Bodhi stood up and put both hands on the sides of his head. "You're really blowing my mind with this!" Bodhi exclaimed.

"Well," Adya said. "Your Higher Self created me to express this to you at this time for the very purpose of blowing your mind. It's all you, buddy. Do you get it?"

Bodhi paced back and forth in front of the bench. "You know," Bodhi stood directly in front of her and said: "The concept is so incredibly simple. But applying it immediately transcends all the bullshit."

"I never thought of it that way," Adya nodded. "But yeah." She paused and snapped her fingers: "Where was I?"

"You were talking about channeling your inner bitch," Bodhi said.

"Don't push it, buddy!" Adya said. "It's the awareness itself that has the power to heal and release. Unfortunately, we tend to point the finger at our partners and blame them for..." Adya made quotation marks with her fingers, "'doing something' that 'caused' our reaction and suffering."

"It's that saying," Bodhi interjected, "when you point a finger at someone else, there are three other fingers pointing back at you."

Adya nodded in agreement and continued: "So that feeling that the world is doing something to you is in fact what is 'apparently' happening. According to Geshe Michael Roach, if your karma allows it, you're able to see further and recognize what is truly happening at a deeper level. At this level, you recognize that you created everything, and the world is nothing more than a mirror in which you are able to see your reflection."

"Wow!" Bodhi exclaimed. "I want us to be spiritual partners." Adya laughed.

"Are you sure?" Adya asked, still laughing.

"Yes, I'm sure!" Bodhi exclaimed. "Let's do it!"

"Okay then," Adya said. "I'm in."

"I'm in!" Bodhi repeated.

"You know there's no turning back, right?" Adya asked.

"I get it," Bodhi said. "If we're here together, then we created each other to have this experience. So, there's no running away because we'd only be running away from ourselves."

"And you know that saying?" Adya paused and raised her hand to indicate that he should fill in the blank. When he looked puzzled, she continued: "Wherever you go, there you are!"

"Right!" Bodhi agreed. "I really get this now. Since your

LOVE IN THE TIME OF CORONAVIRUS

Higher Self wanted you to have this experience and learn something, and you didn't- because you either weren't ready, refused, or ran away- then it'll continue to escalate and bite you in the ass during the next relationship. It's so clear now. I can look back and remember the eerie pattern that each of my partners were exhibiting the very same behaviors that were annoying me. It was as though they were collaborating. I see now that it was all me. I created everything!"

"Here's the most beautiful part of all of this Bodhi," Adya said. "Once you get this, everyone is forgiven for everything because you, your Higher Self, created it all for your benefit. No need for the bullshit or any drama from this perspective. Isn't that so beautiful?"

"It's really the most beautiful thing I've ever heard," Bodhi said. "I'm sure it's not so easy to put into practice, but I can see how life becomes so simple."

Adya continued: "Once you recognize that we all serve as mirrors for one another, you'll try to be the best mirror possible. Imagine yourself floating on a crystalline lake. The more drama you have in your life, usually in the form of thoughts, the more drops that fall into the lake and create ripples, waves, larger and larger waves that turn into tsunamis. These tsunamis travel all the way around the world and return to violently knock you on your ass. So, then what do you do?" Adya paused for effect and continued. "You immediately get up and point your finger at the first person you see, usually your partner, and accuse them of knocking you down. When you can see what's really going on, you understand that it was all you and your partner is simply serving as your mirror. The more ripples that we create, the blurrier the reflection that we offer. Our partners then react to the ripples, waves, tsunamis, and are unable to see themselves clearly. Their resultant ripples, waves, tsunamis then prevent us from seeing ourselves. We consequently end up in a situation where our drama is reacting to their drama, thereby creating even more drama. When you enter in a spiritual partnership, you both try to be the best mirrors for each other, without any ripples that blur your partner's reflection."

"Whoa!"

"Here's one more idea," Adya added. "Imagine a relationship where both partners get this and enter into this spiritual partnership. This is us, right? This is what we're doing, right?" Bodhi nodded yes. Adya continued: "Like I said before, no matter what happens, you say thank you and express gratitude because now you know that your Higher Self created the situation, and your partner's Higher Self consented to serve as the person that will do whatever you requested to create the experience you need, even if it means torturing you. Imagine the sacrifice that your partner is undertaking to torture you so viciously when they, their Higher Self truly loves you so much. This sacrifice in response to your desire and request is a true manifestation of this love. At this level, there's only love and gratitude."

Bodhi pulled Adya up to her feet and hugged her so hard. "I love you so much," Bodhi said. "I'm going to be the best mirror in this whole wide world for you."

"You better be!" Adya joked. "You're a special man. I love you and I'm going to be the best mirror in this whole wide world for you." They embraced for a long time.

"There's a beautiful line by one of my favorite poets," Adya said. "He wrote 'If I could only hold a mirror large enough to show you your wings, your reaction would delight the Gods.'"

SETTING
BOUNDARIES

They were sitting in headquarters and in the middle of a teleconference. The room was filled as well as the computer monitors. Adya had the floor and asked if anyone had any questions. Many people signaled that they had questions. Uzoma, the moderator gave Henri, a Frenchman, the floor.

"What are we trying to accomplish here?" Henri asked.

"I don't understand your question?" Adya asked.

"It's a simple question Adya," Henri stated. "What are we trying to accomplish here?"

"Rebuild the world, Henri," Adya replied. "Build a better world."

"That's so American," Henri said. "So full of arrogance." Adya smiled.

"You're missing the point Henri," Pyotor jumped in.

"Am I?" Henri replied.

"This is not about America, Russia or Europe," Pyotor replied. "It's about creating a future where we, humankind, move forward and prosper while caring for planet earth."

"That sounds like a quaint informercial," Henri blasted. "How can we trust America after such a rich history of abuse?"

"Enough already!" Uzoma exclaimed. "Enough! We don't

have time for this bullshit!"

There was silence. Bodhi sat next to Adya who was standing. They were at the headquarters and sitting at a large desk in front of the wall of screens that showed the faces of leaders from all of the world. It reminded Bodhi of the Zoom meetings everyone was using after the First Wave. This platform looked different but could have been an updated version.

"I'm just raising my concerns," Henri continued.

"Bullshit!" Uzoma blurted out. "You're fomenting conflict."

"I agree," Yuuto added. "We don't have time for this. We're beyond this.

"Am I the only one that can see that Adya is trying create a global government to impose her will over the rest of us?" Henri asked. Adya sat down and buried her face in her hands and shook her head no.

"Henri!" Pyotor exclaimed. "What are you talking....."

"No!" Adya exclaimed. "Henri has a legitimate concern and we must address it."

"But why?" Pyotor asked. "It's clear to the rest of us that this is ridiculous."

"My dear friends," Adya added. "We can't move forward if we leave others behind and leave questions unanswered. These concerns that now seem so trivial will ultimately later percolate to misunderstands over which wars are fought. Henri, let me address your concerns."

"I'm listening," Henri said.

"First of all," Adya said. "This is not about me or the U.S., or any other particular country. This is not about building a global government."

"Then why are we all here?" Henri asked. "There are representatives of almost every country here."

"We are representatives of the survivors of the near mass extinction of the human race," Adya corrected him. "One-half of the human population was decimated along with our institutions- governments, banks, hospitals. We're here to answer simple questions. How do we want to move forward? Do we want to go back and recreate everything the way it was? Hope that things evolve in a different way? Do we agree that the way things were was creating endless conflict?" Adya paused, waiting for Henri to reply.

"This is not about me or anyone else in particular," Adya continued. "Henri. We have an opportunity here. Our history has been undone. So how do we move forward? How do we relate to one another? How can we help each other to thrive in each of our unique ways? We don't necessarily have the answers, but we're asking the right questions."

"But who gave you the authority to impose your will on others?" Henri demanded provocatively.

"If you haven't noticed, Henri," Adya replied, "There is no authority. There are only people interested in moving forward. Everyone is invited to participate. Also, it's obvious that you have a beef with me personally."

"That's not true," Henri denied.

"Regardless," Adya pressed on. "I personally have absolutely no authority to do anything. We are working as a group trying to develop best practices. We look back and take what worked and leave the rest for the history books. What exactly is your problem with what we're doing?"

"Well," Henri said. "It appears that you're trying to develop a global government to rule the world."

"Wow!" Adya exclaimed. "I really don't know how to respond to that. So, I won't. Henri, let's make this simple. We're only trying to develop a vision that will allow the world to move forward in a conscious manner. We've collectively come to the conclusion that in order to do this, we need to do a few things from the start. First, we need to distribute wealth and resources evenly and fairly. Second, education, food, water, healthcare and shelter have to be the priorities. Aside from distributing wealth and resources, everything that we do is based on goodwill and volunteers wanting to make the world a better place."

RICHARD LANOIX M.D.

Henri was about interject but Adya raised her finger and continued. "We've only imposed our will with the foundational rule that no one is permitted to force anyone to do anything without their express consent and no one can forcefully take anything away from anyone else. We leave the rest to human nature and evolution. So, what's the problem?" Adya paused to see if Henri or anyone else had anything to say.

"Unlike former governments that for the most part worked for their own enrichment and benefit, often at the expense of others" Adya continued, "we're coming up with ideas that serve humanity and the planet. They're not my ideas or anyone else's. We're brainstorming, sharing, and doing our damndest to serve humanity. We're allowing ourselves to dream of a brighter future, and so far, we've come up with primary objectives- distribute wealth and resources evenly and fairly, and ensure access to education, food, water, healthcare and shelter. After that we keep on dreaming and everyone is free to be themselves and develop in whatever way they want just as long as they don't cause harm to others."

"Sounds like a Marxist dream," Henri said. The voices came as an avalanche of attacks: "Fuck you!" "You're a troll!" "Drop dead!"

"Wait!" Uzoma ordered. The voices petered out. "Henri," Uzoma said. "It appears that you have a different vision. You are welcome to stay in this group and participate but if your objective is to be a troll, I would encourage you to form your own group of like-minded people and develop your own collective dream. It's up to you."

"I was just..." Henri started to say when Uzoma cut him off.

"Henri!" Uzoma exclaimed. "Do you understand what I said? We have a lot of work to do. We don't pretend to have the answers and welcome differing opinions and all objections, but they have to be constructive. I really want you to take some time to think about this- how can you contribute in a constructive manner?"

274

"Don't you think...." Henri again started to speak and Uzoma again cut him off.

"Henri!" Uzoma exclaimed. "Our conversation is over for now. Please log off and give some thought to what I said. You can join us for our next meeting. Goodbye for now." Henri's face disappeared from the screen.

"Thank you for your thoughtful presentation Adya," Uzoma said. "And thank you for the way you handled Henri. You're absolutely correct that we must make room for dissenting voices. It's the only way to move forward. Thank you." Adya nodded.

"Let's take a short break," Uzoma said. "When we return Dr. Albright will introduce Dr. Bodhi McKenna who will speak to us about the future of healthcare."

ABBATOIRS-
WITHOUT-BORDERS

Bodhi stared out over the wall of computer screens flashing hundreds of faces from all over the world. He was used to speaking in front of large audiences but speaking to hundreds of faces on a wall of computer screens that were each subdivided into many squares was disorienting. He was nervous. It was also different in that what he had to say could be consequential. People were looking for a new direction and they were asking him and others to point them there. Moreover, it wasn't his typical audience. The faces were not limited to North Americans. They were from all over the United States and all over the world listening carefully to what he had to say and weighing it against other ideas. He did not in fact want to do this but Adya encouraged him to speak based on the large following he had in the United States.

The topic of discussion was global health in the post-Covid world. The format was straight forward. He would lecture on the topic and they would then break up into groups to discuss it. They would analyze and debate to determine if there were ideas worth further developing and implementing. Dr. Samantha Albright from Ireland introduced him. "Dr. McKenna is an emergency physician in New York City who has been speaking about optimal health for many years now.

While his message was for the most part ignored in the pre-Covid era, it is highly relevant to all of us today. He's done remarkable work for his community in New York City and his ideas and practices have been widely adopted with great success in urban areas across the United States. It is with great pleasure that I introduce Dr. Bodhi McKenna."

"Thank you for that gracious introduction," Bodhi began. "Please note that my experience is limited to healthcare in the United States, but I believe that the issues that we face here are the same ones that we as a global community must face if we are to move towards optimal health globally. So, let's begin with a thought experiment. Imagine that you won the lottery for millions of dollars. More money than you could possibly spend in ten lifetimes. Despite the fact that you are not a consumer and were quite satisfied with your life as it was except for the inconvenience that you had to work so much to make ends meet, you would most likely buy the car of your dreams. You would purchase this car not because you needed it but rather because you now had so much money. After you donated so much of that money to many causes to help people, why wouldn't you treat yourself to such a gift?

"So now you have this ridiculously expensive and absolutely gorgeous car, would you put less than premium gas or oil in it? Even though in your mind this car is nothing more than a toy, you would most likely take tremendous care of this car and actually take great pride in how well you maintained it. Right? Then after three years or so, even though the car is still in mint condition, you would most likely purchase an even nicer car. Why? Well, why not? You have invested your money wisely and with your profits, helped even more people than ever by donating to worthwhile causes all over the world. Why not again treat yourself to an even nicer toy? And it goes without saying that you are such a generous person that rather than sell the first car, you would gift the car to a great friend who deserved it. The fact that you have so much money allows you to do this again and again and always have a gorgeous car that is in perfect condition.

"What I find so ridiculous is that we would put so much care and attention to a car, or any other valued object for that matter, and yet we disregard our precious bodies. It's the one vehicle that we are given that must last our entire lifetime. It can never be exchanged or upgraded. How is it possible that we put the equivalent of cheap gas and oil into our bodies for fuel and maintenance, when we would never consider doing this to our beloved car? We only get one body in his lifetime and yet most people treat their bodies as a commodity that can easily be exchanged or upgraded.

"The question is why? I believe that the answer to this question is the key to a successful future at the level of the individual, as well as for the global community and planet. Here's some food for thought. Are we any different than the animals that are raised to produce meat and consequently will meet their fate in commercial slaughterhouses? Their life purpose is to be slaughtered, or if you prefer euphemisms, they are "sacrificed" to produce meat for the masses.

"The obvious point to begin this discussion is that society doesn't require the quantities of meat it consumes. The quantity of meat we consume has clearly been demonstrated to be detrimental to our health and even worse for the environment. The environmental issues such as the methane gas these animals produce, nitrate seepage into the water supply, the amount of land and water required, and destruction of forests to create more land to produce grain to feed these animals in relation to the calories and nutrition they produce, are all detrimental to us and our planet earth. These are known facts.

"The counterargument is obvious: People have the right to choose what they eat, even if what they are eating is, at least in the quantities consumed, unhealthy and is destructive to the environment. Please note that I am not attempting to make an argument for a vegetarian diet. I am addressing a more fundamental premise: Choice.

"Are we as a society choosing to eat these large quantities of meat, that 3-liter bottle of Coca-Cola or Pepsi, or that box of Hostess Twinkies? What if we were collectively making those choices through coercion or brainwashing? What if our choices were based on ideas that were planted inside our heads from a very young age by everything presented to us by advertising and social media? If we were aware of this, would we now make the same choices?

"In our prior system of commodification, animals were slaughtered to produce meat for the masses, which provided dollars for... let's call them the Masters. If the premise is correct that we were brainwashed to believe that we "needed" meat, processed food, high-fructose corn syrup in its myriad forms- all of which create disease in humankind- then it follows that we, society, human beings, are being slaughtered to earn dollars for the Masters."

Many voices interrupted simultaneously, stating: "That's complete bullshit!"

Others asked: "That's a stretch in logic, isn't it?" "Who are these Masters?"

Others stated: "What you are saying only occurs in Western Society." "This doesn't apply to us."

Another voice emerged above the rest and asked: "Why are we talking about the past?"

"Please hear me out," Bodhi continued: "I promise I'll address all your questions. Let's look at this more closely. Many of us living in Western Society were raised to live our lives in such a manner so that we consume and in doing so, earn dollars for the Masters. Our inherent value to the Masters was how much we consumed. This was our production, and everyone at every socioeconomic level served their purpose. Many people before the pandemic refused to accept the fact that every aspect of our lives was geared towards production of profits for the Masters. I'm sure many of you now reject this notion.

"Advertisement was ubiquitous to encourage us to live as consumers. We worked longer and longer hours to earn enough money to consume more. We were encouraged to live in debt on which we paid interest, and then had to work harder to earn more dollars on which we paid more taxes while the Masters paid little to no taxes.

"Our food was infused with substances such as high-fructose corn syrup, that enticed us to eat more and more, creating psychological dependency akin to the crackhead who needed his pipe at all cost, and was more than willing to kill for it. Moreover, in the same way that commercial farmers used cheaper products to support their animals in order to yield more profits, the food that we were brainwashed to consume had devolved to the point of being devoid of nutritional value.

"The Standard American Diet, the acronym for which is 'SAD,' was a slow poison that was killing us slowly. However, before we died, our diet resulted in a large variety of illnesses-obesity, diabetes, hypertension, coronary artery disease, cardiovascular disease, metabolic disorders, stroke, osteoporosis, kidney failure, just to name a few. We began to see widespread food allergies such as gluten allergies. Does anyone older than 50 recall ever hearing the term 'gluten allergy'?

"Unlike the poor animals that are fed and maintained for slaughter and yield only one or two sources of revenue- their meat and sometimes their skin and fur- we humans provided a recurring source of revenue for the Masters before our demise. How so? Here are some examples: Health insurance premiums that increased as a person became more ill and developed an ever-increasing laundry list of illnesses. Frequent visits to the healthcare system that simply kept us well enough to consume more in the same manner that created the decline in our health that brought us into the healthcare system in the first place. Absurdly expensive pharmaceuticals that treat the very same diseases caused by the system. Medical supplies. Admissions to the hospital. Heroic, life-sustaining measures for end-of-life care."

Another voice interrupted: "With all due respect Dr. McKenna, these were North American issues. The rest of the world has always viewed your system of healthcare, your lack of some form of single payer system as an anomaly. What does this have to do with our collective future?"

"Everything, I'm afraid," Bodhi replied. "That's the beauty of brainwashing. You don't know that it's happening until it's too late. Don't forget that North America's greatest export was its culture. Why were there so many McDonald's and fast-food chains throughout the world? When did Europeans become such consumers and develop such obsessions with Nike sneakers and iPhones? Haven't you noticed that problems like obesity, hypertension and diabetes have already crossed the pond? How is it that strong cultural habits such as eating healthy food at a table with family were substituted by fast-food chains? I'm afraid the North American disease has already crossed the pond.

"Many people didn't understand the significance of why the French farmer José Bové and his compatriots in 1997 dismantled a MacDonald franchise that was under construction in Millau, France, and before that destroyed genetically modified corn in Nérac, France. He was making a broader statement against this festering disease that was overtaking our civilization. He saw the writing on the wall.

"We are attempting to transform the near mass extinction event that swept the world into an opportunity to create something new. There are others who also see what happened as an opportunity. They would like to use the example of the United States and apply it to the rest of the world."

"Dr. McKenna." Another voice asked. "Do you believe that the leaders of the United States purposefully inflicted these diseases on the North American population?"

"That's a tricky question," Bodhi responded. "I believe that corporations had a product to sell and brainwashed the population to purchase their products. The illnesses may have been an unintended consequence but when it was learned that the illnesses themselves could be commodified, they further embraced, developed, and expanded the idea. The population was dispensable to the Masters.

"Commodifying human lives may not have been a conscious decision, but to take advantage of that situation that produced tremendous profit at the cost of human lives was a very conscious act. The issue now is that those same people that stumbled into a goldmine will now consciously attempt to recreate that system consciously and purposefully. Furthermore, now that the safety mechanisms that every other industrial country in the world had in place, such as universal healthcare, are in disarray, these Masters will try to expand their successful enterprise to the rest of the world."

"That's preposterous!" Another voice exclaimed.

"Is it?" Bodhi asked. "All you have to do is to plot the increase in obesity, hypertension, diabetes and heart disease in countries where it was nonexistent and compare it to its adoption of fast-food culture, North America's number one export. Do you believe that this happened accidentally?" Bodhi waited for a response and then continued.

"What is more compelling was the ingenious manner in which the human abbatoir or slaughterhouse was designed. Through the machinations of advertising, which was really nothing more than a form of brainwashing, we humans at the apogee of Western Civilization have been cajoled to manage ourselves in the abbatoirs-without-borders of our minds. In this regard, we were closely related to the ducks or geese that were submitted to the process known as gavage: force-feeding corn with a feeding tube until their livers fattened to produce foie-gras. However, unlike the duck or goose that was restrained and force-fed, we have been brainwashed to perform self-gavage, and to relish it. We were force-feeding ourselves by an unremitting consumerism that led to obesity, cancer, diabetes, hypertension, etcetera, all of which created revenue for the Masters. Unlike the unwitting animals led to slaughter, we were trained to enter the abbatoir with a hop, skip, and dance, place our heads on the chopping block, and then pull the lever to release the guillotine and chop our heads off.

"As Morpheus stated in the movie 'The Matrix,' we were

bred to become nothing more than batteries, a source of energy, in this case profit for the Masters. The system has now evolved beyond 'The Matrix' to be fully automated. An abattoir where human beings breed, herd, graze, and slaughter themselves without supervision. It was ingenious.

"We had been so thoroughly brainwashed that we believed that this way of life was normal. There was no escape because everything we experienced reinforced the chicanery, and it became more pervasive with every generation.

"There were many who clamored that people had a right to live as they pleased. They insisted on their sovereignty. Think of the backlash against New York City's former Mayor, Mike Bloomberg, when he tried to ban oversized soda in fast food restaurants. There were protests stating that he was violating people's civil rights. From a particular perspective, they were absolutely correct. Yes, everyone has the right to smoke, eat poison, and kill themselves in the manner they choose. The real issue is that we believed that we had sovereignty and were making our own choices. This was patently false. We had been brainwashed. From this perspective, we were worse than the animals led to slaughter. We were complicit. Moreover, what was overlooked was that we were being used as fodder to produce for the Masters. The flesh was not from some poor animal whose consciousness we chose to ignore, but our own."

Bodhi paused to allow the bombshell he just dropped to settle in. He had presented this very same topic many times and the responses were typically the same and predictable. Audiences first rejected his message, sometimes violently. They were insulted and shocked to be categorized as animals in a slaughterhouse. Then as his message seeped in, they began to experience anger at their predicament. This was then followed by the horror of knowing that it was all self-inflicted. In the pre-Covid world, there were enough distractions for them to come full circle and again reject his message. Nonetheless, it had already touched a nerve and the truth of what they had heard set off internal alarms that resonated deeply. It could be avoided but not be erased.

Bodhi continued: "As a practicing emergency physician for the past 30 years, I have witnessed that at least 50% of the suffering that presents itself in emergency departments is self-inflicted by the poison people put in their mouths. Throw in tobacco and that makes about 75% of the underlying cause of all presentations to the ER.

"What kind of argument could be offered for the fact that such a large segment of the North American population was so hell-bent on self-destruction and engaged in activities that constituted nothing less than ritual Hara-kiri performed in painfully slow motion? Even more ludicrous is that we had front row seats to this performance and although we found the performance of the self-disembowelment grotesque and bar-baric, we for the most part stood in line to wait our turn to do the same.

"There are so many examples I could share to show how we committed ritual Hara-kiri as a society and squandered the one precious gift that we could claim as our own- our bodies, our lives. Through the grace of Consciousness, we were gifted this one body, this one vehicle to journey through this lifetime. We were also gifted sovereignty to choose how we use this precious gift, and despite all of those who stood upon the stage of life and performed Hara-kiri in front of our eyes, we actively chose to repeat the process. Moreover, in order to attain more "likes" on Instagram and Facebook, we used longer and exotically embellished swords. We performed this barbaric ritual of disemboweling ourselves in even slower motion to some top-40 hit song and dancers in the background.

"Was it pure ignorance that drove us? As selfish as we were as a society and as human beings, one would assume that we would at the very least take care of ourselves in order to enjoy the rewards of being selfish. Was this evolution at work that slowly over time extinguished our sense of self-preservation and accentuated our self-destructive tendencies for suffering?

"The Covid-19 pandemic has provided us with a great opportunity here. We can now review our past behaviors and their unintended consequences. We can now clearly see how the Masters manipulated the masses into a commodity. By doing so, they took away our true freedom of choice by brainwashing us, blinding us. We now have the opportunity to move forward with eyes open. This is where the Burning Man principle of decommodification is crucial. It states that 'in order to preserve the spirit of gifting, our community seeks to create social environments that are unmediated by commercial sponsorships, transactions, or advertising. We stand ready to protect our culture from such exploitation. We resist the substitution of consumption for participatory experience.'

"This principle and widespread education are essential to ensure optimal health for the majority of humankind. Should we force people to comply? Absolutely not! People must have the right to choose. However, choice must be differentiated from coercion and brainwashing. We have an opportunity here. I for one look forward to our shared future. Thank you for your attention!"

"Bravo!" Someone in the headquarters shouted. Many people on the screens and in the headquarters were clapping. Bodhi blushed and smiled. There were clearly faces on the screens who were notable upset and going through the stages of rejection, anger and horror with which Bodhi was very familiar.

"That was amazing," Adya said as she embraced him. "It was such a powerful message. I wasn't expecting that."

"What were you expecting?" Bodhi asked.

"I don't know," Adya said. "Doctor stuff?"

"Ahhh!" Bodhi beamed. "You thought I was just another pretty face!"

"Something like that," Adya beamed. Dr. Albright was trying to get everyone's attention.

"Thank you, Dr. McKenna," she said. "That was a very interesting and provocative perspective. I'm sure that your presentation will lend itself to lively discussions. We'll meet again in four days to present the group summaries and decide if a course of action is warranted. Thank you!"

PART 9:
KOYAANISQUATSI
REVISITED

KOYAANISQUATSI REVISITED

It was the end of May 2024. Bodhi had consistently visited his mother who was now 95. She remained in good health but rarely went out because she had difficulty walking. He would often take her out in her wheelchair and share time with her. His sister would join them with her dog Mickey. They all enjoyed these moments together. Bodhi was now so busy that he hadn't visited her in almost two months. He stayed in touch via zoom but it was obvious that she missed his visits.

Adya was also very busy with work. They both had a lot of responsibilities and were spread very thin in many directions. They would see each other at the headquarters and sometimes participated in the same meetings, but struggled to find time for each other. Their contact was limited to winks and smiles. By the time they arrived home late at night, they were both exhausted. They made the effort to at least have a drink together to connect before succumbing to the overwhelming exhaustion calling them to sleep. They discussed the challenges they faced on the world stage and the important strides they were making. They congratulated each other with toasts and cheers to distract themselves from what their hearts were screaming to say: "We want more time together!" Their honeymoon was definitely over.

The Covid-19 pandemic presented the world with so many opportunities in the wake of 4 billion deaths. They both recognized the importance of what they were doing. It was an historical moment where humankind for the very first time in its history had the opportunity to consciously author its future. No one had concrete answers but many great minds were galvanized to create a new world based on love, respect, compassion, personal responsibility and stewardship of mother earth. They were unequivocally aware that they would make horrible mistakes along the way, but they had no doubt that they were starting from sound principles on which to rebuild the world. What was key to them was making conscious decisions, assessing the outcomes and then making conscious corrections. What they wanted to avoid at all cost was the path that had led them to their pre-Covid reality where short-sighted decisions based on selfish motives were made that led to future unintended consequences that were too complex to unravel.

They were both caught up as contributing authors of that historic moment that future generations would look back in veneration. There was excitement in being such integral players in such an auspicious moment but something was missing. After their drink they both showered and promptly fell asleep as soon as their heads hit their pillows. They awakened feeling tired despite sleeping enough. They gravitated towards each other in the morning and cuddled. Their lips explored each other's bodies looking for the "on" button. Their hands feverishly roamed over mapped and encoded pathways but the codes were no longer valid. The curve that led to the valley just to the left of a particular prominence that formerly prompted that well-known response was somehow displaced. It was as though the operating system had been upgraded and all the former codes and passwords were no longer functional.

The lovemaking that had given them wings to explore their inner dimensions and outer universes was now grounded and vanilla. It was still physically satisfying, but utterly bankrupt after their prior experience of surfing the energetic monster waves of their chandelier-monkey-sex. This was the life that Adya eluded by dropping out of Harvard Law School and Bodhi so willingly gave up when leaving emergency medicine. The lofty cause of writing history blinded them from the 20/20 vision gifted to them by Covid-19. They were now living the *metro-boulot-dodo* lives that led so many to automated Hara-kiri.

They both rationalized that the lack of passion and their uninspired vanilla sex was the result of working long hours and stress. What they feared was that it was the crash after their wild infatuation. The former offered hope of returning to that state of Tantric bliss. The latter a curse.

"What do you have going on today?" Bodhi asked.

"Arghh!" Adya exclaimed. "I really don't want to talk about it." Bodhi put his coffee down and pulled his chair closer to hers. He gave her a big hug.

"What's up?" Bodhi asked.

"Roadblocks," Adya shared. "Roadblocks after roadblocks. It's fucking exhausting!"

"Believe me," Bodhi offered. "I know exactly what you mean. What's this one about?"

"We're working on ideas for the future global economy," Adya started, "and we're making great progress. Everyone throwing out great ideas. I've never sculpted anything but I was thinking about Michelangelo saying that all sculptures are already present in the slab of marble and the job of the artist is to chisel away at everything that's not the final product."

"Did Michelangelo actually say that?" Bodhi asked jokingly.

"How the fuck do I know?" Adya replied, almost pushing him off his seat. They laughed. "Anyway. You get the idea. We're making solid progress. It feels great!"

"Okay," Bodhi said. "What's the problem?"

"The problem," Adya responds, "is this dick Dutch dude

who used to be a banker working for the European Union. He keeps throwing monkey wrenches in every idea presented and the group came to a screeching stop."

"What is he proposing?" Bodhi asked.

"He basically wants to go back to the old ways of doing business." Adya replied. "He expects every country to pull themselves up by their own bootstraps. No matter what anyone else proposes, no matter how visionary the idea, he manages to bring everyone back to the old 'haves and have nots' anachronistic notions. He feels that he has some obligation to represent and uphold the old guard."

"So, fuck 'im!" Bodhi stated matter-of-factly. "We had a woman with a similar vibe and I finally called for a vote to censure her since she contributed absolutely nothing and impeded progress."

"That's terrible!" Adya exclaimed. "You can't do that. It'll shut others from speaking up and limits inclusivity."

"Really?" Bodhi asked.

"Absolutely! We want everyone's participation, even when we don't agree with their ideas."

"Sorry love," Bodhi replied. He got up and moved his chair back to its place. "I disagree. There's a point where people like this just create paralysis. Isn't that exactly what's frustrating you?" Adya was about to reply when Bodhi stood up and asked if she wanted another Americano. She nodded yes and continued.

"But if we censure people now," Adya continued, "it sets the precedent that we use this whenever someone says something we disagree with." Bodhi smiled and nonchalantly pressed the coffee into the portafilter basket. He then twisted it onto the Venus and turned it on. He continued to look at her with a smile as the Venus hissed pushing the water through the tightly packed coffee. Adya appeared impatient and was not amused by his condescending smile. He waited until the cups were half filled and then steamed water to fill the cups. He got one cube of ice from the freezer, dropped it into her cup and sprinkled some cinnamon into her cup. This was exactly how she liked it.

"I understand and acknowledge your perspective," Bodhi said, "but I disagree. There's a point where your desire for inclusivity gets in the way of efficiency and progress. This is where leadership is most important. It's knowing..."

"Are you questioning my ability to lead?" Adya asked. "Is that what you're saying?"

"No Adya," Bodhi replied. "Not at all. I've seen you lead and you have outstanding leadership skills. What I'm saying is that leadership sometimes requires setting boundaries. Remember the first meeting I sat in with you? That guy who kept trolling you. Remember?" Adya nodded yes. "Well, the way Uzoma shut him down was leadership. You tried to include him in the conversation but it was clear to Uzoma and everyone else that he wasn't capable or, at least at that point willing to move forward. You gave him several opportunities and when he continued to be a troll, Uzoma 'censured' him. She then gave him the avenue to return and participate. That's leadership." There was a long pause and they alternated between staring at each other and sipping their Americano's.

Adya closed her eyes for a second and when she opened them half-smiled and then took Bodhi's hand. "I'm really sorry," she said. "I'm just exhausted and on edge." Bodhi took her other hand and smiled sympathetically. "Now say thank you," he said. She gave him a strange look and asked: "Thank you for what?" Bodhi's smile broadened and he replied: "For being such a good mirror." She nodded yes and smiled: "Thanks for the reminder."

Adya looked at her smartphone and remarked: "Hey! We have a meeting in 5 minutes!"

"I know," Bodhi said. "I was hoping we could skip it and just luxuriate in bed. It's been forever since we did that. I miss you." Adya turned her chair towards him and embraced him. "I miss you too love. Let's make some time soon."

"Now you sound like one of those corporate wellness

gurus," Bodhi said. Adya seemed surprised and annoyed.

"How so?" She asked.

"In those crazy pre-Covid, *Koyaanisquatsi* times," Bodhi explained. "These wellness gurus would come around with advice to help maintain corporate sanity and work-life balance." Adya raised both hands and asked: "And what does that have to do with me?"

Bodhi continued: "One of the things they advised was to schedule time for family and loved ones. They insisted that this time should be scheduled in a calendar just like appointments and meetings. That's *Koyaanisquatsi!* What you just said reminded me of that." Adya just *looked* at him blankly and was about to get up. Bodhi gently grabbed her arm. She was standing directly in front of him. He looked up at her with a helpless look on his face, similar to a little boy who was asking for help from his mother. "Do you think we're slipping back into *Koyaanisquatsi?*" Adya took a deep breath, frowned and raised her shoulders. Bodhi was still looking into her eyes trying to figure out if her gesture was intended to mean that she didn't know, or that she didn't care.

"We have to get going," Adya said as she pulled him up from his seat. "Today's meeting is really important and I don't want to be late." He followed her as she hurried out of the apartment.

LOVER'S QUARREL

Headquarters was jammed packed with people when they arrived and all the screens were populated by multiple participants. Ms. Rethabile Khumalo rang a bell to get everyone's attention. "I think everyone is here. Let's get started."

Ms. Khumalo was a South African woman in her late fifties. She grew up in South Africa during apartheid and dedicated her life to social justice. One of her great joys and accomplishments in life that she mentioned whenever given the opportunity was working with Nelson Mandela. She was highly intelligent, talented, witty, and had the capacity to immediately understand the big picture. She was a natural born leader with great vision that was time and time again thwarted by racism, sexism, political expediency and lack of vision. Consequently, her life could be summarized by repetitively running full-speed into solid brick walls, getting up and doing it again, always hopeful for a different outcome. The Covid-19 pandemic was the blessing she never dared to wish for, but was nonetheless welcomed with open arms for the opportunity it presented. She was further blessed that she was now surrounded by people all over the world that sought another way of life, another modus operandi.

Ms. Khumalo started by saying: "First I would like to thank everyone for their hard work and commitment. We've made significant strides towards rebuilding a world in which

LOVE IN THE TIME OF CORONAVIRUS

everyone can thrive and achieve their full potential. There were many valid concerns raised during this process, the most important of which was the fear of a world government that would impose its will on the world and stifle the sovereignty of individual nations. We were able to convincingly demonstrate that this is not our intention. On the contrary, we all agree that individuality of ideas, religion, culture are crucial breeding grounds for ingenuity and creativity. We want to encourage, foster, and if necessary, fight for this freedom because it is human.

"We now stand at the brink of the history of humankind. Looking back, it seems so obvious that we were not at all living in the present moment. We were simply following paths that were charted centuries before, even when they no longer held meaning and only served a smaller and smaller segment of humankind. Those ancient pathways are now nothing more than sand mandalas and their memory now serve as important reminders of where we went wrong. They have taught us to avoid the anachronistic attitude of rampant nationalism that creates an us versus them mentality. I believe that we can all appreciate that this type of nationalism did not lend itself toward a safe and inviting world that nurtured humankind and the planet.

"Countries are free to do as they please as long as they don't engage in activities that harm others or the planet. Yes to sovereignty and self-determination. Anything else would be an abomination and contrary to human nature. History has provided us with ample evidence that no one can subjugate anyone, whether an individual or a nation, without negative repercussions. Our goal is to build a world that encourages economic, intellectual and spiritual growth. A world that establishes and promotes profound connection with our neighbors and the planet. Will we make mistakes? Absolutely! But hopefully we never forget that what we are doing, that we ourselves in fact, are a work in progress. Nonetheless, we are not operating in a vacuum. We are here today because of the

Covid pandemic. Despite the horror of losing more than half of our brothers and sisters worldwide to the pandemic, it has provided us with a tremendous challenge and opportunity. We are answering that call. We may not know exactly where we are going, but I believe that we can unanimously agree that we don't want to go back to the same path that we were on before.

"As I mentioned before, we've made great progress. The areas that are for the most part settled and ready for implementation globally are the following: A global digital currency; eradication of all debt; free healthcare for all; eradication of world hunger by redistribution of resources and relocating willing communities to fertile areas or cities of their choice; improving the world food supply in regards to both quantity and quality by implementing sustainable farming techniques; addressing climate change with 100% commitment to renewable energy and the eradication of fossil fuels as a source of energy, reforestation and stopping desertification; developing a circular economy; rebuilding communities where necessary; and universal education and vocational schools.

"The following areas have been more challenging: "Universal basic income; establishing a global minimum wage; eradication of borders and open immigration; prohibiting marketing of substances known to cause harm, such as junk food and cigarettes; and redistribution of wealth and resources. Based on our prior discussions, I believe that this last point is going to be the most challenging. I only ask you to keep in mind that much of the wealth and resources that belonged to individuals were liberated by the death of their owners and families. This is similar to the accumulated wealth and assets of some corporations that dissolved secondary to the pandemic. The proposed idea is to redistribute those resources to allow for a level playing field. It also raises the question of ownership of natural resources that for the most part had been usurped by wars and economic coercion.

"Let's break up into our assigned groups and tackle these issues. My advice is to not become discouraged. These are tough issues and we're on the brink of human history without any precedents to follow. Be patient with yourselves and with each other. Lastly, don't lose sight of the fact that all your sweat and hard work is not for the purpose of breaking bricks, but rather, building cathedrals."

Everyone slowly got up and headed to break-out rooms. There was a fog of fatigue that hovered above their heads and visible over the heads of those on the computer screens. The truth of their situation that was previously clouded by the joy of survival and enthusiasm of their common lofty goals had percolated to the surface: World building is difficult!

The meetings appeared to go well. Many ideas were shared and the overall feeling was positive as progress was being made. Adya was noticeably upset and rushed out of headquarters immediately after the meeting without saying goodbye to anyone. She didn't wait for Bodhi. Bodhi started to follow her but someone stopped him to talk about something he had said during the meeting. What started out as a simple conversation between the two of them turned into a major discussion. A large group formed around them and some digital participants also chimed in. Bodhi desperately wanted to catch up to Adya but he didn't want to be rude. Rather than have a piecemeal conversation, Bodhi invited everyone to sit down. He reiterated the background of the conversation, what he had said during the meeting, and then the question that was posed for the benefit of those who only caught bits and pieces. It was an extremely productive conversation that didn't necessarily provide any answers but provided a meaningful context to frame the ongoing discussion. Once Bodhi felt that it was appropriate, he excused himself and rushed upstairs to their apartment.

Adya was sitting on the terrace. There was a beer on the table that was half finished and a sandwich. Bodhi realized that he had not eaten yet and was in fact starving. He walked over to her and bent over to kiss her. Adya turned her cheek.

"Why did you do that?" Adya asked sternly.

"What are you talking about? Bodhi asked. Adya looked at him and smirked.

"Really?" She replied.

"Babe. Just say it. What did I do? Whatever it is, I can tell you that it wasn't my intention to hurt you or piss you off." Bodhi pulled a chair next to her and tried to take her hand. She pulled away.

"You cut me off several times and then contradicted me in public." Adya said.

"Adya." Bodhi started. "Are you..."

"And when I tried to clarify my point," Adya interrupted, "you started to mansplain. What the fuck?"

"Adya," Bodhi said. "That wasn't my intention. I just wanted to..."

"To what?" Adya interrupted again. "To embarrass me? To make a total ass of yourself?"

"Can I..."

"No!" Adya exclaimed. "Would you have done that to a man?"

"Done what?" Bodhi asked. "All I did was to ask you for a clarification? I then went on to state what I thought I understood you were saying. What's wrong with that?"

"It was your constant interruptions to ask questions and then not wait for my response." Adya responded. "It was your fucking condescending tone, asshole. You know better than anyone else what I've accomplished and yet you felt the need to mansplain me. What were you thinking?"

Bodhi leaned over to hug her but she pushed him away so hard that he almost fell out of his chair. Adya got up to leave the table. Bodhi stood up and grabbed her arm with his left hand. She instinctively took his hand and twisted it in such a fashion that his entire body flipped and splattered on the floor. Bodhi was noticeably stunned. Just as he reached for the back of his head where it struck the ground, he screamed out in pain and held onto his left shoulder with his other hand.

"Are you out of your fucking mind?" Bodhi screamed as he rocked himself slowly on his side. Adya just stood over him dispassionately. "So what's next? Are you going to chop my head off? Is that your idea of conflict resolution?" Adya turned around and walked out of the apartment.

Bodhi just lay there for a long while. His shoulder was still throbbing in pain but he was able to move it so he at least knew it wasn't dislocated. He was still stunned and couldn't believe what had happened. He slowly got himself up and sat down. The impact was on his back and his head, and his shoulder was strained, but every part of his body was in pain. He reached for the beer that Adya left on the table with his left hand and a sharp pain shot through his shoulder. He doubled over, gasping. After a few deep breaths, the pain diminished to a low-grade throb. He grabbed the beer with his other hand and took a gulp. It was a bit on the warm side but despite the gravity of his situation, he mentally commented on how really good it was for a home brew.

The pain settled down just enough for him to feel the grumbling in his stomach. He was now starving. Adya had left her half-eaten venison-spinach-tomato-avocado sandwich on the table. He struggled to pick it up with one hand and not let it fall apart, so he settled on lowering his head to the plate and took a big bite. It was delicious. All of a sudden Bodhi started to feel jittery and started to tremble. He wondered if he was hypoglycemic but rationalized that this was unlikely since he just took a bite of food and had some beer. Just in case, he took another big bite and washed it down with another gulp of beer. He was still jittery. He came to the conclusion that it likely the adrenaline rush over having just having his ass kicked by the love of his life and spiritual partner.

Bodhi finished the sandwich and beer and without much thought went upstairs, packed up his stuff, and left. There was no thought process or weighing of pros and cons. It was the violence. He had some male friends when he was younger who had physically assaulted their partners. This was before he became an emergency physician and learned about the psychology and ramifications of domestic violence. He then witnessed his fair share of domestic violence during his years of practice as an emergency physician. He knew everything there was to know about it and he always had a great deal of compassion for its victims. From his younger days, he promised himself that he would rather leave a relationship before entering into the cycle of violence. Well, here he was. He just had never entertained the possibility that he would be the victim.

BACK TO THE 'HOOD

Bodhi moved back to his apartment on the Upper West Side. Upon his return, it dawned on him that this was the first time in his life that he had moved away from this neighborhood. He lived on that same block since he was six years old. What was most remarkable to him was that nothing had really changed. It was as though the entire neighborhood was frozen in time. It wasn't just the time he had been living with Adya, but the time since his childhood. He joked over the years that a pigeon could randomly poop anywhere in the neighborhood and he'd have a story in his lifetime that occurred on that same spot. He acknowledged that there were superficial changes. Stores that were present from his childhood had disappeared and different stores would pop up over the years. Then they were all closed and shuttered after the Second Wave and now life was being breathed back into them. He was sure that everything must have appeared very different from a birds-eye view in light of the food gardens on every roof. Nonetheless, the neighborhood appeared exactly as it did to his six-year-old eyes. What he also recognized was that he had in fact changed.

Everyone was really happy to see Bodhi and expressed how much they missed him. Especially his mother and sister. He accepted invitations to share time with old friends and attended community gatherings when pressed. Everyone was apparently following the global plans that were being discussed on the internet and Bodhi's contribution. They were proud of him and considered him their own. When asked if his return was permanent, he simply said that he needed a break from the intense work he was doing. They must have sensed that something was wrong because no one asked about Adya.

For the most part, Bodhi stayed in his apartment. He exercised, maintained his yoga practice and meditated. Since returning to the Upper West Side, Bodhi was not sleeping well. Rather than tossing and turning in bed, he would take long walks down Riverside Park along the Hudson River. He would often just sit on a bench and stare out over the river. This park meant so much to him and carried so much history. His mother never had enough money to take him and his sister on vacations so his entire childhood was spent in the neighborhood and on Riverside Park. He remembered playing on the swings, slides, monkey bars and see-saw as a child and then played basketball and handball on 110th street when he was older. This was later followed by long jogs along the river with his German Shepard. This was before the bike and walking path was constructed along the entire length of river. When Bodhi later had children, he repeated these same steps with them. By then, the city had constructed "Hudson Beach" at the lower level of the park on 104th street.

Bodhi's feet naturally led him there as he was swept away by his memories. He surveyed the area. There was a large area with sand in which there were two rows of rings on which to swing. One for kids and the other for adults. The sandbox was also large enough for a beach volleyball area and other activities. That entire area was bordered on the north and south by two large fields where Bodhi had played baseball, football and soccer as a kid, and the Westside Highway and Hudson River on the west. The east of the area was immediately bordered by amphitheater style concrete seats where parents would picnic and watch the kids. There was a large area surrounding the sandbox that was simply concrete. There were two concrete ping pong tables just to the southeast of the sandbox and a larger area where people also played volleyball. Bodhi remembered this area when he was a kid. The amphitheater seating was present but the entire area was just concrete. The volleyball games on the concrete were the only activity that carried over. This was something else that didn't change. The people who played volleyball back then and now were Mexicans and South Americans who were for the most part in their sixties. Then as now, they played with gusto and quite well.

The area just above the steps was dominated by a walking area and four beautiful arches. Once the area became very popular and consistently filled with families, athletes, volleyball and ping pong ball players, a restaurant opened up under the arches. Tables were set in the walking area above the steps as well as in the area above the arches. Even more people came now to simply sit, have lunch or dinner, or just grab a drink. It was a beautiful scene.

What made Hudson Beach so beautiful was the swinging area. There were some really talented individuals who would do truly amazing and beautiful things swinging from ring to ring. It was aerial ballet. Everyone lined up to take turns and the children tried to emulate what these aerial artists were doing. One person in particular, David Scott, became a legend. He was one of the aerial artists who was always on the rings and his performances were spectacular. He was recognized by everyone as the best. What made him so special was the fact that he spent most of the day playing with the kids and teaching them how to swing on the rings and do the remarkable feats that he was doing. Bodhi remembered that many parents didn't at first accept his offering. David was black, and it was obvious by the way he moved and spoke that he was from the 'hood. The parents were noticeably uncomfortable that he was touching, lifting and carrying their kids on the rings.

Bodhi immediately understood what was going on because he himself had experienced this. His kids loved to play tickle monster with him. They had frequented another park called the Dinosaur Park when his kids were around the age of four and six, on 96th street and Riverside Park. The Dinosaur Park had great swings, slides and a sprinkler area. Whenever Bodhi was in the park with his kids, they would gather all their newfound friends and insist that Bodhi play tickle monster with them. They loved it and learned to love Bodhi. A few years later, those same kids were now ten years old and still insisted that he play tickle monster with them. At first he did, but then stopped after catching the glimpses of those same parents who knew him for so many years casting disapproving looks as he tickled their children. It was one of the great disappointments for his kids and their friends when he told them that he could no longer be the tickle monster. It wasn't until they were much older that he explained that his fear was being accused of child molestation. Bodhi was saddened but understood, because he certainly wouldn't feel comfortable having some grown man tickle his prepubescent daughters.

Bodhi saw the beauty in what David was doing and it was not surprising how quickly the kids fell in love with him. What was truly remarkable was the fact that the parents got over their initial fears and fell in love with him too. Perhaps they sensed his kindness and gentleness with the kids. Perhaps it was his dedication to teaching them and how quickly they learned. In no time, those same kids were performing remarkable aerial feats. David restored Bodhi's faith in humanity. Through David, Bodhi was able to witness how a community could get over their racism, prejudices, fears and embrace a black man who was a truly remarkable human being. This miracle however, was too good to last. A few years later, after David had already become a legend at the Hudson Beach, he stopped showing up. The kids were distraught. It was learned shortly afterwards that David died. He apparently had some medical problems and died of a heart attack. This shocked everyone because he didn't look a day over 40, but was already 50-years-old. This was a sad moment for the community. His contribution and the love everyone had for him was commemorated with a plaque on the concrete steps in front of rings.

What stood out the most in Bodhi's memory was how this beautiful environment was transformed on Saturdays and Sundays. There was this man who Bodhi later learned always wanted to be a circus performer. His dream was never realized and he instead became a successful Wall Street lawyer. Nonetheless, he never lost the passion for his dream and had a large collection of hula hoops, juggling pins, pogo sticks, and other circus paraphernalia. He also had tight ropes that he extended across the metal beams that supported the rings and a large supply of colorful drapes with which he decorated the entire area. He had an arrangement with the restaurant and they let him store all his equipment in their storage area. He also brought out two large speakers and played music. Hudson Beach was already a very special place and he transformed it into a magical playground for both adults and children.

Sitting on the steps of Hudson Beach, Bodhi's life flashed before him. He was taken on a journey traveling through all the different moments that landed him in the here and now. All of a sudden, he burst into the tears. He realized that this journey had culminated in his relationship with Adya. It was as though every moment in his life was for the purpose of preparing him for his relationship with her. For the first time in his life, Bodhi had felt so happy, whole and authentic. Now there was an emptiness that grew from within and engulfed him. It dissolved whatever meaning or purpose that Covid-19 had temporarily provided.

At first, he considered that his deep love for her was nothing more than an infatuation based on their dramatic meeting. With the instability that everyone who had survived the near mass extinction event was feeling, it would take a truly remarkable and rare individual to come out of that experience unscathed. Falling in love was the last thing on anyone's mind or list of expectations. It was all about survival and then finding meaning in one's life. Then there was the adrenaline explosion of having a noose around his neck. Bodhi remembered standing on top of that car. Its engine was revving and Junior was counting down to the hour of 7 O'clock to have everyone cheer for him as he was hung. This was so intense because there were so many mixed emotions that erupted into an overwhelming feeling of cognitive dissonance. Even though he intellectually knew that there wasn't anything anyone could do in that circumstance, there were still feelings of betrayal over the fact that no one dared stand up for him after everything he had done for the community. There was the feeling of never having felt appreciated as a physician contrasted by the cheering and applause every day at 7 O'clock to honor frontline providers. Now everyone gathered around to cheer for him at 7 O'clock as he died of strangulation from a light pole that he had stood under since the age of six. This was intense enough, but then to have Adya, a beautiful goddess in black leather swoop in and save his life at the very last second, praise him and belittle the community for being cowards for not stepping up to save him. The icing on the cake was the dramatic manner in which Adya chopped Junior's head off.

Was what Bodhi believed to be love for Adya just a form of hero worship? Bodhi then recalled asking her to return so he could tend to her wound and she asked him if he was asking her on a date. Wow! It was as though he were watching himself in an old Humphrey Bogart- Lauren Bacall movie where Bacall threw out those classic lines in rapid fire. Adya had swept him off his feet.

Bodhi's tears flowed as the reel of their romance rolled in his head. It seemed like such a set up in retrospect. First her cinematic entrance into his life and then the starring role of playing doctor to save her life from septic shock. This was as dramatic as you can get and still suspend disbelief. But then again, the boundaries of what was believable had already been stretched impossibly thin with the near mass extinction of humankind. If all of this wasn't enough, she also gave him a much grander meaning and purpose in his life that extended beyond his small Upper West Side community and onto the global stage.

Bodhi wiped the tears from his eyes with his sleeve and blew out the accumulated snot from his nose. Then again, he thought to himself, all of this was complete bullshit when compared to the most mind-blowing sex he ever had in his entire life. It was all too good to be true. The stuff infatuation is made of. Bodhi acknowledged that infatuation may have been the flicker that started the fire, but the forest fire that completed consumed him was love.

So what happened? He thought to himself. The emotions of grief and pain now transformed to anger. *What the fuck? What was all the talk about spiritual partnerships? Serving as mirrors for each other? All bullshit!* Bodhi just sat there crying out his pain into the soft breeze of the Hudson River. He wondered if the breeze would deliver all the emotion each tear carried to some anguished artist who would then transmute them into a poem.

THE BREAK-IN

Two months had passed and Bodhi drifted deeper into his depression. He barely came out of his apartment. He refused all invitations and didn't want to speak to anyone. He was barely eating and had lost a lot of weight. His friends became more and more concerned. They didn't have Adya's direct contact but had some connections in her community. They reached out and expressed their concern. Two days later, a few friends from Adya's Brooklyn community knocked on his door. He didn't answer.

"Bodhi!" Tristan yelled. "Please open the door. We know you're in there. Please." There was no answer. Giovanna stepped up to the door and knocked gently.

"Bodhi," Giovanna pleaded. "We know you're going through a lot. You're not alone. Just open the door. We just want to talk." There was no sound coming from the apartment.

"You think he's in danger?" Dahlia asked.

"This is bullshit!" Phineas exclaimed. "I say we break the door down." They all looked at each other for consensus.

"I'm with Phineas," Giovanna said.

"Before we go Rambo," Tristan said. "Let me see if I can get in through his fire escape. I'll text you." They all nodded.

"I'm coming with you," Giovanna insisted. Giovanna and Tristan walked up to the sixth floor and opened the door to the roof. They climbed down the fire escape stairs to the fourth floor. There were two doors on each landing to two apartments. Bodhi's door was locked. They leaned over the fire escape railing and noted that there was an air conditioner and his window that was partially open above it. The window was at a 110-degree angle from the fire escape. The window ledge was only about one foot away and two feet lower than the fire escape railing.

"What do you think?" Tristan said as he looked down the four flights.

"I don't think it's a good idea," Giovanna said. "Too dangerous. Let's go back and break the door down."

"I think I can make it," Tristan said.

"Dude!" Giovanna exclaimed. "The air conditioner takes up half the window and there's hardly any ledge."

Tristan pointed to the window. "Look on top of the air conditioner. There's a metal bar that prevents it from falling. All I have to do is lean over and grab it. I can then get my knee on the ledge, push the window open and get inside."

"Why, Tristan?" Giovanna asked. "Why take the risk?" Tristan smiled and kissed Giovanna hard on the lips.

"Because I love you," Tristan said, "and always have to find ways to impress you."

"That's some stupid-ass-shit!" Giovanna exclaimed. "Let's go back and join the others."

"Listen," Tristan said. "It's only two feet away. If it looks dodgy once I'm there I'll come back okay?" Giovanna smirked and shook her head no. Tristan stepped up on the fire escape railing. He stabilized himself holding Giovanna's hand and reached the metal bar on top of the window with his right hand. He tried to get his right knee onto the small window ledge but couldn't reach it.

"Abort Tristan!" Giovanna demanded. "Abort now!" Tristan let go of her hand and stepped off the fire escape railing. He was now dangling from the metal bar with only his right hand. Giovanna gasped and tried to reach him but couldn't. Tristan quickly grabbed the metal bar with his left hand and pulled himself high enough to get his knees on the ledge. He then pushed the window open high enough to get his head in and with the back of the neck opened it even more. He crawled into the apartment and quickly opened the fire escape door for Giovanna.

"Cake!" Tristan exclaimed. Giovanna threw her arms around his neck and held him tight.

"That's it!" Giovanna stated. "That's the last time. I love you too much to watch you risk your life for nonsense. Promise me now or we're done." Tristan had his arms around her waist and leaned back to look at her.

"I love you so much," Tristan said as he kissed her face. "I promise. No more risk taking unless if it's absolutely necessary." Giovanna stared at him as though judging his sincerity. "Okay then. Let's find Bodhi." They walked out of that empty bedroom. Tristan went to the front of the apartment to open the door for Dahlia and Phineas while Giovanna looked through the rest of the apartment. It was a mess. She then walked into the other bedroom and immediately saw Bodhi sitting in half-lotus position with his back to the door. He was wearing over-the-ear headphones and eye shields.

"Bodhi!" Giovanna called out. Bodhi didn't move. Tristan, Phineas and Dahlia heard Giovanna's voice and entered the room. Bodhi was perfectly still.

"Bodhi!" Phineas screamed out even louder. No response. Dahlia walked into the room and stood directly in front of Bodhi and clapped her hands loudly in front of his face. No response. Dahlia squatted in front of Bodhi, picked up his smartphone and paused whatever he was listening to. Bodhi's hand reached out to the floor and tried to feel for his smartphone that Dahlia was still holding. Giovanna started to laugh and covered her mouth to contain herself. Bodhi took off his eye shield and immediately saw Dahlia squatting in front of him. He smiled broadly and took off his headphones. Dahlia kneeled in front of him and threw her arms around him.

"We were so worried about you," Dahlia said. They embraced for a long time. Tristan, Phineas and Giovanna gathered around them, knelt down and hugged him tightly.

"How did you get in?" Bodhi asked.

"Through your window," Tristan replied.

"Why didn't you just knock?" Bodhi asked. They looked at each other and laughed.

"We almost broke your door down Bodhi!" Giovanna exclaimed.

"Oh!" Bodhi said as though surprised. "I was meditating with these headphones and listening to surf sounds. I couldn't hear a thing."

"No shit!" Phineas said. Bodhi stood up. He was only wearing shorts and appeared emaciated. His ribs were sticking out and his arms and legs just skin and bones.

"What's up?" Bodhi asked.

"You tell us," Tristan countered. "You just disappeared. We were all worried and Adya's been going crazy." Bodhi started to sit at the edge of the bed but then stood up and signaled that they should sit in the living room. His clothes were all over the place. Bodhi gathered his stuff, threw them behind the sofa and invited them to sit.

"I just needed some time by myself," Bodhi said. "Had to clear my head."

"When was the last time you ate?" Dahlia asked. "You look like a skeleton." Bodhi just smiled.

"I'm okay," Bodhi replied. "Really. I'm fine."

"I have an idea," Giovanna said. "A few of us are going out to the Hamptons tomorrow. It's a small group. Just a chill hang. Why don't you join us?" Bodhi just stared at them blankly. They all looked back and forth at each other as though confused.

"The house is right on the water," Giovanna said. "The fresh ocean air, the water and the food will do you some good. It'll just be a few of us." Bodhi continued to stare blankly at them.

"Adya won't be there," Giovanna added. "The change of scenery will do you some good." Bodhi started to shake his head no. Giovanna moved over next to him and put her arm around him. She continued: "Bodhi. We love you. We're not going to let you sit here and wither away." She jostled him firmly. "Please join us. It'll be good for you."

"Let's make this simple," Dahlia chimed in. "We'll be here first thing in the morning to pick you up. If you don't answer the door, we'll kick it open."

"Are you in?" Tristan asked. Bodhi shrugged and nodded yes.

"Great!" Giovanna exclaimed. "But for now, let's get you some food."

"Thanks," Bodhi said, "but I'm not hungry."

"Dude," Phineas said. "When was the last time you ate?" Bodhi looked away.

"Listen," Phineas continued. "Let's have lunch together. A small meal. Nothing fancy. Okay?" Bodhi nodded yes. Tristan looked through his kitchen and there wasn't any food.

"I have Bri's number," Giovanna stated. "She'll hook us up." Giovanna stepped into the other room and called Bri. After a few minutes, she returned to the living room and gave a thumbs up sign. "Bri's amazing!" Giovanna continued. "I just asked for some stuff to prepare lunch. She said she had just prepared lunch for her family and had plenty. She's going to bring it over."

"Sweet!" Phineas said. "I'm actually starving."

THE HAMPTONS

G iovanna was sitting next to Bodhi in the back of the car. Tristan was driving and Dahlia was in the front passenger seat. Phineas took another car with some of their other friends. It was a beautiful day. The sun was shining and the sky was bright blue with some scattered puffy white clouds. There were only a few cars on the road and they were driving at a good pace that would get them to the Hamptons before noon.

Bodhi was looking out the window. He hadn't said a word since they got into the car. Giovanna held his hand. Tristan and Dahlia were having a lively conversation about the pros and cons of the redistribution of wealth globally.

"Damn!" Tristan exclaimed loudly while hitting the steering wheel with his fist.

"What happened? Dahlia said in a startled tone. Even Bodhi turned his head rapidly toward Tristan.

"I forgot to bring the beer," Tristan said. "They specifically reminded me to bring the beer. Shit!" Dahlia was about to say something when Giovanna put her hand on Dahlia's shoulder, raised her index to her mouth and just smiled. Dahlia understood and smiled.

"We have to turn around," Tristan insisted.

"You're kidding right?" Giovanna asked. "We're already two hours out, which means that it'll take four hours to get back to this point with another two hours to go. No fucking way!"

"I agree with Giovanna," Dahlia said. "Don't worry about it. They'll understand."

"Okay then," Tristan said. "I'll drop you off and then go back."

"Why are you so bent out of shape about this?" Dahlia asked. Tristan sighed.

"Because it's the third time I went to their place and forgot to bring the beer they specifically asked for," Tristan responded. "They're going to think I'm a complete idiot and irresponsible."

"Don't worry about it my love," Giovanna answered while putting her hand on his shoulder. "Everyone already knows that you're a complete idiot, irresponsible and a fuck up."

"What?" Tristan snapped back.

"That's why I love you so much," Giovanna reassured him. "You're so special."

"Yeah," Dahlia added. "Special like the Special Olympics. We love you!" Giovanna and Dahlia burst out laughing and even Bodhi couldn't contain himself and started laughing. Tristan pulled over to the shoulder. He was noticeably frustrated and upset.

"Okay," he asked. "What's so funny?"

"We're just messing with you honey," Giovanna said in choppy words through her uncontrollable laughter. Bodhi was now doubled over laughing.

"Well, I'm happy to see that you're feeling better," Tristan said sarcastically. "Wanna let me in on the joke?" Giovanna took a second to control herself. She leaned forward, reached around Tristan's seat and hugged him really hard.

"I love you baby," she said. "We saw that you had left the beer and packed it. We were wondering when you'd remember." Tristan smiled broadly and nodded his head yes.

"Well, that's a relief," Tristan said. "And by the way, I'm happy to be the butt of your jokes if it puts a smile on my man

Bodhi's face." Bodhi continued to smile. Giovanna put her hand around his neck and pulled him into a hug.

"We're really happy you joined us," Giovanna said. Tristan reached back and scuffled Bodhi's hair.

"Yes!" Dahlia added. "Thank you for coming." Bodhi's head was buried in Giovanna's chest. He didn't say anything but had a big smile on his face.

They drove another two hours and pulled into a large driveway. The sun was high and it was scorching hot. They started to unpack the car when a young man with dyed blond long hair in a ponytail came out to greet them. The man beamed a bright smile and gave Giovanna, Dahlia and Tristan big hugs.

"Did you remember the beer?" he asked. They all burst out laughing as he was obviously in on the joke. He walked up to Bodhi and gave him a hug.

"And you must be Bodhi," he said. "We've heard so much about you. My name is Peter. *Mi casa es su casa*." Bodhi smiled. Peter continued: "It's hot as hell out here. Let's get everything inside, jump into the water, and have some drinks. I'm sure it's 5 O'clock somewhere in the world." They all laughed.

The house was absolutely beautiful. It was spacious and the decor was fabulous. The floors were a very light wood and the style was quite eclectic, reflecting a hodgepodge of modern, contemporary, Art Deco, and even minimalist design. The key feature of the living room were the large glass doors that opened onto a wooden patio that was directly on the beach. There were many windows and despite the stifling heat of the midday sun, there was a cool breeze circulating in the house. The space, large glass door and windows reminded him of Adya's apartment. That single thought of Adya's apartment just started to bounce around his head and multiply into a cascade of colliding and depressing thoughts. Just at that moment, Bodhi felt a tap on his shoulder and was startled.

"Sorry to startle you," Peter apologized. "I was calling you but you were deep in thought."

"I was just admiring your living room," Bodhi said. "It's fantastic. Are you a designer?"

"Thank you!" Peter said. "Only by injection." He was standing next to a tall, olive-skinned man with deep creases on his face and dark salt and pepper hair. "I'd like to introduce you to my husband Maximo. He's the designer." Maximo stepped forward, gave Bodhi a firm embrace and kissed both his cheeks.

"It's a pleasure to meet you," Bodhi said. "And thank you for having me."

"The pleasure is ours Bodhi," Maximo said in a thick Spanish accent. "We're well aware of the important work you're doing. I'm also very happy that you like my interior design."

"It's spectacular," Bodhi said.

"You know," Maximo continued. "I've been an interior designer my entire life. My work inspires me and my greatest joy is to provide people with a living space that inspires them. But this place is what inspires me. It's like an artist's palette that allows me to play and combine ideas whimsically. It keeps the creative juices flowing."

"And I'm sure it goes without saying," Peter interjected playfully, "that your amazing husband and the sound of the ocean contribute a tiny bit." Maximo laughed and gave Peter a big kiss.

"No darling," Maximo replied. "You are my only muse. Everything else just adds the highlights."

"Great!" Peter said. "Now that we're all on the same page, let's get wet!"

"I unfortunately didn't bring a bathing suit," Bodhi said.

"Neither did we!" Peter exclaimed and laughed. "Let's jump in." Peter and Maximo stripped butt naked and ran onto the beach. Giovanna, Tristan, and Dahlia had just come out of their rooms and saw them running into the water.

"Let's go!" Dahlia exclaimed. "Last one in cleans the dishes." They all took off their clothes and started to run to the beach. Giovanna turned around to see Bodhi standing there.

She went back, gave him a hug. She lifted his T-shirt off and started to open his shorts. He stopped her.

"Come on Bodhi!" Giovanna said. "When was the last time you tasted the water. You're going to love it." Bodhi looked at her and dropped his shorts. Giovanni was shocked to see how thin he was. If she hadn't known him so well, she wouldn't have recognized him in the street. She held him by the hand and dragged him to the water. He started to hesitate but she pulled him harder.

"Let's go straight in!" She said. "No hesitation." They got up to their knees in the water and dived in. The water was cold but incredibly refreshing. The waves were strong and tossed them back and forth. Bodhi felt invigorated. He felt great and was so happy at that moment. He smiled.

"Isn't this the best?" Tristan asked.

"It's perfect!" Bodhi exclaimed. They swam for a bit and then bodysurfed. Bodhi instantly felt different. The cold water shocked his body into a reset. The cloud that weighed on him was washed away by the waves, and he felt lighter and lighter with each wave that passed. He laughed and joked with everyone.

They remained in the water for a long time. They were shriveled and their lips were blue, but they were ecstatic. They lay in the sand and dried in the sun. They walked back to the house and cleaned the sand and salt water in the outdoor shower. Maximo gave them towels and they lounged on the deck chairs. Peter and Maximo went inside the house and returned with a pitcher and a tray with lots of small sandwiches, guacamole, humus and chips. Peter poured out glasses for everyone.

Dahlia raised her glass and toasted: "To your friendship and hospitality!" Everyone cheered.

"This is delicious!" Giovanna said.

"Isn't it?" Peter said. "It's my go to summer drink. Just watermelon, vodka, vermouth and mint. Very tasty, refreshing and just enough vodka to remind you that it's not fruit punch."

"He used to make them with less vodka and everyone would get plastered thinking they were drinking fruit juice," Maximo said. "It got ugly very quickly."

"It's perfect," Bodhi said. "Everything here is perfect. Thank you!"

"Thank you for joining us," Peter replied. They all cheered again.

"Listen up," Maximo said. "People will arrive around five and we'll barbecue around 7 O'clock. It may turn out to be a late night so Peter and I are going to take a nap. Feel free to do as you please. There's food in the fridge if you're hungry. See you in a bit."

"Ciao, ciao!" Peter waived as they walked inside holding hands.

"I wouldn't mind a nap," Tristan said to Giovanna. "What do you think?"

"Yeah," Giovanna replied. "Right after we finish our drinks."

Dahlia put her hand on Bodhi's arm. "And you?" she asked.

"I think I'll sit here for a while and then take another swim," Bodhi replied. "By the way, thank you. I haven't felt this great in a long time. Thanks to all of you."

"You're family Bodhi," Dahlia said. "We love you." Dahlia pulled Bodhi to his feet and gave him a big hug. Tristan and Giovanna waited and then each gave him a big hug.

"Rest up," Bodhi said. "I'll be back after a walk and swim." They hesitated to leave Bodhi alone but looked at each other and without words agreed to take their naps. It was already 3 O'clock and the sun wasn't as hot. Bodhi walked to the water and waded in. It was delightful. He swam out until he could no longer touch to bottom with his feet and then swam parallel to the shore. He used to be a great swimmer but was now winded after only 200 meters.

He turned on his back and floated for a while with his eyes closed. He just relaxed with the ebb and flow of the waves and the soft sun on his wet face. His reverie was interrupted by a large wave that tumbled him over. He had drifted out further than he intended and started to swim diagonally towards the shore. His arms were tired so he alternated between a crawl and breast stroke. Just as he passed from tired to exhausted, he felt the strong rip current pulling him out even further. There was a brief moment of panic because despite having been a strong swimmer, he recognized how weak he was in his current state. He allowed the panic to subside and looked at the receding shoreline. The rip current was too strong for him to swim diagonally back to shore so he very slowly swam parallel to the shoreline. He made it a point of not overly exerting himself so that he'd have enough energy to get back once he was out of the current.

Even at his slow pace, Bodhi's arms were getting really tired. He floated on his back for a while to rest. He appreciated the cold water and waves moving his body, and the sun shining on his face. The panic had dissipated. He knew that in the worst-case scenario, he could stay afloat without any effort until someone came to get him. Once rested, he looked up again and noted that he was indeed further out but the rip current wasn't as strong. He continued to swim parallel to the beach. After another 200 meters, he stopped and made note that he was out of the rip current. He slowly started to swim to shore. He was exhausted but now had the waves pushing him to shore. He finally made it to shore and was breathing heavily. He just threw himself on the sand and lay there on his back. *What an adventure!* He thought to himself. He lay there for a long while and even fell asleep for a while. He stood up and started to walk back in the direction of the house. He had no idea how far he drifted and didn't know the address. Nonetheless, he wasn't at all concerned and figured that he would recognize the house.

RECONCILIATION

Bodhi walked slowly with his feet in the water. He felt great. Surprisingly, he didn't think about Adya, his work and even what he was going to do the next day. He was just happy to be alive. His legs began to feel heavy so he sat down on the sand just far enough that the water covered his feet. He lay down again and closed his eyes. His mind was blank. There was only the awareness of the water hitting his feet, the cool sand under his body, the hot sun, and the sound of seagulls and the crashing waves. He drifted off to sleep again.

When he awakened the sun was just setting. He sat up and stared at the red sun as it slowly approached the horizon. It was magnificent. Bodhi thought he heard his name being called. He listened more carefully but could only hear the crashing waves. This thought did nonetheless make him realize that it was getting late and that he should start making his way back to the house. As he was getting up, he heard his name being called more clearly. He stood up and looked around but didn't see anyone.

Bodhi started to walk back with his feet in the water when he heard the voice again calling out his name. He couldn't mistake it. Bodhi turned around and saw Adya running towards him. Adya stopped immediately in front of him. She was panting and had tears in her eyes. He wondered if he was still sleeping on the beach and was having a lucid dream.

Adya threw her arms around him and held him tightly. Bodhi was frozen in time and space. His arms just dangled at his sides.

"Thank God you're okay!" Adya whispered in his ear. "We were all looking for you." Adya pulled away and held him by his shoulders. "I missed you so much." She embraced him again even more tightly. Her phone started ringing.

"Hello," Adya said. She took Bodhi's hand, held it tightly and never took her eyes from his as she spoke on the phone. "It's okay... I found him...He was sitting on the beach... We're not too far. We'll be back soon...Thanks." Adya hung up and let out a sigh of relief.

"We were really worried about you," Adya said. "What happened?"

"I fell asleep and just woke up," Bodhi replied. Adya smiled.

"Should we start walking back?" She asked. He nodded yes. She still held his hand. After a few steps, she stopped and stood immediately in front of him.

"Bodhi," Adya said. "I'm so sorry."

"What are you sorry about?" he asked.

"Everything," she replied. "Everything. I'm sorry about getting so consumed with my saving-the-world ego bullshit. Losing sight of us. Blaming you for something you didn't do. But most of all, hurting you physically." Adya now had tears in her eyes again. Bodhi wiped the tears from her cheeks. Adya continued: "I walked around a bit and when I returned to apologize, you were gone. I was devastated. How could you just leave like that?"

"Adya," Bodhi said very calmly. "You physically assaulted me. I hit my head really hard. You almost dislocated my shoulder. That's not reason enough?"

"I'm so sorry Bodhi," Adya said as she embraced him. "It was a reflex. I wasn't thinking." Bodhi stepped back and looked at her.

"You know," Bodhi said. "Every domestic violence perpetrator I saw in the ER said something very similar. That's the problem Adya. The fact that this reflex can manifest without even a thought is why I left. You're dangerous and I couldn't live with violence as a go-to for conflict resolution."

"I'm so sorry Bodhi," she repeated. "I'm so sorry." Bodhi continued walking with the waves rolling up gently on his ankles. The water felt warm and soothing. Adya walked by his side. They were silent. The only sounds were the waves crashing on the shore and the water splashing as they walked.

"So why are you here now?" Bodhi asked.

"I needed to see you," Adya responded. She took his hand as they walked. "I wanted to tell you I was sorry. I wanted to tell you how much I love you, how I've missed you and that I don't want to live without you."

"But why now Adya?" Bodhi asked. "It's been two months." Adya took a deep breath and blew it out.

"Well at first," she replied, "I felt so ashamed of myself. But when I saw that you packed up and left, I got really angry. I had the opportunity to go to Europe and then South America and Mexico. The purpose of the trip was to meet their leaders and talk about some of the sticking points we were facing."

"That sounds great," Bodhi commented.

"It was," Adya said. "But my heart wasn't in it. I was running away from you, from all the conflicting feelings that were erupting from deep inside. I was running away from myself."

"I'm sure you accomplished a lot," Bodhi said coldly. Adya indicated that they had arrived at the house.

"Hey," Adya said. "I really don't feel like being around a lot of people right now. Are you hungry?"

"Starving!" Bodhi exclaimed. "I haven't eaten since this afternoon."

"How about we get some chairs and some food?" Adya asked. "We can eat out here and talk. I have a lot to get off my chest. Is that okay?" Bodhi nodded yes.

"What do you feel like drinking?" Adya asked.

"Just water." They walked into the house and everyone

hugged Bodhi. He apologized and explained how he got caught in a strong rip current that took him very far away. He told them that he was completely exhausted after finally getting back to shore and then fell into a deep sleep on the beach and woke up to a glorious sunset. They were relieved that he was safe and even happier that he and Adya were talking. It took a lot of planning and effort to get the both of them in the same place without Bodhi knowing. They all gave each other high fives after Adya and Bodhi head to beach for their tryst.

Bodhi carried the two beach chairs and small folding table. In one hand Adya carried a tray with barbecue chicken, lobster, prawns with grilled vegetables and corn. In her other hand she carried a bag with a large bottle of water, glasses, plates and cutlery. They set up just next to the water. The waves were calm now and brightly lit with an almost full moon. They poured out the water and clinked glasses without a toast and sipped. They each served themselves and ate in silence.

"So, what happened?" Bodhi asked.

"I managed to keep myself distracted," Adya said, "but I was really hurting inside. I missed you so much." They refilled their glasses and both stared out into the ocean. Their attention was drawn to the bright white reflection cast by the moon on the shimmering waves that extended from the horizon to their feet.

"Then I had a really crazy experience," Adya said. "I was in Peru and the leader there asked if I was familiar with Ayahuasca. I had heard about it and had lots of friends who did it. There was actually a group that offered Ayahuasca at Burning Man. I considered doing it but changed my mind at the last minute. I convinced myself that Burning Man just didn't seem like the right environment, which was probably true but the reality was that I was just too scared."

"Did you do it?" Bodhi asked.

"I hesitated at first," Adya replied, "but I felt as though I was being called. I was with people I knew and trusted, and what better place than the Peruvian Amazon where Aya-huasca's been part of their culture for millennia. I also appreci-ated that it was done in such a traditional way and with such deep respect."

"What happened?" Bodhi asked.

"We started from Lima at 4am and took a two-hour car ride over shit roads to Pucallpa. We then took a 90-minute ride in one of those really narrow boats to where the ceremony was going to take place. We went really deep into the jungle. Once we arrived, the shaman spent a lot of time with us tell-ing us about Ayahuasca and the unconscious realms we would journey. He also gave us concoctions of what he called master plants to prepare us for the Ayahuasca ceremonies. On the sec-ond day, he gave us the Dragon's Herb, which was the worst."

"What's that?" Bodhi asked.

"Oh my God!" Adya exclaimed. "The shaman put this black powder in some water while blowing into the cup while mixing it. He gave us each about a teaspoon full. In about..."

"Sorry to interrupt," Bodhi said, "but how many of you went?"

"Nine," she responded. "After 15 minutes or so, every-one started vomiting. The shaman gave each of us a 5-gallon bucket of river water and told us to drink at a steady rhythm to keep up with the vomiting. It was supposed to be an energetic cleanse. Boy did it kick our asses." It was completely dark now except for the bright moon that stood out like a globe lamp in the sky. They picked at the food while talking.

"This is delicious," Bodhi said. "I was starving."

"I know it's not my place to say anything," Adya said, "but dude, you look like a skeleton. What's up with that?"

"It's a long story," Bodhi responded. "I'll tell you about it later. Finish your story first."

"Well," Adya continued. "The Dragon's Herb nearly killed me. I'd basically drink three glasses of the river water and it would come right back up. The first few times were super easy and painless, but it got harder and harder to keep the pace of drinking and the stomach spasms were extremely painful on an empty stomach. I drank almost three gallons before the spasms got better. The shaman let us go back to our huts in the jungle but the nausea and vomiting continued. I really just wanted to come home."

"Sounds horrible," Bodhi commented. "Why did you stay?"

"I felt that I was there for a reason and didn't want to miss the opportunity. We then had an Ayahuasca ceremony the following day and every other day after that. It was the craziest experience I ever had in my life." Bodhi was intrigued by Adya's experience in the jungle, but he was distracted by her beauty that glistened in the moonlight. Maybe it was because he missed her so much but she seemed so much more beautiful than before. Her features and mannerisms seemed softer, which made her seem larger than life in the moonlight.

"And then?" Bodhi asked.

"I just got back last week and I'm still processing, but it was deep," Adya replied. "It was an amazing, blissful, talk-to-God experience, and the feeling of being dragged through hell all rolled into one."

"Doesn't Ayahuasca make you vomit a lot too?" Bodhi asked.

"Yeah," she replied. "I vomited a bunch the first ceremony but only once or twice every ceremony after that. There were a few people who vomited nonstop. Holy shit!" She instinctive reached out and took his hand. They both felt awkward and stopped to look at each other for a moment.

"It's a lot to unpack," Adya continued, "but the main thing is that I learned so much about myself. I realized that I somehow felt guilty about my mother's death and wanted to do whatever it took to make my dad happy to make up for it." Tears started to well in her eyes. "I cried so much. I think I spent at least two full ceremonies bawling." Bodhi squeezed her hand and put the other on her knee.

"I never fully realized it but I saw as clear as day that all my dad had to do was suggest something and I'd jump into it. All that mattered to me was getting his approval." Adya was now sobbing. Bodhi handed her a napkin to wipe her eyes. She continued: "The thing is that he wasn't at all demanding and wasn't asking for anything unreasonable. I'm so grateful for everything he did for me and how he raised me. It's just that I was caught up in proving myself worthy that I never really developed a sense of self. It sounds crazy and I couldn't get my head around it but I realized that my sense of self was tied to my accomplishments and external validation. There was no real me. I was so empty inside." Adya started to bawl. Bodhi got on his knees and crawled between her legs. He put his arms around her and held her tight. She buried her head in his neck. He felt the tears running down his back. When she stopped crying so forcefully, he took another napkin and wiped her eyes.

Bodhi sat cross-legged in front of her seat on the sand and held her hand. "I understand so much now. That poor little girl was just trying so hard to make her father happy, but really just wanted to play. As I got older, I got really good at rationalizing everything away to make it work, but I left that poor little girl behind. She was in there the whole time just asking to be loved. She just needed a hug and to be told that she was enough just as she was. She needed so desperately to know that it wasn't necessary to do this or that to deserve love or to be recognized. Ayahuasca showed me, plain as day on an IMAX screen. I saw how I constructed layers and layers of reinforced brick wall to protect myself from the reality of never feeling I was enough and worthy of being loved."

"Adya," Bodhi said. "Did you ever doubt my love for you?" Adya wiped her tears with her forearm. She picked up her glass to drink but it was empty. Bodhi stood up to get the pitcher and filled their glasses. He again sat on the sand immediately in front of her. The reflection of the full moon filled her eyes against which he could see the waves coming and going.

"God! It's so much more complicated than that," Adya

answered as she took a gulp of water. "Intellectually," Adya pointed to her head, "I never, ever doubted you. Never. But subconsciously I'm just beginning to see how I couldn't trust you, or anyone else for that matter, because deep inside I felt that I wasn't good enough. I felt that I didn't deserve to be loved and if you loved me, there had to be something wrong with you." Adya took another gulp of water. "Everything was interpreted through that lens." Adya took Bodhi's face in her hands and kissed him deeply. "Bodhi, I am so sorry about what happened that day. I was so wrong at so many levels. I see that now and I'm sorry." Adya dropped to her knees in front of him and hugged him tightly. She pressed his head against her chest. Her pounding heart beat drowned out the sound of the waves.

"I'm only beginning to scratch the surface on this but what I now understand is that it was all about control. I had to be in control and constantly perform in order to feel validated. You were amazing because you gave me so much love and I felt so validated. I felt real. For the first time I felt truly and deeply loved." Bodhi squeezed her tight.

"It was real Adya," Bodhi said. "It is real." She separated herself from him, again held his face in her hands and looked deep in his eyes. She smiled.

"I always knew it was real," Adya continued. "But I constantly questioned it and thought it was too good to be true. You were too good to be true. Like I said before, I subconsciously felt that there had to be something wrong with you because you showed me so much love. You reached deep down inside, embraced and held space for that little girl that I had ignored and abandoned. I was always looking and expecting the true you to pop out of a box. It was a set up and although it was beyond my control, I'm sorry I did that." She again embraced him and held his head against her chest.

"I ran that scenario at the meeting over and over in my head," Adya said. She pushed her chair back and sat in front of him. They held hands. "Before the ceremony, I thought you were such an asshole and really believed that you were trying to undermine me at the meeting with your questions and mansplaining me. I get it now. I was seeing everything through that lens that was looking for proof that you didn't really love me. That lens allowed me to bend reality and twist your words to fit my narrative. After that it was a runaway train." Adya stroked Bodhi's hair with one hand and placed the other hand on his chest.

"After that it was one thought leading to another that created a boiling cauldron in my head of some bitch's brew of all my accumulated pain and suffering that had been stifled all my life. It was now spewing that poison all over and I couldn't face it."

"So much for spiritual partnerships," Bodhi flippantly commented.

"No, Bodhi," Adya stated firmly. "It was exactly our spiritual partnership that allowed me to see my shit. You were a perfect mirror. I just couldn't handle it." She paused and stared at him. Bodhi looked down at his hand that was filled with sand that he was pouring out in a thin line.

"I know it's a lot to ask," she asked softly, "but can you forgive me? You opened up..." She caught herself and stopped for a second before continuing. "You allowed me to really see myself. I get it now. I don't like what I see but it's me. I have a lot of work to do and I want to do it with you by my side." Bodhi held both of her hands.

"I love you!" Bodhi exclaimed.

"I love you more!" Adya replied. They both smiled. "I don't want to live without you Bodhi."

"I don't want to live without you either."

"You know I have a ton of stuff to work through?" Adya asked. "It's not going to be easy."

"Hey!" Bodhi exclaimed. "That's what spiritual partners are for, right?" They picked up their almost empty water glasses and Adya toasted: "Here's to spiritual partnerships!" They clinked glasses and drank.

"One more thing," Bodhi said. "No more ninja shit on

me!"

"Never!" Adya exclaimed. "Never!"

"Promise?" Bodhi asked.

"Cross my heart and hope to die," Adya said. They leaned into each other and stared at the moon that seemed to wink at them. "I know I'm not in any position to ask, but can you do me one favor?"

"What's that love?" Bodhi asked.

"Please don't run out on me again," Adya asked. "I almost died. No matter what I do. Stick with me and let's work it out."

"No matter what?" Bodhi asked.

"Are we spiritual partners or not?" Adya asked. They stared into each other's eyes and lost themselves in the reflection of their eyes that was itself a reflection. Bodhi nodded yes.

"You're such a perfect mirror," Adya said. "You showed me exactly what I needed to see. It was devastating but I'm grateful because I'm now on the path to loving and accepting myself. To healing. Thank you for that. As I learn to do that and clean my mirror, you'll hopefully be able to see yourself clearer." Bodhi spun his index finger in the air moving it up to the stars.

"An upward spiral," Bodhi added.

"Yeah," Adya said. She took his arm, put it around her and snuggled against him. They both closed their eyes and felt the warm breeze of the moon's kiss on their faces.

"So many blessings," Bodhi whispered.

"Thank God!" Adya said.

"Thank Covid!" Boddhi added.

"What?" Adya said in a surprised tone as she separated from his embrace.

"Well," Bodhi replied. "We never would have met if it weren't for Covid. We never would have witnessed the powerful changes that are taking place in the world, and we would've never had the opportunity to be part of making this brave new world a better place."

"You're absolutely right," Adya agreed. "Aside from the

minor detail of a near mass extinction event, there are so many blessings and opportunities. I would have never body-slammed you causing you to skip out on me and would've never taken the trip to Peru and met Mother Ayahuasca."

"And I would have never known how much I truly love you and can't live without you," Bodhi added.

"Let's jump in," Bodhi said.

"Really?"

"Yeah," Bodhi said. "Let's jump in and wash all the bull-shit away. All of it. It's a new day, a new world, a new life. Look!" Bodhi pointed to the moon. "She's smiling and wants to baptize us. She wants to make it formal and pronounce us spiritual partners for life, till death do us part. Are you ready?" Adya stood up, pulled him up and hugged him tight. "I am and I do Bodhi. Till death do us part." They stripped naked and walked into the water hand in hand. "Bodhi?" Adya stopped and asked. "Can you do me another huge favor?"

"Anything," he responded.

"I really need you to put some meat back on your ass," she said. "I was really into your ass."

"Hmmm," Bodhi smiled. "I'm not sure. I'm kinda digging this new look. I'll have to think about it." Adya smacked him hard on his ass. They laughed, hugged and fell in the water to-gether. They swam out just a little further and stood in front of each other.

"It's done," Bodhi said. "We are now spiritual partners for life, till death do us part."

"Till death do us part," Adya repeated. The water and moonlight washed over them as they embraced.

PART 10: EPILOGUE

SPRING 2025

Adya and Bodhi were riding bicycles through the streets in SoHo. Art was exhibited in a generous, carefree and random manner all over the city. This was borne out of a desire to express the creative energy that was bursting out after such a monumental human experience. It was expressed in the form of paintings hung randomly on storefronts, building walls, parks, as well as directly on walls and sidewalks. Sculptures and interactive art installations were randomly and often strategically placed throughout the city. There were maps indicating the different order in which viewers could experience them, each path telling a different story.

People started to wear costumes as part of everyday life. It was as though Covid-19 liberated the spirit of Burning Man into everyday life. As they rode around SoHo, Adya and Bodhi pointed out to each other interesting sites, art or people who were dressed in a unique style that caught their attention. They occasionally put their bikes down to explore particular art installations and chatted with other interested observers. Sometimes they would encounter the artist who was more than happy to share their perspective and inspiration.

The new, modern, all-glass buildings that had sprouted all over the city just prior to the pandemic, stood out against the older buildings that were more than a century old. The newer buildings either cast shadows or reflected light onto the older ones depending on the time of day. The juxtaposition,

LOVE IN THE TIME OF CORONAVIRUS

shadows and reflections gave these old buildings an artistic facelift and charm found on building facades in Havana Cuba without the inconvenient, crumbling reality.

The sun was shining bright and created intermittent periods of heat and glare followed by shadows and cool as they moved on their bikes from the shelter of buildings to the open sun. There was a paucity of cars. People walked and rode their bikes, but the streets weren't as crowded and hectic as the pace that had defined pre-Covid life in New York City. People appeared lighter. Their yolks had been lifted. Cafés and restaurants were open again and doing well. Covid-19 was distant in everyone's minds but the outdoor cabanas and tables were a pleasant and welcomed residual effect.

There was a freshness in the city, as though the wind just blew life into it and the sun put it in a new light. They felt revitalized. The future was uncertain and there were no promises, but there was opportunity. This of course included the opportunity to mess it up all over again, but how many times in human history did humanity have the opportunity to start all over again. It was a breathtaking realization on the surface, with the subliminal undertones of a tremendous responsibility.

Those devious subliminal voices provided a shortcut back to their pre-Covid *Koyaanisquatsi* reality, to which Adya and Bodhi almost succumbed. Their experience provided them with new insights. They understood now that the future of humanity was not predicated on the wisdom of world leaders, but on the level of consciousness of humanity as a whole. This had always been the case throughout the history of humankind. Major changes didn't occur because of a great leader who showed humanity the way, but rather, the collective consciousness arrived at a point sufficient to manifest its spokesperson. There were likely many incarnations of Mahatma Gandhi, Martin Luther King and Jesus Christ who carried the same messages but the level of consciousness of humankind was not ready to hear and embrace those prior iterations. This understanding was at first depressing and created anxiety because it was too early to tell. But in reality, it was liberating. It was the opposite of *Koyaanisquatsi*. The Covid pandemic taught them that it was only in hindsight, as in the 20/20 hindsight they were gifted in 2020, that it became clear. They were now free to contribute with dedication, passion, and love without any preconceived notions or expectations of the outcome. It was living life as it happened, reading their lines with gusto and trusting the universe would receive their best intentions and provide the best results for humankind at the appropriate time.

Bodhi was riding behind Adya. She intermittently looked back and smiled warmly. He caught up to her and they rode side by side holding hands. They were together. They now understood deeply what it meant to be spiritual partners. They also learned that they were in a spiritual partnership with the universe that they were co-creating in the same manner that they were co-creating each other. Whatever the outcome, it was exactly what was indicated at that moment in time.

They passed by a crowded street on Lafayette and Spring that beckoned them. There were a number of restaurants adjacent to each other. They had tables as well as the wooden semi-open-air huts on the sidewalks that were created during the Covid lockdowns. The huts were artfully lit and the tables, chairs and store awnings colorful like a painter's palette. They parked their bikes against a bike rack and sat with the sun shining brightly on their faces. They ordered two Americanos and almond chocolate croissants. They watched the impromptu performances of the people who sat at the adjacent tables against the backdrop of seemingly unrelated performances of others who passed by. Their movements and conversation appeared to be choreographed to the music that was playing and blended with the music emanating from the other restaurants. They were alive, happy and madly in love. Through those lenses they were able to see the joy and love in others. They took all this in while sipping their Americanos, delighting in their croissants, and exchanging pleasantries. When they finished eating, they sat holding hands. Their gaze alternated between the spectacle playing out before them and into each other's eyes. They were now fluent in the language of communication with only their eyes that developed from the Covid-imposed years of having to wear masks. Their eyes simultaneously asked: "Who could have imagined that in the wake of the Coronavirus pandemic that took 4 billion lives, there would be such an abundance of joy, love, hope and opportunity?"

They continued to gaze into each other's eyes but there was no response. No response was necessary. Someone had stopped in front of where they were sitting and was apparently intrigued with their own performance. He smiled at them and lifted his camera to ask if he could take their picture. Adya and Bodhi nodded yes and put their heads together for the photo. The man took a few steps towards them and took a few pictures. People around them started to focus on them and the photographer, who then gestured that they should continue to pose. It turned into a photoshoot. The man finally stopped to look over the pictures he had taken on the LCD screen. They thought he was done but he asked for one more, indicating that they should kiss. They started with a peck on the lips. The man got closer and continued to shoot pictures. Adya and Bodhi then started to kiss each other deeply to the rhythm of the music playing, punctuated with the sound of the camera shutter clicking as feverish as their kiss. People clapped. The man thanked them and gave them his card indicating that they should contact him for the pictures. The man left and the spotlight moved onto another performance.

Adya and Bodhi continued to stare into each other's eyes. There were no words but Bodhi's eyes beamed: "I love you Adya!"

Adya's eyes laughed and beamed back: "I love you more!"

ABOUT THE AUTHOR

Richard Lanoix, Md

The author was born in Haiti and has lived in New York City for the past 54 years. He is an emergency physician who has dedicated his life to the healing arts and the exploration of Consciousness and creativity. His first novel was "The Twin Flames, the Master, and the Game."

BOOKS BY THIS AUTHOR

The Twin Flames, The Master, And The Game: A Journey To Enlightenment

This is an epic love story and thriller that takes place over many lifetimes and depicts the hero's journey to enlightenment. Orfeo and Carina are Twin Flames, souls that have been together since the beginning of time, and they are merged in Consciousness. At one point, Orfeo can't find Carina, so he returns to the earth-realm to find her. After many lifetimes, they are reunited, and Orfeo learns that it was him that was lost, not her. She makes him aware of the battle of consciousness that is taking place between the forces of Light (the Resistance) and the Dark forces, led by the Master, whom they believe is attempting to obstruct humankind's path to Consciousness and imprison them in the earth-realm. After many plot twists, Orfeo learns about the true nature of reality. He then tries to share this truth with Carina, who can't accept it because she believes that he's been brainwashed by the Master. This impasse jeopardizes their eternal love and return to Consciousness.

Made in the USA
Middletown, DE
19 December 2021

56583484R00195